Mad Girl's Love Song

Rukmini Bhaya Nair

HarperCollins *Publishers* India

First published in India by
HarperCollins *Publishers* in 2013

Building No 10, Tower A, 4th Floor, DLF Cyber, City Phase II,
Gurugram 122002
www.harpercollins.co.in

2 4 6 8 10 9 7 5 3

P-ISBN: 978-93-5029-647-9
E-ISBN: 978-935-029-648-6

Typeset in 11/14 Crimson Regular at
SURYA

Printed and bound at
MicroPrints India, New Delhi

Mad Girl's Love Song

RUKMINI BHAYA NAIR is Professor of Linguistics and English at the Indian Institute of Technology, Delhi. She received her Ph.D. from the University of Cambridge and has since taught at universities ranging from Singapore to Stanford. Awarded an honorary doctorate by the University of Antwerp in 2006 for her work on narrative, Nair has been the recipient of many awards and authored several academic books. She has also published three volumes of poetry and her poems have been widely anthologized and translated into languages such as Chinese, Swedish, Italian and Macedonian. Married, with two children, Nair lives in Delhi and has recently adopted an unprepossessing feline. Her great ambition is simply to continue to write, teach and research. This is her first novel.

ALSO BY THE AUTHOR

Non-Fiction

Technobrat: Culture in a Cybernetic Classroom

Lying on the Postcolonial Couch: The Idea of Indifference

Narrative Gravity: Conversation, Cognition, Culture

Translation, Text and Theory: The Paradigm of India (ed.)

Poetry in a Time of Terror: Essays in the Postcolonial Preternatural

Poetry

The Hyoid Bone

The Ayodhya Cantos

Yellow Hibiscus

For those who died

&

for the teachers, students, readers and
people all over the world
deranged and destroyed, moved and removed
by the English language

I shut my eyes and all the world drops dead;
I lift my lids and all is born again.
(I think I made you up inside my head.)

The stars go waltzing out in blue and red,
And arbitrary blackness gallops in:
I shut my eyes and all the world drops dead.

I dreamed that you bewitched me into bed
And sung me moon-struck, kissed me quite insane.
(I think I made you up inside my head.)

God topples from the sky, hell's fires fade:
Exit seraphim and Satan's men:
I shut my eyes and all the world drops dead.

I fancied you'd return the way you said,
But I grow old and I forget your name.
(I think I made you up inside my head.)

I should have loved a thunderbird instead;
At least when spring comes they roar back again.
I shut my eyes and all the world drops dead.
(I think I made you up inside my head.)

—Sylvia Plath
'Mad Girl's Love Song'

Contents

Sylvia

The Return of Ariel

What's love, anyway? Sylvia asked on the night of her death, her wide mouth curving.

I did not answer her and then she entered the moonlight and she died.

Who killed her? Who killed my mother? Who killed Jahangir the turkey?

You can read the answers in this notebook.

Pari's Book

Sylvia never looked at me when she asked her questions, never. But that night, it was different. The moon had sharpened her voice and it drove something into my heart. A stake, she said. Or maybe she said *snake*. Anyway, I was cold and Sylvia had no time for me. She was going on a hunt to set traps—traps for poems! A poem was a beast, a furred, tawny creature in a cage of words. It was a wild mess of scribbles and lines and harsh talon scratches on paper.

Later, the bars would have to be strengthened, the snarling creature tamed and the poem fitted onto a day-time page where strangers' eyes would come to peer and stubby fingers point. All these things, this *bucolic ghastliness,* she told me she had schooled herself for. What she could not stand, she said, still not looking at me, was the 'nothingness'—the nights when Daddy or Blake or someone stood there at the edge of the woods and picked off the beasts long before they got to her. On these nights, she felt she was the one being hunted. It was then that her impossible questions came to her and she'd repeat over and over, in a hysteria of unknowing:

What's love? What's love, anyway?

Not that Sylvia intended to die. That was an afterthought (or a *murder*). When people are in love with death, they don't usually bother to ask what love is. They know already—Love is Death. But Sylvia never bothered with such simple equations. That is why my wings fluttered like restless window-curtains at her moods.

I was Pari. I was her Angel even if no one believed me. But I knew that it wasn't going to be easy to answer her. This wasn't the first time she'd asked and it got a little worse each time.

Things were happening already—small, bad things.

Just four hours before she gang-planked into eternity, four hours to connect her story with mine (Pari's from Tempke, written in this Notebook) and all the lovers and travel and devastation in between—and every pipe in Sylvia's house chose to go mad! There they were, clicking and ticking and clattering like insanely excited skeletons, like gossiping time bombs, like rigid snakes! And she stood in the middle of it all, shivering in her thin black dress, waiting for Daddy . . .

It was going to happen.

She knew it. *I* knew it. The pipes, they knew it.

This was the night.

I thought of her children, lying sweetly asleep next door. They knew nothing. *They* could not see the flying ash from Sylvia's cigarette staining the smooth innocence of the kitchen tablecloth between us, a smudge of bees in a clear summer sky . . .

I wanted to start another conversation with her, a better one, a *newborn* one, but all she did was blow her smoke-rings straight into my face.

Did I not know that flying in the face of reason was her form of sanity?

I said I did, but she should think of her moth-breath babies.

What did they know? What does any baby know? A baby cannot even read, so could they see me, Pariel, Pari Ariel, unloosed, kicking their wild mother roundly in the stomach as she fell? Did they spot that thin line of red sludge gorging from her every month and driving her crazy in the weeks before? Did they know what she was up to?

Of course not!

She'd tucked them away, she said absent-mindedly, as if everything was normal, as if the pipes were silent. She's wedged wet towels under their bedroom door, so the gas doesn't get to them. They're safe until morning, her darlings.

I felt sadder than the moonlight then but she just blew smoke into my face again.

And the pipes sang.

Indefatigable hoof-taps, clickety clack! went the pipes.
Somebody's done for, clickety clack, clickety-clack!

Ignore them, Sylvia commanded, now looking me straight in the eye and repeating herself above the din, no trace of self-pity in her voice. Tiredness perhaps, and a delicate bubble of terror in the froth that laced the edge of her coffee, but nothing maudlin. Yet, there it was, Daddy-lurking in the doorway, the impossible truth at the edge of daybreak.

For Sylvia, it was a 'fight foretold'. He appeared every decade or so, she told me, her Daddy demon from Hades, hoping to carry her away and she's fought him each time, clawed at him, sent him back down under! Every time!

I said softly, I know you're a winner, Sylvie!

It was not the truth, but it was what Sylvia wanted to hear. London's coldest night in 129 years, and there was Sylvia the Queen Bee, waiting for love red-eyed, as if Ted or Al or William might swoop in any moment through the narrow frosted windows of her depressing Fitzroy Street flat and Superman her into bliss.

There was nothing I could do. This was Sylvia's fight. Hers alone.

Bone-cold, frostbitten, frozen-pipes London! I could feel Sylvia's last thoughts lashing out against the city, about how dank it was, how un-American, what a stupid, stupid wax-house! But even at that moment, I saw how tightly she held on to hope, to the slight glimmer of the hallway light beyond the darkness of the kitchen door. It would happen this time, the reprieve. She knew it! Chance would save her, chance, her keyword, her talisman, unlocking the oven, freeing her for the dance!

And to the end, standing between her and the new babysitter she could not see, the Aussie lass who'd arrived all the way from wallaby land and now stood dawdling, puzzled and wool-encloseted, in the mists of Fitzroy Street, I, stupid Pari, hoped with Sylvia.

I did not cry, not even once.

But then it happened. Chance spoke.

Chance answered Sylvia's question, speaking out of turn—because that was its nature—not to Sylvia, but capriciously, chillingly, to the messenger. And there's chance for you, as the nuns said, never on the side of the angels!

I watched it happen.

The death.

❁

The Australian girl, kangaroo-hopping from the frosty cold outside Sylvia's unfriendly door, made up her mind at exactly seven-twenty-eight in the morning. She came to her decision after the third clanging ring and not the ghost of an answer and all of destiny's weight rested on the slight shrug of her shoulder. She might be a mere babysitter but she would not hang around that deaf door-post a minute longer! She'd phone the employment agency and return after a proper breakfast. And she would complain.

And at that moment, I knew hope was blown.

Then I watched the girl march off, sublimely unaware (messengers always are, I learnt later) that destiny had picked her out. It had chosen her to knock on Sylvia's door for all eternity. Why her, why a stranger from halfway across the globe, descendent of some unknown ex-con from a distant colony? It's a question nearly as hard to answer as Sylvia's own: *What's love, anyway?* The last of her big, WASP questions, a question so crass it required an answer, she'd whispered, of angelic subtlety—and here's the strange thing . . .

I, writing down these things, am an Angel—just like in the nuns' library books.

I am the Lioness of God, Prospero's spirit, Madwoman of Tempke trailing my sari of diaphanous blue across the waltzing stars of Gaia, holy descendent of Summa! The only witness to Sylvia's it-so-nearly-didn't-happen death. The only one. *I have a self to recover, a queen,* she'd written, *with her lion-red body, her wings of glass.*

I am that glassy self—Slyvia's 'truth mirror', her angel.

I am Ariel, very cold, very bad.

Sylvia could make me shiver with her words even though she laughed when she spoke them. That was the funny thing. She laughed and smiled and talked and I shivered . . .

Now I have to try and make you shiver with *my* words. Summa says so.

And then I will be free . . .

Do you know something? Sylvia named her *horse* after me, which was typical—at once an acknowledgment and a dismissal, she said laughing. That's what she always did, but whether she admitted it or not, the men we loved, we *both* loved, were more honest. They put it down in black and white and feathered gold and kissed their manuscripts to heaven, God promise. I was real! Even the stupid boys of Tempke called me '*Angel No. 1: Angrezi Crazy!*' But these men were not the buddhu boys of Tempke, they were famous poets and lovers: William-ji and David Herbert and Ted. Ask them. But if you will not trust a 'besotted male', ask her, ask Sylvia . . .

Sylvia told the truth when it really mattered, even if it killed her and even if it turned everyone around her heartsick. *Sly*-via, I called her sometimes. She knew where to slide the knife in all right. If I was not a pukkah Angrezi angel, consecrated by the nuns of Tempke and by my father's wish uplifted straight to my own high heaven long before I came to know her, I think I might have wanted to be Sylvia—and time was running out for me as it did for her.

At any moment now I would have to connect the dots and watch my story merge with hers, like the lion and unicorn in baby Nicholas' colouring book or like strands of DNA with the genes for schizophrenia marked in bright, bouncing cobalt. COMT, WKL1, Nogo CAA, PPP3CC, all twenty or thirty of them absorbed in their funny, blobby dance.

Now! It was time. I lifted my pencil and I stabbed.

I stabbed and stabbed and stabbed till the dots went still and the whole writhing kaleidoscope came to a dead halt for one whole second—and I was back.

I was back in Tempke.

Lost nadir of the world, Sylvia had called it . . .

Tempke is my town. It has a level-crossing, a Girl's Convent and Biscuit Baba's World Renowned Meditation Ashram. When I came back from England after my long interludes with Sylvia and William and David, cured of my madness forever, I heard a story. One of the little beggar boys who was always hanging round the Ashram had had his hands crushed by the Baba's supporters and the police for trying to steal from the big pile of biscuits kept in the Baba's tent. Of course the Baba had no idea what had been done to the boy; he was observing his maun vrata at the time and nobody wanted to disturb him. But in the end the Baba came to know and he acted *at once*. He arranged for the boy to have the best hospital care and when he recovered—both his hands had to be amputated—he was even given a job by the Baba. His job was to guard the pile he'd coveted. He had no hands now, so there was no question of his touching the biscuits. And once in a while, the Baba would be extra kind. He'd order someone to throw a biscuit in the boy's direction—for the boy had been expertly trained by the ashramites to catch biscuits with his open mouth, just like a dog. Naturally, the boy became the tent's star attraction on Thurdays, the Baba's day for public darshan. When he wasn't catching biscuits and coins in his mouth, this boy never ceased to sing the praises of the Baba. Until one day when he ran away without a backward glance and set up his own holy business in Madhepura. This was a story about disloyalty and how it is hard to know the heart of another . . .

Many other things happened while I was away and I have written them all down. Now I'm almost done and my pencil which was so sharp and stabbing when I began is worn to a stub and rough with bite-marks where I have chewed it raw on wordless days.

Today, I don't need the words so badly.

I'm cured and back in the Convent where it all began, Sister Maria's old red cushion with its tassels of faded gold warm and comforting against my back and the gobar smell of the smoke from the morning chulhas wafting in from the outhouse window.

Now I glance up at the dawning light—and I notice something.

A nosy, noisy pigeon and a tuntunia bird have taken over the windowsill and are belting out a chorus I recognize. Sylvia wrote this poem for me. It was a 'villanelle'. She called it her 'Mad Girl's Love Song'. *I shut my eyes and all the world drops dead, I lift my lids and all is born again, I think I made you up inside my head*—but these birds are shameless, *besharam.* They mix up Sylvia's poem with her question, stick in all sorts of bits and pieces in-between and make up this total crazy hodgepodge! *Anyway, anyway, mae ka khaun, ka piun, ka leke pardes jaun,* they jabber. *I dreamed that you bewitched me into bed, kissed me quite insane. And anyway, anyway, what's love, anyway?* Their twittering makes it sound like it's the easiest question in the world.

Let Afi wake, I tell them, you ridiculous avians, and you will have your answer!

Then I turn towards Afi, my love, though I can hardly bear to look in his direction.

❁

That stone-slab look of him, flat-dead, that awful bluish O of the fish-mouth gaping in his bandaged faceless face . . . Alone with Afi in the unforgiving light of the convent outhouse, I know I'm in need of a miracle. And I am NOT INSANE. The most incurable madness in the world is to live in hope when there is no reason for it. Afi, too, was beaten to a pulp not too long ago and now it's a matter of touch and go whether he survives. Not that the Baba has anything to do with the matter.

Someone else was guilty . . .

Page from New Addenbrooke's Medical File 203 16.8.88: Patient, a healthy Indian woman of seventeen, presents with classical symptoms of mixed schizophrenic and affective psychosis type 295.7. Suffers from hallucinations and believes she can fly. Hears voices and exhibits remarkable linguistic fluency during her aviomanic phases. May also fit profile of the residual and/or restructured schizoid state 296.7.

Referred by Dr M. Treatment first undertaken in India in 1985 when patient was fourteen. Patient has been on a standard regimen of drugs since then, initially Thorazadine, widely used in India owing to its availability and then Prozac to which patient did not respond well. Patient became excited and her aviomania uncontrollable. It was after one such extreme episode that Dr M recommended to her guardian that she be brought to England for special consultations. Prozac discontinued.

Dr M further felt that the patient might respond well to the new drug olanzapine in conjunction with the experimental RTMS neural-pulse treatment that we now have at New A. The detailed case notes we have received from India specifically mention the patient's high IQ (range 100-120). According to Dr M, the patient has an exceptional, although frequently unreliable, memory, reads widely and can hold intelligent discussions, especially on the subject of literature. In view of this noting, I advised her to continue with the practice, initiated by Dr M, of keeping a diary account of her experiences. However, patient merely nodded and avoided eye-contact, as is often the case in these first meetings. Admitted to Ward D for further observation.

In the Library

How did it begin?

This was the first question the English doctor asked me—but it was as bad as Sylvia's question, sort of. There are no beginnings and endings in the history of madness. I know this answer sounds more like hers than mine, but Sylvia didn't say it—*I* did. I don't know how—sometimes the words just come to me. Sometimes I just *guess* that funny things are going to happen. And so, Doctorji, that summer of '84, even before I caught Sister Lydia with the Accountant and she bribed me with the duplicate keys to the Library for the whole vacation, I knew that things had begun to turn peculiar, like you can sometimes taste the moonlight like milk, *touch* it. It was a feeling—not to do with Sylvia because she hadn't appeared yet—but the **Turkey Incident** had happened already and there were other strange goings-on ever since I was released from the Infirmary. And all the while, my wings had grown steadily between December and May . . .

My wings were amazing! If I snake-twisted my body, I could see them at various angles when I took my small mirror and held it up to the big mirror in the bathroom. There were very few mirrors in the Convent because nuns are supposed to avoid vanity, so I was lucky. The mirror in my bathroom was *at least* as big as the island of Nauru about which I'd read in the Encyclopaedia. I think the nuns must have missed discovering it because it was less like a mirror than a whole, entire wall. They hardly came to the part where I lived anyway, but Gowri slept on the floor of my room on her mat, so it was alright. I felt safe with Gowri. Gowri oiled my hair just like Lakshmi did when my mother was alive. Gowri ironed my clothes and brought me *halwa* and *chura* and allowed Mona to come into our room although it was STRICTLY forbidden! I liked Gowri a lot even though she spat betel juice into our sink so that it was permanently stained brown and she mostly spoke Tamil so we could not really talk, but this was good too because she could not tell people about my wings.

My wings had small golden tips. They were glossy blue-black on top and downy grey on the underside and soft like the baby powder brush that my mother used to talcum me with. Some parts were flecked and speckled with green and silver, like Sylvia's eyes. My wings were even more beautiful than the wings of the angels in the Madonna Triptych.

These wings were the most wonderful and secret part of my life. They were *not* a problem. I could handle them, just as I could the sudden blood spurting from my front-bottom. These things had to do with the body. The business with Sis Lyd and the Accountant was more confusing. It troubled my *soul.*

They weren't exactly doing the books when I caught them in the Library. I understood that. But it wasn't my business and I was chicken, as usual. Besides, I thought Liddie far too pretty to be a nun, and—who'd believe me anyway? So, even before she offered me her fatal payoff, I found myself gabbling hysterically: *Promise I won't tell, God promise*! And as I spoke I let my hands move with automatic passion, travelling swiftly from my head to the bony place just between my new breasts and then from the outer edge of my left collar bone to my right in the Sign of the Cross. That was sacred and should have convinced her, but Lydia Sister was smart. She took out an insurance policy anyway.

The next thing I knew, the Accountant had done up his pants and shamble-strutted out of the room, like some stupid cross between a shy bride in a Hindi movie and the horny goats we saw on the streets of Tempke, even though we always pretended not to look. That day in the Library, of course it was the Accountant who wasn't looking. He never met my eyes again after that day. But Sister L the Belle, she was made of a different fibre. She stood there, dangling her spare keys before me just like St Peter and pointing to the neat row of unread Dornford Yates novels on the third shelf of the sixth bookcase.

English Literature, she pronouced, as if she was a grey-haired bozo from some boring old college teachers' outfit instead of a sinful nun with burnished skin, it opens up the world. Read, child, read! Look behind the veil of appearances, and you will discover untold riches!

Who talks like that? I knew perfectly well that L was playacting. She was trying to jinx me with her preachy act. All the same, my tongue refused to move in my mouth. L had power and she understood that she had power, unlike poor Sister Maria. That was the difference, the difference between a human turkey and a witch angel. Sister Lydia's power forced me that fateful morning to back out of the Library—leaving her in full possession. Also, I never told anyone, not even Mona, and so began my secret life—though it took me a very long time to work out the rewards of blowing the lid off Liddie's secret. But when I did, when I did find out what she meant by the untold riches of English Literature, it had changed my life forever . . .

Everything else had changed anyway.

After what my best friend Mona called my idiotic behaviour in the Infirmary following the Turkey Incident (about which I will tell you later), she completely ignored me. As for Afi, my other friend, he had mysteriously vanished. Disappeared completely, without a trace! The nuns said he was studying for his exams but I knew there was more to it than that. They had *sent him away*. I KNEW THIS. Then Sister Maria started to badger me. I had to concentrate, she kept saying. I might be a good student but I'd lost a lot of time. My father would be very disappointed if I did badly in my finals, etc. etc.

I wanted to tell Maria the Terrier that my father would not care if my fingers were sliced off one-by-one and I could never answer a question paper all my life, but of course I did not. I was not *that* mad.

The trouble was, I was scared—not about the stuff Maria was threatening me with, about doing badly in my finals etc. That was just silly stuff. I could still by-heart everything faster than anyone else in the class, even Anuradha Mishra. Anu had private tuition and stood first half the time and I stood first the rest of the time, which was okay but she was not half as good as me at by-hearting and everyone knows that the key to doing well in exams is by-hearting.

So I wasn't worried about not doing well.

I wasn't worried about my wings.

I wasn't even worried about Mona and Afi because I knew they were my friends. They were katti with me now but Mona would need me to pass her exams. Afi would follow Mona and things would become all right in the end.

I was scared because I thought someone was going to kill me, *just like they killed Jahangir the turkey.*

Sometimes I heard the neem and peepul in the yard whispering these scandals, small pointy green leaves gossiping with arcs of silver above and shadows beneath, the dark and the light, talking, talking, talking! They were trying to warn me, I knew, but their voices were oldie voices, always too whispery and muffled to make out the message. Sometimes I saw my father's hand upraised and his MENACING voice, *mere bhoot kore debo, bujhle!* and it froze me even though it was not a true thing. The big clock in the Refectory also spoke to me, always in one, single sentence: *Ding, dong, ding dong, it's time! Time!* And sometimes my strung-up mother came and sang to me, sad as a dove . . .

These were Signs that bad things were going to happen and the awful thing was—*I could speak to no one.*

My mother was losing her strength. I could see that and I became afraid she had grown too weak to protect me, so when my father sent me two crates of the best Alphonso mangoes that summer, I would not eat a single one.

I *knew* the Alphonsos were poisoned.

Of course, I noticed the nuns ate the mangoes, gobble, gobble, gabble, gabble, and they survived—but they were nuns. They lived and died by different rules. Like turkeys.

So I had no option. I ate as little as I could and I tried to read and read so that I could stay awake as long as possible. And this pushed me in the direction of the Library at last . . .

One day I could bear it no longer.

I did it! I crossed my heart before the Madonna Triptych for luck, tucked Sister Lydia's forbidden keys into my pocket and told Gowri to tell the nuns that I was going to take notes in the Library for my exams. Sister Maria would be so relieved she would ask no questions.

The Library was silent as a grave in the moonlight.

I was alone with the Wisdom of the Dead. Not all the dead, though. The books in my father's house, the bound volumes of *Sandesh* my mother read to me in snatches, Robi Thakur in his twenty-five dark red and gold disguises, Michael Madhusudan in green leather, even Sarat Chandra after whose heroine Lolita, aka Parineeta, I was named by my mother: none of them belonged here in the school library. Dornford Yates the Big Conqueror, yes *he* was there, just like P.G. Wodehouse, all the cheery Britishers out in force, not to mention *Lord Jim* and *Lucky Jim*, but *not the ones who wrote in squiggly script with roofs.* The convent roof was not for them. It was for girls to learn to speak correct English, like Mona, Anuradha and me, Pari, whose name means 'fairy' . . .

Then, to the far right, I spotted the big books. Sacred leather-bound Shakespeare and next to him, Thomas A Kempis' *Imitation of the Life of Christ,* which no one had ever been known to touch. John Keay, too—I have to tell you about him soon, he's important—lay in his usual resting place, a bejeweled turkey nestling bang in the middle of his chest, page 119, inside right-hand corner. But the fact was *my* turkey was dead and I was alone, totally alone. *That* was the reason I was here.

Fly, Pari!

So I dived and I fell. I tried to fly until my arms were cut and my knees hurt. But I could not. I could not fly. I *kept* falling. And then I fell near the bookrack—and I knew! It was the exact place towards which Sister Lydia had pointed, the Dornford Yates novels standing like a fortress on the third shelf. I stared and they stared back at me, unblinking.

No blinking.

Somebody had to make the first move. So I picked up one of the fattest DYs and I flicked through its many-winged pages.

Nothing.

Then the next.

The next.

Next!

The Dornford books had formed this small tower at my feet in bands of blue and bands of brown. Sky and flesh and flesh and sky, a squat tower of silence. Squat, so what, *squat,* squat, squat! Do you know about the Tower of Silence, Dr M? It's where the Parsees leave their dead in the open and the vultures eat them and all that's left in the end is a white stack of bones, neat and clean and still. Nothing left to be scared of . . .

Nothing at all.

Until I discovered the second layer, the books behind the

books—but this was not surprising. Everyone hid things in the Convent, because practically everything was forbidden. The older girls hid things like lipstick and love letters and the younger kids hid food and almost everyone hid the Mills and Boons, not only because they were forbidden but because they were in short supply. Mills and Boons were the only books everyone read from class five up. So there are Mills and Boons under mattresses and M&Bs in forgotten classroom cupboards amongst piles of tattered copy-books and also in the Library behind the respectable stuff in front. M&Bs had invaded everywhere—like bacteria—and it was an open secret that the nuns liked to read them too. They'd fine someone five rupees once in a while just to keep us disciplined but that was the end of it.

We all knew the Mills and Boons were too precious to banish. They meant romance, they meant far away lands and handsome, rugged lovers, boys. Not one of us could afford to let them go, not even Mona. *What's love, anyway?* In Tempke convent, love was a Mills and Boons dream, something secret, delicious and indestructible.

The books that lay behind the Dornford Yates stack were not Mills and Boons, though. They were:

Ariel: Poems by Sylvia Plath
The Collected Poems of William Blake
The Collected Poems of D.H. Lawrence
The Psychology of Sex by *Havelock Ellis, M.D.*

The fattest book was the sex book and I knew it was hidden because it had the word 'sex' in it. That was simple. Then I picked up the thinnest book with thin red flower patterns on it and simple writing. It looked unexciting. So I put it down and picked up the sex book again and my eye fell on the name of its author and suddenly I got it—John Keay and Have Lock! The names *fitted*. Another Sign, a sign from my mother and, maybe, even a solution to the turkey murder! I was sure this was the book I was meant to find, the real one. The rest could be put back—but, just as I was about to, the pages of the thin little book fluttered open and I saw a single black word on the page staring up at me—**Daddy**.

And then I saw the words beneath and the temperature in the Library grew ten degrees chillier, god-promise. I did not know it then but it was Sylvia. She had spoken to me for the first time.

Somebody's done for, *clickety-clack*!

In the innocent school library, Sylvia had offered me sweet, poisoned Alphonsos, just like my father. Under the tutelage of Lovely Lady Lydia, Most Beautiful Nun of the Convent of Tempke, she'd slithered into my head and she would not be dislodged. She and her dead Daddy and Havelock, all determined to teach me things I did not wish to learn—English, for example. They'd joined up with Mona and Afi, ringing me around with their concern and their giggles, whispering in my ears and *never letting go . . .*

All I wanted to know was, *who killed Jahangir* and *why my mother hanged herself wearing that stupid, furry hat* and why my father and even the Doctorji cannot bear to meet my eyes—answers to simple questions like that, but their plans included a full education, A-levels in lust and poetry as Sylvia called them when I got to know her.

From that moment on, though I did not know it then, my

life was to change. It was to be ruled by *poetry*. And so I left the Library that night, holding Havelock's heavy weight in the crook of my arm and Sylvia's light fluttering body in my moon-frozen hands as if I was the one in charge, which was a joke.

❊

Smith College to rehab to Cambridge, Sylvia's project had always been to have it all, to be a queen, to recover from the shambles of her chocolate-brittle, torn silver-wrapper, absurd marriage to Ted, a perfectly remembered sweetness. After all, she reminded me, *I* was there, my glass wings rising proudly heavenwards, when she wrote her lines, her 'immortal' lines:

I have a self to recover, a queen.
Is she dead, or is she sleeping?
Where has she been,
With her lion red-body, her wings of glass?

And then I told Sylvia exactly where my lion-red body had been. It had been with William and DH and with Ted in Devon. It had roamed in Massachusetts and Italy and it had lived in India . . .

❊

New Addenbrooke's Medical File 203 20.8.88:
Patient's entrance into consultation chamber was preceded by a minor scuffle, after which she was duly escorted here by Nurse. Apparently, the patient refused point blank to leave her ward without the small pile of books that she had brought with her from India. A struggle ensued when Nurse tried to relieve her of these.

Patient wept and protested bitterly. In view of the excessive distress exhibited, Nurse let patient retain her books.

However, it is noted that, despite every kindness, patient still visibly cowers away from Nurse and, were she not under sedation, would probably try to escape. Sedative effects are also apparent in the patient's gaze and gait. Patient seems passive and cooperative, although Nurse reports that acute symptoms of aviomania continue unabated. For the past few days, whenever her sedation wore off in the Ward, patient would run to the window and spread her arms in gestures of flight. Imp: mother's suicide when subject was seven entered in case-history; but, without further evidence, the aviomanic movements of patient may not prima facie be judged suicidal.

Patient's other gestures seem overtly to relate to her sexuality. She is observed to stretch her hands above her head and spread her legs without displaying the conventional emotion of shame usually associated with such acts, so that Nurse is obliged to cover her with a sheet. At such moments, patient heard to insist that she is 'William's Angel'. On being questioned about this unusual behaviour in consultation today, the patient appeared surprisingly cooperative. In unexceptionable English (she obtained excellent grades in her A-Levels), she suggested that I take a look at certain pages in one of the books she was clutching—the very same books that had been the subject of her earlier tussle with Nurse. The book in question turned out to be a considerable tome called *The Collected Poems of William Blake* but it wasn't the poems she was drawing my attention to. It was the pictures. They had titles like 'Two Angels Descending (1822)', 'An Angel Whispering (1822)', 'Eve Tempted by the Serpent (1807)', 'The Jelousy of Los (1797)'.

Since patient helpfully held open the pages for me, I was able to note these titles and dates in some detail. Each sketch showed a naked young woman with a clear emphasis on the genital area and some showed snakes (obviously embodying the distended male organ) coiling round the woman. The patient's observation to Nurse that she was 'William's Angel' also became immediately clear, for these poems and paintings were by William Blake. To understand the roots of the patient's psychosis, this self-identification needs to be probed.

I then asked to look at the other books which the patient held guarded in her lap, but she would not oblige, so I judged it best to let her be and requested Nurse to lead her out.

Next consultation: 23.9.88.

Wings of Glass

Sylvia's question about love was very hard but I just had to search till I found the answer. There *were* answers and they were hidden in the books Sister Lydia led me to in the Library. I knew that, even if the Doctorji didn't and that's why I needed the books, why I'd brought them with me to England, why I had to guard them all the time.

So when I was taken to see the Doctor-sahib in the new English hospital and he asked me in a low, soft voice—very kindly, not like the Nurse—if I'd let him take a look at my Angel pictures, I showed him William's book at once because I thought from his voice that I could trust him. I thought he would take me in his arms afterwards and stroke my hair like William.

But the Doctorji did not say anything. He just stared silently at William's drawings for a long time and then he asked me to show him my other books. That's all. No love, nothing . . .

That's why I refused to show him my other books—because I saw something in a flash the way we'd sometimes see that a nun had ordinary legs and thighs and even scars like anybody else when she lifted her skirts higher than she should. *At that moment, I saw it was the same with doctors and nurses.*

Underneath the kindness, it was business, as it was with my father and as I suppose it was even with the nuns. But when I talked to Sylvia and William and the others, it was different. I *wanted* to talk to them because I loved them, pure and simple. Fact is, they freed up my snake-twisted mind and allowed me to fly—and that, after all, was what my wings were for.

Of course, the doctors never believed I had wings, so they never asked what the wings were for.

If they had, they would have discovered something strange.

My wings were *turkey* wings. They weren't mine at all. They were just borrowed feathers. Yes, yes, *hiss*, my story began with a set of borrowed plumes, and I could hear Sylvia giggling hysterically in the background already. Go on, she was saying, *do* tell! And I am going to, even if you laugh out loud like Sylvia and I am sad like the sky when the moon goes away. I'm going to tell you my story, beginning with the wings . . .

✿

The fact that I was growing wings—real ones, as real as Jesus' red, illuminated heart golden-inscribed with *God is Love* jumping out at me, throbbing, pulsating, from the walls of the school verandah—did not, at thirteen, strike me as odd. Not in the least and that's God's own truth, as Sister Maria used to say. For one thing, the process was gradual, more irritating than alarming. At first, when the nodules appeared like knots on my shoulder blades, slightly raised and tender, all I wanted was to keep feeling them, like an itch. I'd tilt back on my chair in class and pretend to scratch my back.

Bad form, Sister Maria said, frowning, sit still, girl!

But I couldn't. Because Sister Maria had suddenly *turned into a turkey bird* right before my eyes—gobble, gobble, gobble! I suppose, in hindsight, this too could have been the first sign of my 'madness' creeping up slowly, like a cold. At the time, though, I didn't pay it much attention, just as I wouldn't bother too much about a sniffle. And after a few minutes, it's true, Maria turned back to her old self and we went back to our history lesson on the 'Sultanate of Bijapur' and that was that . . .

Most of the older nuns had always looked like turkeys to me anyhow, their habits bustling and rustling with self-importance, and their necks straggly and curious and beaky. How they managed to keep their wattles on in the heat of the plains, I do not know. To this day, with all my knowledge of the cold English frost, I have no answer to this mystery. *How* did the nuns of Tempke keep themselves from sweating under all those barrels of clothing? No deodorant, no cooling showers, no nothing! If you'd undressed all the Sisters in our convent, I said to Mona years later when all was past, there would have been enough Irish linen for all the babies' nappies from Alaska to Zanzibar, but one thing's for certain. Turkeys have great dignity, and I know a lot about the tough old birds, because there was one led into the schoolyard for slaughter every October, to be eaten at Christmas . . .

If I were to go back to the 'prehistory' (Sylvia's word) of my so-called madness, my flights of fancy, my 'paranoid schizophrenia' (in the English Doctor's notes which I read upside down when he wasn't looking) and all that, I think I'd have to begin with THE TURKEY, the 1984 turkey.

Turkey-eating once a year was as important to the nuns of Tempke Convent as the daily chewing of biscuits and paan to the bhakts at Baba's Ashram. It was part of the life of our town—like Biscuit Baba's fortune-telling every Thursday. For the price of a packet of Britannia or Parle, anyone, rich or poor, could get a *True Palmistry/Astrology/Numerology Forecast!* direct from the Baba, just as anyone could get to learn English from the nuns for a price. Only the price was different, maybe. The other difference was that our Convent was quite far away and school buses or Ambassadors had to take you there; the Baba conducted his operations right in middle of the town, in the main market not far from *Swapna Sweets* where Mona, Afi and I sneaked in once in a while for chaat and mithai and then hung around for some fun at the back of the Baba's tent with the all other escapees from our weekly convent 'outing'.

The Baba could fix any problem. That is why they took my mother to see him when she became mad but she bit his hand so hard the nishaan remained for years and so the Baba had to give her a shaap and because of this curse maybe she killed herself, that's what Lakshmi said. That's the way my mother's problem was solved—solved forever.

The exact same thing happened when I began to shiver and dash around and the girls at school began to whisper and giggle every time I left the room—all of them except for Mona. They took me to see the Baba because he could solve my problem (by the way, 'solve' is 'loves' all mixed up but only Mona could see this joke and they would not allow her to come with me to the Baba, no way). Anyway, I knew about my mother so of course I did not bite him.

I became a stone instead.

I became still like the moon which is actually a piece of rock, everyone knows. Then Laskhmi made me hand over the packet of Kaju-Badaam-Special-Biscuits wrapped up in red with gold patterns, just like my mother's wedding sari, to the Baba. Of course I kept my eyes tight shut the whole time because then I would not see the mark of my mother's bite on his wrinkly hand. I was the moon—still and small and far away.

But I could smell and I could hear.

In the rose-petal silence, I could hear Lakshmi tell the Baba how she and everyone else at home had tried to solve my hush-hush problem by calling in the Jhar-phoonk man. Then the Baba said that all these jatil problems had been caused by the bad karma from my mother's side, from my pichla janam, but my father's side was good, very good. So I would be all right in the end (which was a correct prophecy even if it took a lot of years). He said Lakshmi was quite right to call the ojha because I was just a child. My problem would not become serious if my father sent some daan with biscuits every month to the ashram. No need for me to come again.

Then we touched his feet which had very long toenails like a cat and we left.

After that, Lakshmi insisted that the ojha come every month even though I didn't like him at all. He mumbled away for hours and beat me with his long jharoo of thorns and neem and peepul. Then everyone grabbed me and bathed me in ice-cold water and lit the havan fire and ate prasad except for me because the churail inside me had to be starved for a day and a night—but none of this helped either. I still dashed around madly. I continued to shiver and was quite uncontrollable. So the jhaar-phoonk did not help but I remember the Baba's words that I would be all right in the end and when Sylvia came to me I took her to the Baba because the Baba could solve any problem and Sylvia had many problems.

She was not keen. Kirtans, whatever that strange word meant, in an obscure Indian small town did not 'excite' her, she said. You may or may not know this, but Sylvia loved 'jocks'—she taught me that word—and the Baba was just the opposite. He had the most mottled, creased body you'd ever seen and you could safely say he did not smell of aftershave. Also, his eyes ran constantly. *Cataract,* Sylvia declared at once in her doctor's voice. *Dis*gusting! I tried to tell her that the Baba was famous, that he was our local celebrity and people came to consult him from All Over India, but Sylvia was not impressed. There was a lovely fellow in the street outside, she insisted in her strict Sister Liddie poetry-teacher voice, whose *snakedom of writhings made manifest his manhood*—whereas it was obvious the Baba had no manhood to speak of! Sylvia tugged at my hand and whispered that she much preferred the Snake Charmer.

Shush, I said, the Baba's here. He'll begin telling fortunes now!

At that, Sylvia cocked her neck sideways like a mynah. *Fortunes?* she breathed.

I could tell she was hooked because if anything could beat Sylvia's passion for jocks, it was her appetite for fortune telling. Also, the atmosphere in Baba's tent had changed and Sylvia responded to it as if she was a rupee coin caught in a sudden ray of sunlight. Her brown hair glowed with red, her eyes began to glint and her soul stood stock-still. She didn't even notice that the Baba's rant about maya and moksha etc. had come to a total halt.

The shamiana was suddenly full to bursting. Everyone was pushing and shoving and touching but Sylvia, Angel Sylvia, stood rooted, metallic and cool, a coin-princess among her doting subjects, a Queen Bee being pelted with rose petals. Dead or alive, Sylvia was always a realist . . .

It's good fortune, pushpa varsha, flower rain, I translated like an obedient lackey but by this time the kirtan was hammering in our ears so hard, I wasn't sure Sylvia could hear me, so I just pushed her forward until she was in the front row.

I was right behind where no one could see me. Totally safe. And then, there she was: *Sylvia face to face with the Baba,* staring into his kind, dribbling face and it hit me like a stone from Afi's surefire catapult!

I'd forgotten the biscuits!

What would happen now? What if the Baba cursed Sylvia, what if he turned her into a cow or an earthworm or bird-shit? What if his informers told my father, what if they carried tales to the nuns and I was locked up? *What if?* My whole body began to shrivel in panic and the heaps of rose-petals around us started to wrinkle and smell shit-rotten too. Sylvia's magic sun vanished behind a choking cloud and the dhoop-incense began to clog up my nostrils. I couldn't see Sylvia's face at all and I felt scared to death.

But it was all a false alarm!

For once, for *once,* the Baba seemed to have forgotten his biscuits and Sylvia her jocks. There was something else going on. Love perhaps, or a trance or something, something really serious . . .

The tent was so hushed that if the rose-petals were still falling, I'm sure we would have heard them. And then the Baba, who *never* spoke English, was suddenly talking to Sylvia in her own language and grabbing her and telling her she had Ganga Mata's blessing and that she would be immortal and Sylvia's eyes were full of tears, like a newborn baby's . . .

The first time I told this story, it was to Dr M back in Tempke who made neat notes in his book, taking in my rigmarole about the Biscuit Baba and Sylvia without saying a word—but I could *see* he didn't believe me. It made me want to yell at him:

If you don't trust me, Doctor-sahib, you can read the history books!

They all say the same thing. Through her short life, Sylvia's interest in ouija boards and palmists and the future never waned. It was one of the things she and her poet husband Ted had in common, like planchette. Or read Ted. Read his *Birthday Letters,* addressed to her, to Sylvia, in the year of his own death. These are his words:

I was there. I saw it . . .

What did Ted see?

Well, for one thing he saw me—

Sylvia's 'Indian midwife,
(Of all your fairy godmothers the timeliest,
for you she was a deity from the Ganges,
Black with alluvial wisdom) stroked your hair
And made you weak with relief, and stowed you aboard,
Folded you from yourself, lulled the passage
With monkey-fine dark fingers delivered you
In a free floating crib, an image that sneezed
And opened a gummed mouth and started to cry . . .

Also, he saw the nuns at the convent—a 'sorority' he called them.

He saw the turkey murder.

He saw the faraway landscape of India, of Nauru, of Tempke.

And he must have caught glimpses of Biscuit Baba's tent. Otherwise how could he write so exactly, tell me, Doctorji?

It was your membership
Of a sorority of petals and creatures
Whose masonic signs are beauty and nectar
In the love-land, the Paradise
Your suicide had tried to drag you from . . .

And it was you that escaped death
In the little woven vessel
On the most earthly river
Of that Paradise.
Of yourself from your bleeding self
With the face mask of nitrous oxide that was empty.
With yoga breath . . .

Ted saw these things with his poet's eyes.

Like William, he saw Paradise. Like David, he saw me . . .

He saw I was there with Sylvia at all her finest moments, helping her draw her deep huffing happy yoga breaths when Frieda and Nicholas were born and at the exact gasping moment of her suicide. I was there in Sylvia's dreams, her angel of petals and creatures—and she in mine, *interfused.* You call it madness, Doctor, but for me it was real. It was *real* for Sylvia and it was real for Ted. Ted saw these things and in time he was able to write about them and *absolve himself.* In time, Ted answered Sylvia's persistent question about love and the whole word read it—in time . . .

Tempke was different. Time was never a problem in our town, as it was with Ted and Sylvia, so pushed by desire and ambition they were like American boxers, battering their bruised love to bits as if it was a punching bag. Sylvia and Ted, fighting in the eye of history, their own eyes purple and swollen and bleeding, what *chance* had they? But in Tempke, it was different. Mostly, we lived outside time in Tempke because none of us had any ambition. I don't think we knew what the word meant—1984 or no 1984.

1984: The year Mrs Indira Gandhi was shot, I remember that. She looked like an Egyptian mummy all wrapped in white or a ship about to be launched or something, sideways on the front page of all the newspapers for weeks and Doordarshan remained switched on endlessly, but did we care?

Then some gas leaked in some factory in Bhopal and we saw this dead boy with his glassy eyes covered in dust with no one to pick him up because his mother and everyone else had died, running, running, running from the gas and then Moscow pulled out of the Olympic Games in 1984, but we didn't care about these things either. Not much, anyway. It wasn't our business. Of course we knew they were Tragedies, they were Blots on the Fair Face of Indian Democracy, like the Emergency (not Moscow, of course, which was the opposite (A Blow in the Face of Western Dominance!), but they were too far away to matter. These newspaper things were never part of Tempke's story, not really.

However much weedy Father Sinha (sin, *sin*, ha, ha!), adjusted his wobbly eyeglasses over his oily, noble nose and lectured to us about Nehru and Gandhi and Foreign Policy, we knew he was only acting. Just as we knew he ran Sunday School (for Hindus only because they didn't go to Mass, so where would they get their morality from otherwise?) because he was too poor and too weak to be a politician. Naxal marches, gheraos, the lockouts and the shouting, Father Sinha managed nimbly to keep away from all that tamasha. So who would listen to him except us captives? We all knew FS had to settle for priesthood because there was nothing better on offer in Tempke. Father Sinha the forgettable, he lived outside history, too.

Personally, I was more involved with the turkey. (*Don't laugh, don't stand there beside me giggling, Sylvia didi, you heartless about-to-die wench! It's your story, too, after all.*)

That year, 1984, the nuns' Christmas turkey was wonderful. He was magnificent, just like the turkey painting I'd found in

India Discovered by John Keay. *Key*—get it? Like so many things in my life then, I saw it as a Sign. I loved that book. It was brand new and the pictures in it glowed like my mother's eyes when she wore her jewels. Before she hanged herself, that is, and my father began to hate me . . .

About my mother's jewellery, by the way, this is what I remember. She didn't *wear* it much. It only appeared at weddings and festivals before being put sternly back into the bank. I wanted to play with them, my mother's mega-jewels. I wanted to play with her. But they would not allow me to. So I think they were 'prisoners of the dark' both, my mother and her jewels, guarded, shut away. My wings hurt when they came into my mind—but the book was just the opposite.

It always lay out in the open—sunlit, beckoning, bathed in Englishness and in security. *India Discovered,* with a picture of the Taj Mahal on the cover, as untouchably white as the Taj inside Doctorji's glass paper-weight but minus the upside-down snow. Only a brilliant blue sky above and John Keay in sharp black below . . .

There was also another book which sounded the same in our Library, which was by a very famous author, Jawaharlal Nehru, Prime Minister of India. (Btw, Doctor, *Letters from a Father to his Daughter* is also by the same author but *my* father never wrote me any letters, not a single one—not even when I came by myself to England).

Anyhow, this other book called *Discovery of India* was prescribed for our history class and it said: *India is an ancient palimpsest upon which layer upon layer of thought and reverie has been inscribed and yet no succeeding layer had completely hidden . . . what had been written previously.* I thought that was beautiful, so beautiful I memorized it—I can memorize anything in a jiffy—but Mona said who cares whether India is a Palimpsest or a Potato, it's all boring stuff! So John Keay was the winner in the end, Doctor-sahib, I think. He had pictures and JLN has only words—tons of words.

They bury you, words, so you've got to be careful when it comes to words. I learnt this from Sylvia too. Pictures were safer, less *incendiary* than words, that's what Sylvia said. And later, when my mind began to disintegrate, when it felt like a heap of dry leaves, piled up for burning, a few bits and pieces of it flying away each time a breeze blew, it's true—I'd think of John Keay's book and feel calmer. Nehru was fine—but he didn't calm me down, and neither did Sylvia. They both spoke too much, like a pair of Freddy Mercurys, rock stars from Mona's precious firang album jabbering away in my head.

India Discovered was different, very smooth like Kishore Kumar or Mohd. Rafi singing. It slid over the surface of my mind like honey. Someone called Chartered Bros. had presented it to the Convent. He'd written on the front in a curly hand: *In Gratitude For Services Rendered.* I wished I could thank him back, but there was no address and we weren't allowed to borrow the book. It was in the *Encyclopaedia Britannica* category—'read only'—but that was good enough for me. I'd sit in the deserted library and turn to page 219, which was mostly about this English person called Havell (Have- hell: *and he within this snakedom makes manifest his writhings,* Sylvia had written. Get it?).

Anyhow, I think Havell was the one who (according to John Keay, page 119) found the Turkey picture first. It was a really beautiful picture, the turkey's wings shining in the sunlight like Sylvia's halo of hair, like my mother's eyes, like poetry even. The English in the book was quite difficult, though. I had to copy out the whole passage in my Vigyan notebook. Then I underlined the difficult words and looked them up. It was a struggle—but even at thirteen, there are things you have to do . . .

New Addenbrooke's Medical File 203 5.9.88: Patient readmitted to stricter security Ward F earlier than scheduled appointment. Experienced psychotic episode when home for the weekend and brought back to the hospital by relative (aunt) who claims the patient began to behave very strangely in the evening when the aunt returned from work. Patient's appearance was markedly disheveled. She had a page of handwritten text pinned to her chest and talked and laughed uncontrollably throughout dinner to an invisible interlocutor whom she referred to sometimes as Mona and sometimes as Sylvia. There was, apparently, no mention of 'William'. From her conversation with the patient, the aunt gathered that she was upset by a television programme she was watching which showed home-range fowl being culled on suspicion of disease.

After her meal (patient's appetite was reportedly normal), patient ran excitedly to her own room and tore out some pages from her notebook, which she repeatedly attempted to attach to her shoulders, making gutteral, gabbling sounds all the while. When asked what she was doing, patient said she was trying to fix her wings so she could fly and approached the window. At this point, the aunt decided to call for an ambulance, as she thought patient might damage herself. Paramedics reported within the half-hour.

Patient's state described by paramedics as hyperactive but not violent. Since patient has a history of self-inflicted wounds, this was a concern. Was sedated immediately by the Nurse on duty and is under observation. The torn pages clutched in patient's hand are blank but the page on her chest is hereby attached to her case file:

> INDIA DISCOVERED BY JOHN KEAY, page 119, FOR SYLVIA, MONA AND AFI. PL. INVESTIGATE THIS CLUE. 'Take the famous picture of a turkey cock commissioned by Jahangir . . . Here was a turkey, not from life, but as the mind's eye saw it . . . hence the result, which says a lot more about a turkey cock, from the precise markings of the feathers to the absurd swagger, that could any accurate painting from life. It was a turkey as one imagines a turkey, but it would never win a poultry club prize.'

Who Killed Cock Robin?

My turkey—the one whose wings I had inherited, the one I fed every day from October to the BLACK DAY he was stolen and murdered—would have won any poultry prize he was entered for. He was Mr Swagger-and-Strut, he was Badshah Jahangir, Emperor of the World and he would eat out of my angel hands. *Please,* you must believe me, Doctorji.

Of course, we both knew he would have to go soon, but we tried not to think of it. We lived for the moment, the Badshah and I. Until the holidays, I'd whisper to him under my breath, until the holidays. I said it like a charm, repeating my words every day for weeks—*badshahrukjahbadshahrukjah jamumkhashahtutkhabadshahturukjah!* And it worked. Not exactly in the way I expected, but it did work in the end. The charm *worked,* that was the point—and that's why you must listen to my story.

Usually the killing of the school turkey was discreet, typical of the nuns. He was there when we broke up for the Winter Vacation early in December and he wasn't there when we returned to school in January. Painless, but this time—all hell broke loose.

First of all, get this—*there was no Assembly*. Unheard of! No

Assembly in the winter of 1984 in Tempke—shocking, more shocking for us than the faraway murder of Indiraji by her bodyguards, which had filled the front pages of the newspapers for weeks. The no-Assembly day would go down in the history of Tempke. It *has* gone down in history though you will not find it recorded in any paper. The nuns hushed it up and the police thumped it down and the parents connived but everyone in Tempke heard about it all the same. How could they not? No classes, nothing! The whole school milling around outside like bees in summer—Sylvia's bees—but we will come to those . . .

Sylvia's honey bees, buzzing around at the very end of my story, wreaking havoc. In this story, almost everything happens in the last few days. Love, sickness, revenge, but the fact is you cannot understand the meaning of these things until you know the small things too—the small, silly, meaningless things that happened first. Droning first and honey after, that's the rule, Sylvia said.

That day, anyway, there's this huge sarkari Black Maria parked in the yard and two real live policemen patrolling the scene of the crime. They wouldn't let anyone near. It was like something out of *Sholay,* I promise you, Doctor-ji. Those inspector-jis—you should have seen their lathis and enormous khaki half-pants—like helicopters! On top of which, one had a moustache that came down almost to his knees, while the other with the pockmarks, guess what he was doing. The badtameez was pacing up and down with his hands locked together right in front of his goolies. Obviously on purpose to impress the nuns who'd gathered in a helpless clutch on the back verandah. I'd swear I'd never seen them so dumbstruck, even sharper-than-scissors Sister Liddie.

Then suddenly, as if by magic, Mona appeared by my side. She said, *Come, I'll show you. Buddhu poleece, idiot geese! They think they know everything!*

Have I told you, Mona was my ulta, my opposite. She didn't have a meek-Jesus bone in her body and she was very clever, as clever and outward as I was slow, stupid, *inward.* It's true I was always top of the class and Mona was middle or bottom but that was because she had no time to waste on mugging. She had more important things to do—and here she was now, smartly summoning Afi to our aid and I'm surprised at how quickly he comes, almost as if he was waiting for Mona to summon him.

Afi: we can go no further without him. He's at the centre of my story. AND I HAVE NOT IMAGINED HIM, DOCTOR SAHIB, WHATEVER YOU SAY. What? Why have you never set eyes on him? Well, that's because the nuns sent him away to study in Ireland after school and then he came back and all these terrible things happened. Just listen, Doctor sahib . . .

Back in school, Afi was the nuns' great darling and, in a way, he, too, was my ulta. I was royally paid for all right, but (I've told you this already) I was peculiar and I was Hindu whereas Afi had always been—I think the right word is 'cherished'. He'd been baptized and cherished by the nuns from birth.

Afi belonged and he was beloved as I was not. Mostly the nuns (except for Sister L, of course) didn't like men but Afi was the great exception. Afi was a boy touched by the Angels. Everyone knew his story—how his Adivasi mother had stumbled into the nunnery in the throes of labour and died giving birth to Afi before she could tell them who his father was or anything. So the nuns had reared him since he was a baby and now he did a lot for them, too—he chopped wood, he gardened, he went to the market, he cleaned up the schoolyard. Plus, he studied, plus he could sing.

Plus he was handsome—which may be hard to believe but it's not Mills and Boon. Promise. It's *true.* Afi had long limbs the colour of the best ebony my father (who is in the wood business and many other businesses) smuggled in at great expense from China via Burma for his richest customers. Afi also had curly hair and slanty eyes that crinkled when he smiled—but the greatest thing about him was that he was a genius with animals. He could splint a dog's broken leg so that it would be running around in less than a month and he could charm squirrels off trees.

Was Afi perfect, then? Was there nothing wrong with him? Oh there *was*, of course there was. Because the main thing about him was that, all said and done, he was a *servant.* Just like Emperor Jahangir was a turkey and meant to be roasted one day. It was like the colour of our skins. Afi was born ebony black, I was born milkish fair and Mona golden wheatish. This was our Fate. We did not speak of it but we knew that these things mattered and that no one could change them, not the nuns, not Jesus, not even Sylvia so 'hag-haunted' by the colour black—not *anyone.*

If Afi had other faults, they all came from this basic flaw. He was a servant, so it was expected that he would tell a few lies now and then—and of course he did. Afi obliged. He always did. As you will see, Doctor Sahib, the key to understanding Afi was his obliging nature. He did not return every single paisa from the shopping and worst of all, he smoked, scrounging bidis off his friend Ramu, the panwallah's second nikkamah son—but the nuns were indulgent. It was normal and to be expected. What was wrong with that? It wasn't as if they'd caught any of the girls in the school lighting up! Any girl from a decent home who did such a thing would have to be expelled, disgraced, fined!

Afi was a different proposition, though. He was only sixteen, a fatherless boy who was a gift from God and so all eleven of his mothers forgave him without a thought, because they had such enormous hopes for him. Servant Afi may have been by birth, but he would be the highest kind of servant—Jesus' servant. Jesus was poor too, born in a manger, didn't we know?

Mona once asked whether Afi was like the dog in the manger perhaps, but the nuns shushed her up at once. They could bear no aspersions cast on Afi, even as a joke. They had struggled to teach him all they knew and then they had consecrated him to God. Mona, be quiet! And Mona was, because she was generous as well as intelligent, my friend Mona, and she did not hold it against Afi that the nuns were so gaga over him.

They'd given him a thunderbolt of a name, too, to match their hopes. ATHANASIUS FRANCIS IMMANUEL, the keeper of the creed. Sister Maria never tired of repeating that they'd spent a whole week praying over the name before they decided: Athanasius meaning 'deathless', Francis for gentle St. Francis and Immanuel meaning 'dedicated to God'. This boy would be undyingly dedicated to God, like St. Francis of Assisi. St. Francis had been merry in his youth, boisterous, full of pranks, not so great at his studies, but then he heard Angelic Voices and was converted to the Service of the Lord. Afi would be the same.

Next year, when he finished school with the Jesuit brothers, they'd raise the money to send him to Dublin to study medicine and become a priest, after which he would come back and help them convert the Poor to God. Best of all, the eleven nun-mothers had no doubt that everything would come to pass exactly as they foretold. Afi is an angel, they'd exclaim, with a benign glow on their cowled and innocent faces—and the funny thing is that not *one* of them had any idea at all of how truthfully they spoke . . .

Anyhow, the angel had by now meekly unlocked the gate to the roof at Mona's bidding and let us up the outside staircase to the roof of the nun's quarters. It was beautiful, this staircase, a sort of winding coppery green, carved and trellised. On its inside edge were the words: *Sen & Company First Indian Ironworks, Estbl. 1885.*

No one paid the slightest attention to us, least of all the strutting policemen, so it was as safe as playing Chinese Checkers in the last few rows of Miss Gupta's Hindi class. Miss Gupta was shortsighted, she could not see anything beyond the first six rows. We could have staged all of *Godaan* in dumb charades at the back of the class as she droned on about Premchand's virtues in the front. On the day of the turkey murder, I guess you could say everyone had turned as short-sighted as Miss Gupta—and Mona could do *exactly* as she wanted.

Mona had POWER that day, she could have flown like an

eagle if she wished—but Mona was not like me. Her feet were always firmly planted on the ground.

The roof was warm, with a white light spreading everywhere—white from the rows and rows of flapping washing, white from the sunlight falling on the whitewashed parapets over our hidden kingdom of bird-shit all the way from Nauru, white from the painted water tank in the far corner. The green trees swayed gently at eye-level around us. It was calm, like Paradise. If I could, I would have stayed up on that roof forever—but we didn't have much time.

Come, said Mona, tugging at my hand, so I shuffled behind her to join Afi where he was already posted, looking comfortably down on the policemen below.

Then I saw Jahangir. Or rather, I didn't . . .

I saw just an emptiness, the silence of a nunnery parlour, Biscuit Baba's maun vrata before his demented prophecies, the gaps between the words on a page, the huge distance between my crazy madness and Mona's clear-eyed planning. I, Pari the Fairy, saw all these things. From my roofy place very high up, I saw everything as clearly as Ted had seen Tempke. I saw the space where Jahangir *might* have been. Wings without a body between. A pair of great wings, spread-eagled across the dry winter grass, their white serrated edges sharp as razors in the sunlight, and a little torn rubbery piece of red beside . . .

I began to shiver and *no one* could stop my shivering, not even Mona.

Would I not have known them anywhere, those wings, that bloody mutilated wattle?

❁

There is a white wall, above which the sky creates itself—

Angels swim in it . . .
The sun dissolves on this wall, bleeding its lights . . .
A grey wall now, clawed and bloody . . .
Is there no way out of the mind?
Steps at my back spiral . . .
There are no trees or birds in this world,
There is only sourness . . .

Convent Days

The next thing I know, I'm lying in the sickbay and my mouth smells of vomit and tastes like yoghurt gone stale, sour, bitter and *cold*. My head aches terribly. Little fishes swim in and out of my skull into the blue Oceania of the Infirmary walls.

I keep seeing visions of my mother.

It's very silent in this room with ten identical beds—of which only two are occupied. I'm in one and then two beds away, the epileptic girl who's been put in here after she had a fit. There is a silver spoon on her bedside table and they stick it in her mouth whenever they think she is going to have a fit. So that she won't bite off her tongue, Sister explains to me kindly, but this only terrifies me more. What if she bites off her tongue when I'm alone in the room with her? I imagine the blood gushing out of her mouth and flowing onto the bed and then her silence. I imagine her tongue-less silence and my mouth dries up and my breath stops in my chest . . .

The epileptic girl's breathing is rasping and uneven. My mother's eyes are wild and sad. Bird-shit spatters the world! *How can I sleep?* The pain will not go away. No hope. Then, finally, *finally,* Sister comes in and gives me some aspirin. I swallow the pills and my head begins to feel heavier and drowsier, but then, just as I'm dozing off, *Mona* suddenly creeps up on me from somewhere! Somehow she's managed to persuade one of the ayahs to smuggle her in.

At first, I'm not sure whether she's real or not but that's only for a second because then she pinches me and I'm sure it's Mona because she has no mercy, as usual. She shakes and pummels and yells.

Oye, get up! she says. *Get up!*

Then she leans over me, her breath warm and moist over my face. Somehow this is very comforting and I sit up.

Don't you remember what happened? Mona hisses—but I don't.

I remember nothing but the wings . . .

The police have gone! They found nothing!

I stare at Mona blankly.

Then she says, in the same dramatic whisper: *We did it! We did it!*

But I'm past it. My mother has appeared again, standing just behind Mona. She's weeping but the jewels round her neck glitter like stars. At last, I manage to find some words—but they aren't the right ones.

What to do, what to *do?* I say weakly, not daring to look at Mona. It's my all-time favourite phrase when I'm miserable, my wringing-hands mantra, *whattodowhattodoto dotodotodo* . . .

Shut up! Mona says to me. *She's dead, okay baba, forget it!*

All Mona's sentences end in exclamation marks and second to 'Shut up!' her favourite phrase is 'Forget it!'

Now she marches off in a huff. I know she despises me and

will never trust me again. Still, I love Mona. She's my best friend, whatever happens.

We didn't talk much those days. But we did things, we did things all right. Every time I whined *what to do*, Mona thought up things to do. She didn't hold with empty words and memories. Mona was the original action heroine. She was Nadia the Fearless/Take 2.

Mona was a Forgetter and I was a Rememberer. I remembered everything, the Heineken poster, the Triptych, the Glaxo Baby's toothless smile, so many useless things. I even made up things to remember. This was my madness, Doctor M told me. I couldn't separate past from present, he said. I couldn't tell the difference between fact and fiction, between memory and imagination, between Mona and Sylvia, etc. etc. They're phantoms, just phantoms, they cannot hurt you, Doctor M kept saying, but what I wanted to ask that white-faced firang sahib was—how did *he* know? Was he Einstein or what?

The truth was that Mona, Sylvia, Lydia and the others were always around those days, waiting to pounce! Sometimes it was a game and sometimes it was real, but I could never be sure, so I had to watch out all the time, just to be on the safe side. Some months, I couldn't sleep for days because *I* saw them, even if others couldn't. Sometimes, I would get so tired just trying to keep my eyes open that I would say things to Dr M that I didn't intend to. Once I said out loud, without thinking:

Please, Doctorji, did *your* mother kill herself and did *your* father freeze every time he looked at you?

Then I grabbed the Doctor Sahib's coat and clung to it, jabbering.

Listen please, Doctorji. I'm *not* mad like Ma. Please, *please* stay . . .

Dr M did not reply but I could see he was shocked. His body spoke to me even if he didn't. I saw his shoulders drooping and his leathery eyelid flickering the way it did every time I spoke of my mother—and I guessed it was because the Doctorji was like everyone else in the end. He didn't want to be embarrassed by the scandal of my mother's suicide. No one spoke about it, so why should Dr M? But that day, he did speak after all, firmly disengaging my hands from his coat and muttering and sighing almost to himself: *No, you're not mad, Pari, not any more than the rest of us . . .*

It was a few weeks later that my father arranged to send me to England, but I never forgot what Dr M told me before I left. Remember to keep your diary fresh, Pari! Write down the facts as clearly as you can because *you* see things that we don't . . .

❁

So here you are, Doctorji.

I remember this. *Fact:* my mother has been dead ten days. I'm squatting happily with Lakshmi in the servants' quarters, sipping tea from her battered old aluminum mug, and my father suddenly stalks in and orders Lakshmi to get me cleaned up, jaldi. Then he scoops me up, drives to the convent and dumps me with Mother Superior. No explanations.

I remember that drive, Doctor. My father doesn't say a

word in the car. He doesn't even look at me. Of course, he doesn't *touch*. Then we get off and I notice that one of the pots with the bright purple begonias is broken and the mud oozing out of its side like thick blood. I notice that some of this mud-blood clings to the black heel of my father's shoe as he climbs up the steps to the MS's office. I notice the Brylcream glistening on the sharp, spruce hair at the back of his head and the confident swing of his arm as it moves up to ring the bell.

Mother Superior is out in *twenty seconds flat*. She must have been listening for us, the cunning old sweetie. Then we move quickly to the parlour. *More private,* Mother Superior whispers. And so I sit there, invisible, even though I'm wearing my best pink-lace party dress sewn by Hamidullah Tailor. I sit comparing my father's toothbrush moustache to the feather duster on Mother Superior's upper-lip, my father's low solemn baritone to her surprised Irish pitches while they talk on as if I didn't exist.

Seven, I was only seven then, Doctor, but did they think I was stupid or that I couldn't hear? *Fact:* mad people are not stupid and for your information, they can hear. Take me, Doctorji. I'm a *hyper hearer*. Where you hear only one voice I hear so many—Sylvia, Afi, Summa . . . You want me to go on, Doctor Sahib? Mad people aren't blind either. In the days before I left, I saw your fingers doing violence to your stethoscope each time I came to you. Maybe you wanted to hit me but it was that poor instrument being mauled instead. *Transference*, Doctorji, remember? Last point: mad people aren't dumb either.

There weren't many voices in the Parlour that day—only two, my father's and Mother Superior's and she's speaking. She's saying in a low murmur that she isn't sure she can keep me that long, they don't have a hostel. If they had the means, they would've started up a Girl's Hostel. Maybe some contribution to the Building Fund . . .

Then, all of a sudden, my father *acts.* Abrupt and powerful, he lays MS low with a single stroke of his Sword of Silence. One lakh, he mutters and the numbers spread across the room like melting chocolate. I can taste the sweetness on Mother Superior's tongue. Visions of good works flood her brain, giving her a chocolate high. I see it—Mother Superior yielding in silence and my father winning. In the end, he always does. He's rich and he's used to winning. He'd won my mother, too, before she managed to escape. My mother was one of my father's few failures and it cut him up like crazy. I see that now.

As for my mother, she punished my father by putting him in Cold Storage forever. Me, she blessed by giving me my shivery Voices. That's fate—or you can call it chance. Which is why, when I summon up Mr Bee-stung Bishnupada Dey, my poor father fresh from the honey-freezer these days, I just feel sorry for him, not mad. But he was mad that day in Mother Superior's Parlour, I could tell—not mad like Ma or me, but *angry,* furious chilly undefeatable angry.

You could *smell* my father's coldness after my mother climbed up to the ceiling fan and floated up to heaven. Lakshmi showed me the picture. She had torn it out from the *Dainik Dastaan* and one of the jagged edges had amputated my mother's foot from the photograph. Still, her face, you could see her face very clearly, white and strained like a clown's, with her eyes popping and her neck tilting sideways like a broken bird's, the folds of her red wedding Banarasi hanging neatly down as if she is about to go out to a party. She almost looked ugly in that photograph, my beautiful mother, with, of all things, her big, English fur hat which she never ever wore perched upon her head just like a circus clown's topi but much uglier—which shows that you cannot trust anything, not even a photograph. The world lies to you—and that's the truth.

Now I hear my father issuing final instructions to Mother Superior. I can have as many glasses of milk a day as I like, he'd pay for everything. I was to be taught correct English and convent manners. When I finished school, he would come and get me. He was leaving the country on business next week, but this was his address, she could phone if there was a crisis. He would open a Bank Account for me before I left and the convent could draw on it for expenses. No strings, except that he wasn't to be disturbed unless it became *absolutely necessary.*

And I see that Mother Superior has been reduced to mere nods, clutching the first installment of her *ek-lakh* cheque and meekly ushering him to the door.

And that was how I became a **Convent Girl**.

No difference between me and the charity Anglos from across the railway tracks or the Adivasi basti recruits, except that their parents were poor, Christian and alive (as far as I knew) and mine were rich, Hindu and dead (or as good as). I'd spent six years in the convent already like this and had only three to go before my father came and fetched me, when the turkey thing happened. Or so I thought before things came to a head in the winter of '84 . . .

❁

The funny thing is, I hardly remember my mother at all, only drifting bits and glimpses. How she dressed up at Puja time, how beautiful she was and how she crouched in corners and no one could pull her out her room or she'd *bite* them.

Sometimes I think I've made up my mother's shining beauty and the Dracula sharpness of her teeth, but it's hard to tell. She's lived in my head for so long, I don't know, but one thing I DENY. I have *not* made up my mother's voice or her sparkling laughter—like soda water! These things are real, as real as you are, Mr Whitie-Mighty Doctor Sahib, believe it or not like Mr Ripley.

Abol-tabol, her nonsense rhymes. Sat bhai champa, jago re, kaeno bhai parul dako re? I cling to them, these pieces of her, her language, just like Sister Maria's 'mannafromheaven'. Because the more perfect my English, my convent manners, the more I feel my mother leaving me and her voice fading.

She is very sad.

That's when I cut myself.

I cut myself to make the pain go away. It's not so original maybe but it's simple. I hurt, hurt, hurt, so who cares whether I remember my mother or not? I miss her anyway. So this is what I'm trying to do: I'm trying to make a perfect circle pattern with her name and mine—SONALI and then PARI spelt backwards with the two 'I's at the end of our names joined up forever. But I can't manage it, I'm so stupid! I try all sorts of things—a knife from the Refectory, safety-pin points or stones, anything! When you are miserable, anything will do, but *broken glass is the best.* That is why, all my days in the blessed convent of Tempke, searching for my beautiful-as-the-full-moon mother, I leave behind this trail of broken crockery.

Clumsy, *awkward* child! Sister Maria scolds, rapping me hard with her ruler.

I do not blame her. It must be the ninety-fifth time I've let my glass slip through my fingers and hidden away a sliver in my handkerchief. But my father's money flows into the convent like an endless supply of antiseptic. It's such a salve that I know the nuns will never complain about their lost crockery or the mysterious bleeding cuts on my arms and thighs, my bloody stigmata. *Christ, Christ, a man on a cross and a cross man, my Father.* Because my father is my father, I know the nuns will endure their trials with me uncomplainingly and silently replace their broken china out of his bottomless bank account. And I'll endure too and hug my broken mother to my heart.

Empires are built out of such collaboration, Ariel, Sylvia whispers suddenly in my ear. Tell him, Pari! Go on, show some guts. *Your father's as bad as mine.* My father was a Nazi, your father picks the pockets of the poor. Same difference! My father died before I could punish him properly, your mother died for revenge! Tell the Doctor, Pari, *tell* him how your mother died of her ridiculous, fur-hatted grief. Tell him about your perfect Triptych holy family, same as mine! *Go on,* Pari girl, brought up in your never-never English nunnery, *tell* him . . .

I'm shivering by now, really scared. Sylvia's mocking me

and I know I have to obey her or AFI MIGHT DIE. So I try to tell Dr M about the English business in the Convent even though I know he isn't really interested.

The nuns say it's their duty to teach us to speak English. That's why they've come all the way from Ireland, from Australia, from Kerala, and even—once—from Papua New Guinea. Boys want to marry well-brought-up, convent-educated, English-speaking girls, that's why your parents spend a-little-bit-more to send you here. You should be grateful, girls, you shouldn't let them down.

Me let my parents down? Who's done the letting down, Doctorji, you tell me. I'm not *that* mad! Some of the girls are fined 50 paise by the nuns—for their own good—every time they break into Hindi or Bengali, but not me. Because the fact is, in spite of my A1 memory, I *just don't know* enough Bangla to dream in it or gossip in it or joke in it, just as I can't remember my long-ago, perhaps-beautiful mother. So I'm mad in English, Doctor Saheb, and you are sane in it and the nuns pray in it and how smoothly like honey we all get on together . . .

Ourfatherwhoartinheaven—when I was seven, I thought it meant, our father, his *heart* was in heaven, then I thought it meant, our father was *art* in heaven, like a picture, then I gave up. Prayers are not meant to be understood, Doctor. They are like Sylvia's poems. *Incantations*—that's what she said they are.

Anyway, I feel like telling you a joke—it's Afi's joke really—and it's about nuns. There was this very beautiful nun like Sister Lydia and there was this boy like Afi who wanted to kiss her, so he asked someone like Father Sinha, could he please kiss Sister Lydia. No, said Father Sinha. Please, *please,* said Afi. Well, I told you Father Sinha was weak, so after some time he gave up and said—okay, Afi, just this once, but *don't get into the habit!*

Habit. You could say that, after a point, I cut myself from habit.

It didn't make the pain go away or anything because in the end NO EDGE IS EVER SHARP ENOUGH and, in any case, knife-like things were carefully kept away from me. Still, this is the secret I learnt in the convent and you can't take it away from me. **Sonali will be joined to Pari her daugnter forever**. I will make a perfect circle for my mother one day whatever anyone says. Mantra-tantra: *language drives out language and pain blunts pain.* It's the simplest remedy of all. That's why I cut myself, Doctor—simple!

BTW, WHERE AM I? I DON'T KNOW WHERE I AM.
SOMEONE, PLEASE HELP.
PLEASE HELP PARI.
SILEN . . .

New Addenbrooke's Medical File 203 15.9.88: Note: Patient's outpatient appointment for 23.9. stands cancelled. Patient still admitted in Ward 11, suffering from what seems to be a severe panic attack. Could not settle all morning and began to cry and wring her hands, saying that she wanted to go home because she had to 'find Afi'. Kept repeating that she had to go to Afi, but when her aunt was contacted, she said she knew of no one called Afi of the girl's acquaintance. Moreover, when her aunty visited at lunch time, the patient buried her face in her pillow and would not have anything to do with her. It is presumed the patient was referring to her home in India and not to her Cambridgeshire residence. Since the case is a complicated one and the patient's regular consultant away on holiday, the Ward doctor suggested that the old regime of medications be continued and patient kept under hourly observation. Next consultation on priority basis: 17.9.88.

English Lessons

I just don't know *where* I am and I'm too scared to talk . . .

Sometimes I think I'm with Sylvia and sometimes I think I'm back in the convent and leaning against Sister Maria's vacant chair. I've pulled down her warm red cushion onto the cold stone floor of the outhouse and I'm hugging my knees against my thudding chest and thinking of all the crazy things that have happened—of my English books and my shivering madness and all the bad things I have done. Because of these terrible things, I know there will be no flying any more, no cool superior conversations with Sylvia, no smart *putter-putter* in English, no second chances. That world is done for, *clickety-clack!* Only rubbishy memories left, cramming my head as if it is some overfull waste-paper basket, or like the bottom of Afi's bed, an unofficial *raddi*-dump. From the corner of my snake-pit eyes, I can see crumbly bits and broken pieces of memory, how they lie there, stored under the high old convent bed, abandoned but still *there*, still waiting—and one can see it all at floor-level, the way one cannot from higher up.

Take that old **Heineken poster**. I see it mocking me from under the bed, its long insolent length lounging against the cold wall where the white-sheeted bed pushes up against the whiteness of our convent plaster. What business a Heineken ad ever had in a rustling-pure Convent, the nuns never said. It used to hang in one of the outer corridors and I remember it clearly, as clearly as I remember the Glaxo baby in Dr M's room, but somebody must have taken it down sometime because it's under the bed now. In the end, everything and everyone falls from their angel heights, haina? However high they hang, however close to the stars, all things come down to earth sooner or later, even drunks, mad people, *everyone*. I don't know, but I suppose that's the truth the Heineken poster was trying to tell us.

It had pictures of four giant beer-mugs. The first mug was half-empty and it said '*Pessimist*'. Now, in my mind, waiting endlessly by Afi's sickbed, I give that mug to David, to DHL 'Drunk-on-Hate-and-Love', always so down on everyone. Another mug had lots of foaming froth and bubble and it said '*Spiritualist.*' That mug I unhesitatingly allotted to William, God's Demonic Prophet. The third mug said '*Realist*' and, despite everything, despite her extravagant exit from the Stage of this World, I wanted Sylvia to have this mug. She saw things so sharp, I felt she deserved it.

I also have to tell you what the Heineken poster declared at the end, in the biggest, boldest letters: ***ATTITUDE IS EVERYTHING IN LIFE.*** *AND IN DEATH,* I can hear Sylvia adding dryly. But I never had Sylvia's Heineken courage. I was more like DHL. I hated myself, I could not fly but I still wanted to live. That was the main difference between Sylvia and me. Sylvia could dismiss hope unflinchingly. She called it 'hope's illegitimate blanket'. I never could, I was too stupid.

So, to myself—Pari of Tempke, Ariel or mixed-up Pariel, I had to give, I could not help it, the silly *Optimist*'s mug, full of memories and half-forgotten clues.

Under the bed, other shapes had begun to emerge.

Now I saw them dimly, a heap of broken-spine books, maybe endlessly reread Mills and Boons, maybe Dean's Classics, Abridged. *Twenty Thousand Leagues Under the Sea* and *Tale of Two Cities* and *War and Peace*, books like that. Afi above and these torn English books below—Humpty-Dumpties from my past, you could call them. Suddenly I think how everyone complimented my *English*—of all things!—when I was sent to England for my 'cure'. It was funny. 'What wonderful English you speak, dear!' the Addenbrooke's nurses said. 'Where in the world did you learn it?' my Homerton teachers asked. *In a convent*, I wanted to scream, out of misery—and, by the way, many of the people who wrote the books I read were not English! If you really want to know (no one did, of course), that's how I learnt my English, because my mother died and my father put me in the Convent 'to get a good education' (that's what he said anyway, the truth was he hated me). The main thing was, I had no friends—except Mona (and Afi, if you counted him). That's the way I read my English books, and that's how I found Sylvia and David and William—but now that I'm cured of my madness, I know something else.

My English books *made me blind*. When I entered their world, I did not see what was right in front of my eyes, for example my father's khani-eating bodyguards or the things he did for a living. English houses with pointy roofs and English gardens with gnomes in pointy hats were more real to me than Tempke people. All through my childhood, the truth is that everything that happened around me seemed *remote,* as if it was happening in Africa or somewhere very far away and I was looking at everything from the wrong end of a telescope. That was what my English books did to me. *I shut my eyes and the world dropped dead.* The ones outside who lived in small, peeling huddles in the fly-haunted clusters of colonies dotted all around Tempke, I simply did not *see* them . . .

When Lakshmi took me to see Dr M, there were always the others, waiting and waiting for hours. But they lived outside the pages of my books, always fluttering, fluttering like *wings,* and they did not matter, not to me, not then. Lakshmi and I were the only ones and we always got to see Dr M first because THAT WAS THE RULE.

My father was the richest man in Tempke with the sarkar in his pocket. Karpoori Thakurji, Jaggnath Mishraji or President's Ruleji, whoever, my father knew all the high-ups. He was, he is, Mr Total Fixer. Bhumihars, Yadavs, Rajputs, ask anyone. I heard he buys and sells mushahars, they eat rats and he eats them—yes! My father has six servants, one just for tel malish, two cars and a cowshed glistening with buffaloes. Plus he had married a Sen and Dr M is the Sen family doctor. My mother was a Sen and her family has been in Tempke for generations. Of course, my mother killed herself, which was not a good thing. Still, even at seven, I was at the head of any queue in Tempke. In Tempke (Major Attractions: Girl's Convent School, Biscuit Baba

World Renowned Jyotishi, Elephant Wood Company owned by my father and stretching blue-green Adivasi farmlands well beyond the level-crossing, also picked up by him one by one and of course the old Ironworks belonging to my mother's family), I was just like Queen Sylvia. Everyone knew this: Dr M, the nuns, Lakshmi, everyone. So when I read my English books and wore my English frocks sewn specially for me by Hamidullah Tailor who sat on our front verandah all day long pedaling his Usha-Singer machine and copying English patterns out of *Women's Own* with total exactness, it was easy for me to forget that I belonged not to England, but to Tempke—and in the end this madness addled my brain . . .

Those days, I was a top, mostly.

I spun and spun, always aiming for the ceiling, my English dresses spreading and my turkey wings trailing over-pitched to the ground and hitting what I suppose was Sylvia's 'void'. I was weightless and unbalanced and I would scream for hours when I was stuck up there in the air and I just didn't know how to bring my body down to earth again. Sometimes my knickers would be wet and my face was covered in tears without my knowing. Nothing helped, not the ojha, not the beatings. And Biscuit Baba had already told Lakshmi my 'cure' would take years. Then I saw people had begun to point at me just as they had done at my mother. Also, they had began to call me Pagli Pari, the crazy one, not just behind my back but to my face.

Finally, Lakshmi complained to my father and that was how I started visiting Dr M. He was the one, Dr M, whose idea it was that I should tell the whole story from beginning to end about how I grew wings and began to hear voices and everything. At first, I thought it was a really stupid idea and would not agree—but now I think only telling the story can save me—and Afi . . .

I am to tell you the story of my madness. Unabridged.

So, if you can, please stay with me while I finish because my story is about real things too. I will tell you who killed the turkey in the schoolyard and why my mother hanged herself.

I will tell you about my father and Afi and the nuns . . .

I'm nearly at the end now and back in Afi's room, as I told you and—at this very moment—I can see small pieces of these puzzles right here under the bed, like the Madonna Triptych poking its head out boldly, though I think I won't tell you about the Triptych yet. It's just a set of three hinged pictures, not so important. Maybe I'll tell you later, if I have the time.

The main thing is to finish before Sister Maria comes at 9.30.

We only have three hours left, I think. It's early in the morning, about 5.30 or something, and I'm still doing the 'penitential' job the nuns have assigned me. I'm keeping watch over Afi's maimed body. *Afi is in this state because of me.* I alone am responsible and I can do nothing but sit and watch, perhaps for All Eternity. The nuns (Sylvia said they were 'past masters at chastisement') know this. This is my punishment. And here is Sylvia's cold December sky, drifting unstoppably into Afi's sick-room, just like Fate. *Tempus fuckit*, Sister Maria used to say, never caring for the stately Latin nor noticing the dirty wordplay lurking beneath, because that was how it always was in the Convent.

I try to shut my eyes as tight as I can against the ever-brightening morning light and do my best to remember the faraway English scenes. It's a matter of life and death, Summa says . . .

New Addenbrooke's Medical File 203 17.9.88: Patient's outpatient appointment for 23.9. stands cancelled. Patient still admitted in ward. Patient's state apathetic and sullen. Typical symptoms of depressive stage following manic episode. BP, Blood, Urine: normal.

Note: Aunt does not have resources to attend to patient at home. Is trying to arrange for a full-time home nurse or return patient to India, but until then has paid in full for patient to remain in ward till the end of the month.

Consultative expert panel arranged for 10 a.m. 12.10.1988 to assess patient for RTMS treatment and commencement of Zyprexia. Meanwhile, patient is on a lithium regimen along with mild sedatives to be administered by ward nurse in charge as and when necessary.

Nurses' Rhymes

These days, I've been banished to England, did you know—yes, to *England* . . .

It is shuddery wet and freezing and I've been in hospital the whole week and my aunt's only been to see me once and that time she kept herself far from me as if I had rat-plague. I *know* my rich father has given her money to keep me here, so that he won't have to be shamed by my mad behaviour in Tempke: mae ka khaun, ka piyun, ka leke pardesh jaun! Besides, Badshah Turkey is stone-dead and I don't even have Mona's address. But what does my aunt care, what does *anyone* care?

No one comes to Addenbrooke's Hospital, not even my dead Madonna mother. It's white and safe and I am Snow White or something in a glass case, not dead, not alive, not free, only germ-free in my (or, rather, Sylvia's) *bell-jar.* This is a castle place guarded round-the-clock by Sylvia's nurses—food nurses, trainee nurses and matron nurses with red lipstick and crackly faces, temperature nurses and false smile nurses, sheet changing nurses. *Nurses curses!* Changing, changing, the nurses are changing! What are they changing into? Not into their uniforms, no. They are changing into *a bad dream.* Sylvia's gone but I can feel her 'dwarves' surrounding me and I can hear their little, hard thoughts beating like drums in my head. *To the person in the bell-jar, blank and stopped as a bad dream, the world itself is the bad dream.* Sylvia! Her voice! *Whose* hospital is this? Where? Then, other voices . . .

You're a lucky girl today.

The young nurse comes in. She clears my breakfast tray and leaves me wrapped in my white blanket like a passenger taking the sea air on the deck of a ship.

Who's this? Who's talking? I have never been on a ship. My *mother* went on a ship with my father for her honeymoon. I have a picture of them on the deck of the P&O Strathnaver, smiling. She is wearing her English fur hat. But that was long ago and that was my mother, not me. So Sylvia's back and she's asking, smartly:

Why am I lucky?

Then, a nurse's voice says, *Well, I'm not sure if you're supposed to know yet but you're moving to Belsize.* Belsize, what's Belsize? That's the trouble with Sylvia. She speaks in code. Maybe Belsize means my aunt's house. But I don't want to go back there. I don't want to eat her food. It's poisoned! What to do? Now Sylvia's looking straight into the nurse's expectant face and declaring:

Belsize, I can't go there.

Why not?

I'm not ready. I'm not well enough.

Of course you're well enough. Don't worry, they wouldn't be moving you if you weren't well enough.

Sylvia's speaking to herself: *After the nurse leaves, I try to puzzle out this new move on Doctor Nolan's part. What was she trying to prove?*

Who is Dr Nolan? My new doctor's T and he's a he. I know that much. Sylvia's trying to tell me something. Maybe I shouldn't trust T . . .

Sylvia says:

I hadn't changed. Nothing had changed. And Belsize was the best house of all. From Belsize people went back to work and back to school and back to their homes.

Home! Oh God, I did not want to go back home. I did not want to eat my aunt's food which was poisoned. What to do, what to do? Sylvia's trying to tell me something. I've got to listen. Sylvia is speaking again, very fast and distinct.

At least at Belsize I could forget about the shock treatments. At Caplan a lot of women had shock treatments. I could tell which ones they were because they didn't get their breakfast trays with the rest of us. They had their shock treatments while we breakfasted in our rooms and then they came into the lounge, quiet and extinguished, led like children by the nurses, and ate their breakfasts there. Each morning, when I heard the nurse knock on my door, an immense relief flooded through me. I knew I was out of danger for that day. I didn't see how Doctor Nolan could tell you went to sleep during a shock treatment if she's never had shock treatment herself. How did she know the person didn't just look as if he was asleep, while all the time, inside, he was feeling the blue volts and the noise?

Sylvia's right. It's crazy to think the Doctorjis know everything: Dr M said so himself: you know what we don't, Pari. So Sylvia's telling me something *I* don't know—about trusting the doctors, about *the nurse without a breakfast tray.*

She's warning me about the blue volts to come. They don't have shock treatment nowadays, I know that, but Sylvia's not being literal. Shock is like love. It comes in many shapes and sizes.

Sylvia nods. I think she's agreeing with me. Then she continues in her conspiratorial whisper. *Listen to this, listen to the nurse talk about her hard life!*

You ladies don't know what it is, holding down two jobs. Nights I'm over here, watching you . . .

Then Sylvia's friend Loubelle (she's like Mona, only not so smart) starts to giggle. *Oh we're good. We're the best of the lot and you know it!*

I wish I could ask Loubelle: what's the point of comparing one bunch of lunatics with another? If we're all mad, then no one's mad, but Sylvia's pal Loubelle's too wacky to have figured this one out. The nurse says to Loubelle:

Oh, you're all right. You're all right, it's those boobies at the state place that worry me off my feet.

Do you work in both places, then? That's Sylvia, sounding really interested.

You bet! And the nurse gives Sylvia a straight look back.

I can hear Sylvia thinking: *This nurse thinks I've no business to be in Belsize at all.*

Then the nurse says: *You wouldn't like it over there one bit, Lady Jane.*

At this, Sylvia makes a funny face at me: *Isn't it strange that she should call me Lady Jane when she knows* perfectly *well what my name is?* Then she gets back to the nurse.

Why? Sylvia asks her.

Oh, it's not a nice place like this. This is a regular country club. Over there, they've got nothing. No OT to talk of, no walks . . .

Why haven't they got walks?

Not enough em-ploy-ees. Believe me, ladies, when I collect enough do-re-mi to buy me a cat, I'm clearing out. And now I can hear the chatter of all the other mad girls joining in, egging the nurse on—but I can tell Sylvia's stopped listening. She's figured out that the nurse is a Messenger just like the Aussie babysitter on the night of her death. She's been *sent.* Sylvia's clear about this. This is what she says to me.

I felt the nurse had been instructed to show me my alternatives. Either I got better, or I fell, down, down, like a burning, then a burnt out state, from Belsize, to Caplan, to Wymark and finally, when Doctor Nolan and Mrs Guinea had given me up, to the state place next door.

And I knew then that Sylvia's returned to show me *my* alternatives. First the sessions in Tempke with old Dr M, then to my aunt's care which is my Belsize, then here to Addenbrooke's which is Sylvia's Caplan and then finally, when my mind turns into a heap of dry leaves, ready for burning, down to the lunatic asylum in Ranchi, where the mad people are chained to the floor. Parallel tracks, all leading down, down, **down . . .**

I'm shivering now, but I make myself look up and Sylvia's right there. She's gathering her blanket about her and pushing back her chair.

And I must do the same . . .

You cold? the nurse demands rudely.

Yes, I say and move off down the hall. *I'm frozen stiff.*

There's **no** difference now. Sylvia's here. When she wakes, I wake. My words are her words. Now she's speaking again:

> *I woke warm and placid in my white cocoon, a shaft of pale, wintry sunlight dazzled the mirror and the glasses on the bureau and the metal doorknobs. Mrs S's sleepy voice boomed out and the nurse went in to her with the jingling tray. I thought, with a mild stir of pleasure, of the steaming blue china coffee pitcher and the blue china breakfast cup and the fat blue china cream jug with the white daisies on it.*
>
> *I was beginning to resign myself.*
>
> *If I was going to fall, I would hang on to my small comforts, at least, as long as I possibly could.*
>
> *The nurse rapped on my door and, without waiting for an answer, breezed in.*
>
> *It was a new nurse—they were always changing—with a lean, sand-coloured face and sandy hair, and large freckles polka-dotting her bony nose. For some reason, the sight of this nurse made me sick at heart, and it was only as she strode across the room to snap up the green blind that I realized part of her strangeness came from being empty-handed.*
>
> *I opened my mouth to ask for my breakfast tray, but silenced myself immediately. The nurse must be mistaking me for somebody else. New nurses often did that. Somebody in Belsize must have been having shock treatments, unknown to me, and the nurse had, quite understandably, confused me with her . . .*

> *Oh, the nurse smiled at me, you'll be getting your tray later this morning . . . But I didn't wait to hear what the nurse said. I strode blindly out into the hall, not to my room, because that was where they would come to get me, but to the alcove . . .*
>
> *I curled up in a far corner of the alcove with a blanket over my head.*

No one can see me now.

I feel safe under my blanket. Sylvia's gone. The nurses have gone.

The world is silent. Softly, under my breath, I sing to myself.

I sing the convent rhymes I learnt with Mona and Afi back home.

Oranges and lemons sold for a penny
All the school girls are so many!

Ring-a-ring-a roses, a pocket full of posies
Hush-a-hush-a, all fall down!

Three blind mice, see how they run
They all ran after the farmer's wife
She cut off their tales with a carving knife
She how they run, see how they run . . .

The songs calm me down. I feel I could hide here in the alcove for years. It's so peaceful. But of course they manage to find me! They always do. The mice feet are closer. The nurse's flat-soled, padded feet and I cannot run anywhere . . .

I hear the feet stop.

My heart stops too.

I can see two of them now from under my blanket. Feet standing stock-still and I'm still as a mouse. *Oranges and lemons, hush-a, hush-a, all fall down!*

I'm frozen stiff.

It's Nurse Standish. I look up at her from my crouch on the floor and she looks about nine feet tall. I notice how her stockings have creases in them, like fine English toilet paper. She has a paper face, paper clothes, paper charts in her hand. I remember the scene long ago in Dr M's office when I *dropped the paperweight* and just at that moment a sudden desire comes to me to *write* on Nurse Standish, to write my stupid life on her blank white uniform. I almost laugh to myself under my blanket, the thought is so funny, I giggle . . .

Then she yanks my blanket off my head and nothing is funny any more. The morning light is cold and harsh.

What are you doing here? Stand up! says Standish.

She pulls me to my feet and then—I bite her.

That's the end. No more chances, just like my mother. I'm back in the ward with needle jabs in my arm and a dull haze in front of my eyes. SHOCK—this is the shock Sylvia came to warn me about. Now she's gone and they have taken away all my things as well.

They have taken away my blanket, my books and even my thoughts. I feel dull, dull, dull, like a rag-doll, like a piece of dead animal skin. I am Jahangir. My *wings* have been torn from my body. But Sylvia *will not give up*; she hammers away in my head:

> *Be smart. Catch that insistent thought at the back of your head, use it, Ariel! This ward reminds you of something, does it not, bunnykins? Meditate!*

Okay, so it's not the convent Infirmary, no. Not the rooftop, not the Refectory, not the . . .

Got it! This place is like the *Library*. It's so obvious. Sylvia's been telling me I have to treat this English Hospital as a place to get myself 'sorted out'. I have to figure things out as I did in the Library before my father sent me to England to die. I have to have a PLAN before they kill my mind with medicine or the pain creeps up on me like a snake . . .

I have to *remember* and if I can manage this, then, despite everything, I may be a lucky girl today. Like Sylvia.

Memories, Sylvia said, were *relentless* like bees. They came in swarms and there was nothing you could do to stop them and she was right. My memories are like the mosquitoes in Tempke from Dhulia swamp at dusk, Anopheles, Culex, Aegypti and all the other names we learnt in Nature Studies, or like fireflies buzzing and breeding in my skull. Sometimes I try to wave them off and they dance back delicately into the marshes—but they always return.

The first memory that I manage to swat down is about Dr M again.

I think I'm about seven and being shooed *relentlessly* by Lakshmi down a long corridor reeking with the smell of tincture iodine. Rows of red plastic chairs with screechy iron legs line the corridor. They scrape and grate with a terrible sound every time somebody moves. Patches of the floor are sticky and wet and I begin to feel a bit vomity, but Lakshmi just holds her head high and her sari higher and shepherds me past the old men with elephantiasis ankles and mothers dripping with babies as if they didn't exist. It's the same old story. Lakshmi and I are being supported in our royal progress down the dispensary corridor by both sides of my family—my father has money and my mother has ancestry and that's that, although at the time, it's true, *I really didn't see it.*

Anyway, here we were, entering the doors of Dr M's chamber and the sounds and smells vanished like magic! Instead, gurgling noiselessly over us from his sky blue perch behind the doctorji's desk, hung that awful, rolls-of-fat **Glaxo baby**, gap-tooth happy, the Pond's Dream-flower talcum smells wafting from him like holy dhoop. I hated this infant! He always looked as if he had never done susu in his life but *where was his mother*? I didn't trust him. Come to think of it, this fat old Glaxo Putr in the doctor's surgery looked quite a bit like the Triptych baby in my convent room, but most of all he looked like moon-faced Krishna, bathed in his blue glow of unearthly happiness, which somebody had pasted over one of the real Triptych pictures, I don't know why. (I think it must have been Gowri, because the nuns couldn't have done it, they *knew* it was wrong to stick a heathen god's picture over a Holy Christian painting and you could be Punished in Hell for it.)

The Glaxo Baby was just like Krishna, like Jesus. He was also a bit like Afi—he specialized in being 'too good to be true', as the nuns said. All we had to do was to gaze up at him from the door of the surgery and the whole world would turn suspiciously calm and Lakshmi begin to mutter Hai Ram under her breath, which meant she was too impressed to talk—and then all we heard was the whirring of the fan and a slight, *very* slight, rustle of paper, just like a krait through the brown, dry grass of Doctorji's huge, dark desk as we waited. And then we waited and we waited—but Dr M did not look up at all.

Then we waited some more.

I began to feel I would burst because I could not bear the silent chortling of the Glaxo boy any longer—what was he *laughing* about, the silly fatso?—so I stared into the big round glass paperweight on the Doctorji's desk with the big Taj Mahal in its middle and tried to listen to the silence inside to calm me down. I listened so hard that I did not even notice that my vomityness had gone.

Dr M was still writing away busily. And finally, it was not me but Lakshmi who lost her patience, *Hai Ram* or no *Hai Ram*. She pulled the pallu of her cabbagy Terylene going-out mustard yellow sari firmly over her head and whispered, soft but tense,

Doctor Sahib?

This made Dr M's hand stop at once and his head jerk up like a cobra's. He said:

Oh, Pari. Your father phoned.

Then he asked Lakshmi in his strange firang Hindi:

Kya hua? What is the matter?

And Lakshmi of course, being Lakshmi, did not lose a moment. She launched into her long story about how I hadn't talked for nearly a week. When a little mosquito bit me, I scratched and scratched at it until it became a boil. It was only a mosquito, she said, flaring, but I behaved as if an elephant had trampled on me! Sometimes I would get hot and flushed at night and refuse to wear any clothes. At other times, I would talk bakwas nonsense. So, finally, she complained to my father and here we were!

Dr M waited till the tirade was over and then spoke straight to me. His voice was tired and kind.

Pari, it's not your fault. I'll give you some medicine to make the pain go away.

How did he know about my pain? I decided then and there I couldn't trust Dr M either. Why did he have that idiot Glaxo boy hanging over his head? So the best thing was to keep quiet. I let Laskhmi take the medicine from him and concentrated on the paperweight with the Taj Mahal inside.

When you turned the glass over, this paperweight snowed! It wasn't snowing now. But I wanted it to. It was beautiful when it snowed whitely, whitely, all over the white Taj Mahal and so I tried to make it snow with my mind at first—but I couldn't. Then a very strange thing happened. *My hand acted on its own.* It reached out and tried to pick the globe up from Doctorji's desk. And then it dropped the globe which rolled off dumpily into a corner and Lakshmi started to shout! Some papers flew off the desk at the same time and I saw Dr M frowning.

Paper, paper everywhere, white swans flying, white swans with blue writing on their backs flying and flying and flying, and Lakshmi diving round the room until she finds the paperweight and thumps it back on the desk! The funny thing is, it wasn't broken at all, the Taj Mahal still had all its minarets and Dr M didn't scold me. He just *frowned* but that made me scared and I just shut my eyes and wouldn't let them touch me.

No one could touch the Taj inside its solid wall of glass, no one could touch the pure snow swirling inside, so why should they touch me? In my mind that day, I became the snow, I became the Taj.

No one could touch me.

I suppose it was the beginnings of my madness but at that exact moment I swear I heard the Glaxo baby hooting with laughter.

Then, with my eyes still shut, I heard the Doctor tell Lakshmi to bring me next week and he would talk to me—which is funny because Dr M never talked. *I* talked and the snow fell. I talked and it rained. I talked and Dr M listened and once I started talking, it was hard to stop and I'm still talking, you see. Talking, talking, buzz-buzz, quack, gobble, cackle . . .

Now it's a different scene again, disconnected, flying off . . .

I'm sitting on the Convent parapet with Mona and Afi. I'm seven, Mona is eight and Afi is twelve and the nuns are in recess and the convent belongs to us. We're happy and loud. We're singing the song of the poor tuntunia bird of Bihar: *mae ka khaun ka pijun ka leke pardesh jaun* and we don't care for anyone! Three pairs of bare feet dangle over thin air and emerald grass. It's the world as it was before Sylvia and I'm speaking to the sky. I'm looking down at the ledge below the parapet and then up again at the fleecy, blue shamiana-tent above our heads and I'm saying:

> I think we have the biggest guano deposits in the world, apart from the island of Nauru. We could be *rich* if we collected all this and sold it, I'm telling you!

Mona and Afi don't respond, but this is usual. All I have to do is wait. Mona's curiosity will get the better of her sooner or later—and it does. What's guano, she wants to know.

Bird-shit.

Afi's beginning to listen too. He knows about bird-shit because he works in the garden.

Manure, says Afi, bird-shit's manure.

This is a cue for me to show off. I become All India Radio, I become AIR. I carry the heavy bulk of the *Encyclopaedia Britannica* effortlessly on my angel wings and I say

> **Nauru,** smallest independent state in the world, situated in the South Pacific, total area 21 sq. km, 032 5 S, 166 55 E, possesses the biggest bird-shit economy in the world. I by-hearted it. It's true!
>
> So what, says Afi.
>
> Birdbrains, listen, you can *live* off bird-shit, that's the point! But now Nauru's eaten up too much of its bird-shit. There's only just enough left and Nauru's sliding. Nauru's slipping into the deep Pacific ocean! That's the point!

Don't talk nonsense! Mona's voice is sharp and she's about to swing her body off the ledge and step back onto the roof. I'm going!

But I can see Afi's mind working. He's thinking, if I can collect this stuff from the Convent ledges and sell it, I can make some money and it'll be mine, because who owns all this shit anyway?

Meanwhile, *I'm* flying. I'm gliding high over Oceania, past Australia, and then swooping down over Nauru, full of phosphate rocks and tropical jungles. Look, a snake!

Where? Afi asks.

Where? *Where?* Mona says.

And now they see it too—small, glistening, green, a little garden snake.

Mona's irritation is forgotten. Let's go see him, she says.

So we abandon the parapet, we abandon Nauru and we come down to earth. Fast, fast, says Mona, or he'll disappear! Spotting a snake is exciting and Tempke is snake-paradise—harmless grass snakes mostly, but also kraits and even cobras. Ask me, because *I* was the one who taught Sylvia about snakes.

In England, Sylvia was queen, but in Tempke, I was the one. I led Sylvia through the gullies of the town, God-promise. I knew how to bargain with the rickshaw-wallahs and how to find a place within the inner circle of watchers, the closest ones. *My* father was Mr Fixer, so I was the one—me, Ariel. Would Sylvia have written her snake-charming verses without me? No chance, Afi!

He pipes a world of snakes,
Of sways and coilings, from the snake-rooted bottom
Of his mind.

His mind? It was my mind, the snake-rooted bottom of my mind into which she'd stared, from where she raked up her Indian snakes, her eastern demons. The text of *my* dreams: *And now nothing but snakes as out of Eden's navel . . .*

The problem is, they are *her* snakes in the end, not mine.

These are not the nagas of Tempke, these are not the jade dancers of the Convent or the big brown fatties who taste like chicken, Afi says, when they are chopped and eaten. No, those snakes have drilled down and gone under all the way back to Nauru the Guano Paradise of the Pacific Rim and it is I who am at Sylvia's mercy. It is *her* voice insistent as a phone ringing inside my head and I know I have to pick it up sooner or later . . .

Phone calls: phone calls are not about remembering, they are about talking to people *now and here.* They're about sounding normal, even when you can't be sure whose voice it is at the other end. How can you be sure? All you hear on the phone is a *voice.* How do you know there's a body there? That's what's scary. It's hard to answer the phone because it could be anyone pretending to be anyone—like the voices in my head, so many of them, David, *Pessimist,* William, *Spiritualist,* Janhangir the Turkey and my English books all jabbering away. So, on the phone you need to be like Sylvia the *Realist.* You can't just say, excuse me, I'm an Angel. You have to say your *name,* which is difficult if you are confused. **Confusion + Fear = Craziness.**

Of course, in Tempke the phones are regularly 'Out of Order', so you may miss some parts of the story and get confused if you don't listen carefully and also you'll get lots of cross-connections, because some peculiar boys, God knows from what cheap mohalla, are always ready to butt into your conversation and get smart with you! This makes everything terribly mixed-up and you want to hiss just like Mona 'Shut up, just *shut up,* okay!' and disconnect, phatak!

Then there are the afternoon callers, the professor uncles from Burdwan or Jamshedpur who happen to be friends of your father. They don't really care *who* you are, they know the Ramayan better than you. You could be Adolf Hitler but they know more about concentration camps than you. All they want is to tell you the entire history of the universe, which bores you so much you end up holding the phone six inches away and trying to strangle yourself with the cord just for a little relief, arre baba!

Love happens when lives interfuse. I think I read this in a Mills and Boon type novel once but it is the truth and because the telephone's been around for ages, it *knows* this. The telephone knows exactly what it is doing when it slides like a snake in the sky and goes underwater from country to country and town to town, setting off voices like little Diwali sparklers, *phut, phut, phut!* in people's heads. That's why you can't trust phones just the way you could never trust Afi—not completely, anyway . . .

One time, Afi, Mona and I were playing **L-O-N-D-O-N** near the Convent grotto and Afi was the den. That day, Mona and I were *perfect.* We kept freezing into Statues each time he turned around. Afi wasn't fast enough to catch us at all and I managed to snake right up to him and was about to smartly tap his back when he suddenly whirled round with his eyes still tight-shut and caught me. Shock! I don't know how he did it but I tried to twist and turn very silently to escape him. I squirmed this way and that so his grip would loosen and I could slide out, but Afi held on tight. With his eyes shut, he kept repeating *Who is this? Who is this? Is it Mona?* But Mona and I didn't say a word.

Then Afi asked, his voice shaking: *Is it Anu?* which was really stupid because Anuradha was always doing her tuition and *never* played with us. I nearly began to giggle but I held my breath and waited and waited like we did at the Doctorji's haspatal until finally Afi was forced to open his eyes! But as soon as I looked into them I could *tell* he had been fooling me all the while.

I saw that day from Afi's eyes that he knew that I knew that he knew I knew he *knew* who I was from the beginning. So was there any need at all for him to open his slanty eyes wide and say *Oh, it's you, Pari!*

Yes, I was.

Afi knew it, everyone knew it: Pari was the daughter of the richest man in Tempke, who put her into a convent to get a good education after her mother killed herself. My mother named me, by the way. She called me Parineeta, 'the married one' out of her favourite novel by Sarat Chandra, which is quite funny because I was a child and not married but the good thing is everybody always called me Pari for short, and Pari means 'fairy'—which is exactly what I am.

❁

Why should I lie to you?

I am not Afi who could charm a tuntunia bird into a snake's jaws with his smooth, smooth talk and get Ms Tuntuns to pay for it to boot. I am not Mona-sona, Tempke's golden girl. I am silly, shivering Pariel. Listening to my story will confuse you, it will bore you, maybe it will even make you angry. After all, I've *seen* the expressions on the faces of people, doctors, nurses, nuns and all, who were forced to listen to me because they were paid to do this by my father. And I'm paying nothing! So I can hear you saying to me now, just like the rest: Hello, who do you think you are, Pari, handing us this crazy angel-tangel hodgepodge. No, this is too crazy, forget it, girl! Why get mixed up with these *mleccha* English writers with their cow-leather boots and hats, God knows if they had baths every day, why not Rabindranath or Jibanananda, respectable Bengalis like that, great poets from your own country? Are you a TRAITOR, Pari? What do you, half-wit motherless child from some half-price convent school understand about these English people anyway? Can you even speak their language, has anyone checked your khatas for spelling mistakes, haan?

But I don't believe much in this 'us-them' business! History is history and truth is truth. What happened, happened. As far as I am concerned, I entered the lives of my William and David by chance the time I caught Sister Liddie doing something she shouldn't have and she gave me the duplicate keys to the Library for the whole summer—just like the Aussie girl crossed Sylvia's path by Chance. Then I started reading and reading and I got into their lives and they got into mine. That's all.

Anyway, I had already begun growing wings by then. So I was always a pure angel when it came to William and David. But then there was Sylvia, who was American. I was never certain about her because she danced and moved about like Aedes Aegypti and asked me 'stinging' questions the whole time. With Sylvia, I was confused and I never touched the phone when she was with me, but when she was away I'd sometimes pluck up the courage but my voice would still tremble a bit. I'd just say Hello, then stop dead while the person at the other end went on talking and talking and after some time I'd stop listening, but that is not what I wanted. What I really wanted was to tell them my story, which was the story of so many lives twisted together like telephone wires . . .

Are you still holding on? If you are, please hang on just a bit more . . .

Some people call me mad because they think I talk to myself but the thing is—I'm not talking to myself, I'm talking to THEM—and to you. Of course, you can put the phone down any time and end our conversation once and for all. You have the power, but if you do, just remember what Sylvia said because she always told the truth when it mattered: *It is not every day an angel calls and talks to you of love.*

Which brings me almost to the last point now: it's about my MEDITATION, which Biscuit Babaji called dhyan. The Baba said anyone could become a great sant if they could do dhyan properly but Sylvia thought it was all a big joke. Anyway, I *have* to meditate and when I do things are not up to me exactly. I have to zoom off to strange destinations on orders. Voices come to me and I must listen. That's the difference between the others and me. They can hang up any time. *I* can't, especially when *Summa's* involved. I'll tell you who Summa is later, but the gist of it is: angels have to meditate, just like nuns have to pray, and I'm not very brilliant at meditation. I just flit here and there and you can't see the point. *I* can't see the point, Sylvia could not see the point, sometimes I think even Jesus God can't see the point! So I'll just *say* the point now. *The point is to find an answer to Sylvia's question.*

That's why I have to tell you about William and David and many historical things and my story will get stuck in the mud of history from time to time just like the wheels of my father's Ambassador when it rains in Tempke. The car goes grrr-grrrh! and you see the murky wheel-marks clearly but the car does not *move.* You think you'll be stuck forever, looking out through the plastic-glass and the raindrops will slide and slide downwards forever, which is *another* problem—these little rain-pools and puddles of POETRY right in the middle of my story for no reason. Well, there is a reason, sort of, but it's very irritating anyway! You have to walk around the puddles if you don't want to get your feet wet and ganda. All you want is for me to finish my story quickly, to get to the end, to go home, but there's all this 'poetry nonsense' in the way.

What can I say about this? Maybe, like Mona, you can just avoid the poetry. Mona always scolded me the loudest when it came to poetry: listen Pari, how long do you expect us to stay cooped up inside your stupid makes-no-sense story? Are we chickens or what? Let's go now, chalo!

Mona is my friend, my only friend and when she says be normal, no point getting choked up by poetry-shoetry, I know she is being wise. But I have no choice. I *have* to tell this story my way.

Here by Afi's bedside, staring away at the half-hidden debris of my long-lost English books, the half-hinged Madonna Triptych and the dust-disguised Heineken poster, I know I have to answer Sylvia's question.

Or Afi might die . . .

Of course Mona would say I'm being dramatic, I'm *spooking* you—but I'm not. Paranoia, Dr T calls it, but that's too easy. It's doctor talk. The truth is that if you hold tight, *tight*, just like Afi, you will see them. You will see Sylvia and Ted, William, David, you will see Summa . . .

And I'm standing right beside you now and my wings are brushing your shoulder. Look!

❁

New Addenbrooke's Medical File 203 30.10.88: Patient escaped from private room and hid in the alcove yesterday. Sedation advised. Even after strong sedation, patient's behaviour continued to be exceptionally erratic and unstable. At intervals, she wakes in a state of fevered excitement, her hands continually plucking at the sheets and making animated gestures. Talks constantly to the poet Sylvia Plath with whose life and work she seems well acquainted. Says she is 'investigating' the 'love-hate' relationship between the poet and her husband, Ted Hughes.

In one of her brief lucid interludes between manic attacks, patient mentioned what could be a valuable insight into her pychosis. She remarked that she had read many books on Plath and each asked why the poet killed herself. Patient said she had the same question regarding her own mother's death. The two suicides thus seem **related** in the patient's mind. If Sylvia loved her children, why did she deprive them of a mother, enquired the patient lucidly. She said she had addressed this question to 'Sylvia' herself (patient is convinced that she is in regular communication with the poet, as in the case with many classic schizoid sufferers) and the poet had parried with a counter-question about the nature of love. In the patient's interpretation, 'Sylvia' had indicated to her that the mystery of her mother's death could only be resolved if the patient was first able to answer the question: what is Love? Patient seems certain that the answer lies within the covers of the books that she protects so zealously, which is perhaps why she is observed to peruse them day and night and to display hysteric symptoms if they are out of her sight for a moment, as when nurse temporarily had to confiscate the patient's belongings following her escape from her ward (29.10.88).

There may also be a second connection between the patient's insecurities concerning parental rejection (her mother committed suicide and her father 'sent her away') and the growth of her sexual fantasies. It is noticeable, in this connection, that among the patient's small pile of personal books is a rare edition of Havelock Ellis' classic *The Psychology of Sex*, while her edition of the poet William Blake's *'Poems'* contains many explicit drawings of naked males and females sometimes engaged in copulation and at other times in sexual foreplay. Many of the beings depicted in Blake's sketches are drawn with wings extending from their shoulders, which could be related to the patient's basic aviomania and her repeated claims of being an 'angel'.

Advanced schizophrenic symptoms, seemingly not amenable to the regular drugs, but have advised nurse to keep the olanzapine up in controlled 0.05 mg doses. Patient is not violent although she is showing great resistance to eating anything at all and will only eat fruit and drink water from the tap, which must be poured out before her eyes. She will try nothing brought in from outside by her relative, for whom she seems to have developed a morbid mistrust. Overall, patient still not judged entirely suitable for RTMS treatment as drug treatments are still being experimented with. Constituted panel in October should consider if Prozac might be tried again or a new cocktail.

Court Green, Devon 1962

Ted reenters their bedroom again at exactly 12.33 a.m. I see him clearly . . .

He's looking fraught, a dark strand of 'Heathcliff' hair falling across his forehead like Cary Grant. Handsomer than usual, but for once neither he nor Sylvia are conscious of their bodies, the pheromone scents that pull them together and then drag them apart just as brutally.

Sylvia lies still in bed, her eyes closed, but there's a freshness about her face. The lines of her recently unburdened figure beneath the bedsheet are tense and firm. This is a woman ready for action.

Ted gazes down at his wife, and all the worry of the day slowly leaves him. Those long, rasping gasps, the terror of the moment when the gas ran out and Sylvia could only claw at the midwife for relief from her pain, fade from his mind. He has already spent hours in his study distractedly trying to read D.H.L.'s *Collected Poems* and failing. He has been very apprehensive about disturbing her. One could never tell with Sylvia, but now, standing here, he is of a sudden so taken with her damp grace that he almost forgets the cause of that newfound serenity.

Their son, Nicholas Farrar Hughes—9 lbs 11 ounces at birth—was a long time coming into the world. Now, he lay there, tightly swaddled, beside Sylvia, as calm as a Christ child in his crib, asking for no special attention, demanding nothing, but Sylvia has grown tall as a goddess—special, blest.

Outside, the three great wych elms shiver in the January cold of Court Green, Devonshire.

Ted moves round on tiptoe to kiss Sylvia, aware that things are far too bright and warm and preternaturally still around here for a winter's night in Devon. True, this is their bedroom he's standing in, a familiar enclave, rattling with memories of quarrels, infidelity and ferocious love-making, but, with Nick's birth, he senses, even in this early moment, that a transformation has been effected. She's somehow succeeded in making this space her own. For months after, it will be full of maternal odours, milk, patchouli, a tumble of urine and talcum. He will have to share his space with that little pink fellow in the corner, contentedly asleep. And Sylvia?

She seems asleep, too, but with Sylvia one could never be sure . . .

Love. What Ted feels for his wife and newborn son at that moment is pure, unadulterated love.

Then he leaves the room, as he must, without kissing Sylvia, but looking in on little Frieda on his way down and spending the rest of the freezing night downstairs, waiting for me to come to him—but I do not.

I spend that night with Sylvia.

Her new poems—she does not know that they are nearly her last—have one thing in common, she tells the BBC interviewer later. They are all written at four in the morning. She describes this hour to him in detail. She calls it that still, blue, almost eternal hour before cockcrow, before the baby's cry, before the glassy music of the milkman settling his bottles. If these poems have anything else in common, she says, perhaps it is that they were written for the ear, not the eye. They are poems written out loud—but Sylvia does not need to tell *me* this. I know it because I was there already at the birthing cry of these poems—not just afterwards, but *before*. All night from about 1.00 a.m., when she's ready to push down into a deep post-REM slumber, into the state she later describes as *stasis in darkness* but not before she has muttered under her breath, in a fall of half-done words:

Rubbish, Ariel! That story you've just told me—that's not love at all. It's exploitation! Vanish, Ariel. Into the blue, go! You're talking through your hat . . .

❁

Ah, the hat!
I talk through it.
But so does everyone.
Including you, Doctor Saheb.
If I'm as mad as a hatter, so were Sylvia and William.
When I wear my mother's hat, my language changes to theirs.
And I'm back with William today and this is about a *hat-trick*, Doctor.
Pay attention to the hat, I'm telling you, because it holds all the secrets, *sine die* . . .

❁

Pari's Book

I am growing up.

The colours of my wings are changing.

I am to become Willam's Angel.

I know this because I am wearing 'the hat'.

That hat meant a great deal to my William and me, always. It was the perfect symbol of our love for many long years, but in my heart I knew it was not the only clue, so I waited and waited for a Nurse Standish-less day and when it finally came, I wasted no time.

I begged a pencil and a piece of paper from Cathy the cleaning lady at Addenbrooke's Hospital, whose whooshing machine was so Thunderbird-loud that she could hardly hear me but when she finally understood what I wanted she brought me up the stuff at once, sporting Mona's unguilty smile and unsuspicious as William's 'Lamb'. And then at last, I tried to write out as neatly as it is possible when you have no book to rest your paper on, all the Questions and Signs that I had, the **Questions** on the first side and the **Signs** on the other, underlined:

Questions

Why was my mother wearing her fur hat when she hanged herself?

Why did my father hate me?

Why did Dr M's leathery eyes flicker when my mother was mentioned?

Why was Badshah Jahangir the turkey murdered?

And, most important of all, Sylvia's question:

What's love, anyway?

Signs

The Heineken Poster

English Books, especially the ones Sister Lydia directed me to in the Library

The Hat

Snakes, Bees, Turkeys and Other Creatures

My Wings and my Voices

The Madonna Triptych with the pasted-over picture, covered by Glaxo Baby Krishna

A Poem I Found which was not by an English person but by an Indian

Then I did a calculation:

TOTAL: Five Questions and Seven Signs = Twelve

5 + 7 = 12 12 = 1 + 2 = 3

Three! which means that it's time I mentioned the Madonna Triptych and even maybe the Poem I found addressed to me, *directly*, by one A.K. Ramanujan, Indian Poet. We were not encouraged to read Indian writers in the Convent (except for Great Leaders like Nehru or Gandhi) but this writer's book with the flute-Krishna sketch on the cover had escaped the ban somehow and found its way to the Library where I managed to read it that fatal summer. I knew it was a Sign, a final clue for me. Because, you see, this poem was supposed to be an 'Anonymous Fragment', written by an ancient Tamil poet according to Ramanujan and translated faithfully by him—but the funny thing was: *it was addressed to me by name.* Here it is, by-hearted by me from page 50 . . .

Pari! Pari! they cry
these poets
with their good red tongues
praising one man
in many ways
    yet it's not only Pari
    the rains too
    keep the world going
    in these parts

Pari! Pari! they cry, these poets. Are these words not prophetic? How could an ancient Tamil poet have spoken them and they have found their way to Tempke in an English translation by a Living Indian Poet if they were not *meant for me?*

It's true, what William said: an Angel flies on the Wings of Chance. Do you remember how I told you about the wheels of my father's Ambassador stuck in Tempke mud and about how my story would sometimes get just as stuck in the slush of history? Well, that's exactly what's going to happen when we walk into William's story of nearly two centuries ago. *It's not only Pari*—just as the ancient Tamil poet said.

The rain, the cold English weather, Chance and the good red tongue of William the Spiritualist are responsible too. For they have confused Pari into madness. In just a few moments, we will enter William's world, where Madness and Poetry and Prophecy exist in equal measure and where he will be the Leader. His Voice will take over and his overpowering Gaze will colour everything. Because William was just like Sylvia.

William saw Visions of Angels (me) and Demons (naked

ones whom he drew with such accuracy that no wonder the nuns of Tempke found it necessary to hide his book away). And I must come to William's story very soon. It's been *commanded.*

No one has come by yet, by the way, and it is almost seven. I calculate in my head that I have about two and a half hours left to tell my story, to connect all the dots. That isn't much time at all, and I have no anwers yet to Sylvia's question or any of my own, but there's one deep thing I've learnt from the Madonna Triptych that I have to tell you before William's tale begins.

Random things reflect perfect symmetries: *the Heineken Poster, the Madonna Triptych with its pasted over picture of the baby Krishna, the hidden books by Sylvia and William and David and Havelock that Sis Lyd led me to in the Convent Library, John Keay's* India Discovered *and the Ancient Tamil Poem in English Translation Addressed by Name to Me, Pari*—all these things make a Poetic Chain of Love binding the Truth together. Join them up with *Biscuit Baba's prophecies, my mother's English hat, the green garden snakes, Sylvia's bees, Jahangir the Turkey (murdered 1984) whose wings magically reappeared on my shoulders, the upside-down snow-flake glass paperweight with the World's most perfect Monument to Love jammed right inside it* and *so many other bits and pieces of* **evidence** *and you will see that I am not so mad after all.*

My Voices point the way to the truths already apprehended by William, Sylvia and David and the broken-hinged triptych in my room shows William's immense contribution to solving at least three of the five questions I simply *had* to answer if Afi was to live . . .

What had William to do with the fur hat my mother donned before she hanged herself?

Why did my father banish me to William's distant island?

How was Dr M involved?

William

Dropped Mercury

Sylvia's still around . . .

I see her silhouette sharply outlined at the desk by my hospital window, gazing out at the elms and typing out her notes for her BBC interview as I walk over to her. She doesn't stir at all. She's so absolutely immersed in her work that I can read over her shoulder as she types, the words jumpy on the old typewriter:

> This poem–'Death &CO.'–is about the double or schizophrenic nature of death–the marmoreal coldness of Blake's Death-mask, for instance.

So she knew about William! No, more than that. Sylvia was *directing* me to William, William who haunted her poems and whom she could never escape as I could not escape her. That's the message! *William* is the next link in the chain: I need to go to him to find the answers to my questions. I think I get it, but Sylvia's still concentrating on her manuscript and pays me no attention. At last, though, she's done, and swivelling towards me, the green flecks in her lion's eyes dancing with mischief:

> Tell me about them, Sylvia says. Tell me about your men!

As if she didn't know, as if she was not as involved with those men as I was! I remember one time I plucked up the courage to ask her straight out: what did Sister Lydia mean by leading me to William and David? Of all the 'untold riches' that English Literature offered, why get involved with *them*?

Some things I knew better than Sylvia. I knew that Sis Lid the Kid was the smartest nun in the Convent, future Mother Sup. Material and so the old Mother Superior had enrolled her for an Honours degree in Eng. Lit. at the local college and given her an allowance to buy all the books she needed for her Honours essay (Chosen Topic: Poetry—William: born 18th century, David born late 19th, Sylvia born 20th century, it said in Liddie's own clear hand on the inside covers of the library books). The hidden books belonged to Lydia—that much was established. It was also true that the nuns had put her in charge of the school library so that she could 'study while working.' If Sis Lyd did extra work with the Accountant in her spare time, well that was her own business, but how did Sylvia, William and Ted come into the picture? That's the question I asked Sylvia.

Sylvia answered by telling me about a boy she knew called Buddy. Buddy was an all-American blond boy from a good family. He could do nothing wrong, just like Afi. He could even discuss poetry with Sylvia. *Do you know what a poem is?* he asked her once. *No, what?* said Sylvia. *It's a piece of dust.* That's the kind of smart boy Buddy was. *Buddy's father was a teacher,* Sylvia told me, *and I think Buddy could have been a teacher as well, he was always trying to explain things to me and introduce me to new knowledge. Suddenly, after I'd finished a poem, he said, have you ever been with a man? No, I said, only statues.* Then Buddy said, *Well, don't you think you'd like to see me?* This shocked Sylvia a bit at first. *I didn't know what to say. My mother and my grandfather had started hinting around a lot to me lately about what a fine, clean boy Buddy Willard was, coming from such a fine, clean family, and how everybody at church thought he was a model person, so kind to his parents and to older people, as well as so athletic and so handsome and so intelligent.* (This Buddy was beginning to sound more and more like Afi!) *All I'd heard about, really,* Sylvia continued, *was how fine and clean Buddy was and how he was the kind of person a girl should stay fine and clean for. So I didn't really see the harm in anything Buddy would think up to do.* So Sylvia said to Buddy, *Well, all right, I guess so.* Then she watched *while he unzipped his chino pants and took them off and laid them on a chair and then took off his underpants that were made of something like nylon fishnet.* Buddy was nice enough to explain the underpants to Sylvia. *They're cool and my mother says they wash easily* . . . Naturally, I couldn't help thinking of Sis Lyd and the Accountant when Sylvia told me this story about Buddy. It was as if the two scenes had melted into one in my mind.

But Sylvia hadn't finished.

Then he just stood there in front of me and I kept staring at him. The only thing I could think of was turkey neck and turkey gizzards . . . And the minute Sylvia uttered these words, I got it! I didn't need to hear the rest.

I had loved Badshah Jahangir the Turkey and he was dead. All that remained of him was turkey neck and torn wattle. Sylvia was dead too. William and David were dead but if you wanted to learn about sex and the spirit, there were still no better teachers. They could turn 'statues' into living Buddy Willards, which was a very big deal, especially if you were stuck in a convent dedicated to teaching pure convent girls like Mona and Anu and me, pure, unpolluted English.

In the course of her Honours degree, with no immediate prospect of flight, Lydia had chanced upon this singular truth. William and David and Sylvia were the purest of the pure; they were high Archangels in the pantheon of modern English Literature. They were white-skinned. They were Christians, they went to church, but when it came down to it, there was this lurking, gizzardy thing below the surface that they were all obsessed with—sex, which is love's shadow. Of course, Lydia carried out her own practical experiments on the matter too, as I've told you, but she was intelligent enough to guess that William and David—and Sylvia and Havelock—were immeasurably her masters when it came to sex and angelic spirituality. *This* was the bittersweet book-buried secret that she passed on to me when I caught her in the convent library and it was this knowledge that I had to use somehow to answer Sylvia's trick question about love. And here she was now, wickedly repeating: tell me, Pari. Tell me about your men!

What follows is the chronicle of the things I told Sylvia in the tumultuous hours preceding her death, and I could not have had a better listener—smarter, or more avid for what she called 'new knowledge'. Unlike William or D.H. (or like Buddy, her fine, clean mentor sporting cool nylon fishnet underwear), Sylvia had been a straight-A student all her life and that strain of method and discipline never abandoned her. For instance, on this occasion, she already had her notes on William lying neatly typed and gem-clipped on the table beside her, library-referenced and cross-checked, full of dates and events and ready to present to me, as if to say—I'll *know* if you're faking it, Pari. Buddy Willard was my tutor after all!

WILLIAM BLAKE'S LIFE

1757-	0 years	Born in the year that Swedenborg proclaimed that a new natural order on earth was to begin. Clive wins the Battle of Plassey in India
1765-67	8-10	Saw angels in a tree in Peckham Rye and God putting his head through a window
1767-71	10-14	School
1772	15	Swedenborg dies in London
1771-77	14-20	Apprenticed to James Basire, engraver
1776	19	*American Declaration of Independence*
1778-81	21-24	Royal Academy, hanging around London.
1782	25	Marries Catherine Boucher, 18 August
1783	26	Publication of *Poetical Sketches*
1784	27	Rents studio in Broad Street with Flaxman's help
1787	30	Death of brother, Robert, from consumption
1788	31	**ARIEL ENTERS THE STORY** exactly 100 years after Swedenborg's

		birth. Blake invents method of hand-engraved text and picture on the same plate
1789	32	Publication of *Songs of Innocence*
		Move to Felpham. The French Revolution
1793-1802	36-45	Literary activity. Prophetic books
1803	46	Charged with sedition at Chichester
1810-1817	53-60	Insane and unhappy years. Visions
1818-1823	61-66	Happiness again. Felpham
1824-26	67-69	Illness. Nagging jaundice, gallstones
1827	70	Death, Catherine by his side
1831		Catherine Boucher dies. No children

What's this? I asked her then, eyeing her proffered sheet of foolscap with what I thought was a look of perfect innocence—but Sylvia saw through my trick at once. Nothing, she said flatly. Just a reminder . . .

And she stood up and deliberately walked away from me, her secretary's heels click-clicking on the cold ward floor like heartbeats.

We're voyeurs, you and I, she announced, bright as a knife. It's our version of love! We make love through key-holes and we see what we see. So if you want to begin to solve all those crazy mysteries in your head, begin with that damned hat, Ariel! Blake's hat, your mother's hat, Ginsberg's crazy karma hat, whatever it was. You were there, remember? Although I can't imagine why, except that we poets are compulsive hoarders, we're the malignant magpies of humanity, Ariel. *We just can't throw away a feeling!* We save it up until it begins to smell and then we salt it in the red meat of language. Turkeys eat other turkeys in their confined coops, did you know that, Ariel, Pariel, whatever you call yourself? But we're more civilized! We are *language* cannibals. And so there you were, talking helplessly to William in his awful eighteenth century dodo-dead language—or passable imitation of, anyway—and watching over him with doe-eyed devotion even before he set eyes on you and was busy bargaining with you-know-who . . .

Oh, yes, I *do* know who and here's her story, which is also my story and William's—who drew naked angels and was prepared to bide his time in a convent behind a sedate row of Dornford Yates until the opportune moment came . . .

William was a poet, like Ted, like Sylvia.

❁

POETS ARE RETARDS. Even the sharpest among them possesses an embarrassing belief in words, as if these bits and pieces made up of wind and vocal chords really *matter*, as if they are charms. Like babies with rattles—or women with hats . . .

First question: *Why did my mother die wearing an oversized English fur hat? Why?* The truth is, countless things happened on account of that karmic hat in her life, in William's and in mine. The affair of the hat was to result in a poem almost as famous as *The Tyger* and it was to lead to Disaster and Redemption. Complicated, yes, but then a Poet's Life is always messy and that hat set things in motion all right and here is the inside story, rimmed with gummy mercury and tears, of that ubiquitous fur-hat. I, Ariel, was *there* when it first came into the picture, although neither William nor the jade knew it. I was there, talking in William's quaint archaic language, reading his quaint archaic verse, marveling at his Engravings and waiting for him to notice me . . .

But Sylvia is getting insistent now . . .

Cut short the reminiscing, will you, bunnykins, she commands. She has other things to do, like decorating the Fitzroy Road flat that had once, she said, belonged to Willam Yeats. Haunt of the priapic poets, the daddy mavens! But she will show them. She will let her poetry leak into their mouths and stopper them up like over-filled bottles. She will win!

What Sylvia doesn't know, not consciously, anyway, is that she has only eight weeks to live, but she feels it within her, the pressure of dying, building up in her all those eight impossible weeks. Eight weeks to spew out her poems, eight weeks to decorate her new home, eight weeks before what she calls the 'lopped blood-caul of absences' envelops her. And about this sudden lopping off her mortal activities in the Fitzroy Street flat, she writes with cool foreknowledge:

All night I carpenter

A space for the thing I am given
A love . . .

The glass cracks across,
The image

Flees and aborts like dropped mercury.

On the night of her death, the mercury dropped without mercy in winter's barometer. London's coldest night in 129 years and there was Mercury with her curving Aussie boomerang, waiting at Sylvia's doorstep.

❁

Once, Afi showed me a funny poem about a boy called Willie who *died* because he did not know where cool Mercury hid out. Of course, I didn't know either at the time that it was really a Destiny poem about *my* William and Sylvia that Afi was presenting me with. The poem:

Little Willie from the mirror
Licked the mercury right off
Oh, it was a chilly day for Willie
When the mercury went down!

Okay, message received. Sylvia was reminding me that there are many kinds of madness and that none of them is a 'tea-party.' Get on with it, she was saying, get on with your story, however unhinged it sounds! *Make a space for the things you love before the images flee and abort,* go on, Pariel!

Like dropped mercury, Sylvia repeats, as she prepares to leave. She has things to carpenter, she declares with a casual shrug of her stylishly furred American shoulders. It all happened before she was born, anyway, that business with William and David—what had it do with her?

And then she's gone and will not return until I'm done with William . . .

❁

New Addenbrooke's Medical File 203 3.11.88: Since episode where patient tried to escape and bit Nurse, she has occasionally had to be restrained. Patient in danger of damaging herself as she has a case history of aviomania. Change in treatment following the current examination is indicated and olanzapine is the drug of choice to be administered as of today.

An interestingly complex case of a high IQ patient with several combined psychoses. Currently most attentive when under the influence of the 'voice' she calls William. Often converses with physician as if 'William' and his world are tangible and visible to her. Grows excitable at times and speech betrays astonishing manic fluency and clarity af articulation; tape-recorded sample:

> Doctor, the hat! The harlot's [??] going to sell him the hat, I can see that. I have to warn him—but not on a telephone. Not on a phone! You can't dial the dead, Doctor, especially not William! William hated—he hated machines. A hat's not a machine, it's a . . . [indistinct 10 seconds approx]. *She* doen't even know who William was, the hussy! William was a poet, a great one and I was his angel. I was his Recording Angel and his Guardian Angel, appointed to watch over him . . . What? *Who* was William? Let's be frank, Doctorji. I *lived* William for forty years, so let's not beat about the bush. William was a Poet and he loved me, Pari. But, as he said to me once, quit if you don't have the Passion, angel! So quit, *quit* Doctorji, if you have no taste for the stench and cold [??] of London streets. My affair is more than two centuries old, can you believe it? Plus, there are no doctors and nurses in William's [garden? Eden?] . . . Only he and I, Doctor, he and I wandering about and crying out to each other, mad as ghosts . . .

Patient began to rock back and forth and croon to herself at this point and the signs of her wailing are clearly audible on tape for a full eight minutes. Then a fifty-second silence after which the patient breaks into speech again, but this time her voice is calm, measured, tonally quite distinct from the hysteric pitches of her former outburst. It was observed that the patient sat bolt upright and her body took on a rigid posture during this phase of her mania. Transcript of tape-recording continued:

> Pariel [?] is charged by Someone [Summon? . . . articulation unclear] to tell you William's story and I will do so most diligently. I will tell you how Williams' poems came to be written, poems as radiant as London and The Tiger! You will behold me flutter luminously [tape unclear 35 seconds] . . . I will be his Angel. Sometimes, sometimes, sometimes [word repeated thrice with clear intonation] a robin redbreast in a cage, sometimes, a snaky-haired daughter of Lost [?] . . .

Pause and indrawn inhalation on part of patient: 45 seconds approx.

> Sometimes a tiger from Bengala . . . !

Pause: 1 minute approx. Sudden resumption of high pitched delivery.

> The matter was decided long ago, I tell you. Long ago in Tempke! There's no escape for Pari. I am to show you marvels and stars! Just hold on tight like Afi [ice?] and I will *show* you how William learnt his best techniques of engraving and how he died in ecstasy singing and praying in my arms . . .

Pause: 1/2 minute approx. Voice very low, almost inaudible.

> I will show you myself—his forbidden Love, his London harlot and his Heathen Angel. I will tell the story of the hat . . .

Pause: End of tape. Patient's eyes glaze over and she seems oblivious to her surroundings. Remains in this withdrawn and inward state for a considerable time, although she is observed to make excited gestures with her hands from time to time. Deep schizoid symptoms. Next appointment scheduled for 12.11.88.

Cheapside, London, 1793

Pari's Book, written in the Eighteenth Century in Eighteenth Century language:

Watch it now! Here comes the harlot about to traipse her way into William's life . . .

William's been sauntering down the pavement for a full half-hour already, lazily enjoying the bustle of the afternoon. He takes this route often, abandoning his Spiritual Madness for a while to admire the speckles of sunlight falling gently on bales of fustian and loosened crepe. The truth is that he's always been, at bottom, an honest hosier's son and he cannot resist a Good Bargain in clothing. So, although he hasn't quite spotted the Young Hussy as yet, his mind is primed and when at last she calls out to him at the Whitechapel flea-market, just as she is destined to, he does not turn away but glances over her wares with a practiced eye, his attention caught by two items in particular—a wide Phrygian bonnet in pink chenille with dangling satin ribbons and a fur-hat of thickest beaver-skin.

William thinks of the handsome pair Catherine and he will make strolling down the street, Sunday mornings after church, attired in the said items—and he makes up his mind.

As for the pretty jade (though William, locked in his eighteenth century thoughts, was mind-blind to the premonition), she was Sister Liddie personified—or Mona. She knew a Good Customer when she saw one and she wasn't half bad-looking herself—which is why, catching William's speculative eye that afternoon, she chooses to lift her petticoats just that fraction higher and invite him to her quarters later that evening.

'I will give you a good price, Sir. I will play you for the hats and a little treat,' said the minx. 'If you win, you get the goods free, and if *I* do, you pay me five pounds full. No discounts!'

'What will you play me?'

'You choose, Sir—cribbage, twenty-one, pinochle, faro, fan-tan, bezique. I will play you all!' She was flushed with excitement.

'*Ange-bete,* angel-beast. Do you know it?'

'*Ange-bete?* But I have no angels' She sounds disappointed—and at this point even the good Doctor at *my* bedside is mystified. Angels, he enquires, interrupting my reverie and making me sit bolt upright on my hospital bed, while I explain some history to him. Dr T cares for me, I know, but he knows no history and he doesn't read novels. As for poetry, one line from Sylvia would destroy him entirely! Sometimes I feel sorrier for him than I should—though he's the doctor and I'm the patient.

Angels, I inform Dr T, are rare and valuable coins and only a few survive. First minted in 1465 in the reign of Edward IV, angels bear the stamp of the archangel Michael slaying the Dragon and were thought to cure people of the scrofula or the King's Evil, as the disease was known.

'Really?' asks Dr T. He seems interested by the medical reference.

'Yes, really, Doctor' I reply grandly and continue in my AIR-Britannica voice. 'By William's time, they were stakes in card-games among the dandies, making it highly unlikely that any poor Whitechapel strumpet would possess them, but William, William still chose this game involving angels because, Doctor, it was the only one he knew really well.'

This I knew from personal knowledge, though I did not confess it to Dr T, for who had William learnt *Ange-bete* from but his own private flyer, his beautiful beast, his nut-brown maid, his personal dragon-slayer, his own Pari? And I suppose these cuddlesome endearments were ringing in his ears as he answered the wench that sunlit afternoon:

'You need no angels. I will play you for the items.'

'Done!' This was going to be easy.

It wasn't easy, though, not by half, as she discovered. William was a past-master at the only card-game he knew and he played it with the furrowed concentration of a saint. The fact is, you cannot stack the decks against a true loner, because he does not see you. He sees only the goal as he marshals his host, the reds and whites in serried ranks, closing in and closing in till they vanquish you completely! Naturally, William won. He won the bonnet and the fur, he won the single silver candlestick in the corner, he won her white body in that narrow germ-infested chamber of hers. He won till she had nothing left to gamble. Or so he thought.

Until he heard the infant, a faint mewling in the night like a cat's . . .

'What was that?' His booming voice, unexpectedly loud.

'Nothing!' And I saw the jade cup one expert hand over his mouth, her second caressing his organ in quick rhythmic strokes, but it was his *ears* she should have held. For William was quite ready to give in to her, his organ a firm loaf of bread freshly baked, oozing honey and ready for the taking, when the baby whimpered again, still weakly but more insistent this time. There was no mistaking it for an animal any longer.

'Is that your baby?'

It was an idiotic question and William was not an idiot. He did not expect an answer as he watched the girl swing herself, sheets and all, out of the bed in a flash and crouch dimly in an abandoned corner of the room. It was full of rubbish—rags and baskets and pre-Heineken beer-mugs and broken chairs—yet somewhere in that mess was this living thing! The girl had picked up the tiny wraith now and was rocking it back and forth furiously. William, who knew few worldly things apart from *Ange-Bete* and the price of cloth, nevertheless knew these signs. He was no Allen Ginsberg, world cocaine connoisseur, no Havelock Ellis, MD, but that sagging head and limp body meant only one thing. This baby was doped to the gills. He said:

'Your baby needs a doctor.'

'No doctor!' She was screaming now, if it's possible to scream under your breath. *No doctor*! Holding her infant with one hand, she picked up William's clothes with the other and threw them at him.

'Go, sir, *please*! Leave us!'

Then William said something he did not know he was going to say until the words were out of his mouth.

'I will take the baby with me.'

This simple statement had an electrifying effect on the harlot—who, at that moment, no more knew what she was doing than William knew what he was saying. They were both beside themselves. Luckily, *I* was also beside them both, although they did not know it.

What happened next: the girl literally *flung* her infant at William with the same abandon as she had done his clothes a few moments ago, accompanied by a stream of the most superb invective.

> 'A pox on your wilted caterpillar, you buncombe pooper, you! Shite and ordure, the deuce kiss your Dame's fanny! May Jiminy shrivel your poke to cinders! May he hex your squawking tiddlers and blight your unborn babes with the killing rat's plague! Steal my baby, would you, you sodding brigand, you cutpurse ghoul, you sausage poke! Beshrew you for a cockless turkey, sir!'

❁

Among the things Pari knows:

William and Catherine could never have managed to bring up the kid. They were far too unworldly. The girl needed her baby much, *much* more. He was her reason to live, as Afi was the nuns', so whether she knew it or not, it just would not have done for William to walk away with that infant as a part of his easy winnings. And that is why, as I, Pariel, watched the girl clasp her baby to her once more, I was as sure of the rightness of my decision as I have ever been of anything.

Mona-Liddie was now repeating her earlier message with renewed conviction.

'Go!' she rasped fiercely. 'Take your winnings and go, sir!'

But William did not take his winnings, at least not all of them. Instead, he turned out his pockets. They contained ten shillings and a glittering gold Angel, his good luck charm. It was I who had given it to him but now he unhesitatingly left it with all his silver on the table beside the silver candle-stick. One thing you could bet on—William, in the end, always got his priorities right. And he gave that singularly articulate harlot a second gift as well—one that all the gold angels in the world could not have bought.

He gave her one of his most unforgettable poems.

I wander thro' each charter'd street,
Near where the charter'd Thames does flow,
And mark in every face I meet
Marks of weakness, marks of woe.

And the lament ends:

But most thro' midnight streets I hear
How the youthful Harlot's curse
Blasts the new born Infant's tear,
And blights with plagues the Marriage hearse.

His peculiar sense of justice induced William to take the fur hat and the Phrygian bonnet, though. He thought he'd won those fairly. The fur hat, of course, he gave to me, but you'll be hearing a lot about that! And there's a tailpiece.

William did not present the Phrygian bonnet to Catherine directly. First, he decided to wear it himself for a full week in broad daylight in the open streets of London! A woman's bonnet, trailing pink ribbons! All the records of his life mention this. Of course, as usual, everyone thought he was having one of his mad fits, but, they were misinformed. William wore that bonnet as a sort of Christian penance, deliberately calling down ridicule on his own head for the wrong he had done that poor jade.

No one ever said William was not a brave soul.

It was his insane courage and his sadness, those incredible clouds of depression shot through with blinding starry points of light that he shared with Sylvia that first brought me to William so many years ago and finally blew me, grown-up Pari, into his waiting arms.

❁

New Addenbrooke's Medical File 203 12.11.88: Patient engaged in writing almost non-stop in her diaries. It is observed that she writes in not one but **two** identical exercise-books—sometimes in one and sometimes in the other. One is labeled in large capitals: AN INVESTIGATION INTO LOVE (SYLVIA'S QUESTION) and the other: AN INVESTIGATION INTO DEATH (MA'S & THE TURKEY'S). However, patient refuses to part with either book and often insists on sleeping with them clutched to her. On the rare occasions when she responds to questions during ward-rounds, she asks not to be disturbed as she is 'meditating'. However, aviomania and sexual displays have shown distinct signs of abatement under the influence of the new drug. Olanzapine 0.10 mg to be contd. and patient to be scheduled for concurrent RTMS treatment from 30.11.

Engraving

I cannot say I recall well the first words that David or Sylvia said to me, but I remember very clearly William's first phrase. *Get away!* he said.

He said it with great despair.

Then he said it again—bending this time to pick up a poker from the cold hearth. The poker had an exquisite brass *fleur de lis* mounted with a little Cupid flexing his toy bow at one end and a cruel-looking arrowhead at the other. The latter was the end directed towards me. Yet, I remember inching closer without the slightest hesitation. For all his clenched fists and the violent tongue that often got him into dangerous situations, William was a gentle soul. True, he had a reputation for insanity, just as it was true that he was charged with high treason and had to appear before the magistrates in Chichester because he shouted *Damn the King!* in an excess of passion at a passing soldier he'd caught urinating in his garden, but it is also true that he was acquitted.

Besides, I was by no means a soldier, and I knew even on that first day that William would not hurt a woman any more than he would think of injuring a bird even if its claws and beak were tearing into him.

As I came forward, my dark hair a streaming waterfall and my bangles of engraved gold and red glass tinkling, I began to sense a palpable softening in William. He could not help himself. His heart was flooded with the same tenderness that he had shown when he let that tiny black-face out of its owner's cage without a thought for the fact that it was not *his* monkey to release! It was his way—too impulsive really for a man whose reputation was founded, even in those early days, for being a Spiritual Poet.

Then I smiled at him. *So you've made a monkey of me, have you?* I said softly. The phrase became a joke between us when he came to trust and know me better: *My beautiful nut-brown monkey!* he used to call me.

The light in the studio was fading at the time and the fire quite gone, but then a quiescent ember sparked suddenly for a moment in the gloom. It was all the encouragement William needed. *I know it, I know this true!* He slammed his fist upon his knee. *You are a Vision sent to me by Robert.*

My heart broke for William.

It had barely been a year since his beloved brother Robert had died. He'd died in William's arms, streaming with consumptive sweats, barely conscious, but William's reaction, as always, was unexpected. He looked upward and announced: *He's happy as a lark in Heaven!*

Catherine, standing by the bedside, was quite startled out of her weeping. All the others gathered round the sad bed stared gape-mouthed too, but William remained calm. *This is no occasion for sorrow,* he declared. *I have seen his pure soul! I have seen his soul ascend heavenward clapping its hands for joy!* But for all his protests, he missed his brother sorely and tried each day to communicate with him in the spirit world. This day, 17 April of the Year of Our Lord 1788, he had found *me* instead. Robert's emissary? It was for William to decide.

I shifted ground ever so slightly so that my anklets sounded—like distant, reminding cowbells. One day, we were to argue about those cowbells, about the mystic differences between the dappled heifers lowing contented on William's familiar south Sussex downs and the white cows of India, revered and distant. But for now, my anklets did the trick as efficiently as any bells. I saw William turn instantly towards me, his hands shading his eyes as he strained to make me out against the flickering background of the studio shadows.

> 'Tell Robert I am stalled. Tell him no angels sing since he is gone. My manuscripts need illumination! They need the Saints! They need the Saints to shine in them. Tell him I cannot write in the old way anymore!'
>
> 'Old way? Do you speak of *Poetical Sketches*?'
>
> 'Bah! They were child's play! I am a grown man now. I need a new technique. Ask Robert, ask Robert . . . He will know.'

I could see the strong muscles in William's neck distended. His eyes bulged and his agitation was apparent. I wanted to lay my cool hand upon him but he was still too far. I murmured soothingly to him across the abyss.

> 'You wrote of loss of inspiration in those poems too. It may pass, this feeling.'

'Vision, do not harp, do not harp on those early effusions. If the money had not been raised for them by kind friends, who would have published them, pray? *The languid strings do scarcely move! The sound is forc'd, the notes are few!* I was fourteen when I wrote those lines. Fourteen! I knew not loss, nor sorrow. I was merely copying the great masters. It is different these days. My business is utterly in ruins and we must leave Broad Street by the month's end! Flaxman can help no more. Tell Robert I cannot do without him!'

'You can do without Robert but not without the corrosive acids that eat into the soul.'

'Riddle me not! Do you speak of engraving?'

'I do.'

'Come closer. Closer! Whisper to me Robert's secret.'

'If the doors of perception were cleansed, everything would appear to man as it is: Infinite. This you shall do by printing in the infernal method by corrosives, which in Hell are salutary and medicinal, melting apparent surfaces away and displaying the Infinite which was hid.'

'Infinity! *This* is the sign that you have come to me from Robert although you speak of Hell. We talked so often of Infinity but he has arrived there sooner than I. God bless him!'

'William, you are to find your Inspiration! Before the month's end, you will see the happy marriage of

Heaven and Hell in your art, I promise you that.'

'Vision, I thank thee! You are the Sign I have awaited these past six months.'

'Take each copper plate and bathe it in acid.'

'Yes.'

'Begin with an opaque medium, the ink of a single colour.'

'Just one colour? Vision, it will bore me.'

'At first. Once it's done, the design will stand out stark, don't you see?'

'Aha.'

'After that is done, anything is possible! You can colour each page by hand to the height of your Imagination! Use all the hues of the rainbow if you will. Clouded greys and green sycamores, the sun's bright gold! Think of it, William.'

'I am dazzled . . . it will take me awhile. Does Robert approve?'

'He will be the first to read your books.'

'Tell me more!'

'One other matter. Your poems and pictures must nudge each other on the very same page! Lay your drawing and writing down side by side like a true loving couple! Let them exist, co-eternal like Heaven with Hell. Do not make breaks in your design.'

'I have seen no book of this nature.'

'Yours will be the first. Once your hand is set in this, William, you will use no other technique. It is to be a Revolution in printing!'

❁

History: history, dull as ditchwater. Once past, revolutions are no longer revolutions. They're just history in a dead language. So why should you care? Why should you follow me through these old eighteenth century pathways?

Well, you do not have to, Doctor Saheb. You can luxuriate, you can take off on your Thunderbird motorbike, but I am *chained* here for now, Summa says. I am bound to recount William's story because he was not just a poet. He was a man I loved.

William does not know it yet but there is to be another thunderous Revolution very soon. **1789**: the year of the French Revolution, is the very same year that he uses his new technique and publishes the *Songs of Innocence* and *The Book of Thel.* In that year, his dreams of liberty are to be etched in relief on his mind just like his eternal designs on paper. These etchings will go so deep that he will draw on them for the rest of his life. William is a man who has dreamt of other places far-off from his own since he was a boy—of Jerusalem, land of myth and of America, land of promise, where 'Washington, Franklin, Paine and Warren' decide on the glorious shape of the Future for all Time.

William was just eighteen—young like us, Afi!—when the American War of Independence broke out. He was so elated by the news that he fell in a swoon. He felt as he had on the day that he saw those exquisite angels nestling in the sere oak at Peckham Rye. *So what if his own father doubted his word?* So what if others strolling the commons at the time saw only a bunch of wild boys swinging from the strong old branches and bending them to their will so that the leaves parted wide to let in the large swathes of dazzling April sky?

They saw a tree alight and William saw Raphael's putti. Afi, think! I, his Sylvia-angel from the outer wilderness of Tempke, visited William *exactly* one hundred years after his master Swedenborg's birth—that is another thing he does not know, an unseen blue periwinkle in the commons of history. William has always been vague about dates and times, forever lost in his ethereal worlds, among the poets and mists of the past, but if he were to touch me without warning, he would succumb too soon, and then where would it end?

Where would it end?

❁

New Addenbrooke's Medical File 203 16.11.88: Patient insisted last week that she must acquire a particular book on the Swedish philosopher, Swedenborg, because she 'had to get to the end of William's story.' In the short session I had with her, she begged me piteously to help her and when I enquired how, she immediately extracted a page from one of the diaries she always carries with her (the one labeled AN INVESTIGATION INTO LOVE in which, Nurse informs me, she is still scribbling furiously every day). Carefully copied on the page was a long book title *'WHY MRS BLAKE CRIED: SWEDENBORG, BLAKE, AND THE SEXUAL BASIS OF SPIRITUAL VISION'* By Marsha Keith Schuchard. Given previous evidence, this choice of reading material did not surprise me, since it is evidently connected with the patient's continuing deep-rooted sexual pyschosis. By this morning's session, I discovered that the patient had already managed to read through the entire text (kindly obtained for her by her relative at my express request). Large parts of the book had been underlined and one amongst these that the patient explicitly drew my attention to was the following quotation from 'William':

> . . . the Female lets down her beautiful Tabernacle; which the Male enters magnificent between her Cherubim: And becomes one with her.

Patient then informed me excitedly that it was she who was Blake's beautiful Female, his second 'wife', pointing to a passage in Schuchard's work as 'evidence':

> Once in a patriarchal mood he [Blake] did propose to add a second wife to their small and shifting household, and was much perplexed at meeting with tears and remonstrances. In 1893, William Butler Yeats repeated the rumor, noting that 'It is said that Blake wished to add a concubine to his establishment in the Old Testament manner, but gave up the project because it made Mrs Blake cry.'

It is striking how consistent and coherent the patient's psychosis is and how she manages to settle on that 'evidence' that most suits her delusions. She has repeated to me several times that 'Sylvia' has commanded her to discover love through 'William's' eyes. That is why, she said, she had to cause William agonies and 'make Catherine cry', even though it hurt her to do so. Patient wept as she said these words.

Patient scheduled for concurrent RTMS treatment from 30.11.88.

❁

These days, I spend all my time with William and Catherine, night and day . . .

When I get the chance, I try to explain to Dr T who is

always questioning me about my life with William and Catherine, that I cannot help this. I know that I am split in two when I am with them. It's as if I have turned into someone else entirely. I'm in a different *zone.* I speak in a different language and words come into my mind that I didn't know I knew. Sometimes the thoughts I think are bad thoughts about kissing and other things but I *cannot help it.* When I am with William, it's exactly like it was with Sylvia. The whole world vanishes. The hospital, the bedpans, the nurses! Even Tempke seems like a dream town. I forget my *investigations.* I forget everything except that I am William's Angel . . .

The trouble is that I don't really know if Dr T believes me, because he's always asking me trick questions like what was Catherine wearing last Sunday or what William's special name for me is. Simple questions like this I can answer but there are things about William's life that I don't know so much about—such as what he learnt from his master Swedenborg. So the other day, I asked Dr T for a book on the subject—and he got it for me! But later he began to shower me with questions from the book as if it was an examination. What was Swedenborg's exact relationship with William, the Doctorji wanted to know, and where exactly did *I* enter into the scheme of things?

Of course I had read the book page by page and by-hearted many passages, so it was not difficult to answer the Doctor. William Blake had learnt of Swedenborg's teachings when he was still a boy 'at his father's knee'. Then in the 1740s and 50s Swedenborg came to London as a secret agent for a pro-Jacobite party in Sweden called **'The Hats'** (this is *true,* it's written in the book) and began attending some Jewish Kabbalistic services in Fetter Lane, London (not far from where William met the jade).

Swedenborg was a lifelong bachelor but he 'kept a mistress in Sweden and, by his own admission, another one in Italy'. His 'many descriptions of prostitutes and sirens and his advocacy of legal brothels make clear that he was widely experienced in earthly sexuality; moreover, his writings on these subjects were studied by Blake'. So the book confirmed what I knew already in my bones: *When William went to the Harlot, he had Swedenborg's blessing in a way—just as he did in his dealings with sweet Catherine . . .*

William's Swedenborgian friend Thomas Butts once reported that he had walked in on Catherine and William 'stark naked' in their London garden acting out 'the return of Adam into Paradise'. (Butts did not know about the Madonna Triptych, of course, or that it was Raphael's painting of Adam and Eve that William had etched in his mind but this is no reason to believe that he was lying about Swedenborg's influence in the matter.) Swedenborg recommended mental telepathy and religious union as conferring the highest perfection on married love. Conjugal love, according to Swedenborg, could be raised to cosmic significance if husband and wife followed certain meditative practices. This he recorded in his book *The Delights of Wisdom Concerning Conjugial Love*, which William had certainly read, and also in his journal, where he wrote:

> Conjugal love, or that which exists between two conjugal partners who love one another . . . is the inmost of all loves, and such that partner sees partner

> in mind (*animus*) and mind (*mens*), so that each partner has the other in himself or herself, that is, that the image, nay, the likeness of the husband is in the mind of the wife and the image and likeness of the wife is in the mind of the husband, so that one sees the other in himself, and they thus cohabit in their inmosts [61].

Where were you when William was with Catherine? Dr T asked me cunningly. I was right there, I told him. Sometimes William went through Hell with Catherine and sometimes he was in Heaven but *I* was always there, I said, pointing to my own inmost, whereupon Dr T looked very shocked and called in Nurse, who was sitting just ouside the open door and she came and took me away to the Ward—but I didn't care. I had my story to tell . . .

Fifteen years after I, Pari, had first imparted it to him, in the failing light of the Broad Street Studio, the technique for engraving that was always to remain uniquely his own, William went through a patch of Hell. He was miserable from the sedition charges and sick at heart over his repeated failures at business. They had been intimately happy at Felpham, Catherine and he, but now he had decided to return to London.

The thought depressed him so much that all through the first decades of the new century, he struggled to write and failed. Struggled again and failed again. It became a vicious circle, an envenomed design, and even I could not help him. The gap between us was greatest then . . .

Once back in London, William found himself victim of the same malady. He *could not* bring himself to write at any cost. So he went back to his painting and engraving. In this he was encouraged by all his grand London friends, Lady Caroline Lamb and William Hayley and Sir Thomas Butts, but I thought it a great mistake. William's writing and painting were part of one another, a happily wedded couple, as I had told him already. He could never aspire to peace when one excluded the other—and what William needed at the time was *peace,* the sort of peace only Catherine or I could give him. And sure enough, when his Show opened the critics attacked him most cruelly! I thought he would die wrestling with his 'devilish battalions'. Worse, no one bought his studies. But William was always strong and stubborn as an ox.

After that disastrous 1809 exhibition, he retreated into a shell of such protective toughness, it reminded me of the picture of a giant Galapagos turtle I'd seen once in one of our books in our convent library in Tempke. For nearly eight years, William Galapagos hardly spoke to anyone at all, except Catherine and his Apparitions—John Milton and Edward the First, egalitarian king of England and maker of her 'Model Parliament'. Of course, everyone insisted it was the madness in his family come out at last. William could not help his damaged heredity, but I managed to whisper a contrary message in his ear:

> 'No, it is not madness. It is your friends who drive you crazy!'

I could see William was listening. He quickly pulled a scrap of paper out of his pocket and wrote out a couple of lines.

Then he grinned at me. His eyes were the sanest then that I have ever seen—and this is the verse that William penned for me that day to prove he was not mad:

Thy friendship oft has made my heart ache
Do be my enemy, for friendship's sake
This frenzied plea was plead by
WILLIAM BLAKE!

And he started to laugh with me again. That was when everyone thought he was maddest, laughing so uproariously and muttering to himself all day! They did not know that in fact he was getting better moment by moment, nor that I was with him constantly. It was me he was laughing with!

Most evenings, during this convalescent time, William would gaze out at the treetops from his narrow London window and gently meditate with me beside him. Catherine would tiptoe round the house, not disturbing us and keeping the curious out. She was a treasure! Without the self-effacing protective Madonna cordon she spread around us, how could we ever have conquered William's blues? Meanwhile, wrapped in constricting blankets, a piece of fresh toast spread with Catherine's most delicious blackberry jam untouched beside him, his precious notebooks full of sketches, scratched drafts of poems, prose harangues and all sorts of scribbles lying inert beside him, William would absorb my serene thoughts . . .

Then, in his sixtieth year, the wisdom of my message suddenly became as transparent to him as the glass in his window—nay, clearer. He would return to Felpham . . .

We did so the very next year and were a wondrously happy menage once more—he and Catherine and I—for the next five years. It was only his nagging jaundice and the gallstones that so wracked his body in his late years that finally drove us back to London and it was there he died. He was exactly seventy. Catherine was with him—and I. No other, just his Angels—Catherine and I. *There are always two,* Sylvia's words come echoing back to me . . .

Catherine spoke to William every day after his death. He advised her on all the practical matters of her life but not on the politics of civil war or the constitution of a Mughal garden as an image of Paradise, nor vegetarianism in India nor Raphael's frescoes. These remained my territory. I was the one charged with urging him to look through the Windows of his soul at the glories of his own Future Redemption . . .

Windows: A Meditation on **God and the Future**.

Windows were always important in William's scheme of things.

At seven years of age, William saw God Himself peering in at the window of his father's house. God, he said, 'put his head to the window and set me a-screaming.' And that terror never left my William. He fought off Jehovah as another might battle with the influenza or typhus. For the most part, Summa said, humans tended to lose this battle but William was among the chosen few who won. At the ecstatic end of his life, he won, but it remained difficult for most others—his fellow poets and the sincere, bent scholars who spent their lives poring over his works—to quite grasp this terror of his. Yet, it was on this very madness that his creative frenzy relied. Contorted with my own madness, I saw that clearly and I was even grateful for it, for without it he would not have needed me . . .

William needed me most to assist him with his fantasies of the Future and whenever I found the windows of William's mind even a little ajar, I admit it was a subject to which I constantly returned. I took pleasure in provoking him with little tidbits of information from this faraway place that he could not quite absorb. The future entranced William because he saw it as a vast arena of freedom, a Utopia. It followed, Summa said, that it was my duty as his Angel of Experience to complicate this vision of his until he reached that fine edge of frustration when a Poet truly becomes a Seer . . .

So I began to taunt William just as Sylvia had mocked me. In the twentieth century, I told him, a great empire would be built in America and across the world by another who bore his own name—William. He ought to be interested in this empire for it was the sort of kingdom of which he had himself dreamt—a Virtual Empire—yet it exceeded all his dreams.

If William had made a type of Engraved Book that no one ever made before or since, not Caxton, not Gutenberg, this other William had also ushered in another sort of revolution—an Information Revolution! And were not revolutions William's passion? In this future empire, I continued enthusiastically, you could travel anywhere you wished, as freely as any Angel. You could make friends with Chinamen and Arabs and language posed no impediment. For each man had in his home a silver screen—often more than one—where he could see his words instantly translated into many unknown tongues. You could open up as many

Windows or Gates as you pleased in this world and peer out of all of them at once. At the click of a button you could change sex and age and nation in multiple chat-rooms or roam space in search of a Soul-mate or a Type-face—all the while sitting back in the comfort of your own studio!

'Type faces?' William's attention was caught. He was a printer through and through all his life. Mention Indian ink or a Gothic font and he was hooked. This, indeed, was the first occasion on which he had displayed the slightest curiosity in any of my perorations and I saw I must seize the opportunity at once! Loath as I was to resort to cheap magician's tricks, it seemed I had little choice, and so quickly, out of the liquid London air, cold as frozen nitrogen, I managed to conjure up a smart computer right in front of William's goggle-eyed gaze. And equally speedily, I typed his name—nothing fancy, just plain 'William Blake, Esquire'—and ran it though a full dozen fonts: regular, bold, serif, sans serif . . .

William Blake, Esquire	Arial Narrow
William Blake, Esquire	Bookman Oldstyle
William Blake, Esquire	BrshScrD
WILLIAM BLAKE, ESQUIRE	COPPERPLATE GOTHIC
William Blake, Esquire	Comic Sans MS
William Blake, Esquire	**Franklin Gothic Medium**
William Blake, Esquire	**Haettenschweiler**
William Blake, Esquire	Microsoft Sans serif
William Blake, Esquire	*Monotype Corsiva*
William Blake, Esquire	Nimbus Script
William Blake, Esquire	Sydnie
Ωιλλιαμ Βλακε, Εσθυιρε	Σψμβολ Γρεεκ

William was transfixed. *This* was a window he would have jumped through without the slightest hesitation—but it was a reaction I had anticipated of course, and I made the silver computer disappear from his view in a trice! It was cruel, but should I not have pressed my advantage?

Despite inventions as miraculous as the one I'd just demonstrated—or *demon*strated—I prattled on, giving William no pause for protest and throwing in a superfluous pun to boot, it was not a perfect world, by any means. The world to which this wonder belonged was a world of Rank Commerce where the most powerful dominated and the rest of the world remained enslaved. This was not the Utopia he had longed for. America, his dear America, now qualified as *the* Authoritarian Dictator! That was one of the Great Surprises of the future . . .

Just at this crucial point, however, when I thought I was making some headway at last in apprising William of the Truths of the Future, I found myself rudely interrupted. A scruffy one-legged pigeon—one of William's less attractive familiars, though to him an emblem of the bravest Resistance because the tough old bird had Survived a Human Trap!—came and settled comfortably on the windowsill. That was it!

I saw William grow distracted. It was not my futuristic rant that had held him, after all, it was the practical wonder of a Microsoft screen. When I took *that* away, his attention was lost once more. The bedraggled pigeon that now made its appearance on cue was only a crude earthly Sign of this complete disintegration of focus on William's part.

'Catherine!' he bellowed. 'Breadcrumbs, dear!'

'*What?*' yelled Catherine piercingly from below.

'Breadcrumbs! General Wallace honours us with a visit!'

General Wallace! I may as well have been conversing with the walls. They had better ears than William's at this stage in the proceedings, so what was left for me to do but vanish into them, less conspicuous than a shadow—and about as important to William for the time being . . .

My William was unparalleled as a Poet but he was innocent (not like Sylvia). He was convinced that he could travel freely into the future and learn its mysteries without barriers, but *could* he? Could he, my Sylvia voices taunted, comprehend a Nazi concentration camp or the burning flesh of humans in Hiroshima and Vietnam? Could he visualize his America, Land of Free Love and Free Speech, transformed into a War Machine? *Could he?*

Cluster-bombs and landmines, embedded battles reported on prime-time, a musical band that called itself *atombombpocketknife*—would these fit into the surreal landscapes William was so brilliant at conjuring? My task was to discover the limits of William's imagination, where it could be breached and where it would spiral into helpless incomprehension. *For it is at these breaking points that things get really interesting.* What would William make of the realities of warfare at long distance? I could hear Sylvia mocking and I reminded her then of William's triumphant words:

Bring me my bow of burning gold:
Bring me my arrows of desire!

I will not cease from mental fight . . .
Till we have built Jerusalem
In England's green and pleasant land.

When William imagined bows and arrows, it was the Illuminated Page that was his battlefield. He saw beauty in a Holy War fought with legendary warriors by his side, William Wallace and John Milton his able generals. In William's mind, there existed not a shadow of doubt that in the Paradise of the Future, America would triumph. But *I* knew that no such future would easily transpire and it was my especial challenge, Summa said, to convince William of this disturbing Truth, to rattle that overweening confidence in him that is the mark not of fools alone but often of Poets . . .

I decided on another trick.

I would return William to the world as it is sometimes startlingly glimpsed through a Window! I, Pari, would take him to the start of a new millennium in which flaming wars rent the ancient deserts of Ur and destroyed the dusty province of Babylon. I wanted William to witness these strangely beautiful repellent sights because I was consumed with curiosity to see what he would make of them—but somehow my meditation went wrong.

Instead of landscapes of futuristic destruction, I managed to bring William to a very different site. It was a 'Blake Page' kept by some American. *Yikes!* this person had written. Did William really see His Maker Staring at him through a Glassy Pane? What sort of experience was *that*?

So it slowly dawned on me that it was as hard for William to enter the world of the twenty-first century as it was for the young of the future to understand William's eighteenth century mind packed with ghosts and apparitions. It wasn't a matter of individual zest or doughty willingness to venture beyond the confines of one's own time. William was an intrepid poet, but not even he could help being trapped in his own time, the Spirit of his Age that moved, as he said, a perilous mist into each man's soul and prevented him from entering the Next Age . . .

The truth is that a word like 'yikes!' could *never* have figured in William's vocabulary, nor the attitudes that went with it. 'Yikes' lingered beyond William's reach like Tantalus' fruit, like Christ on Raphael's ebony cross above the reach of the grieving Madonna below—but it took me a long while, as I have confessed to you, to accept this . . .

New Addenbrooke's Medical File 203 21.11.88: Patient appears more communicative. She came in today complaining of pain in her left big toe but in a prolonged session it emerged that it was a classic phantom pain associated once again with the text of Swedenborg that she is obsessively reading. Patient herself obligingly pointed me to the relevant passage in the book:

> Pain was felt in the great toe of the left foot . . . that great toe communicates with the genitals; for the genitals correspond to the Word . . . It has been often granted to sensibly perceive that communication. Reinforcing the sexual significance of foot and toe were certain Yogic rites, in which the great toe plays a crucial role in breath control.

Swedenborg had apparently some knowledge of Yoga rituals of the sort long practiced in the patient's own country and it seems she has somehow taken in this fact and converted it once again so as to fit in with the mental narrative of her 'romance' with William. One of the remarkable features of this case is the patient's ability to negotiate cultural barriers. Patient is of Indian orgin, raised in India, but seems completely absorbed in Western literature, of which she displays a formidable grasp, especially notable in one so young. The 'voices' she hears are consistently western: Sylvia, William, etc. There is just one generalized cultural reference repeatedly noted in the patient's vocabulary during the time that she has been at New Addenbrooke's and it consists in her frequent references to meditation. Apart from this, it is striking that the patient hardly ever refers to her own cultural roots, so the present instance where she reports a pain in her left toe is unique and may be interpreted as a subconscious recognition of her social affiliations which she overtly appears to suppress. What is interesting is that, according to the patient, Swedenborg also refers to techniques of meditation to control sexual pleasure, especially when copulating with 'angels' and other supernatural beings.

Patient's aviomania and her belief that she is an 'angel' have been noted. In view of this, Swedenborg's views of angels, also subscribed to by the poet William Blake, whose 'voice' the patient is much influenced by, are significant. Swedenborg apparently declared that he had

> heard from angels, that when these delights ascend from chaste partners on earth, they perceive them to be exalted from themselves and infilled . . . Angelic love of sex is full of inmost delights for it is a pleasing expansion of all things of the mind. Through proper meditation, the regenerated man becomes angelized and achieves superhuman sexual pleasure.

Patient tells me falteringly that she herself had experienced such 'pleasure with William' by controlling the 'cremaster' muscle which is part of the generative organs. When I ask the patient to repeat herself, she obliges calmly by spelling out the word:

C-R-E-M-A-S-T-E-R. I am a doctor, I tell her, and I have never heard of this muscle. Patient looks up and smiles at me directly: maybe that's why you never see angels, Doctor! I refrain from responding to such deliberate provocation and after a while the patient continues as if she is giving me a medical lecture. She seems to be enjoying herself:

> The cremaster muscle is hermaphroditic. It runs down round the sheath of the spermatic cord in both sexes, terminating in the tunica vaginalis testis and drawing up, sustaining, compressing and expressing them. Angels can change sex at will because they can control this muscle. Swedenborg the master first learnt of the muscle from his contact with Yogic masters from China, India and Tibet, who told him that it functions like 'the yoni place between the male organ and anus.' Later, William drew on this Eastern knowledge when he described Urizen's palace whose 'temples for entertainment were China, India and Siberia, continually creating the World out of the Hermaphroditic Generation.'

Most of this session tape-recorded and transcribed in order to keep a record of the patient's extraordinary fluency and ability to recite from memory, which is a salient feature of this case. RTMS treatment to begin 30.11.88: Appointment scheduled.

American Beauty

This part of the story is about Passionate Love, white like the Taj—William's and mine . . .

We were two of a kind reversed, William said. He wanted me to wander hand in hand with him across an unexplored 'American Continent' he idealized and I wanted to show him that his shining America was to revert to the dark hands of his Urizen, the ancient Jehovah, supreme authority personified. America's voice was to echo so powerfully in the future that all other nations were in danger of being silenced.

William could be charming as no other—and also logical. There were days when he would woo me with enchanted verses and demonstrate to me line by line an inescapable truth. *I* was the heroine at the heart of all his poetry. When he wrote of America, it was I who was his Muse, for America was the Daughter of Los the heavenly Blacksmith, Creative Power of the Imagination. *I* was the America he loved, so how could I persuade him that I was to become his enemy in some far off and not terribly plausible future? Was that not uncommonly perverse? And so, said William, he could not possibly accept my script!

And he laughed.

> Perhaps I would be so kind as to leave the poetry to him?

I could never resist William's laughter—it was so utterly unselfconscious, the laughter of a Laughing Buddha. Things happened when William laughed. I found that I could approach him without danger and I remembered unbidden the words of the ancient Tamil poet revealed to me in the Convent Library long ago: *It's not only Pari, the rains too keep the world going . . .*

A man's body is a porous thing. Air enters and leaves it night and day without a stop. Salt water streams from it in the heat of exertion or of summer and when it is done with its stay on earth, it returns quietly to earth. Air, water, earth—and fire!

William and I were about to burn . . .

William's body lies in an unmarked grave somewhere in the boroughs of London. It is a body that has known love. That love was so deep that William's spirit is assured a kind of freedom that no longer requires a name, a headstone or any earthly attachments. This man had felt my angel wings curve over his head. He has moved within me. I am an angel and William and I never made love to procreate. We made love because we loved and for no other reason, although I will not hide from you here that William's organ was a special one—*made* for lust. For the most part, it lay quietly at his centre, light brown and lightly speckled, soft and smooth as a pouch of rolled tobacco and as supple to handle. It was a wonderful instrument—not of light piper's joy but meant for church-music and when it reached its crescendo, creation sang with the thunder of Beethoven's Fifth, unbearable in its beauty and its mortality. At these times, I felt a fine, radiant spray like cool scintilla of fire light up my whole being. I was most an angel when William and I were most carnal in our love. That was our paradox.

Later, he would pull me into the wavering lamplight or the sudden dawn and read to me in his husky monotone his newly composed poems—for I was the angel at the heart of all of them . . .

It was me he had engraved on the frontispiece of *Preludium to America: A Prophecy*, William said, pulling open the book to the right page to prove his point.

> 'I do not lie, Muse: *The shadowy Daughter of Urthona stood before red Orc!* I am Orc and you, Urthona's dear Daughter! You came to me out of the shadows. *Invulnerable, though naked!* You brought me news of my dear Robert and revived me from my misery, showing me the way forward from *Poetical Sketches.* But for you, I would have despaired entirely. Entirely! You were with me always, my Dark Angel! At fourteen, when I felt the first stirrings of my manhood, you were there. I sensed your Presence, but you were dumb then, dumb until *I assay'd my fierce embrace . . .*'

Here William turned to me with a wicked gleam in his eye—and all was lost once more . . . Like most of William's poems,

America: A Prophecy was written between bouts of ecstasy and excited conversation. Read the poem closely and you will see that its very form is unrhymed and dialogic—a talking poem, we could call it—and the Angel to whom William is talking is *me*. Each of *America*'s eighteen magnificent plates is faithfully engraved in the manner *I* taught him all those years ago in Broad Street. Did that not pleasure me, he asks.

What it did was make me distinctly uncomfortable, I answered grumpily, struggling to escape from the circle of William's arms. There was a huge problem with his Prophecy! Elevated it might be, exalted even—but it was not entirely to be trusted.

Oh *that*! William replied, perfectly mimicking my own airy sarcasm. That was a minor crotchet he'd already fixed, had I not noticed? And, just as Afi had done, or was to do, in a convent garden many years hence, William held me firm in a steely grip . . .

We were shamelessly light headed at the time. How? I enquired, continuing the conversation and tilting back into him so that he felt the whole weight of my woman's body at once. Nor did William resist this pressure, but buried his face in the arched hollow of my neck. *You* were my Inspiration always, he answered, his voice cunningly muffled to hide his delight, but I could see his shoulders shaking . . .

But of course—of *course*! I'd forgotten that I'd tempted William into a wild bout of wordplay—at which he always managed to trump me. His model for Orc—Loki of Asgard—is not just any Norse god. He is the god of mischief.

> 'Not entirely to be *trusted*!' intoned William, amused.
> 'Chained hand and foot in a Secure Cavern beneath a

> High Mountain, but not for long! None could keep Loki down for long, Mistress. That is why I chose him as my Image of Defiance—the one who sets his laughing face against Jehovah's Ten-fold law, those tedious, restrictive, pitiless Commandments—and survives! Like old General Wallace on our windowsill whom you so love, my Angel. So will our Prophecies survive because they are Brave. I see you doubt it, Angel, but this is my Truth. You must accept it! '
>
> 'But if it is Loki of the North you admire, why call him Orc?'
>
> 'Orc—the word comes from the Latin for Hell, *orcus*. You of all beings should know that, Angel! My American Truth is not that simple after all! It is another Marriage of Heaven and Hell, coupled side-by-side. Your own advice to me, dear one, but not only yours! I have dwelt for many years on these ideas in the most august company. I have heard Edmund Burke perorate on American Liberty in Parliament. The prophet Ezekiel himself has appeared to me! I have consulted the great Mr Paine . . . You must learn to trust me, Divine One!'

There was no denying that William had studied the American experience keenly ever since the States embarked on their war against England's unjust taxation.

William was always on the side of the Libertarians. He had been thrown into a swoon at eighteen by the American position on justice and equality. Then, the very next year—1776—America went thrillingly further and declared

Independence. By this time, William had read with the minutest attention Mr Paine's stirring pamphlet *Commonsense* published that very year and made his crabbed notes in the margins.

The American affair no longer made him feel faint with inchoate joy. Instead, it stimulated him to make copious notes, notes that were to result in the long poem he would finally print almost eighteen years later—in 1793—*America: A Prophecy. My* poem . . .

I had appeared in his poems from the beginning in glimpses, William said. He did not know it in those early years—but it was I who had guided his pen.

> 'I wrote about you in the *Poetical Sketches*! The lines are forgot, it was so long ago! But I do not forget the sight of you in my first youth. Listen!

I meet my maiden risen like the morn . . .
Like an angel glitt'ring in the sky
. . . my black-eyed maid

> 'My black-eyed maid! How I have burned for you! Set me free, Muse, set me free!'

William's voice was growing hoarse with pain with each passing instant. I could see his nerves stretched taut. Then he spoke and his words surprised and puzzled me:

> 'You alone are the fitting mother of my children. Have I not joy'd thee? Tell me, Angel. Speak truly!'

What Pari read in the History Books:

> William and Catherine had no children, an affliction that was attributed by some to the infertility of insanity in William's family and by some to Catherine's barren womb. Unlike most couples however, neither Catherine nor William ever betrayed the slightest disappointment in all their forty-six, long years together at this trick of fate. Catherine had her gardening and William his poetry. This poetry he peopled most richly with intriguing animals and with children, and not only the jade's—with chimney sweeps, choirboys, cherubs, putti . . .

Whose children were these? Pari leaves you to search for the clues to this puzzle. They are there, harsh and plaintive as a peacock's cry, in William's story and in the cathartic struggle of the Thunderbird on his imagined American plains.

In the course of our 'fantastical relationship' (Sylvia's phrase), William's grief at my every withdrawal remained as spectacular on each successive occasion—in 1771, 1792, 1793 and all the years of our acquaintance—as it was on that original enchanted evening in Broad Street of which I have already told you.

> 'Do not leave, Muse. Not yet! I have so much to ask you.'
>
> 'You are to explore the senses and their relationship to Imagination. You are to explore the deep connection of Man with nature, as it was of old. You

will awaken your society from the sleep of reason and lead them into the Future . . . That is your mission. I will return to guide you in this!'

'When? When will that be?'

Once again, I could not answer William. His eagerness was endearing and piteous as a child's but I was commanded to attend an Angel meeting and I was an hour late already. I had no choice. And so I began heartlessly to dissolve in the customary shimmer of starlight—and as I left, I saw William's great massive head go down on the table.

He was weeping.

Tipu's Tiger

Pari's History Book, written in the Eighteenth Century:

Change of pace again, take it or leave it, history's muck's a-gathering and gathering, as William put it once.

1757: the year of William's birth, announced by Master Swedenborg as initiating a New Age of Liberty—was a momentous one for colonial England. At the very beginning of this year—2 January, to be exact—Robert Clive, former servant of the Company and later known as 'Clive of India', finally took the city of Calcutta, key to the rich province of Bengal. Chandernagore, until then under the rule of the French, was subsequently secured in March, supported by heavy bombardment from Admiral Watson and his fleet, parked in the Bay of Bengal—but the final stroke was the Battle of Plassey fought in the hot, pestilential month of June.

Nature itself was on the side of the colonial powers, it seemed to the people of Bengal. Torrential monsoon rain accompanied by lightning and thunder destroyed most of the ammunition stores of Siraj-ud-Daulah, ruling Nawab of Bengal and supported by a force no less than 55,000 strong.

Clive, in contrast, had only 3000 men at Plassey—but he also had a Secret Weapon.

This was the man whom the Nawab trusted as his own son, namely, Mir Jafar, the Nawab's first lieutenant. *Trust,* trust is the key, as William often maintained, but sometimes it unlocks the wrong door. In Mir's case, he confounded everyone by crossing over to Clive's side at a time when he was most needed. Perfidious Mir! The records tell us that he paid gratification to the tune of 2,340,000 pounds—no mean sum!—to the British for his elevation to the status of puppet ruler of Bengal. But then again, perhaps he could not help himself. It was his nature. Call it the Stockholm Syndrome or what you will. Sometimes we fall in love with our captors, the shiny buttons on their red coats, the dreams they present us with or the spangled tones of their poetry—though we know in our bones it may destroy us. *All through this morn and through this night, some are born to endless night . . .*

Meanwhile, over in Awadh, Sardar Jang, the grand Mughal governor of another province that was stubbornly holding out against the British, also confounded everyone in a different sort of way—simply by laying down and dying when it was least expected! And slowly the fabled riches of the Indies fell like ripe plums into the hands of Company and Crown. So who would deny that Nature herself played a part in the early colonization of India in 1757?

By the year 1800, when William was forty-three and at the height of his poetic powers, Clive's ragtag Company had grown fine and fatted. It held control over large tracts of the Indian subcontinent, helped by various Natural and Unnatural Forces. Siraj's erstwhile Bengal was now the epicentre of colonial rule. In Calcutta, the Supreme Court set up by the British managed to extend its jurisdiction right up to the district of Varanasi, where the most sacred of Indian cities, Benares, lay. Many other developments that would have far-reaching effects also took place in the same year. For example, plumb in the middle of Calcutta, the Bengal Presidency Bank set up shop directly financed by capital from the East India Company and with the bulk of shares purchased by Europeans, all natives being sternly discouraged. In the outlying areas, the district of Serampore saw the first multilingual Press being established, while back in Calcutta again, the English School and the Fort William College laid the foundations for a whole new educational project . . .

Okay, alright, but what's with the history lesson, angel, Afi wants to know. Why is this frantic activity in a remote part of the world at all important to our story? Well, first off, I must draw your attention to the fact that these events established the foundations that would ensure that William's '**Tyger**' would one day be immortal, immortal in a way he'd not dreamt of! Immortal in a convent in Tempke, immortal even in Nauru . . .

Tyger! Tyger! burning bright
In the forests of the night,
What immortal hand or eye
Could frame thy fearful symmetry?

Those long hymnal measures—*aabb, aabb, aabb*—that William used in his *Tyger* were to hypnotize brown-skinned schoolchildren across the length and breadth of India a whole century later, while a thousand real tigers annually vanished to the tune of scattered gunshots in night-forested Bengal. Magical! One day, irony of ironies, William's verses would be loved by a people he hardly knew but his own knowledge of the verdant Bengala of the Indies came from a more elevated source. *He* saw it refracted through his guru, John Milton's, early seventeenth century gaze:

As when far off at Sea a Fleet descri'd
Hangs in the Clouds by Equinoctal Winds
Close sailing from Bengala . . .

Much had changed, however, by 1800. By then, endless Englishmen, attended by loyal Maharajas in the Mir Jafar mould, had dedicated themselves to pursuing the subject of William's poem with the utmost zeal until he'd been relieved of his Royal Bengal hide once and for all. They then dispatched some of the most impressive of these hides home to England to awe the Great British Public.

Some such displays William and I saw with our own eyes, as I went about diligently following the angelic advice I'd received from Summa and Afi back in 1791 or thereabouts. Since that time, we'd visited the menageries many times and written many poems together. It is of those incredible trips that I want to tell you now and I guess I may as well begin with Tipu's Tiger, also brought to London by the Company in 1800.

End of history lesson, fitful start to story . . .

We'd got to hear of Tipu's Tiger from William's jolly friend Sir Thomas, who had financial interests in the Company and kindly brought home to William a generous clutch of the bills and posters strewn about the city like bright angel confetti. Eye of the needle, this was enough for me.

I began at once to pester William, convinced that a visit to the Company Headquarters would educate him further in the dark colonial history of which he was so blissfully unaware and thus pave the way for him to admit an equally wicked Future—but at first he would have nothing to do with my blandishments.

William, you see, had already published *Tyger* some years previously after a disastrous (but not unproductive!) visit to the Change (also, needless to say, prompted by me)—and the incident brought back bittersweet memories. It all *ended* fine but the path was rocky and I suspected that William did not want to repeat the experience. He'd been so disgusted at the captive beasts I'd forced him to confront then that he grew sullen and intolerant, resentfully enquiring as we entered the portals of the Change:

> 'Why do we come here? Why do we *have* to come here?'
>
> 'To learn, so that our poems truly are poems of experience.'

William whispered back fiercely:

> *'Great things are done when men and mountains meet. This is not done by jostling in the street!* You force me into a Scene from Hell!'

'Then describe it! You are a Poet.'

'I cannot. The air is sick. It fills my head with Chaos. We are all sick! These animals, these multitudes—sick, sick! Angel, you too are sick to drag us here!'

There was some truth to William's accusation. The sticky June afternoon we'd chosen did not augur well. Huge crowds thronged about us, rough and boisterous and seemingly quite untroubled by the fetid air from the cages. They were there to enjoy themselves, despite the Corn Laws, despite the Factory Acts and, by God, enjoy themselves they would—all except for poor William, who was growing redder and more irritable by the minute.

What's more, much to our dismay, there were no signs at all of the star exhibit from Bengala. **'Cruel Flesh Eater of the East! Twenty Hands from Tail to Ear! One of the Largest Beasts Ever to be Shewn in the Western Hemisphere!'** It was this advertisement that I'd especially used to lure William, who for all his learning had not ever set eyes on a live tiger before. And now we could not find the creature!

Catherine had wisely refused to come with us. This had become usual and William never forced her. I think he preferred her to wait for him at home with her tender ministrations, the camomile tea and hot buns she had steaming for him when he got home. Oh yes—and his footstool! Catherine cosseted William like a child and he loved it, but like most men he was too perverse to be content with unquestioning love. *That* was where I came in . . .

Most readers still do not grasp how unconventional a

poem the *Tyger* is. For almost all of William's contemporaries, the *lion* was undisputed king of the jungle, noblest among the beasts of the wild. A tiger, on the contrary, excited universal odium as a cowardly flesh-eater. It was cunning and prone to greed, apparently given to annihilating whole fields of sheep in its orgies of destruction and wantonly leaving off feeding on one carcass to insouciantly kill another.

Only fools were deceived into thinking a tiger beautiful! In actual fact, there was *nothing* handsome about this 'most cruel, rapacious and destructive animal in creation'. It was but 'an emblem of savageness and brutishness'. 'No discipline can correct the savage nature of the tiger, nor any degree of kind treatment reclaim him', proclaimed William Holloway and John Branch in *The British Museum or Elegant Repository of Natural History.*

Wherever you turned in rapidly colonizing England, the tiger stood as villain—and yet I had somehow persuaded William that he should look at the tiger from *my* point of view. I insisted that the tiger stood not for serfdom but for the unfettered, unconquered spirit of the Indies, a spirit that had not quite died even when Siraj was defeated at Plassey and Mir fell in love with the Union Jack. *What's love, anyway?*

I wanted William to see the tiger as a creature symbolic of the bright yearning for Liberty that was such a passion with him. That was my ambitious goal and that was why it was so important that he saw a real tiger—not just some painted or printed monstrosity—but now it appeared I'd miscalculated again.

Still no tiger. Instead, we passed by an enclosure of snarling civets, one of them wounded and moaning. William, naturally, could not be prevented from moving towards her at once but somehow the heat and the horror got to him before he got anywhere near the cats' cage. I saw him retching and reeling. He was going to be sick, *literally* sick—unlike me or those vulgar multitudes he'd castigated just a few moments earlier. I took one look at his face—and pushed him hard towards the exit gates.

Now, I am angel-strong, stronger than any man when I have to be, and as I drove William along, what people saw was a man pitching forward and stumbling like a drunk and talking wildly to himself. It must have been a very odd sight. Of course, he was arguing with *me*, as usual, for even *in extremis* this was not a man who gave up—but they didn't know this, and I was invisible to them. So what they heard was William yelling in great agitation:

> 'Call the Keeper! Call the Keeper!' and again:
>
> 'The humblest of God's creatures is not meant to suffer in a Cage!' and:
>
> 'The man is a criminal! He should be hanged!'

O, blow! *Exactly* this sort of incident led to the frequent accusations that William was insane and also to his trial for sedition. There were occasions on which it was clear that he had lost his head—and lost it *in public.* Fortunately, I was with him during several of these crises—as indeed I was now, as I was with Sylvia too—and I just knew we had to get out fast before some upstanding member of the public delivered William into the hands of the Law. But William *never* yielded without a fight.

I found him now suddenly stock-still, digging in his heels and managing somehow to resist the tremendous pressure I was putting on him. It was a miracle his backbone didn't snap! Summoning up what must have been every ounce of strength in his body, he announced:

'Where is the King? I must see the King!'

It was dangerous to mention royalty in a crowded place, especially when that King was the vindictive George III against whose tyranny of the Americas William had written as long ago as in his youthful *Poetical Sketches.* Who knew what spies were around us today? Anyway, why would William want an audience with his monarch all of a sudden? I clapped my hand over William's mouth and breathed into his ear:

'Do not mention King George!'

William gagged. I was asphyxiating him, and he couldn't talk back. I released my grip slightly, just enough to let him gasp:

'Not His Highness! The Tiger, I meant the Tiger!'

My fault again. Was it not my rhetoric on behalf of the wounded Indies that had led William, in total contradiction to the prevailing opinion of his time, to crown the tiger king in his heart? And now the plan appeared to have magnificently backfired. William had turned hostile and would not leave without a session with Bengal's Royal emissary. *What was I to do?* Break my promise to William I could not and yet I did not want him arrested or incarcerated. But just then, Fate intervened.

An urchin danced past us. I could not see his face but I smelt a familiar odour . . .

'Five pence, sir, to see the tiger! Five pence only!'

William never could resist a kid. Despite his sorry state, he fumbled in his pocket and declared authoritatively:

'Let's go!'

Afi! I'm sure of it. It was *you*, Afi. Now you lie there playing dead, but that day, it was your whirlwind energy that delivered us against the bars of the cage before any of us knew what was happening, least of all William, still very groggy, although, as ever, unbowed. I don't think he even noticed that Afi was *not* your common-or-garden shaver, begging for survival. I bet he thought he saw an ordinary chimney sweep, a Little Vagabond, because that was the image in his beholding mind. As I'd said to him before, presenting the popular philosophy of the Indies, whether we saw a serpent or a rope on the ground before us depended on the frame we brought to the experience.

William's vision of a peppy little London tyke, a child-survivor versus my image of Afi lying bandaged in Tempke, which was the more real? Perhaps we were both deluded, but when I turned to check, Afi had vanished. And I was alone with William—and the Tiger . . .

❁

He was all I could have wished—huge, golden, eyeball-to-eyeball with William and totally at ease. Lounging, almost. The silence was profound. Somehow, the crowds had all melted away, and we stood, it seemed, out of time, in some forest out of legend—William, the Tiger and I.

Then at last William spoke slowly, the sickness quite gone from him:

> 'He tells me he's here because he wants to be. No one captured him, no one *could*! They who imprison him are themselves the prisoners, he says. He came only to see me and tomorrow he will be gone, back to his Kingdom!'

It was typical William-speak and absolutely convincing. This was a King far removed from the ones described in Willliam's *Song of Los.* There, he wrote:

And the Kings of Asia stood
And cried out in bitterness of soul:

Shall not the King call for Famine from the hearth . . . ?

On Famine and the Kings of Asia, William had been personally educated by his master Swedenborg, who brought to William's shocked notice this devastating fact: that, in the year 1770, within just two decades of the Battle of Plassey which established 'the rule of law and liberty' over Bengala, a famine—not entirely natural—carried off **ten million people** or one third of this Eden province. At that time, William had groaned with despair at these revelations, but now he seemed liberated from that dark vision.

He had met the King—who was not George, by any means—and all was well. Hallelujah, hallelujah! And that I suppose would have been that—were it not for the fact that I read a few weeks afterwards that there *had been no tiger* at the Exhibition. The specimen that had been advertised had died on the voyage out, but the organizers had suppressed this news for the first few days on Commercial Grounds—in case it put the crowds out and retarded takings.

I suppose it was not particularly angelic of me, but when I read this delayed information, I just could not bear for William to learn of it, so I whipped away the paper for eternity before Catherine could take it up to William. I did this of my own free will, so help me Summa!

And William never did learn that his tiger was an illusion.

Thanks to Afi's miracle—as real for me as for William—and my subterfuge, he wrote his great poem satisfied that he had seen a kingly tiger—and yet I must confess that he caught me foolishly lachrymose when he showed me his first draft of *Tyger. What was I crying for,* William demanded. He was on a high. He knew he'd written an immortal poem. *I don't know I don't know,* I snivelled, *I was just being silly!* Well, that episode ended in the usual way, with us blissful in Felpham, out merry *Spiritualist* and *Optimist* beer-mugs clinking happily over William's work-desk on a rainy July weekend and it is not strictly relevant to the progress of this story . . .

However, what I do know is that the following stanza found its way into the final version of the poem:

When the stars threw down their spears,
And water'd heaven with their tears,
Did he smile his work to see?
Did he who made the Lamb make thee?

Anyone who has the slightest acquaintance with William's poetry knows that in his vocabulary the word 'star' is synonymous with 'angel' and so, there they are—my tears, and duplicate-Afi's, I suppose—glistening towards the end of William's poem. And I guess, too, that it was because he did not want the embarrassment of those inexplicable tears repeated, at the very instant that himself was so pleased with his poem, that William was now so unwilling to come with me to see Tipu's famed Tiger of the Indies. But then again, as the Psalms say, water weareth away stone and so, in the end, we went . . .

I *loved* Tipu's Tiger. William hated it. As usual, we fought bitterly.

Tipu's Tiger did not resemble in the least the sometimes mangy, sometimes magnificent great cats occasionally to be found in English menageries. It had nothing at all to do with William's 'divine forges' but was emphatically a man-made marvel. It was the 'ultimate anti-colonial statement' that had found its way into the hands of the colonizers and you can still see it on display at the Victoria and Albert Museum. As an automaton, as a symbol, Tipu's Tiger is unsurpassed! (I read this, God promise, for an assignment in Miss Marsh's Homerton English class, about which I will tell you later.) The tiger is made of wood and *is* mounted atop a supine Englishman. Inside its body is concealed a *secret spring*. When wound up, the box within reproduces both the cries of the prone Englishman in mortal pain as well as the satisfied growl of the tiger. I loved Tipu's Tiger—but it left William cold. He said it was too 'Industrial', a favorite term of abuse with him.

Only my sober estimate that the commotion caused would be major prevented a most un-angelic display on my part when I heard this statement from William. I confess I would cheerfully have caused Tipu's Tiger to sail through the air and hit him right between the eyes at this point, so that it would be *his* English groans we heard!

William could be *exasperating* and here he was now, asking me earnestly whether the tiger astride the English soldier was in fact *female*. Did, he continued, female tigers from the Indies have more of a taste for Englishmen, perchance? His queries *sounded* innocent enough—but then I realized that this was a danger sign. So I had no choice then but to look into William's eyes, as I had once looked into Afi's in a convent garden during a game of L-O-N-D-O-N, William's betraying Mir Jafar eyes, full, just as I suspected, of a most uncalled-for ardour . . .

I replied with dignity:

> 'Colonial tyranny is no joking matter!'
>
> 'No, indeed, but it could be a choking matter.'

William's remark, of course, was intended to remind me of that time I'd almost strangulated him at the Change by stupidly misreading his words, and it found its mark. I decided not to argue, but *I would have my revenge.*

I would follow Summa! I would bring William a tiger poem—but not my own. I *could not* write poetry, I would *never* be able to. Nor could I offer him some light limerick about a young lady of Riga who went for ride on a tiger for he would squash it in an instant with a playful thump of his own tiger's paw. No, something more serious was needed, a leaping attack. Then the answer came to me in a flash! *Sylvia*—her poetry was guaranteed to ricochet off the page. It would hit William in the solar plexus and wrestle him to the ground. My tiger, or rather, Sylvia's, would finally break free of William's hold, his language, his influence, his *patriarchal* views. It would assert Liberty from Colonial Domination after its own fashion! So now you know: Tipu's Tiger holds a special place in this story because it provoked the first lines of poetry I ever presented to William, which was also a poem *against* him.

The whole world knows William's poem—but here's that other tiger, all three lean lines of her—half devouring lily, half stalking animal and the rest fearsome woman—carefully rescued from the tangles of Sylvia's verse, that I let loose on William . . .

Cold folds of ego, the calla

And the tiger embellishing itself
Spots, and a spread of hot petals.

Summa in her wisdom had assured me that William would be taken with poetry, his judgment swayed and his mind beguiled, but William, as contrary as ever, roared with laughter as loud as any tiger when I submitted Sylvia's elliptical lines to him. He bid me sit on the arm of his chair, hugged me tight and then insultingly declared the poetry I had so hopefully released into his ken as ragged as General Wallace's tail-feathers!

Hey, I answered, bristling in Sylvia's defense, that was sort of *intended.*

Sylvia's poetry was in the best traditions of modernism, even *post*-modernism. This sort of poetry projected into the blank space of insanity, *touching and melting nowhere,* as Sylvia put it herself at the end of that poem. This was a great Advance on his own neat stanzas, a sort of Poetic Revolution! These verses were *meant* to be jagged and broken, their enjambments signalling unease, desperation, terror. Could he not see that? *His* monolithic, macho rhyme royal was *not* the only way to go!

To which impassioned pleas William coolly responded that he suspected me of making a virtue of necessity. These lines were a heap of broken bones because the right words had escaped the poet. Was *I* perhaps the poet? Was that why I was so protective?

> 'No!'
>
> 'Happens it, my angel, that you left those couplets in rhyme-less disarray because you lost your Art at crucial points? Or maybe it is just the work of a female.'

Well, *that* it was, but that was not the point, was it? I was not keen to discuss the authorship of these lines with William. That way lay trouble and God knows to what revelations such an exchange might have led. On no account did I want our conversation, which had already descended into childishness, to get so out of hand that I would regret my initiative, but how could I let go? It was the first time I had done anything so momentous as pluck a poem out of the future and bring it to William—and this was the result! Summa's advice had bombed. But I decided to try one last time. I entreated him:

> 'Take a good hard look, please, William, my love, and you will discover that the point of this poetry is *not* smoothness of rhyme, it is not spit and polish. It is *feeling*. Do you not feel the agony in it, the night dancing at the edge of consciousness, the stalk of the tiger-lily?

William looked, and then he looked again. He glanced from Sylvia's poem—which had rapidly become *my* poem, so intimately connected did I feel to it—to me and back again. He did this more than once, letting the deflationary seconds tick past one-by-one. Then he conceded:

> Alright, I give you *that*, Angel.

But William had seen to it that there was no longer any triumph in my achievement. He accepted, I think, the force of my argument that Sylvia's were couplets too, but of a nature stunningly different from his own, but I could see he didn't think much of this sort of verse. Poetry, he now chose to announce grandly, is a matter of Inspiration, of Discipline, and of Truth! And even if one had not an iota of these, one ought not to be a mere *Augustan* jingle-master! I do not condemn Pope and Dryden, said he, because they did not understand Imagination but because they did not understand Verse. To rhyme with neat precision is mere prissiness, it is Child's Play, but not to rhyme *at all*, ah, that is Woman's Folly!

Oh, I replied, stung. I *was* inspired, inspired by rage against his calm superiority, his strutting arrogance. *That* was why I let him catch a glimpse of a tiger in Sylvia's poem. How marvelously different was her hunt from his male hunt! Did William understand that, *could* William understand that, *could* he? But William's answer was unexpectedly gentle. He said:

> 'I do, my angel. You know that. I would die for a child myself.'

And one more time, William's sweet ambiguity derailed me. *How* had he managed to sense the presence of Sylvia's babies in her poem? She does not mention them there at all. Yet one thing was certain. Sylvia's poetry *did* have an **anachronistic effect** on William, for in the great visionary epics he wrote and etched later in Felpham, *Milton, Jerusalem* and *The Four Zoas,* there is neither traditional plot, characters, rhyme, nor meter. These late poems envision a new and higher kind of innocence. In them not only is the human spirit triumphant over reason but *wisdom inheres in the state of childhood.* What does a baby know? I had asked this question about Sylvia's babies once—and now William has answered my question. A child had the unassailable self-confidence of a being whose spirit is entirely independent even as it is physically dependent on the care of others.

Like me on you these days, Doctorji.

The one thing I knew with absolute conviction about William, Doctor Saheb, was how much he cared for children, for animals, for Truth. Perhaps I was doing him an injustice then, perhaps he saw much, much more than he let on. But William was still speaking:

> 'Not your sentiments, but it is your *language* eludes me, Spirit. The *words* are alien, not the woods. Do you get my meaning? My King and your Tiger Lily, they inhabit the same forest, but we describe them in separate Tongues. And you have the advantage of me here, my Muse. You are familiar with my language, you have *seen* my King. Was he not magnificent?'

I nodded silently. I did not have the heart to tell William the truth about his King. Yet my offering of Sylvia's poetry to him had brought home to me another persistent Truth: that world of the Future I was so keen to bring to William, 'a broken postcolonial world of fragmented truths' Miss Marsh called it, that world knew William's verses very well indeed—yet William himself had *no idea of this.* He did not know his own assured place in the future. He had no idea of the other voices that echoed there, of others quite as demented as he himself who held his verse in the highest respect in other times, other climes . . .

❁

New Addenbrooke's Medical File 203 22.11.88: Patient's state stable. She had responded well to olanzapine and although currently in an acute manic phase where she talks continually to her 'William' voice, she has bouts of absolute lucidity between phases. Earlier conversations with her indicate that the patient believes that she is in communication with the spirit of the poet William Blake. Last month she made a request to be allowed her books and possessions. Among these were a volume of the *Collected Poems* of this writer and nurse has observed that the book hardly leaves the patient's hands when she is awake and is at her bedside constantly. Patient also requested her mother's 'fur hat' along with her books but permission was not granted for the same as there was a chance that she might asphyxiate herself with it.

Next appointment: 26.12.88.

A Universe Out of Control

I have to admit it. I felt calm in William's company as I'd never done in Sylvia's. My stupid shivering had almost stopped. No longer was I trapped in a breathless bell-jar. Life was *not* a bad dream anymore. I did not feel the need to cut and jab at myself so often. There was both contentment and excitement in our relationship. I was always afraid to tease Sylvia but it was different with William. I knew in the core of my being that William did not just believe *in* me, his angel, he believed *me.*

William took me seriously even when he mocked me and I felt I was learning from him things that no one else could have taught me, not even Summa. His madness and my madness were 'cut from one cloth' as he put it, and yet, and yet—I was also confused. I felt more and more remote from the world each day, from the doctors, the nurses, even from Sylvia. I recognized this feeling and its treacherous sweetness. It was the same faraway contentment that my childish English books had induced in me in Tempke.

Now the only world I knew was William's world, the only truths we lived by were his truths since he could not and *would not* live by others' values. He had made all my other voices disappear, almost. This absolute dependence on one single dead human male made me nervous somehow. It unsettled me *within*, though on the surface I was, at this time, 'improving' miraculously. Dr T said so himself. He was pleased with my 'progress.' I'd be ready to leave the hospital soon, he assured me, his eyes reliably square behind his square, heavy-rimmed glasses.

Happy New Year, Pari!

It was apparent to me from all that he said that Dr T did not foresee any bumps in the road ahead; no crashes, no accidents. So if I was uneasy, I'd have to fend for myself. *They* were just going to let me out at the soonest and send me back to my aunt's poisoned food! And so, I began to look around, to ask for books from the library, all of which Dr T, the poor innocent, saw as part of my advance towards sanity. He had *no* idea what I was looking for, of course.

What I was after was the 'Blake sightings' I had read about.

For this evidence would *prove* once and for all that I was not mad and I would be free to go home to Tempke. You won't believe this but William was one of those poets who *materialized* frequently. He appeared to Catherine and to Sylvia and to William Butler Yeats, owners both of the Fitzroy Street flat—but those sightings could have been fated. I wasn't there when William's apparition came to his part-namesake, William Butler, who always maintained that his incandescent half-phrase 'a terrible beauty' came *straight* out of Blake's mouth . . .

But there was 'independent evidence' from another very flamboyant acolyte of William's, Summa said. This man was a contemporary of Sylvia's and he had left an unexpurgated account of his ghostly encounters with William. He was the American poet, **Allen Ginsberg**. Allen Ginsberg was as unlike Sylvia as it was possible to be, Summa said, except for three things: one, his 'madness'; two, his exposure to electric shock treatments; and, three—his Blake sightings.

Wandering in 1963, the very year of Sylvia's death, by the most sacred of India's rivers flowing though the most sacred of her cities, Benares, so high on crack he was almost an airborne angel, his head bursting with the 'iterative chants' of Brahmins reciting their prayers for the dead, this Allen Ginsberg saw a vision which he said changed his life, recording the experience in his *Indian Journals.* Just like William, Ginsberg talked to angels and like William, he was judged insane on this account. But I also read that this Ginsberg was a confirmed *junkie.* William never needed any assistance from drugs to speak to his angels! But Allen was like William, like Sylvia, in another way. He had awful 'intuitions' about terror, about *a universe out of control.* It was mainly because of these fears of Allen's hat I was present on this particular occasion though Summa told me I'd missed out on an earlier, equally spectacular, meeting!

Twenty years before his Indian travels, back in the nineteen forties, the same Allen had reported a mind-blowing revelation. In the throes of amphetamine angst assisted by 'onanistic sensations of release' which came to him while 'idling over' William's poem *Sunflower,* he recounted that he had 'heard Blake's voice' at the very moment he grasped the poem. He had heard an 'earthen grave voice', full of 'infinite tenderness and anciency and mortal gravity of a living creator speaking to his son.'

William's voice! Yes, I could confirm that it was capable of an infinite tenderness. But Ginsberg was right: sometimes there could be flint in it, and gravel and cruelty, just as his exopthalmic eyes often managed to convey sheer wrath under their cool grey veneer of assured reasonableness. What made William 'God-like', I think, was his ability to hold in his heart all these contradictory feelings without inhibition. William thought he was like Jesus-God. He could just go over everyone's heads and talk to Angels! *That* was why Summa's American, this Ginsberg, confessed that Willam was *his* 'God' and that his famous poem *Howl* was 'Blake-inspired'. Now I understood. I read Allen Ginsberg's poem and I got it!

My God, this Allen did not know how prophetically he spoke when he said that 'Asia is rising'. William would recognize those words all right. In the flaring temples around Benares and Assyria, Asia is rising—now, *today*! So, can you blame me if I could not resist the temptation to hang around Benares when informed by Summa's ever-efficient minions on the angel circuit that another replay of the original Blake-Ginsberg contretemps was in the offing. The only thing I'd *not* calculated that this Ginsberg person would actually spot *me*!

He was looking, as he says in his stoned-out poem, in the *opposite* direction, but Summa explained to me that when it is *that* doped, a human mind sometimes breaks out of its prison. After she told me this, I suddenly saw that Allen Ginsberg understood my William well—his 'dread of being torn apart', his terror of a God who sent the universe into such a spin that the only way to regain control was to *write it all down.* These were William's tricks!

In an age before electricity and spark-plugs, William knew nothing about cars, of course, but that 'crashing in the head' that Allen wrote about in his poem, *that* he knew most intimately. It was at these times that he clung to *me* most intimately as well! It was also the reason why I positioned myself so close to Allen that evening in Benares. I knew there was a real chance he might summon William up in the depths of his hashish dreams. True, I had shamelessly disappeared at the very hour of William's death, never to be seen in London again until half a century had past—but now I returned with my memories fresh and their unexpected vividness brought a sudden rain of tears to my eyes. I'd come to William when he was thirty-one, in the prime of his manhood and ready for love of a kind he did not possess with sweet Catherine and then stayed with them both for the next forty years. So is it a surprise, Doctorji, that our great devotion brought me back to the strangest places whenever I was needed to keep his Record?

The day Allen spotted me, it was clear to me at once that Allen in his cross-legged 'Hindu transcendency' had managed, just as Sylvia once had, to see William as surely as he saw me hovering in the mirror behind him minutes earlier. But the odd thing was—William himself seemed quite immune to these goings-on. Allen says in his poem (which, by the way, William would not call a poem at all because he would say it lacked 'form'!) that he saw William's 'white life-mask eyes' closed. And I saw that he was very shaken by this moon-cold look of William's, so distant, so remote, because now William, too, lay like Afi all plastered up and white in his faraway Tempke hospital bed. Then I saw Allen's hand get shaky as he wrote but he bravely scrawled on still, asking if the face he saw in the mirror was 'real'. Was William 'inside' the 'mass of images' in the mirror or outside, he wanted to know! (Well, I could answer that one. William was outside, right out of Allen's psychedelic dream-frame. Coke-trips in the alleyways of Benares were beyond him and he *would not* open his eyes for Ginsberg. And I saw how clever William was at the game, managing somehow to evade all Ginsberg's Tantric mantras. It was amazing.)

But this Ginsberg was almost as stubborn as William himself and the next day I watched him trying again, with all the concentration of a yogi, to speak to William—or at least to get him to open his eyes for one moment, just for a moment. And this time he scored . . . he looked into the eyes of Blake, his 'Guru'!

And what did he see? William's elusive Mir Jafar eyes, what did they show Allen? *Where did they lead him?*

The answer is simple, very simple. They led him back to my tumultuous Indies, they led him to what he described as 'indescribable horror' beside the Ganges and then they led him to a dream where he saw me once again, and yes, also saw *Afi* . . . an 'apparition' who gave him 'the sensation of a living presence . . . a non-human, implacably alien presence'.

Afi was good at this, I have to say, at bringing the whole sky tumbling down around one's head. I knew that all too well . . .

As for Ginsberg, seeing Afi in his mirror was his 'last sign' from his Guru William Blake, telling him to 'shut up' and live in 'the present temporary Form'. It was William's message that 'all Form can be is what it at present is—till it literally dies'. Allen was, I know, quite distracted by other visions at the time. Sometimes he saw 'Vishnu's many pink arms rotating', he saw Asia rising and America failing and falling, he saw 'red plastic begging bowls', at times he even thought he *was* America! A mad kaleidoscope but Allen Ginsberg still managed to read his last sign correctly. I, Pari, born to look for Signs, can assert this with confidence, for just a few days later, still stoned besides the Ganges, on 17 January 1963, Ginsberg got to see us both. Ask Summa. This is what he recorded in his *Indian Journals*: Not only did he see Afi—as ever, headless and faceless!—but *me,* his 'Dream Lady Guru' wearing my mother's fur hat . . .

And how did Afi appear to Allen? He came like this: 'a tall red robed figure- a large man in heavy Tibetan robes- with seemingly no head but held by his hand a small bright hose where his head should be'. Afi could be terribly wicked, God promise. He told me later that he was not sorry he had pleasured Allen so unblushingly that day—with a *hose* where his head should be. And it needs no Freud to work out *this* sign, on par with William's heavenly organ or 'Ganesha's resplendent, elephantine trunk sitting atop the beheaded body of Vishnu's son'. It reminded me of the time I'd discussed this 'deep Hindu myth' with my teacher in England (Miss Marsh, Homerton College) while talking about another poet named David Herbert Lawrence, a deep admirer of Freud's, who'd written a 'wonder-poem' on the ponderous pleasures of elephant sex in the jungles of Ceylon—but that day was set in another lifetime, so I will come to David's story later.

Closer to Ginsberg were other funny memories: of Afi pulling at my precious hat and of his attempts to show me that his hose had deep significance. It was not just a 'penile message' (Sylvia's words) but a piece of advice to Ginsberg to 'beat it and cool it!'

And how about *my* hot fur hat, Ginsberg spotted it right away, did he not, Afi had asked teasingly, and what kind of metaphor was that, O Dream Lady Guru?

❁

Well, that hat was a very confusing thing is all I can say. It is now a matter of history that William presented Catherine with the lady's bonnet with pink ribbons, which made her smile her shy smile and pack it away in lavender as the most treasured of her possessions.

What is less well known is that he gave the fur hat he had won from the jade to *me*. He said he could never again abide to wear it himself. Keep it, he cried, placing the fine headpiece over my head. where it stubbornly refused to remain perched but slipped absurdly down over my eyes so I could see nothing. Yet it is about the stunning insights as well as the sightlessness that came from that persistently restless hat that I am committed to telling you next. I know, I know, Afi, my dearest love, that there's very little time left for us and you must be fed up to the gills by the endless saga of my mother's hat even though you cannot speak and tell me so. But, please, *please* listen. My mother's hat is soon to give us a very important piece of information. Listen!

❁

New Addenbrooke's Medical File 203 26.11.88: Patient's consultant physician, currently on vacation, is of the opinion that there is a small buried incident in the patient's childhood memories that could unblock her sexual obsessions and lead to a 'cure' if the site of trauma is identified. The patient is highly conflicted because, despite her excellent memory and her wide reading in literature and history, she is as yet unable to recall this small personal incident. Dr. T believes that, after several sessions with him, the patient is currently on the verge of recovering this memory. A complex case of a high IQ patient with several types of combined psychosis—but not unamenable to treatment.

Note: we are ready to increase the dosage of olanzapine and combine it with valium for maximal effect on the return of her regular physician. New variation of treatment drugs to begin next week along with the RTMS regimen from 30.11.198

Hat Trick

Wearing hats was never common practice in India—everyone knows this. Only cockaded Clive and his marauding ilk wore hats but the native population of India went bare-headed for the most part. The women covered their heads with their saris, it is true, a few of them bearing an uncanny resemblance to Raphael's Madonna, and the men wore pugrees, also like the worthies in Raphael's paintings, but the population as a whole never took to the practice. *Which is exactly why my mother's hanging from the roof wearing her blood-red wedding Benarasi and an outmoded fur hat makes no sense at all.*

There was only one other person who wore a hat in Tempke and that was Dr M. Dr M, with his long, leather limbs and his straw hair and eternal stethoscope was my mother's family doctor, the high-class Sen family doctor, a proper Englishman, no less, who'd treated my mother long before he began to treat me.

Something nags at me now, something I *must* remember about Dr M . . .

His hat! That's the first thing I think of, but it is a boring old beat-up affair, like him, and I can tell it holds no secrets, not even Dr M's. No, it's something else about him, something about Lakshmi and me at Ratan Talkies. I am about five, I think, and Ratan Talkies is one of the most exciting places I have ever been to. It has a big, round entrance-hall with coloured bulbs circling the top like a circus tent, orange and green and white which are the colours of the Indian flag, and then it has huge black and white pictures of film stars in flowery gilt frames. Nargis and Raj Kapoor and the others line one half of the semi-circle and Cary Grant and Ingrid Bergman and the Hollywood contingent the other. All of them look like angels, they all have cupid-bow lips and wavy hair, even the men, and although at five I don't know the names of the stars, I can tell the ones from India from the one's who aren't. *There are always two, it's perfectly natural.*

I know that we aren't supposed to be in Ratan Talkies with Lakshmi for a matinee show without permission from my parents but Lakshmi says she has to meet her friend who's come all the way from Ranchi to Tempke just for the day and how can she look after me and meet her friend at the same time? Her friend is rich, they are going to see a fillum and she will buy us the best tickets and I can see the fillum too but I must not tell Sahib. Sahib ko kuch mat bathana, han! So I go with her, it's much better than staying at home and playing in the back-garden anyway and of course I am *not* going to tell my father anything.

We queue for tickets. The line is long but not impossible because the film we are about to see has been running for three months already and the huge poster of the hero and heroine gazing at each other with agonized lovelorn expressions has begun to peel off at places on the grey stucco wall in front of the cinema.

I spot a paper hole in Meena Kumari's chest like a bullet wound. It's a must-see, this film, *Phool aur Pathar* ('Flower and Stone') with Meena Kumari and Dharmendra, but at five, I don't understand much. I register that Meena Kumari is beautiful with a milk-white, dhop-dhope skin and long dark eyes and that Dharmendra is a thief and they love each other. Still, by the Interval, I'm looking around the long, shadowy theatre for other kinds of excitement. Lakshmi and her friend, who is a tall, gaunt woman in a shiny purple sari, have bought packets of chana for themselves and a Fanta for me and are chatting away to each other. They've seen the movie twice before and are no longer interested in Dharmendra's and Meena's every move—or in me. So I squint and adjust my eyes to the darkness and look around.

My mother!

It's *my mother*, four rows up in front! I can't believe it and she is with old Dr M, of all people. I can't believe it!

Then I see more.

I see that the doctor has his arm draped around my mother's shoulders and that their heads, silhouetted against the flickering lights from the big screen, lean against each other. Sometimes my mother's head descends and falls crookedly onto Dr M's shoulder, just as crooked as it was many years later when she hangs herself wearing that stupid hat, but at five, I do not foresee any of this.

At five, all I see is Dr M and my mother joined together four rows ahead of us in Ratan Talkies and I am so amazed, I can't say *a word*. I want to tug at Lakshmi to tell her but her friend is seated between us and when I begin to think about it, something warns me that I should say nothing, that I should keep this secret to myself—*which is what I do.* For years and years I tell no one and slowly, very slowly, I teach myself to forget, and in the end, I *do* forget—until now.

Now I see it.

Lying on my snow-flake cold English hospital bed, the November sky the stained and battered gray of Lakshmi's aluminum tea-mug the day my father deposited me in the Convent, a sky that has forgotten that it ever had another nature, cerulean and sunny, *I see the truth.*

I see why my father, always a businessman with an eye to the main chance, nobly married my aristocratic mother whom no one else would touch despite her beauty because of the madness in her family and I see why he whisked her away for a honeymoon voyage to England almost as soon as they were married and why they did not return to India until after I was safely delivered in an anonymous nursing-home in Croydon. Croydon! Havelock was born there too and Havelock, usually taciturn unless he has something really important to reveal, had something to tell me.

Jealousy slays love under the pretence of keeping it alive, he says evenly, and I, Pari, chosen angel of Tempke, have to admit there's no quarreling with this proposition. I have had occasion to witness its painful truth in the havoc wreaked by the emotion in Sylvia's life. Now I see it starkly in my own. I see fate in a fur hat—*my* fate. I see that my father bought my mother that cheap old English hat, a flea-market bargain, motivated by a single inexplicable emotion—*jealousy,* which is itself a deadly concoction of rage, resentment and sheer frustration.

That hat, my mother's English hat, William hat, the jade's hat, was a fiend for the truth.

I see now that when my father made my mother wear it, his protective arm around her shoulders in a grotesque parody of Dr M's and when he forced my mother to smile her fake smile in the P&O liner photograph, he was getting his own back on his humble beginnings. In my father's hands, that hat brimmed over with hostility. It became part insult, part punishment. With this one masterstroke, my father broke my mother's spirit. He managed to take her dignity away and at the same time earned the reputation of a caring husband. He won his place in history and was named inheritor of a large part of my grandfather's estate, his beloved foundry, founded by *his* grandfather in 1885, in the exact year of David Hebert's Welsh mining-town birth—a company that made lovely trellised iron stairways that took you all the way up to heaven's convent roof only to cast you down again . . .

My father, I told you, is a very clever man.

As for Dr M, I see now why his eyelids twitched and his stethoscope suffered so much in my presence, the betraying whiteness of my skin, attributed by everyone to my mother's luminous, fair-skinned beauty, a sign of his lasting guilt. No wonder both he and my father connived to send me away to this prison cell in England, a certified mad child.

Who will believe me now even if I tell them of my discovery? No one!

I want to kill them both, my father and Dr M I *am.* I'm *going* to kill them!

My mother got her own back on her tormentors the day she named me Parineeta—'the married one', ha! Then she rebelliously hanged herself—her second triumph. And I can see *something else* now, though I have no proof of it. I can see curled up inside my mother's high, trapeze artist's body a small, living thing—a still-to-be-born Glaxo baby, my little brother or sister, the one who got no chances. *Two, there are always two, it seems perfectly natural now,* Sylvia's message in 'Death and Co', how *exactly* it fits!

The day she hanged herself wearing that absurd hat and her wedding red and all her sparkly jewels was the day my mother sent me a final message. That day she taught me that madness can be defiance and that defiance can be very cool, rational and true—but now that I have managed to work things out, I've learnt one other thing that is just as important. *I don't have to be scared anymore.* Just because my mother killed herself and Sylvia killed herself, and my embryo brother-sister died speechless, doesn't mean *I* have to die. It doesn't mean *I* can't speak.

I will survive and I will get my revenge.

The hat has spoken: I DID NOT KILL SYLVIA. I DID NOT KILL MY MOTHER.

Fate assigned me the *Optimist* Heineken beer-mug in Tempke convent long ago for a good reason. I know this now, thanks to two documented 'lunatics'—my clever, mute mother and Sylvia whose words cut through jiggery-pokery like acid. Also, I shall have to hold my counsel—for now. *The place where optimism flourishes most is the lunatic asylum,* Havelock wrote, and once again, he was dead right though he may not have foreseen the irony of these circumstances that would prove the final truth of his words. But I am freed now, that's the main thing! My relief is so immense, I can't tell you. It's greater than my anger, it overwhelms my sorrow, it shines! There have been many deaths but I am going to live . . .

I am saved!

I feel as if I'm floating, floating in the upper air . . .

The transformation I feel within me these days is real. I have found out the truth and suddenly—*I'm in charge*. I don't have to bite and I don't have to throw tantrums. I just have to lie here quietly and plot. I *have* to get out. I have to return to Tempke—that's the goal.

These days, the nurses hardly ever bother to strap me down because of what they have started to call my 'cooperative behaviour'. Dr T is very pleased with these reports. He says I am going from strength to strength and tells my aunt that I can have as many books as I like from the library. Reading is good for me. My aunt, remote-controlled by my father (who is of course not really my father any more but *she* doesn't know this) is also cooperative. She brings me my books every week with unfailing regularity and a long-suffering air and leaves as soon as she decently can and I don't mind.

I have got my life back although I have no one to share it with.

Sylvia's not back and William is too distracted by ill health and his own insanity to pay any attention to my discoveries. So, last week, out of sheer relief, I asked for a book on hats, since they still will not allow me to have my mother's hat for fear I shall choke the breath out of myself, which is a joke because if anyone's going to have the life choked out of them, it isn't going to be *me*!

I can afford to wait for that hat now—my immediate problem is just to get out of this hospital, to convince Dr T that I am as sane as him or Nurse Standish or my aunt. Meanwhile, I can just relax and read my book and *plot, plot, plot.*

From the book on hats, this is what I learn.

Hats

There's madness in the history of the hat. Take the mercury that still lies buried in the sediments of the Still and Housatonic rivers, near Danbury, Connecticut. Where do you think that mercury came from? It came straight from *Hat City*—Danbury, Connecticut.

The hat trade was brought to Danbury by immigrant European hatters at just about the time that I found myself sporting with William and the jade in London, and it became such a successful industry there that King George II, grandfather of the very George III whom William so detested, actually *banned* exports of hats from the colonies to benefit hatters in England in 1731—just as the textile workers of Bengal were banned in their time from exporting cloth to England. Monarchs may change, as William said, but the policies of tyrants do not change, whichever the continent.

Danbury was burned by British troops in 1777, during the same American Revolutionary War which my William supported so vociferously, but another revolution, this time Industrial and roundly condemned by William, brought hat-making back with a vengeance to Danbury. Abe Lincoln's famous revolutionary stovepipe hats, made of beaver felt, were very likely Danbury-manufactured. Lee, Stetson and other branded cowboy hats, the State Troopers' broad-brimmed hats, so many of these were made in Danbury, which had all the makings of a successful hatter's town—abundant water, plentiful labour transportation and, above all, a vast reserve of rabbit and beaver and so, who could stop it from becoming the hat-making capital of the world in the 19th century?

Zoe Benedict. the first Danbury hatter, who plugged a hole in his shoe with rabbit fur and 'discovered that pressure and perspiration had transformed it into felt', opened his shop in 1780, making beaver hats at the rate of three per day, but at the peak of the industry, *five million* hats a year were produced in 56 different Danbury factories. The only fly in the ointment—and it was just a small fly at first but much, much more vicious than the fly in William's famous poem of that name (which I shall have occasion to match with my own poem in the not-so-distant future)—was carroting.

Carroting had nothing to do with carrots. What it involved was 'washing animal fur with an orange-coloured solution containing mercury nitrate, which helped separate the fur from the pelt and made it mat together smoothly'. The fur was then shaped into large cones, shrunk in boiling water and dried many times before the final shaping, smoothing, and finishing. The point is, unbeknownst to them, many hatters suffered severe mercury poisoning from this process.

Mercury poisoning is no joke. It attacks the nervous system. It causes drooling, hair loss, uncontrollable muscle twitching, a lurching gait, and difficulties in talking and thinking clearly. Hatters with mercury poisoning stumbled about in a confused state with slurred speech and trembling hands. Some were mistaken for drunks, some experienced hallucinations. Ah, you're beginning to recognize the symptoms! When my mother wore her English hat, she became just that little bit madder and so did the jade and so did everyone.

Anyhow, around the time of Sylvia's birth, the hat trade began to decline and mercury was no longer used in hats following agitations by hatters' unions. Little by little, the 'Danbury Shakes' disappeared, but the mercury remains in the heart of the country soil of America, menacing—and it has travelled to other places too.

Modern estimates inform us that the levels of mercury in a remote Danbury children's park still measures 25,000 ppb. where normal levels are around 400-600; and other strains of Danbury mercury have found their way to the nearest rivers, where they accumulate in the innocent bellies of fish and wait quietly, one day, to be carried straight to Long Island Sound, so close to Sylvia's home, if perchance a hurricane comes—which, incidentally, it is almost *bound* to sooner or later. History does not give up so easily and *what we call progress,* as Havelock says, *is merely the exchange of one nuisance for another*—a sentiment with which William would most heartily agree.

❁

William, by the way, is back and *fighting* fit.

Perverse as usual, he's still bent on foisting that hat, my mother's hat which once belonged to a jade and that my father bought, moth-eaten but still serviceable in England on their 'honeymoon' trip, to humiliate and kill her, on me. This fatal hat that he won from the minx and that she'd earlier flicked from a wandering American sailor from

Danbury town with her amorous tricks, William insists on giving to me, of all people.

> 'Keep it, and let it be a Talisman forever against Blind Greed and Folly!'
>
> 'I cannot. It's too big for me, and besides, the thing reeks of cruelty! Think of the animal skinned alive to produce this object!'

And it was this impulsive statement that led to the animal rights debate, for if there was something of the penitential Christian in William, there was a bit of the Hindu Pythagorean in him too. William believed in metempsychosis and was instinctively sympathetic to the doctrine of the transmigration of souls which I'd laid out for him in great and gory detail in so many of our 'philosophical discussions'. Unlike many of even his most liberal friends, William was quite prepared to accept the Hindu belief that he could inhabit the soul of a flea or a tiger.

> Then why, I demanded, following up on the matters raised by the Danbury fur, do you continue to consume Catherine's lamb-chops with such lip-smacking delight? You eat the very Lamb whose soul might be bleating out to you. What is the point of your tender poem, pray, when you devour lamb every night for supper?'
>
> 'Tigers eat lambs too!'
>
> 'Not for *pleasure*. Only for sustenance but *you* could live without eating meat. You could be a vegetarian and happily survive.'

> 'It would weaken the constitution. We would fall prey to illness'
>
> 'Weaken you? The continent of the Indies lives on a vegetarian diet. *They* manage!'
>
> 'Not as well as the English. You told me so yourself. You told me of the conquest of the colonies. The Indies would not have succumbed so easily if they had been flesh-eaters!'

Hoist with my own petard! But I did not give up. I tried to explain to William how the Indian subcontinent was not the same everywhere. It has many thousands of meat-eaters as well as vegetarians. In Bengala, even the high-caste Brahmins ate meat. Siraj-ud-Daulah, crushed by Clive, was a lusty meat-eater. This had not prevented him from being soundly defeated. Ergo, meat-eating was no great guarantee of strength.

William countered.

> 'You should blame the butcher then! *I* killed no Lamb to make me stronger, but once he's dead, best not to waste the remains, eh Angel?'
>
> 'That is a weakling's argument! It *proves* that eating meat helps one neither mentally not physically. Why do you hide behind a butcher's apron, William? And why do you invoke bourgeoisie thrift in your defence of murder? Are you not by this argument a greedy murderer of lambs yourself? Have you not read your own master Voltaire?'

Voltaire! I *can't* abandon him, for the Great Rationalist has a significant part to play in my William's life. *Please be patient.*

William had the greatest respect for this man, not because he always agreed with him but because he *didn't.* He longed to meet Voltaire's Spirit one day so that they could have it out in honest argument. If any agency could win my animal rights battle for me, it would be the words of Voltaire. William admired Voltaire for his unwavering rationalism and his wit, for his French rebelliousness combined with an English pragmatism acquired, William believed, during Voltaire's three years of exile in England when banished there for insulting a young nobleman.

Voltaire's merciless criticism of the Church also meant that he was denied burial in church grounds, another feature which earned him William's boundless admiration. When, two years after the French Revolution, in 1791, Voltaire's remains were finally transferred from their remote Champagne abbey to a grand resting place at the Pantheon in Paris, I remember how William rejoiced! To him, it was a symbolic victory of the youthful forces of Liberty over the 'Ancien Regime' debauchery of the Duke of Burgundy, dripping in purple wines and blood, whose excesses William had thoroughly castigated in his poem *The French Revolution. What's love anyway* but unstinting regard? So to please William now I produced out of the air, just as I'd once charmed him with Microsoft typefaces from an American heareafter, a pretty scroll unashamedly culled from Voltaire's famed *Philosophical Dictionary* of the past. Not only that, I considerately highlighted with a **thicker nib** for William's benefit the relevant sections on animals and other 'notable facts'. (His eyesight was no longer reliable and part of that far-sighted, all-seeing effect in portraits of William in these last years derived, I have to tell you, from his acute hypermetropia.)

The passage I chose for William's edification was from the section on the *Brahmins of India* for whom Voltaire had an altogether curious respect far removed from the rude attitudes he exhibited towards 'negroes' and other coloured races. Voltaire had read translations of the Hindu holy books and was as informed as Ginsberg about the ancient deities he called 'Birma, Brahma and Vitsnou'. Not that he had found these sacred texts free of 'contradictions' but in the selection that I now placed before William's eyes, Voltaire wrote unequivocally:

> ***Is it not probable that the Brahmins were the first legislators of the earth, the first philosophers, the first theologians?*** *Do not the few monuments of ancient history which remain to us form a great presumption in their favour, since the first Greek philosophers went to them to learn mathematics, and since the most ancient curiosities collected by the emperors of China are all Indian?*
>
> *It is incontestably from the Brahmins that we hold the idea of* ***the fall of the celestial beings in revolt against the Sovereign of nature;*** *and it is from there probably that the Greeks drew the fable of the Titans. It is there also that the Jews at last took the idea of the revolt of Lucifer, in the first century of our era . . . But it must be carefully observed that in this revolt of celestial beings against their Sovereign no blows were struck, no celestial blood flowed,*

> *no mountains hurled at the head,* ***no angels cut in two****, as in Milton's sublime and grotesque poem.*
>
> *One remarks a singular contrast between the sacred books of the Hebrews, and those of the Indians.* ***The Indian books announce only peace and gentleness; they forbid the killing of animals; the Hebrew books speak only of killing, of the massacre of men and beasts; everything is slaughtered in the name of the Lord; it is quite another order of things.***
>
> *The 'Shasta' . . . is the first book of theology of the Brahmins . . . anterior to all the other books. According to the 'Shasta,'* ***God placed humans in our globe on condition that they should not eat animals****, and that they should not copulate with the males of their new species, under pain of returning to* ***ondera*** *(darkness).*
>
> *Those are the principal articles of the Brahmins' faith, which have lasted without interruption from immemorial times right to our day:* ***it seems strange to us that among them it should be as grave a sin to eat a chicken as to commit sodomy.*** *This is only a small part of the ancient cosmogony of the Brahmins . . .*

My sudden Brahminical zeal, backed by an authority no less than Voltaire's, had William worried. I saw a frown appear on his brow. After all, the London in which Catherine and he lived was not so different from the one in which a few decades ago, James the First had ordered his witch-trials or a woman hanged at Tyburn for bestiality along with her partner in crime, *a dog*. Both, I'd read, were held equally guilty, so small was the space separating human from animal in that age. If human beings could be tried and hanged for their crimes, why not animals, that was the wisdom of the age. Now William spoke slowly, measuring his words:

> 'The Papists eat the body of their Saviour in Church. They drink his blood. My Lamb is Christ himself. *For he calls himself a Lamb, He is meek, and he is mild, He became a little child. Little Lamb, God bless thee!* To eat a lambkin is no less that to unite with Him and seek His blessing. What do you say to that, Muse?'
>
> 'I say there is a difference between a real animal who bleeds when he dies and a mere metaphor. The Papists do not drink blood but only something that stands for it—wine! If they were to eat real human flesh and grind on bone, your own Mr Paine would be the first to dismiss them as devilish barbarians, not to mention Voltaire!'

But I was on perilous ground. No one is better positioned than an angel, Summa had told me, to know how permeable is that wafer-thin wall between words and world. And William pursued his initiative:

> 'I have heard tell, and not only from Monsieur Voltaire, that they worship cows in the barbaric Indies and will eat no beef on this account.'
>
> 'Some eat beef, many don't. It is a matter of custom.'
>
> 'So is my eating of lamb! It's customary in England. *All Religions are One.* I have always believed this, Angel, even before I met you.'

William is right about this. He has always been interested in far-off rituals and mythologies, never shutting them out of his poems or from his mind. Mention strange creatures, oddities, and William's attention is caught at once. I remember his confessing once:

> 'When I was a boy, my Peri, I saw a freak cow preserved in a bath. It was an Awful, Monstrous thing, with a Leg growing from its back, and equipped with the udders and entrails of a Second Cow! I have never forgotten it.' He shuddered. 'How can anyone worship a Form capable of such Distortion?'
>
> 'That Nature sometimes produces anomalies only highlights her consistent Perfections. The cow of the Indies is a most lovely animal. A far cry from your English kine! You should *see* her, William, this wish-granting goddess, her eyes long-lashed and ringed with collyrium. She is a Poem!'
>
> 'Like you, Muse!'

William, I noticed, had magnanimously chosen to ignore the insult to his native cattle—but I was not so forgiving:

> 'Oh yes, but you know how ill I can be treated by those who profess to love me. Like you, William! That goes for the cow of the Indies, too!'

William lifted up my English fur-hat and kissed my blinded eyes, getting by slow degrees, by *very* slow degrees, to the tip of my nose. This would have to stop if we were to have a serious discussion. I said quickly, fire-fighting:

> 'The word for 'cow' in India is *gau*, cognate with your own English word.'

Etymological detail captivated William. It pushed ardour away and replaced it with intellectual hunger. To my mind, William always had the makings of a cranky scholar, despite his unbending disapproval of Dr Johnson and despite the fact that his own schooling could be severely faulted. He was now all eagerness to hear about my cow, beautiful, mistreated, alien. This outcome was predictable.

> 'Tell me more, Spirit!'

With my hat drawn safely over my eyes once more, I regaled him with my catalogue of oddities:

> 'In India, cows wander about in the streets of her biggest cities and no one stops them. Imagine your heifers off the fields and loose on the streets of London!'
>
> William chortled: 'They have more rights than our English cattle, then!'
>
> 'In a way, but customs that seem liberating do not always liberate. This is as true of the custom of eating beef in England as it is of the custom of worshipping cows in India. It's a paradox.'
>
> 'How so?' William is puzzled.
>
> 'I will explain myself through poetry.'
>
> William produces a mock groan. 'Your own poem, Muse?'

> 'I will recite to you from the annals of the Indies. Here is that poem—*Gau*!'
>
> 'I don't want to go. Why should I go? You are to recite your poem!'
>
> 'Oh, I didn't mean go, I meant *Gau*! That's the name of the poem. It's the Sanskrit word for "cow", remember?'

For some unfathomable reason, William seemed to like my poem on the Gau although I have long since forgotten its meandering lines. He did not, he declared, quite understand it but he found it atmospheric. I responded, pettishly:

> 'But my poem is too long, too pointless! It wanders all over the place, just like India's cows!'

And then William answered me, seriously:

> 'Why in heaven's name should a poem be short, Muse? It can be as long as a heavenward journey, as long as Life itself! Have you forgotten Milton, Dante?'
>
> 'I am not Milton or Dante!'
>
> 'You must aspire to the greatest, not pander to Commerce like Sir Joshua.'

And that was the end of that, for when William got onto the subject of his bête noire, Sir Joshua, all sane conversation ground to a halt.

Voltaire's Prophecy

Sir Joshua—William's evil angel. I had not wanted to get him started on the subject but now he was off and away at his favourite past-time: hounding Sir Josh, just as I would one day hound my father and Dr M. Hound them and kill them *dead*!

When Sir Joshua Reynolds died
All Nature was degraded
The King dropped a tear into the Queen's ear
And all his pictures faded.

William smoothly slid into his rant by reciting his own verses. Then he continued his attack with evident relish:

> 'The old Humbug knew *nothing* of Form. He lacked the very elements of Soul! Are Rubens and Rembrandt to be elevated over Raphael? Are artists' rules to be drawn from the work of two manifest Fools? Then God defend us from the Arts! Accursed Venetians! Colouring is no substitute for Line. Only a dog would tolerate such rank foolishness!'

And he's off scribbling rank doggerel in his notebook:

Perhaps this little fable may make us merry
A dog went over the water without a wherry

Outline! There's no outline, there's no such thing
All is chiaroscuro, poco-pen—it's all colouring!

I was powerless to stop this tirade. William could go on for hours in this vein. He had abhorred his training at the Royal Academy, leaving the august School early and in disgrace, and he frothed at the mouth until the day he died if anyone so much as mentioned Sir Joshua's 'Boy in Blue'. His hate for Sir Josh was matched only by his love for his Master Raphael, for William was exactly like Sylvia and David in one thing: he loved and hated with unconcealed passion.

The blue boy, no populist Glaxo toddler or blue-skinned Krishna but a proper English lad, had been painted in response to a challenge that any painting that reversed the 'background' hue of the sky and made it massive and central was bound to be a failure. As a low-brow angel, not fit to touch the hem of Summa Sukkalin's gown, I, Pari, must say I found myself in sneaking sympathy with this attempt of Sir Joshua's to bare-facedly challenge artistic dictum—and the world, for once, agreed with me.

Once done, the 'Boy in Blue' was widely considered a masterpiece—but *William* did not think Sir Joshua's famous oil challenged anything at all. To him it was an act of Cowardice, a devilish Blob by a man who, like the dog in his poem, could not distinguish shadow from substance or commerce from art. William's prejudices in this respect, alas, were all too well known. Study William's canine verses closely, though, and you will find buried within a juicy bone, a telling item of vocabulary that belonged to a future not yet foreseen. This is the cunning reference to a *'poco-pen'* or that *'chiaroscuro* postcolonial consciousness' so loved by Miss Marsh that had followed like a miasmic shadow upon the eventual demise of Clive's empire—and it *came from William's prophetic pen.*

Need I say more about the role of angels in a poet's work?

❁

William holds my hand up to the light.

> 'A lovely hand, translucent, glowing! It is all Form.'

My hand looks waxy and bloodless to me, not elegant at all, but then I'm not sure where this conversation is leading, so I hold my peace, not distracting William.

> 'I know so little,' he confides, 'of your strange and distant world, where it exists, how it turns. Muse, will you try again?'
>
> 'Why, what do you mean?'
>
> 'I need more sweet evidence to decipher your language. You fly in unfamiliar skies. It is like hearing from an Oracle—heavenly but obscure. Be kinder to me, Priestess!'
>
> 'How?'
>
> 'I celebrated you in the *Book of Thel,* my Angel. You were the unborn Soul foreseeing the future, looking back from her Grave, travelling through the states of Imaginative Creation—but I was not ready for you then.'

And here William grasps my hand once more and picks off items on my fingers. He speaks in a rush:

> 'You foresaw everything. As my Lily, Cloud, Worm and Clod, *you foresaw your own death* and how that terrified me! I was a coward! I could not accept that you rejected the very *possibility* of living in a world where the Imagination was set about with Curbs. Now I see it! *You* chose not to be born in *Thel,* because *I* was a mere boy, not man enough for you. It is different now. I am ready for you, Muse, ready for your Singular Creations. I will place no curbs on you. Give me but more years with you, one each for the fingers of your lovely hand, and I *will* decipher you!'

I reply, my emphasis echoing his:

> 'I cannot give you time. I cannot, my love, but I *will* give you another poem.'

The poem I gave William then as a sort of consolation prize is inconsequential, an exercise tossed off that night as we lay abed side by side, post-coitus contented, and I would not mention it but for the fact that it illustrates so well William's oft-repeated point about Inspiration. I was an Angel, maybe, but I lacked Inspiration. Read our poems lying side by side, matching stanza for stanza, abcb rhyme for abcb rhyme, sufficiently alike yet different—a well-adjusted couple, his English 'Fly' and my Indian-American 'Spider'—and you will see this at once:

THE FLY

Little Fly
Thy summer's play
My thoughtless hand
Has brushed away

Am not I
A fly like thee?
Or art not thou
A man like me?

For I dance
And drink and sing
Till some blind hand
Shall brush my wing

If thought is life
And strength and breath
And the want
Of thought is death

Then am I
A happy fly
If I live
Or if I die . . .

THE SPIDER

A spider subtle in sunlight
Each tentacle matched by shadow
Now clear against concrete
Now lost in a tubular hollow

Parabolic hills and bridges
The irrepressible desert grass
All California's faulted earth
Centres on its tremulous mass

Silicon sharp, never in focus
Smaller, softer than my eye
That views it, gossamer slews
Slung up like steel pitched high

Girder-strong, a Golden Gate
Sheer in earth's ascendant
The hulking mass of Half-Moon
Rock, precariously pendant

Falls within its netted throw
Towered cities toss to bays below
And at last the sea sinks also
Down yellow, Tolumne meadow . . .

Those who care for poetry will perceive at once from this example that *it is not rhyme and structure alone that make a poem.* Technically, you cannot fault me if I claim that my effort is as good as William's, but *his* sparks with life. It is as light as a fly but of a profound simplicity, squarely confronting matters of life and death, and never shirking that issue of animal murder that we had discussed so often before. My poem sits much heavier on the page, a clayey thing, tied to the gravid earth and to a weird American landscape of the future that William has never set eyes on—but he is unfazed.

> 'Ah, dare I say it? You are getting better, my Fairy. Your Tiger and mine, my Lamb and your Cow, my Fly and your Spider—we dance a perfect cotillion. I prophesy it. We shall be One for Eternity.'

An exchange of poems, what does it signify—a love story, a learning experience, a bargain, a dance of the imagination, eternity or THE END? I, Pari of the faraway Indies, trained to fly on the wings of my English books, was no match at all for William when it came to poetry—but I *would not refuse his gauntlet.* He had reminded me of my mission. I was to introduce him to the future via poetry. And now I was being reminded by William that he'd come some distance too from the point that he wrote *Thel* for me. He said so himself—we danced a perfect cotillion. So I decided to tease him a little about those early days, recalling a poem he'd once written for me:

> 'Do you remember *The Fairy,* William?' and I recite it softly to him.
>
> *A Fairy leapt up on my knee*
> *Singing and dancing merrily*
> *I said, "Thou thing of patches, rings*
> *Pins, necklaces and such-like things*
> *Disgracer of the female form*

> 'You doubted my very sex, William, you Unbeliever! Male or female, human or divine, what *am* I? Still a gilded worm, perchance! Is your mind made up at last?'

It's my turn to be surprised. William says absolutely *nothing*, his expression a comical mix of doubt and discomfort—but perched as I am on his knee, my intimate wing brushing his thigh, now as then, I reckon I am in a position of advantage. I exclaim gaily:

> 'Why do you not bravely discover once and for all if my form's female enough for you?'

I expect, of course, that he will grab me round the waist and prove to me that he's familiar to the exact inch with the contours of my female form but, to my astonishment, William continues to look wretched, not essaying a word.

> 'What is the matter? Why will you not speak?'

But William resolutely turns his face away from me and my light-hearted, heartless banter and reaches out for his beloved notebook. I have not said it in so many words but he gets my message all right. I am to leave him once again—and he cannot bear it.

William's notebook is, as ever, covered with sketches and scribbling with hardly a bare space, but he manages to find one at last. The poem, one of his very last, is crisscrossed with tell tale lines and marks. William has brutally scratched out the whole first stanza—he did this in front of my eyes—and replaced the word 'seek' with 'pain', which may not make much sense, but is some indication of his tortured state of mind. The poem:

Never seek to tell thy love
Love that never told can be . . .
I told my love, I told my love,
I told her all my heart,
Trembling, cold, in ghastly fears—
Ah, she doth depart . . .

When William is done, he holds out his lines dumbly. I see that he is too proud to repeat his former pleas to me. It is not that he suspects my female qualities or that they do not 'joy and please' him; it is that each time I have left him, he had gone down on his knees proclaiming his desperate need for me—and in spite of it all I have cruelly vanished!

The pattern is self-evident, destructive. For what is a poet without inspiration, without Imagination? Nothing, a suicidal mess, a hollow fool! Sylvia knew this. Her poems flowered from this root of terror. Now, William's terrifying fear also communicates itself to me in all its helplessness:

Soon as she was gone from me
A traveller came by
Silently, invisibly—
O, was no deny.

To lose his Muse, who flies from him time and again without explanation is like staring insidious Death in the face, Death the stealthy Traveller who creeps up on William each relentless day and leaves him exhausted, wordless . . . Once it was enough for me, Pari, to jingle all my Indian 'rings, pins, necklaces and such-like things' and allure him out of his despair and keep his spectres at bay—but now he cannot take it any more.

Suddenly, he's broken, with the dramatic suddenness of the *opera serie* of his time, the altissimo crises in the works of Adolf Hasse or Metastasio's hugely successful *Alessandro nell'Inde*—except that this crisis is dauntingly real.

❁

William lies inert in my arms like some wounded animal, a Dürer sketch of a deer, an arrow in his eye, bleeding slowly to his death or like a side-speared Raphael Christ or Afi deathly motionless in his convent bed. Occasionally, he babbles . . .

Catherine is pale with worry, rushing up and down the stairs with cold poultices and hot. We are at the mouth of the bad years. If we do nothing they will gobble William up sure as hellfire. She knows this as well as I.

How little it takes to bring a man to breaking point! There we were jogging along nicely, discussing the trifling matter of getting me up a speed of maybe five poems, never mind William's five hundred. William appeared in the best of humours—and now this! I *know* I have not killed Sylvia, I have *not* killed my mother but I feel like a murderess now. *What should I do?* I am, once again, in need of desperate remedies to revive the victim I have destroyed so carelessly, but I cannot ask for Summa's advice. We are bound by the 'once in a lifetime' rule. And Sylvia's not around, nor my mother, nor Mona the Queen of Action.

The only solution that occurs to me is a non-starter. I curl up yogi-like in a corner and meditate, following the age-old practices of the Indian subcontinent, but you already know how *hopeless* I am at dhyan. I sit there cross-winged for weeks and nothing happens. My mind is a volatile whirl, worse even than Ginsberg's; it just refuses to float upwards into saintly transcendence and William remains suspended between life and death, gall-stone-ridden and without the slightest will to live. He is in great pain (*as Dr M and my father will be one day*).

❁

General Wallace the pigeon turns out to be my sole companion during this period. He does not seem to leave his post on the windowsill on any account. I wonder vaguely when the old battleaxe eats and for how long he can keep this up. I am an angel but he is only a bird. Then, one day out of the blue he cackles at me, most un-birdlike and peremptory:

'We should consult Robert!' and disappears off the sill.

Life is full of wonders. After some days—I can't say how long, Catherine and I have both lost our sense of time, which is ironic considering how demented I am about punctuality when things are normal—Wallace returns. He is carrying an olive branch in his beak in daft imitation of a Biblical Dove, the absurd codger! I guess no one has ever informed him that he is a pigeon, not a dove, and that the two species are distinct! Never mind, I suppose this is not the time to be concerned about the delusions that a most peculiar member of the *Columbiform* order labours under. I eye General Wallace warily.

> 'Hop closer!' he commands. Cheeky bird, does he think angels *hop*?
>
> 'I have a message from Robert. He says William's time is not yet come. He will not die but he needs desperate succour for the soul or he may slip into madness forever. A preternatural conclave is advised.'

What is the ancient squab maundering on about? Wallace mutters conspiratorially:

> 'It has been arranged. For this evening—a meeting with Master Voltaire himself! Robert was doubtful but I persuaded him!'

Robert, I felt, was right to be doubtful but General Wallace is fluttering about in a fever of excitement, leaving a trail of shameless droppings on the windowsill—so I say, in order to calm him down:

> 'I'll enlighten you with wise saws, shall I, General, to while away the hours until evening—just as I do with William?'

'Do, do' he purrs obligingly, so I set about entertaining him with all manner of sayings from John Keay and Havelock Ellis both, first showing him radiant visions of Royal Jahangir the Indian Turkey, of Native American Thunderbirds and the like and then tailing off my performance with Havelock's most enlightening of lines—*the art of living lies in a fine mingling of holding on and letting go.* But once I'm done, all the old boy does is to produce a hail of guano to show his appreciation! I've taken a lot of trouble over this venture, equipping myself with pigeon-vision and grimy pouter feathers to get into the right mood for General Wallace and all he can rise to in return is to royally desecrate my offerings. Forget it, as Mona would say. I decide to save the saws for when William is better.

When William does finally recover and I tell him about my efforts to keep the Mad General calm at this harrowing time in his life, the only comment *he* makes, rather dryly, is: *what on earth was I doing serenading General Wallace, pray?* To which all I can say is, Wallace's methods might be a little suspect and perhaps saluting an angel's theatrical talents with guano is not everyone's idea of the best way to acknowledge a gift, but hey, the bird is a brick, a Braveheart—and never mind the mixed metaphors. He richly, *richly* deserves all the accolades he gets.

Besides, it all took place with military exactness, precisely as General Wallace had said, my histrionics and the other routines of the day only interludes until the clock struck six.

Catherine had been told of the imminent visitation. She was never interested overmuch in William's intellectual pursuits but even she knew how much William longed to engage with Voltaire's spirit. Maybe a meeting with this master of the *bon-mot* would cure him! I let that cunning thought buzz around Catherine's head, insistent as one of Sylvia's bees till she was bitten by it and could not resist. Four in the afternoon and she was down already, tidying up the front parlour which was so little used it smelled like a gigantic mothball. By five, she had nervously readied tea and condiments and heaved William into the front-room (albeit with some unseen help from me).

There he lay now, stertorous, on his cot in the corner. Catherine would have been glad of some support from her sister Beth or Nancy Flaxman in such a crisis but the General had decreed secrecy ('The Spirits must not be Disturbed'), so now Catherine sat there alone (or so she thought), her hands in a flutter, waiting for Voltaire.

Then he walks in, calmly, without warning, paying no attention at all to William in his damp corner but bowing briefly in her direction. He goes briskly up to the large central window and pulls apart the curtains—which is uncomfortable for me, because I'm up there doing a bat impression, my favourite disguise when I want to hang around unnoticed. Fortunately, the great man pays me no attention either. He has located William and is examining the books that lie neglected on a small marble-topped corner-table beside the somnolent patient: Thomas Boreman, *Description of Three Hundred Animals* (1698, first edition, 1762, eighth reprint); Louis LeClerc, Comte de Buffon, *Histoire Naturelle* (1749); Oliver Goldsmith *History of the Earth and Animated Nature* (1774); and Thomas Bewick *A General history of the Quadrupeds* (1790). As it happens, William had borrowed these from the Public Library before he fell sick, apropos our great disputations on animal rights. I must remember to spirit them back some time, I think to myself—but that's not my immediate concern. Voltaire has begun to speak . . .

This is worrisome. Catherine knows no French and I know that William's French, unlike his self-taught Greek and Latin, is *atrocious.* I doubt if he will be able to follow half of what the master's saying, especially in his present state—in which case, what would be the point of the whole exercise? Monsieur Voltaire, meanwhile, has inaugurated his speech with an exquisite disquisition that combines reflections on authorship with thoughts on animal freedoms. It is clear to me that he has taken in both the fact that William is a writer and that he has lately been reading books on animals.

> 'Real authors are those who have succeeded in one of the real arts, in epic poetry, in tragedy or comedy, in history or philosophy, who have taught men or charmed them. The others are, among men of letters, what wasps *(oh Sylvia!)* are among birds.'

I'm immediately worried. Is William a bird in Voltaire's estimation? And what kind of a bird would he be—noble eagle or inconsequential sparrow?

> 'An eagle, of course! Undoubtedly an eagle.' Voltaire answers my unspoken question swiftly.

I breathe a sigh of relief. If William has heard this, he will be truly gratified. Voltaire and he might differ in their beliefs but the Frenchman has shown how Great Souls can soar above petty differences. His next sentence, however, is calculated to take our breath away.

> 'Yet it is quite clear that man and the other animals can exist very well without any of the arts—without bakers, without novelists and painters, without theologians; witness the whole of America, witness three quarters of our continent!'

Mankind can do without the arts, witness the whole of America? I am wondering what William will make of these sentiments when I hear a sort of rumble from him, an early volcanic warning, as it were. Amazingly, he is attempting to struggle to his feet—which, I have to say, even at this fraught moment, is *entirely* in keeping with his character. Praise may not succeed in rousing William but provocation will bring him back from the dead.

Voltaire seems to know this. He calmly props up the heavily staggering William with his strong arm, plonks him down on a chair and begins a lengthy mussitation in his ear. A scatter of indistinct words and phrases falls untidily about the room, like a fine drizzle or dust storm. A word that sounds like 'impression' is repeated several times, I catch 'art', 'form', 'line' and 'America', of course, and the word 'museum' and then a long unclear line about poetry. All this from Voltaire in his French tones and once from William in English, hollering and distinct: *Mock on, mock on, Voltaire and Rousseau . . . 'Tis all in vain! You throw the sand against the wind and the wind blows it back again!* and again: *Bring me an easel, Catherine, be quick!*

Catherine would do what William ordered even if he commanded her to take off all her clothes in public. Now she unquestioningly trips up the stairs to bring down William's little practice easel and the emergency palette and brushes which he keeps in their bedroom for when sudden inspiration strikes him. As soon as she sets up the contraption, William lunges towards it. He seems to be in a trance, but he's painting all right, in quick, determined strokes. Soon, a windblown prospect emerges on canvas—a large building in the foreground with what seems like a light dusting of sand blowing over it, lakes and a waterfront in the distance, an old beggar in the rain huddling on a park bench . . . and there are children, carefree children on a beach, playing ball in a summer's idyll . . .

Interpret these images as you will, but what struck me at once about this creation was that it was far removed from William's usual allegorical style—almost like an impressionist painting from much later, where colour and form merge, not to be told apart. *Impressionist*, yes, *that* was Voltaire's word, not *impression*! Obviously, he had taken over some of my duties and given William a whistle-stop glimpse into the future of French art.

Much to my regret, when he came to his senses, William chose to destroy his one-of-a-kind pre-Impressionist painting. It seemed to upset him, perhaps because it would not fit in with his strong ideas, learnt from Raphael and the greatest of the Old Masters, of what Art should be—or perhaps because there were themes in it that he would rather lay concealed forever in the sandy mists of the future. But, coy as he was about displaying his canvas to them, William could not resist informing his friends of the fact that he'd at last received a visitation from the great Voltaire himself, this being an elegant feather in his cap (or his Phrygian bonnet). Whereupon Flaxman, all the nuns of Tempke bless his soul, foxily asked the very same question that has been plaguing me.

How did William catch Voltaire's meaning? Did the great man speak in English? And William answered with a metaphor still to be found on record in the history books:

> 'To my sensations it was English. It was like the touch of a musical key. He touched it probably in French, but to my ear it became English.'

Just like my English books! *Around the World in Eighty Days, Heidi, Anna Karenina, Grimm's Fairytales* and all those other stories written in French, German and Russian but magically translated in my head into the rhythms of Tempke—what language did they speak? At last, I understood. It was William's 'imaginative music' that I really heard when I read them, not English, nor French, German, Hindi. So *that* was how Art crossed over, how Raphael's Madonna had stolen into Tempke Convent, how William managed to look into the Impressionist future of French art and how my Voices spoke to me. Simple enough, I suppose, but for me, Pari, the revelation was *stunning* . . .

William's reply to Flaxman was of course given months later, when William was quite recovered. What is worthy of note, though, is that his recovery began the instant he fell into his deep, revivifying sleep after he'd laid down his brushes on that momentous night, ultimately justifying Wallace's bizarre feathered faith in him. And Voltaire? Well, I followed him out of the door that moonlit night, reluctantly shedding my warm bat disguise and putting to him a few last questions, spirit to spirit . . .

> 'Will William be all right?'
>
> 'When he awakens out of that slumber, he will be a different man—and he owes it all to you, Muse. I am a Rationalist but I salute you! It was your wisdom I used to bail this English poet out from the depths of

> his depression, so deep, so *grande*—deeper even than the Indian ocean.'

I am as dumbstruck as William was not so long ago. Is Voltaire poking fun at me?

> '*Non, non,* it is as I said, but now you must leave your friend. He is becoming too dependent on you . . . '

How dare this Frenchman tell me what to do! He may be William's hero but I can't abandon William when he's so sick. What will Catherine do without me? *I will not* leave them!

> 'You can still see them, surely, but this was Summa's plan. Your role was to set William free, put him in charge of his own Destiny—which you have done, which you have done magnificently, *ma belle.* Now you are as free as he is—*voila*! *C'est meilleur des mondes possibles.*'

He has spoken of Summa! How does he know her? Is he *duplicate-Afi* again, perchance? My mind goes into its usual series of somersaults but we are almost at the end of the street now and it is time to say goodbye. I resign myself to not getting to the bottom of this particular mystery. And meanwhile, here's Voltaire giving me a quick, Gallic peck on both cheeks, wishing me happiness in this best of all possible worlds and departing as mysteriously as he'd come, never to be seen in the vicinity again.

Exit Seraphim

In time, William recovers and it is true—he is a different man, subtly, completely different. *It is like the touch of a musical key.* Change the note and you move from ecstasy to bromide calm in the flap of a sparrow's wing. William is still affectionate, happy to be in my company. It's just that I have lost the power to drive him mad anymore. He does not need me with the same ragged desperation—and he *never once* asks me to stay by him. That time is past. Summa's plan has worked far better than I'd anticipated. *So where do we go from here?*

'To America. *Fly on by, Sweet Angel!* answers William wickedly, as if nothing has changed and that he has all the right in the world to skip a couple of centuries and bid me goodbye with the words of a Jimmy Hendrix lyric, belted out in the smoky dives of Harlem and Chicago, circa 1960! And so—it is exactly as the superior angels prophesied. William has become in his final years a poet freed of the burdens of history, eliding centuries at will, a poco poet par excellence. He has brilliantly outgrown his Muse—me, Pari! A Pyrrhic victory? William obviously does not think so. He speaks, undaunted:

> 'And do you not still owe me, my nut-brown monkey? Men differ from animals only in this. They can plan for a far-off Future, they can speak of day-after-tomorrow or fifty years from the Present as not even the wisest Owl can. Be assured, Muse, I *shall* need you to guide my hand in the next century and the next and the next though you may think it a Fiction!' And William had the audacity to wink.

The rest, I see, will be up to me. But as I prepare to leave them, redundant as a used notebook, it is evident that my charges—William and Catherine both—have little need of a third party betwixt them. A Raphael reproduction adorns the mantelpiece and William is seated at his desk, revising an old draft of a poem from *Songs of Experience,* utterly relaxed and confident in his newfound freedom. Catherine bends over her cross-stitch by the fire . . .

Bliss. The scene is one of the almost unbearable domestic bliss embroidered on morality samplers by convent nuns or stamped on greeting cards at Christmas. Any angel is entitled to feel justly proud of such a denouement, to leave a hearth behind so tidy and serene! I should be happy (and I suppose I am) especially when I take note of the poem that William is battling with as I depart, for it does seem to suggest that I, Pari of the Indies, am not quite erased from his memory as yet. That key poem used to be called *The Human Image* but you will see from the Rossetti ms., published only after William's death and containing most of his latest, most private thoughts that William had in his final years tinkered with it and altered its title.

In its final avatar, this poem is called: *I heard an Angel Singing . . .*

❁

New Addenbrooke's Medical File 203 30.12.88: Since episode where patient tried to escape and bit nurse, she has occasionally had to be strapped to her bed. Initially showed considerable resistance to this procedure, but has lately shown signs of accepting it. Patient might damage herself as she has a case history of believing she can fly not just physically but 'across time and history' as she recently declared to her consultant doctor.

Under the circumstances, the Medical Panel constituted for the case has unanimously agreed on the suitability of RTMS treatment for this category of patient who responds only partially to drugs. The latest research studies show that Repetitive Transcranial Magnetic Stimulation can result in almost total cures in some cases. Change in treatment following the panel's examination is indicated and olanzapine is the drug of choice to be administered as of today.

RTMS to begin and continue for a month at regular intervals from 30.12.88.

Interval

First Meditation on Angels

Pari's Unreachable World in RTMS

Love, love, love! Sylvia, Ted, William, Catherine, Afi and me. What's the difference between love and madness, Afi sweetheart, *tell me, tell me, tell me.* You seem so dead, SO DEAD, I cannot bear it. These days, I'm madder than Sylvia. And as for the poetry—enough already! It is drivel, as Mona said. And William

Do what you will, this life's a fiction
And is made up of contradiction.

Contradiction: that's the KEYWORD, Afi. When one meditates, one is not oneself. One does not sound like oneself; one does not feel like oneself. One is someone else—*but who?* And how can one be both oneself and not oneself? Is *this* what Sister Maria used to call *speaking in tongues, being 'touched'* and all? The truth, Afi, is that I don't really know, because this is my first real biggie! Practice meditations, I've had those—but this one's really important. Summa says: pontification's boring but it is good for the soul. And who am I to contradict Summa, so here's my first angel insight, Afi, just for you . . .

Try this, anyone: rub your corporeal finger hard against the stuff of this page. You might find the print blur and grow a bit grubbier but it *will not disappear*—and neither will I—I, ANGEL PARI! That friction you feel on the tip of your finger, the rising heat—*that* is the Sign of my presence, as it is of the imaginative fire that forges a Lady Macbeth or Juliet dying. Ask dead Sylvia, ask Sister Liddie studying her English books in Tempke Convent's Library, ask important critics like Sir Wilson Knight: was Lady Mac a real historical figure? Just how many children did she have? Do these questions really have to be answered for you to believe in her? Did Shakespeare make her, did her parents, did HISTORY? *Does it matter?*

Truly, you need no more proof of my existence or of my Voices than you need of the fact that you yourself exist and think and believe in this or that fact. Trust is the key Afi, and poetry the divine expression of that loving trust, as William said. Angels dance about us at all times, and if only we trusted our intuition we would see them just as he did. Afi, Afi—do you love me, do you *trust?*

PROPHESY! Life is most true when it is an Angelic Fiction, according to William. All poets revel in this contradiction. They deal with the messy world by turning it into poetry—and into love's liquid cauldron. Think of it, Afi: *why did I, Ariel Pari, who could have had any man in the wide world, choose William and David and Ted?* If one has the Angelic Capacity to love at will, why alight upon a group of men with decidedly flaky views, and all confined to a single small island floating desolate somewhere off in the North Sea?

Why not choose Karl Marx, who wisely advised the world

to 'doubt everything'? Would not such a man have proven a rare and marvellous challenge? And why choose Will B. over the greatest Will of them all—Will S.? Is that not perverse? Or how about the anonymous tribe: a fire-walker in Singapore, an Alabama truck-driver, a Chemical Ali in Iraq? St. Francis or Raphael, Master Painter? Other poets—stone Homer, stoned Omar Khayyam, a stony Rabindranath Tagore staring defiantly into a colonizing camera—could I not have brought them to life with a kiss?

POETRY AND PROPHECY! These trajectories are infinite and I would not deny their charm, nor that each could prove so fine an opportunity that I hardly dare think of them without agitation. But even angels do not fly entirely free, Afi. The Imaginative Chains that William spoke of always bind us. Not my limitations alone but theirs, enslaved by history's endlessly blazing regimens—those benighted men driven by their times and their contingent natures to consort with beasts and angels, their coin the *Ange-bete* . . .

Stranger still, or perhaps not so strange because it does establish a continuity of taste and desire, is that the men to whom I, Pari, appeared, had THINGS IN COMMON. Each was an **Englishman** of humble origins in the high-noon of **Empire**, each an ironically situated Luddite. William was a hosier's son, David a miner's and Ted a farmer's. Each married an invincible woman without whose support he would *wilt*, whether he admitted this or not: William Catherine, David Frieda and Ted Sylvia. Then, each was a lover of animals as well as a poet, although I don't mean to imply by this that they had a penchant for bestiality or that they were perverted. Nothing like that—well, perhaps they were a bit perverted, as all true thinkers must be—but not in *that* way.

Havelock Ellis, MD, who documented the sexual love of man and beast so explicitly in his books that for a long time *The Psychology of Sex* was available only to MEDICAL PRACTITIONERS knew this when he wrote: *it is only the great men who are truly obscene. If they had not dared to be obscene, they could never have dared to be great.* Ted, William, David, were very great poets who dared to be great and I was amongst the last of their animals, the most enduring and the dearest, so I should know . . .

✿

But of course you will tease me, Afi. You will say that I make no sense at all in these hyper moods of mine, when my wings are all made up of **other peoples' words**, when the wild sharp feathered thoughts fornicating in my mind just cannot be controlled. At these times, I babble and rant and struggle so hard that I can only be put down with an injection, with jabs and with stabs straight to the heart. I cannot even decide if I am an angel or an animal. So how can you help turning cold towards me at these times? Now I'm a foul animal! I'm a rat in the mushahar's belly. I am my father devouring every poor mushahar without pity and snapping my mother's bones in two! I'm Turkey Jahangir too and so *you* have to be like Drs M and T. You have to maintain your distance, you have to lie there stiff and cold, you *have* to doubt my sanity—or how else can you preserve your own?

The whole story's been wildly unconvincing so far, you're thinking. Conversations between a psychotic angel and a bunch of dead poets, Pari: *what next?* And I see Sister Maria's good old skeptical serpent wriggling its Eden-way into your mind already. Oh yeah—an *angel*? Where have you *been*? Oh, a convent in Tempke, India? Flying over the island of Nauru, Australasia? Get this, winged creature. In the civilized world today, poetry's a proper turn-off. No one needs angels anymore (whatever *that* means). These days, all we need to be TRANSPORTED is to hit a button. Down Ginsberg, up Google!

Where did I learn to talk like this? Afi, it was in England, ENGLAND! I could not eat my aunt's food there, Afi. IT WAS POISONED! So I had to gorge on fortune cookies, God promise, I had to exchange 'Utamaro Prints' with a gent in downtown Tokyo, check out coy Asian Brides from Indonesia, become 'Indi-Pari'. This isn't false talk, Afi. It's *multicultural*. I was multicultural! *Porn-scorn-popcorn*, they called it in my English College, Afi! I speak the truth. No one needs angels in such times of plenty . . .

Sylvia already *had* her zillion critical guardians, her university high priests—and so did William and David. Where did *angels* figure in this scheme of things? Nowhere! I learnt so many words in England—Post-tech, Post-mod, Post-colonial. POST-PARI, also! Post her straight back to Tempke! Because my teacher told us we had reached the 'end of history'—but I think Sylvia knew this already. The twentieth century was not for poetry.

It was not a time for *Birthday Letters*. When *split lives congeal and stiffen to history*, Sylvia wrote, a birthday comes to mean nothing and a birthday present even less: *I should be sixty by the time the whole of it was delivered and too numb to use it*—and she was right. The Sixties are gone forever, *kaput*! Sylvia, ever the Realist, declared she would've been a middle-aged matron by now—how sexy is *that*? Had she lived, *had she lived*—but that's another story, Afi.

Afi, Afi, Afi, *please* don't go and die!

Don't leave like Sylvia. *He* lived, she didn't: *Ted, Ted, Ted, her Teddy bear, hunkering down in his wintry lair, so sad is life and so unfair, Sylvia dead and he still there, Ted, Ted, her Teddy bear!* Birthday letters for dead paramours, ugh! Afi, let's forget it: *No one's* a *hero* these days.

ANGELS! They're the unrequited lovers of our times—discarded pieces of intellectual junk! So why do I persist in hanging around, why don't I just shut up and take off *now, this moment,* like Sylvia?

Yes, I, Ariel, hear you, Afi. I hear you, Afi my love, I hear these thoughts blowing about in your head like a desert sirocco but the situation isn't quite as black and white as you think. On the contrary, it's squigglier than the script you're squinting at with your blinded eyes this very moment—just like Dr T, like Dr M. You're trying to figure me out—but that's impossible! *Angels are indecipherable.* And by the way, mistake you not, Afi love, the dictum applies as much to angels of the sweetly cumbersome traditional variety. The ones on the walls of our convent, these exquisite creatures decked out in medieval spandex by Fra Lippo Lippi. Raphael *et al,* or the amorous beauties clad in irresistible see-through pyjamas who appeared each night to Prince Murad in his cups—mere figments of a vanished imagination. *Figs!* That world is dead—D-E-A-D. Ergo, seraphs, cease to flood us with flat wine and discard the mouldering casks, as Sylvia said. Besides, Afi, if you could speak, I know what you'd say with your eyes slanting: you never could understand how anyone could abide poetry, especially full-grown adults. Imagine grown men rabbiting on about unseen forms paddling overhead. Insane!

But INSANITY—that is the heart of the matter. Angel meditations belong to the upper air. If you want to understand me, fly with me! *Fly with me, Afi my love.* It's the only way. Smug and neg responses to poetic bolts from the blue, to manic starts, that's just being normal, that's *ordinary.* For instance, that knee-jerk reaction—there can *be* no angels. To which I say: well, good, *very* good, we shall see, Doctorji. You're exactly the sort of sceptic I need. No passionate fancies, just a lifetime of sitting on fencies! What a wonderfully cross-hatched derriere you must have, I hear Sylvia snorting—but in her innermost heart, Doctor Sahib, Sylvia was always serious, DEADLY serious, a Realist.

Sylvia knew there were *always two,* the angel and the beast, pulling at a person. The face in the mirror was her face but the body was mine. Her twisted American, my Indian accent, love and mania, false words and poetry, they came in pairs. DING! The Refectory clock in Tempke Convent spoke every hour without fail but the silent second hand had the real message: second hand, *duplicate*! The Madonna Triptych and the Heineken poster, William's common jade and my aristocratic fur-hatted mother, the Englishmen whose hands stretch out to me in friendship, the doctors and the nurses, their gifts were all *double-crossing gifts.* History repeated itself first as chance and then as fate—*contradictory.*

Two, Sylvia says to me firmly now at the end of my meditation, ignoring the fact that her very presence in William's story happens to be a bit of a contradiction because she'd *assured* me she'd never come here. Then she repeats those lines of hers I already know so well, dragging my hand over her prickly yew-berry verses and crisscrossing my fingers with many heartless scratches:

Two. Of course there are two.
It seems perfectly natural now—
The one who never looks up, whose eyes are lidded
And balled, like Blake's . . .

❁

Yes, William's unforgettable, lidded eyes—it was when I saw myself reflected in them, a double angel, that I first made the observation that still has the power to shock me. Despite my glorious aureole I, Pariel, was, for this man, *no better than a kitten or a lamb.* No worse maybe, but no better. The fact that he might have been dead at the time does not make this insight a jot less true. He was an eighteenth century eccentric living at the edge of penury and madness and I was a supernatural sensation, an angel who could recite his poems backwards, even the ones he'd not yet written, but when all was said and done—it came down to this.

I'm being serious now. I was *other than human*—and that's the first sadness about being a creature of the spirit, Afi.

Inspiration never lasts and love is the rose within a circlet of worms. That was William's theory and it was Sylvia's story: you know this well already, I have repeated it so many endless times but fly with me now, Afi. Come! It's a matter of life and death, after all—*yours . . .*

Second Engagement with Angels

In which Pari meets Summa

Flying is easy, see! So easy that, even as we chatter, Afi, here we are at our destination—*GABRIEL'S GAZEBO,* already packed with ice-guzzling angels.

This is my other world, which even William and Sylvia cannot enter and certainly no ordinary mortal. In this universe of superior madness, human ties mean nothing, *nothing.* Everyone is intimate and everyone's a stranger. The more fantastical the voices in one's head, the more coolly rational the tone of one's voice. But I see you shaking your head, Doctor. I'm babbling too much again. *But fly with me just for a bit and I'll* ***show*** *you . . .*

We have to be quick, though! As I mentioned earlier, I'm royally late.

Well-trained angel girls, my nuns taught us, are loath to curse, but nothing to my knowledge prevents them from urging expletives on their *hearers* and I urge them upon you now. You've guessed already that I am a punctuality fiend (by the way, you must not take the word 'fiend' literally here, or then again you may, depending on how far you want to carry your scepticism). Anyhow, transgressing a time-line distresses me. It could be my upbringing but being late makes me hyperventilate like some nervous teen, the paint hardly dry on her toenails, and—more to the point—it makes me *far less inclined* to play the angelic party animal. The other thing is that I'm a low-grade angel only a breath away from humanness myself, so I have to be adept at practicalities too and I do know that the first thing to do at crushes like this one is to get rid of wraps, wings and other paraphernalia. I do this at once—and manage immediately to catch the disapproving eye of a Matron.

I also guess—rightly, as it turns out—that this particular queen-sized, pearl-girt member of my clan is no Swedenborgian *proceeding ever to the springtime of her youth.* No chance of that! Big Momma here clearly revels in the authority of her age. She says:

> 'We haven't met. I'm a Miltonian, collateral branch. You?'
>
> 'Swedenborgian.'
>
> 'Region?'
>
> 'South of the Himalayas—the peninsula of the Indies.'

The matron has not said so in so many words but she wears her high Seraphim status on her ample chest. She's right up there with the Sistine Madonna and probably on backslapping terms with Gabriel, Uriel and Zadkiel and other old-timers, none of whom have the remotest idea of my existence. I can see that her micro-processing unit is in fine working order, too. She's thinking, so *that's* what accounts for her uncommonly brown skin. What's she doing here then, so far from her native shores? Really, they shouldn't hand out plum assignments to these young rookies without so much as a check! I must have a powwow with Michael about it one of these days. Perhaps her thoughts do not articulate themselves in precisely this language but that's about the gist of it. She does not approve.

Swedes like myself belong to the angel proletariat, to those nether regions of the angel hierarchy where Milady Titania would never descend. Three steps down Jacob's ladder and she would surely do an about-turn. That is her nature, while I belong to the ragtag bands swarming up and down the high swinging ropes with the careless ease of trapeze artists, a caste-less subversive bunch untidily drawn from every quarter of the globe—and there lie's the rub, Afi!

While I wait politely for the matron to make her next move, I decide on another little meditation to calm me down. I will need my wits about me in this encounter. I can see why Angels are advised to meditate in these strenuous situations (that's what the rule-book says) but the thing about meditation is that it's always terribly lonely. You fold your wings back, hold your breath and dive inwards without pause. Mind-expansion, what does it mean after all? Totaling all my experiences together, my blinding wisdom from all my English books, I, Pari, declare this: **meditation means finding your own patch of infinite blue**, encased in glassy walls, untouchable as Doctorji's paperweight Taj Mahal. It means believing in Raphael's serene Madonna and scheming putti with all one's strength even when one is strapped to a hospital bed; it means tranquility without tranquillizers. Meditation is the incalculable sum of all the arguments one has with oneself and oneself alone, and if that sounds pompous, it's because it is, but we have to accept it anyway because it also happens to be true which is why it's no good waiting around while *someone else* meditates because that other person's in some unreachable place already. So, all that happens is that *you* end up feeling bad, lonely or embarrassed or irritated or just plain foolish . . .

The grande dame, I notice, has come up very close behind me as I thrash about trying to stabilize myself. Clearly, my pathetic attempts at meditation have had an effect on her, for she seems to have decided to take me under her wing—and what a wing it is, resembling in its majestic curvature Raphael's best efforts or one of Da Vinci's finest engineering models for flight, securely trussed and impressively tensile!

'Refreshments?' she warbles serenely, a warship proceeding towards its unquestioned port. I'm impressed by how the little schooners amongst the crowds give way as she sails by—oh yes, and the clouds too! She is *somebody*—that's obvious, but *who*? And we have moved by now into the most exclusive part of the ceremonial space. Gabriel himself is positioned there, declaring:

'Hello, Summa! This is an honour.'

Now I get it. I might have been frivolously calling her Titania, but my companion is no mere Fairy Queen of light Shakespearean extraction. She is **Summa Sukkalin**, of the most ancient Babylonian stock. Her line is older than Gabriel's own. Even I know that the Baylonian sukalli are the rarest of rare angels, appearing in ancient Minoan inscriptions on par with the stars and moon. They correspond to the messenger spirits of the Bible who bring the tidings of the Lord to earth, but far exceed in antiquity anything in the Hebrew Bible. The rustle of legend has it that the sukalli have always had the most direct access to their Maker and some are rumoured to be more than mere messengers—they are sanctioned *viceregents* of the Supreme Being. In short, you cannot get much higher than supralunary Summa. You see members of her kin alongside the Sphinx and in the enormous winged bulls and lions that have long guarded Assyria's palaces. Those strange winged men with hawks' heads on Sumerian temple walls are Summa's own brothers—and what's more, I am about to meet one of the freakiest descendents of her clan shortly—very, *very* shortly . . .

First, though, we have to get through the formalities. By now, I have become quite successful at avoiding the eyes of the storm when I'm forced to attend these things. It is true that my invitation read: *The Most Holy Archangel Gabriel desires the pleasure of your company to meet a Visiting delegation of Afreets,* et cetera, et cetera—but this did not mean I had to meet them. No such thing! Still, this time there's no avoiding the contretemps . . .

There they are now, the Pulchritudinous Persians—about fifty beauties en masse, glittering with sparkly gems and floating gently on a dawn-pink cirro-cumulus sea, sipping their genteel sherbets—not a wing ruffled or out of sync. It is an extraordinarily pretty sight—too pretty for me. I hang back, feeling more and more unkempt and anti-social, but Summa has no such qualms. She ploughs forward—with me firmly in tow—relentlessly exchanging salaams with everyone in sight, until we get close, really close.

I sigh. The ones I *really* want to get close to are the farthest off, afloat in their zones of absolute independence, high and unreachable. The free-spirited **Apsaras of India** will brook no man's ownership and never enter into the slavery of marriage. They have their own private concerns and cannot be bothered to circulate politely at parties, because as Urvashi once said to Arjuna, why *should* they? O Son of Indra, she said, cool as a snowflake, we Apsaras stand free and unencumbered in our choice. We have no husband, no sons, indeed, no relations. So there! And this evening the Apsaras are running true to form. None of them pays the slightest heed to anyone at the gathering, not even to Summa, and each one's doing her own off-beat thing in her own off-beat way, this breed of nymphs apart. There's Mishrakesi caressing her partner's you-know-what with her long tongue in *full* public view, and as for Viprachitti, Purvachitti, Sahajanya, Karnika, Punjikasthala, Viswachi, Rithisthala, Umlocha, Pramlocha, Swayamprabha, Janapadi, Adrika, I can't even mention to you the things they were up to. The nuns of Tempke would die if they saw and Raphael's serene Madonna *drop* the Infant in her arms!

Plus, there's one at the very edge of the Aps circle with a distinct resemblance to my glittering mother, but I cannot make out the man with her, he's groveling so hard. In fact, most of the Apsaras are trailing some poor smitten Celestial Musician or Sage along! Rambha has Tumburu in tow, Menaka Vishvasu, Urvashi Vibhandaka and Ghritachi, the darling's come with not one but two bearded wise fellas,

Vyasa flailing on one side and Bharadwaja fuming on the other. I want so much to watch, just to *watch* them but finally they disappear from sight, as I follow mutinous in Summa's unstoppable wake . . .

And it's worth it, after all—this ice-counter, this glassy snowflake garden to which Summa's instincts have unerringly led me. It's piled high with flat Antarctic fillets of translucent glacier, soft Alpine snow-drifts set about with tiny red berries, perfect rounded hailstones served in salty iceberg ramekins. The central table is embellished with overhangs of stalactite and the transparent gold of stalagmite so lovely you can hardly bear to break off a piece and pop it in your mouth, but I note again that Summa has no such compunctions. *She* is gorging herself on Andean ice—those coruscating slivers of light collected from the mountain baselines guarded by William's eagles and spirituous thunderbirds and fresh Himalayan croquets springing with exquisite amaryllis flowers . . .

William often reiterated that the periods when I vanished without explanation were agony to him. He would stamp about London red-eyed. He would turn on Catherine for no particular reason, raging. Their relationship was at its best when *I* was around, he said—which was another contradiction! Catherine was a fine cook but still he starved when I was gone. Only I brought him soul food, only I brought succour. Without me, he was blind and inspiration-less, shivering in a fathomless abyss, the spirit gone out of him. These were the emotions he had registered, without equivocation, in *America* and in all his other poems. *Why* then did I desert him thus cruelly for no reason?

That question had no simple answer. I *had* reasons. An angel has her duties, her social engagements and her shocks and these cannot be openly revealed.

The day I return to William and attempt to detail this scene which offers food for the eyes as well as the soul, he transforms it, as he is invariably inclined to do, into a quick love-plea to me. What I saw before me was an enchanting repast for angels—that is all, *no more and no less*—but William's 'Soft Snow' is much more a paean against a sort of heart-hunger, the 'sandy' abstinence he has to endure during my inevitable disappearances. Such is the Creative Imagination:

I walked abroad on a snowy day
I ask'd the soft Snow with me to play . . .

Abstinence sows sand all over
The ruddy limbs and flaming hair
But Desire gratified
Plants fruits of life and beauty there.

And I hear Summa now, vociferously urging me to attack some of those self-same ambrosial fruits. 'Come, eat!' she commands—but I'm riveted by the ice-sculptures . . .

Third Enigma of Angels

Pari in the Vale of Tears

The sculptures surrounding me in this unearthly Paradise are like nothing I have seen. They belong to dream-time, they are the stuff of Sylvia's 'waxy stalagmites', those circling wombs of marble, chilly, barren and perfect. I cannot seem to tear myself away from them.

Not the usual theme-park lot, the world-weary leprechauns, naiads and folksy elves, with the Greek Muses thrown in for good measure that are wont to please the hoi-polloi. No, here's a whole other exotic encyclopaedia: Androgynous Faro, water goddess of the West African Bambara peoples and Aztec Xolotl, dog-headed sun-sniffer, Kurukulla from Tibet holding aloft her blood-red lotus in poised conversation with Siberian Mayin whose job it is to post souls in the bodies of new-born children. An outer ring of messengers and trickster gods, Esu-Elegbara of the Yoruba, Greek Iris and Roman Hermes, their heads bent together in mischief, Tuli the bird postman of the Samoa in beady-eyed conversation with Ratatosk, Northern Squirrel, tireless runner up and down Yggdrasil's Life-Tree, carting around his endless sound-bites of gossip—these I recognize. And right next to me stands Irish Bress, muscular old agricultural god, hand-in-hand with Holy Brigit, daughter of Dagda—but many others I cannot even begin to identify. I appeal to Summa:

'Whose idea were these?'

In reply, Summa produces a raised eyebrow and a curiously tangential but blunt counter-question.

'How strong are your nerves?'

'Tempered steel.' But it turns out these boastful words are spoken too soon.

'Here he is now. Meet . . . '

Something steps out from behind a frieze of Valhalla Valkyries.

I do not know if he is demon or angel for he has no face. *No face*—where there should be indented features, a bridged nose, angled jaw-line, is grim obscurity, a kind of withering mist. Staring into the fumes that make up his—what shall I call it?—his non-countenance, his visage, my eyes begin to prick uncontrollably. The stench is choking too, a blend of cadaver rot and hospital disinfectant, days-old clothing soaked in piss and the vomit-sweet reek of tropical durian-fruit. Yet, through it all, I smell, of all things, tears. I swear I can smell tears, although until this instant I did not know that they had any kind of scent at all.

'*Sunt lacrimae rerum*', he offers politely.

Another blow out of the water! The creature's voice is light and jaunty, a young man's baritone. Reading my thoughts could not have been difficult. He must, after all, have run this party-trick before on other unsuspecting souls—getting them to catch a Virgilian whiff of tears through a miasma of abattoir odours—but to produce that voice out of *that* face. I'm winded. I have no words left. No, correction! I have no *thoughts* left. Desolation sweeps through my mind like a sandstorm. I can't see, I can barely hear, so it's strange that William should suddenly pop into my head at this confusing moment! Perhaps *this* is how William feels each time I leave him. The thought hurts and I decide to abandon it for the time being but discover that my head seems to be hurting too. Best leave the talking to Summa . . .

'My nephew', she explains. 'He does these ice-sculptures to relax. Most of the time, he's away. Travelling!'

I play desperately for time.

'Where does he travel?'

'Into the future.'

The Future: I am reminded of my repeated conversations with William about America. Perhaps I should seek advice from Summa's oddball nephew on the matter.

'Ask him!' says Summa in response to my unspoken thought.

'He's incorrigible, never still for a second—drives himself too hard. Look at his face.'

I'm appalled. Both Summa's casual tone and her logic are out of line. How can she ask me to gaze upon an absence, how can she so lightly refer to the cauterized, cauterizing, *sickening*, void that is her nephew's 'face'? I say slowly, with deliberate, great yawning gaps between my words:

> 'He—has—no—face.'

> 'Why do you suppose he needs one? Why does anyone need a face?'

What a peculiar question! Trust Summa to stymie me. I'm quickly reduced to a stammer:

> 'Because—because he needs to speak . . . To—to see . . . '

> 'You've heard him speak already. Shall I ask him to describe you now? That should prove that he can see—and you have the evidence of the ice-sculptures to boot! Hard for a blind individual to produce those, don't you think?'

Summa is stringing me along nicely. She's won all the points so far. Her nephew can indeed see, talk, hear and I'm *convinced* he has a developed olfactory intelligence. What's left—taste, *touch*? I'm not sure I want him to exhibit his sense of touch, not yet, and certainly not with me as his touchstone! It's true—what does he need a face for? I try again, tentative this time:

> 'To display his emotions . . . He—he needs a face for that. And because it's—well, it's normal. *Everyone* has a face. It's shocking not to have a face.'

'Okay, let's take the point about the emotions first.' Summa sounds like a headmistress confronted with a particularly obtuse student. Maybe, I think, it's time I quit the scene. The crowds have grown thin, the sprites are packing up, and I'm totally out of my depth, but she insists:

'Look at him again!'

So I do. I glance towards her revolting nephew and at once I feel him smiling, like the sun through louring clouds. He's amused—that's the odd thing. You can actually sense his thoughts, his pain, his uninhibited delight. I guess you could say he sends out vibes, *powerful* vibes—again, not a word William would know, but surely appropriate under the circumstances. And Summa's made her argument. Her nephew may not have a face but he manages to convey his feelings all right, perhaps even a little *too* well. When I first saw him, it's undeniable I was knocked sideways, but I notice I've recovered quite a bit and it hasn't taken *that* long. Specifically, I find I've recovered enough to notice that the nephew has a body that matches his voice—athletic, lithe, *bonny*, one that could streak across the sky in a flash, with or without wings. And what's more, he's wearing **sneakers.** How in the world have I managed to get used to him so soon and so easily?

The very fact that I'm asking this question means that Summa's right again. *Look beyond the veil of appearances.* How simple and basic the tenet is and who has not lived by it?

✿

As early as 1788—the fateful year I came to William and we first discussed his unique method of engraving—he practiced hard with many hundreds of short, apprentice engravings. And one of these proclaimed exactly this message:

> *Man's Perceptions are not bounded by Organs of Perception: he perceives more than Sense (tho' ever so acute) can discover.*

Looks are secondary. Natural scientists, poets, detectives, where'd they be if they forgot this basic truth? Take the fairytale of the Beauty and the Beast, or the present case of Summa's ghastly nephew. It's apparent Summa dotes on him. Ergo, sooner or later, love or persistence ensures that one crosses superficial external barriers. One gets over a person's looks. It's what he *is* that matters . . .

Still, my problem remained, what *was* he exactly, this alien production, this morphed biped? Beast or Angel? Where exactly would he stand in the Great Chain of Being? Could Summa answer me that? No she can't, I hear her silent, stubborn refusal inside my head. I have to get there myself—and almost straight off, a famous contradictory phrase swims into my consciousness. *Darkness visible.* I know to whom these words belong. He was William's mentor, one of the Glorious Dead with whom he held untold conversations and the revered subject of his monumental work, *Milton: A Poem in Two Books to Justify the Ways of God to Man.* If there are any images that I see when I confront the terrifying facelessness of Summa's nephew, they are out of *Paradise Lost.*

Summa's nephew is *Paradise Lost* personified—that's it! I recall the painstaking anatomical realism with which William etched Milton, his rippling muscular body, but what I am now drawn to of a sudden are the *angles* he chose. Milton is always caught facing sideways, looking down at a map, studying his toes, almost as if William cannot bear to *look him in the face,* either so effulgent or so blind is Milton's vision. *Just like my English books.* Am I getting somewhere at last?

Summa says, not missing a step:

> 'There are things far more shocking than a face expunged. Look you—this time he's back from warring Somalia, helping child-soldiers exit.'

I guess I look confused because the nephew chips in. The words are clear and fast like running water, gentle, unstoppable:

> 'I'm there when they die. Exit—it means, to die. Not that I can help, I can't really. Don't believe Summa, she's family. She has an exaggerated idea of my importance! These children die in pain, horribly. How can anyone help? Septicemia, that's one hell of a killer! Diarrhea, land-mines, homelessness, *shall I count the ways*? They're tough, these kids, and they did not choose their fate but they die anyway. I can't say why. Do you wonder then that I've lost face, lost face entirely? Oh, you don't like my joke, little Angelica, my Farishta, Pari? But take my word for it. Somalia, Afghanistan, Iraq—these are *not* situations where you can Justify the Ways of God to Man—or the other way around—so I don't know why I go. *I don't know.* It's a type of masochism, I suppose . . .'

Odd to hear an angel so bent on emphasizing his ignorance! Imagine if Gabriel had similarly fretted during the Annunciation! Supposing he was assailed with doubts about how much of the future to reveal to Mary. Should he have told her that the Divine Christ Child would be murdered and mocked some thirty years into His Reign? Should he have mouthed William's brutal couplet composed centuries down the line into the Virgin's gentle ear? *Should* he? Exactly how far can an angel go in exposing the grail-pure certainties of myth to the destructive facts of history?

Nail his neck to the cross: nail it with a nail
Nail his neck to the cross: ye all have power over his tail.

Until this moment, I had accepted *unquestioningly* Gabriel's Principle. An angel acted with restraint in these matters. Our role was inspirational, to guide and to reveal, as I'd attempted to do with William (well, sort of)—but it *hits me now.* I haven't attained conspicuous success in my mission, have I? William's led *me* for the most part, not I him! He's had power over *my* monkey tail, as he sometimes crudely put it. Perhaps I should rethink my premises, but the words that tumble out of me, unwilled, do not seem to reflect this newly acquired self-knowledge. They are cutesy imbecilic, spoilt bratty and oh, *just plain inane.*

'I couldn't do what you do. I couldn't bear to watch and do nothing!' Had William heard me at this moment, I suppose he would say I've gained honorable membership of that society he hated most of all and often bitingly referred to as the idiotic *Slobbering School.*

'Really? Tell us how you deal with your Poet then.'

That's Summa responding and, as usual, she's sharp, detecting my weakness in a trice. I guess I have to forget my appetite for lucent angel-ice this day and confine myself to eating humble pie instead. I say,

> 'Well, actually—I, I was thinking of asking your advice on how best to be William's pathfinder. His works are works of Prophecy, as you must know—but he will pay no heed to my warnings that the future is dark—just as your nephew says. What should I do?'

At this, Summa, super-angel, and her nephew, face of the faceless future, turn to each other. They speak in unison, sounding a bit like Tweedledum and Tweedledee. For the first time in our encounter, I'm the one who's amused.

> 'We're only allowed one recommendation each every encounter.'

I can imagine why. Summa and her nephew would be *swamped* if they were to turn into agony aunties for lost angels. The formality of their set-piece sentence shows they've been through this hoop often.

> 'Every encounter?'
>
> 'Once in a life time.'

Lifetime? Not a usual angelic parameter! We use the word often enough of course, but casually. In actuality it's understood that we are eternity-vendors, omega-merchants. So what does Summa mean? I'm being serious here—but is she?

'Don't be literal-minded, youngling! I don't mean *your* lifetime. I mean his—your Poet's.'

'Oh. But he has many years left. How may I help him?'

Summa says, 'We need to know his passions—and I don't mean you, young lady!'

To which I reply without a blush.

'That's easy! **ABCD squared**—America and Art, Birds and Beasts, Catherine and City-life, Destiny and Desire. But William would say: naming subjects two-by-two like this conforms to the dull principle of Ratio, which lambent Poesy must fly beyond!'

I am momentarily pleased with the eloquence of my reply. For once it surprises me with its unexpected facility, but then Summa's riposte comes back to me, straight and accurate as a lance.

'Desire and Destiny—I conjecture those are still pseudonyms for you in some wise, is it not? '

This time I do have the grace to blush. Summa, meanwhile, is pushing on.

'That leaves the As, the Bs and the Cs. My advice: he is a poet, so ensnare him with poetry. Cast about him a beaded net of poems. Do not be inhibited. Catherine you may spare. She can fend for herself, and has found her own ways of influencing your Poet, has she not? Don't worry your pretty little head about her. Just produce the poems!'

Produce *poems?* Has Summa lost her head? William's the poet. I've never written a poem in my life! My mind is in a whirl. This is not the kind of advice I was expecting.

> 'Come on!' says Summa cheerfully. 'Everyone can manage a poem or two! Your William declared it himself. He made it his very first Principle in *All Religions are One.*'

I'm so confused by now that I've forgotten everything that William did or didn't say and here's Summa quoting William like a pro. My world's turned turtle, it *has*! I need Sylvia.

'Remind her!' Summa instructs her nephew and at once he recites William's injunction for me from the depths of his smoky being:

> *'That the Poetic Genius is the True Man, and that the Body or Outward Form of Man is derived from the Poetic Genius. Likewise the Form of all things are derived from their Genius, which by the Ancients was called an Angel and Spirit and Demon.'*
>
> 'You see! Just take the word of one your William rightly calls an Ancient—me, Summa Sukkalin! The Poetic Genius is within you, Angel, as he says. Do not be confounded by Outward Form and you shall be able to release your Genius—and William's. What—do you not believe me? Then ask him!'

And Summa triumphantly resorts to her favourite trick of appealing to the Darling Nephew once more, flipping her great wing in his direction. They are a class act, these two! Do I stand a chance against them? It's his turn now:

> 'Summa's right. You've just got to take courage in both hands and fly! It's dire, I know, but if you don't take any risks, Farishta, how will you ever know the heights? But my advice is simpler, see. If your Poet's heart goes out to animals, all you have to do is lead him to them. Point your postcolonial pinkie in the direction of the London Menagerie, the Exeter Exchange, my dearest! Convey him to the India Museum. And if it's the City of London that haunts your Poet, well, then—walk with him through London's howling streets. Go! Take courage and show him the Allegory of the Future in his own backyard. That will bring out his essential nature and help him confront his Destiny—and yours! Angelica, you can do this!'

Well, at least what Summa's Dear Boy recommends is practical, though I can't say I care for his patronizing tone but I decide to show some grace at last, especially as we seem to be the only ones left at the party.

> 'Thank you.' I gabble. 'It's been most enlightening. I'll do my best. Will I see you again soon?'

'Unlikely.' says Summa, never one, as I've discovered in the course of this meeting, to mince her words. 'But we'll be keeping watch. If you really need us, we'll be there. And maybe next time Ari will show you his face.'

❁

Ari, did she say Ari?

'Come, Ali. Say goodbye to Angelica. We must be on our

way.' Summa hugs me briefly and vanishes with admirable efficiency. Ali! I guess she said Ali . . .

The nephew says hurriedly, from a safe distance, 'We must keep in touch. I'll call you.'

'But your name? *What's your name?*'

Everyone needs a name, as I discovered when the phone rang in Tempke ages ago . . .

Summa's nephew edges just a bit closer. I can smell him now and feel the sulphurous lighting and the stinging rain that punctuate his staccato bursts of speech. All around us, his ice sculptures drip away dolefully as if they can't bear to say goodbye to him.

'Afi. It's *Afi*. Shh! Summa will have a fit if she knows I've told you. Remember me?'

Afi? *How* can he be Afi? Afi lies maimed in a convent bed in faraway Tempke because of me and *I must save him*. It is for him I've braved winds tramontane and cismontane and come to these weird places where no mortal travels and now this faceless angel, this *shadow*, claims *he's* Afi. How can that be? An imposter, maybe, a Tempke *duplicate*?

I am stunned speechless. Nothing in my English books has prepared me for this, this *resurrection*—what else can I call it? But the nephew's continuing undaunted:

> 'There's some ridiculous custom that no woman must utter my name, except *nuns* of course. Or disaster befalls! Thunderclaps from the sexist sky, bolts from the blue, you know the sort of thing . . . I'm to be called "the one above"—or so they say. Just to be on the safe side. But what's in a name—or in a face—Angelica? Afi's my name among the Abkhaz of the

west Caucasus. Others use different epithets. As for your Poet, he calls me Urizen, but—I could be his Loki, or his Los. His loss, my gain, ha-ha! That's why Summa was so jumpy. She was nervous she'd slip and then . . . '

I find my tongue: 'Then—what?'

'Sorry. Have to go. Catch you later!'

And he's gone.

I'm alone among the weeping ice-sculptures and my inchoate thoughts. Although I cannot reveal it all to him, this—*this* is why I leave William. Because I need to learn, because I cannot help him or Afi or fight my own terrible madness if I do not first educate myself. Life's mysteries are deep and though there's never any saying who one will meet at an angel gathering, there's always a chance of bumping into a Summa and um, well, her nephew with the unsayable name and the unseeable face: Afi maybe (don't forget he mentioned *nuns*) but he also called himself Los. Los, Loki, *Urizen*? But William *hates* Urizen.

Bred from his forsaken wilderness
Of beast, bird, fish, serpent, and element . . .

I can see now that the picture William draws of loathsome Urizen is not dissimilar to the feeling of pure terror that overcame me when I first set eyes on duplicate Afi. The only problem is, I end up liking, almost respecting, this Afi, whereas for William Urizen is ever the hateful tyrant who proclaims:

One curse, one weight, one measure
One King, One God, One Law.

It's confusing! Now I think—what's so awful about Urizen's unitary vision? Well, William's point is simple. Going with Urizen kills individuality, plurality, joy. It stifles new beginnings and hello, it's just too pious! And I can't say I disagree with William. I am his angel *because* he holds these views. But pity, compassion, forgiveness, the bases of Urizen's laws, are these not ends in themselves? And surely one cannot employ child-soldiers even if one is fighting a Just War on behalf of Liberty—which implies that there must be *some* universal principles.

Besides which, there were the stranger Afi's tears . . .

Afi-Los's mercurial tears and Summa's straight-talk—these were for me, at the end of our peculiar encounter, the indefinable clinchers, illogically persuading me that I'd made a couple of friends for eternity. Of course, the next step which I would have to take would become more complicated for this very reason. For it goes without saying—*I would now be put to the test.*

The true exercise of my angel liberty would be tried to its limits. Since it was freely asked and freely given, I was now 'by honour' bound to give, whether I liked it or not and *whatever* the risks, due credence to their alarming advice. That was the code and I was not allowed to duck the difficult bits but as Afi-Urizen the Thunderbird so nobly maintained—*where was the thrill without the spill?* Amen to that . . .

Pensively, I found myself breaking of a last melting spoke off the Goddess Fortina's sculpted wheel. Delicious! For me, this was the best feature of Afi the nephew's angel art: it was touchingly consumable and entirely ephemeral. These objects would never enter the annals of history or the portals of a museum. Like the gleaming images of the Goddess and her Children at Puja in Tempke immersed in the Ganga muddy and drunken after a mere week of festivities, there'd be *nothing* left of Afi's intricate ice-sculptures carved in so much caring detail in a few hours—only an extra trace of moisture in the air and an evanescent hint of rain or tears. And what could I do about that but make my way out of the angel asylum and into the sky, flying low between the steady constellations—safe Orion to my open left and friendly Cassiopeia on my right . . .

New Addenbrooke's Medical File 203 15.3.89: Patient's recovery under the drug regimen of olazapine combined with valium and a full three months of RTMS-pulse treatment is remarkable. She appeared fully composed before the Medical Panel and was able to answer all questions with ease and facility. She admits her aviomania is a delusion. This frank recognition of her disability is itself a sign that the patient has enough maturity to manage her illness. Patient admitted the necessity of continuing her medication for the foreseeable future and said she was willing to sign an affidavit to this effect. She is keen to return to her own country and meet Dr M by whom she was first referrred. We see no objection to this move. If necessary, patient may, on the recommendation of Dr M or any other qualified psychiatrist, be admitted for RTMS therapy in any major hospital in her own country. For the present, her guardian, with whom she resides, has been advised to contact the hospital on an emergency number should patient refuse medication or otherwise begin to show signs of uncontrollable manic activity. Barring such untoward incidents, outpatient visits at regular intervals of six months are recommended. Patient discharged.

FILE VOIDED.

David

Beloved

Pari's Last Notebook

Dusk in Taormina at the end of the War. William is gone! I sing to **David**.

No one else calls him by this name. He is Lorenzo to Frieda and Bert to his mother, but I think David suits him best. I have been reading all about him. A rebuff—Heinemann's rejection of *Sons and Lovers*, for example, in the difficult year before he married Frieda—and David is just as foul-tongued as William's London jade. *Curse the blasted, jelly-boned swines, the slimy, the belly-wriggling invertebrates, the miserable sodding rutters, the flaming sods, the sniveling, dribbling, dithering, palsied, pulse-less lot that make up England today!* And down comes a giant, destroyed by David's furious slingshot! But others are 'liberated and enamoured'. David (Hebrew, *beloved*), eternally embroiled in conflict, eternally in love, how can his first name not suit him best?

David, beloved, to whom I gave a *Pessimist* beer-mug in a Tempke convent long ago, is the **third and last** of my poets, his drawn face that of Raphael's Jesus with a bloody wound in his side and nails piercing his feet. David is the hero of the final panel of the broken-hinged Madonna Triptych—but I do not have any idea yet why he was part of that pile of books that Sister Lydia directed me to in the faraway convent library. Why *him?* If ***ATTIDUTE IS EVERYTHING IN LIFE*** as the old Heineken poster said, then maybe it was just his sheer boldness that put him in Sylvia and William's company. Or maybe it was Chance that connected him to me. The simple truth was that I had no choice. Attitude or Chance or Destiny, I had to follow the path of David's poetry just I did with William so that Sylvia's question could be answered. *Or Afi would die . . .*

These days, I am out of hospital and living with my aunt, with only 'occasional supervision' by the health workers—which leaves me with plenty of time for my investigations. Also, I have learnt an important lesson from my experience at the hospital. *I have to keep my secrets to myself.* So I do not breathe a word to my classmates at Homerton or to my aunt about my brand-new assignment with David. I do not tell them that I have discovered the truth about my mother's suicide or that I am an angel (though if they knew Bengali, they would have realized it from my name!). Addenbrooke's has taught me that as long as I behave 'normal', the doctors and the nurses would be satisfied. They'd take the straps off and I could talk to whoever I pleased.

As long as my lips did not move and my hands remained still, as long as I didn't run from the nurses even when I could see they were trailing long mouse tails or turkey tufts behind them, I was safe. So I would lie there and practice and practice the Afi-art of *living in my head and being dead in my body*. In my last three months in the hospital, I became quite an expert at this. I saw that it was the same as reading a book, after all. If a person could imagine scenes from a story in her head without moving all around with the characters in the story, why should I become agitated when Sylvia or William or David came to me? This was the vital lesson I learnt in the hospital.

I told the doctors on the freedom panel that I still heard voices but I knew they weren't 'real' (which was a lie) and that I would continue to take my medication because it helped me to stay calm (which was the truth). They were impressed by this and let me free. They did not ask about my wings and I did not tell them . . .

My wings were growing out again.

When I was first admitted to Addenbrooke's, my wings were bent out of shape, and although I could not see them because I needed two mirrors to do so and there was only one small mirror over the bathroom sink, I knew they were becoming brittle and losing their colour. In hospital, my wings hurt most of the time and when I tried to sing, all I could manage was a croak, but now my wings were beginning to glisten again and other good things were happening.

I had started to go to Homerton College because I wanted to be an English teacher when I went back to Tempke and my grades were good. Also, my aunt and I had declared a kind of truce. I would eat in the college canteen and buy groceries from the supermarket so I could cook at home. This meant that I did not have to eat my aunt's food just in case my father ordered her to poison me without notice.

Because I had never shopped for kitchen things in Tempke—the servants always did that—shopping was really hard for me at first. The English supermarket was huge and there were packed chicken-hearts and goose-livers and frozen bloody mutton chops lining the shelves and I wanted to scream when I saw the cling-film-wrapped packets of meat with blood congealing in the corners of their bone-white Styrofoam bases but I learnt to control myself by digging my nails *hard* into the palms of my hands and pressing the poky edge of the steel-grocery basket into my stomach, which definitely helped.

Afterwards, I discovered the frugal shelves of dal and rice and pasta in the middle shelves of the big Sainsbury's Central on Sidney Street. They also had plastic-packed Indian meals like 'Dal Tarka' and 'Biryani' which you could just put in the microwave for five or ten minutes. This also helped a lot. I stopped looking so often over my shoulder when I shopped as if I was a shoplifter waiting to be caught. Bit by bit, I became *freer* and I was really happy my aunt had this new microwave because I was *not* going to use her Baby Belling oven whatever happened, first because it had this scary name which reminded me of the *children* cooked by the witch in Hansel and Gretel and second—this was the important reason—because Sylvia had stuck her head in a gas-oven and killed herself. So there was no question of my using an oven, but I used the microwave a lot. It was fast and clean and looked more like a TV than an oven.

Slowly, I began to feel confident. Some days, I even went to the Saturday market in the middle of the city where they sold fresh vegetables and false jewels side by side and called me Ducky. But when I went to the market, I did my shopping as fast as I could and fled because I wasn't sure whether they *really* thought I was a duck and if I gave them time they would catch me and cook me. English people *ate* ducks. I knew that.

Walking down from the market to Sidney Street where Sainsbury Central was also quite tricky. I had to keep a lookout all the time because this street was a *two-faced juju street.* On one side were ordinary bookshops and colleges, and though it was funny to think that *Sylvia* used to walk down the same pavements and see maybe the same things, I knew they were just ordinary places, but the *other* side, just before you came to Sainsbury's, were some *new shops.*

One of these shops was called 'Office Angels', just to tempt people, I suppose. This shop sold nice paper and staplers and scissors and different-shaped boxes. You could have lots of fun in this shop but I knew at once from its name that it was not a real shop but a *trap*—a trap for people. If I looked in that direction, I could get caught. Maybe Summa would appear with her great wings flapping and ask me why I was wasting my time at the supermarket. So I had to rush past this place but as soon as I crossed it, there was *another* dangerous shop that had to be avoided. Now you can see what I mean. This shop was called 'Flight Centre' and it had a big shining statue of a man wearing a pilot's uniform and a silly smile just like Afi. There he was, shameless as ever, inviting me to come into his shop and take off with him to enchanted destinations like *Kingstown £345! Hanover £125! Bali Bargain Holiday £215 inclusive!* But I had to push away this misleading dream because I was sure I could not look in Afi's direction either—not yet anyway. I knew I still had to be tested, so all I could do was hold my breath and keep my eyes down and resist his blandishments, just as I had done when we played L-O-N-D-O-N in the garden. Resisting the snares of Sidney Street and returning hurriedly each evening to cook for my aunt—I *knew* that was the only safe alternative.

The trick was to walk eyes-down every single week *without looking* and *without bumping,* to pass the confident mallard ducks with green-blue stripes on their wings like soldiers who would hog the strutting path and then pass the sleek fearless swans ever ready to fly straight out of the water and right *at* you across the thistledown fields and then the crowds of giggling tourists. It was a challenge, but I had to manage until I was finally ready to take off on my own and go back to Tempke!

Tempke was the goal, but cooking at home for my aunt and me was just like the shopping in the beginning. It was hard. I had hung around in the kitchen in Tempke but I hadn't really cooked at home because my father was rich and the Thakur did that, so for the first few weeks I made a lot of mistakes but in the end I did learn to cook from the big recipe books my aunt had but that she never used. Madhur Jaffrey and Katie Stewart, I spilled *haldi* and vinegar on them, I wept onion tears on their chests but I learnt. And I learnt to heat up all the readymade stuff in the microwave, which I liked much better because it was also like magic almost!

Instant food, no one in Tempke could even *imagine* instant food, and by the way, my instant cooking suited my aunt well because she came home very, very tired from work, poor thing. I think she worked in the British Telecom telephone company because all her friends were from there. I noticed that she spent many hours talking on the phone but I never listened because the conversations sounded boring. Anyway, I didn't *like* phones but I was beginning to like my aunt . . .

My aunt was severe-looking with sallow skin and heavy straight dark hair which she wore in a plait down her back just like a little girl from Tempke even though she was *old,* maybe forty. One thing I really liked about her was her smile. It reminded me of my mother's. My aunt had white, even teeth that made her look beautiful when she smiled and when I heard her laughter on the phone, it cheered me up somehow. I *still* didn't trust her because she was my false father's real sister but I decided to live with her and be well-behaved—an 'Angel in the House'—until I finished my degree at Homerton so that I could go home to Tempke at last and be independent and revenge myself on Dr M and my father. *They* were my real enemies, not my poor, enslaved aunt. I saw that now.

The final good thing that happened after I was let out of hospital was that I began to read **David's poems** from the last of the books that I had carried with me all the way to England from the Convent Library. I have already told you this but even here my stay at the hospital influenced me . . .

I was far more circumspect with David than I had ever been in my affair with William. I took care to study him before I approached him and when at last I did so I took pains *not* to reveal my angel form but disguised myself as a *bat,* as I knew well how to do! This resulted in instant friction but also a very good poem. And so I learnt slowly, as with my cooking for my aunt and suffering many burns of the spirit in the process, how to exploit a man's love to wrench poetry from him. Since this was my mission, I did not finally grudge it. Nor did I grudge Sylvia's long disappearance because she had left me her immaculate voyeur's methods. Sylvia came to Cambridge because of the exactness of her *notes.* So this time, I began well-armed with a neat fact-sheet on David's life, just as Sylvia had taught me. I even managed to find a type-face on the computer at Homerton that would mimic the old font Sylvia used when she laid out William's poetic balance-sheet for me all those years ago . . .

But I know what you're thinking, Afi. You're lying there thinking that a story is a *flight of the imagination*; it is not a *history book.* Dates and facts and things of that sort have no place in a story. One thing I've learnt, though, not only from my days at the English hospital but from Havelock and John Keay and Jawharlal Nehru in the Tempke library—and even from my poets—is that dates and times really *matter.* They matter because without them, we live in immortal animal time, as David maintained a little bitterly—for *how could a mere miner's son afford that?* That is why some record of David's life cannot be avoided. It appears below just as I typed it, slyly interwined with the career of another now forgotten writer, **Dornford Yates** (no miner's son, he), born the exact same year as David, whose books formed the solid colonial wall behind which David and William and Sylvia once crouched in a convent. *Two, there are always two, it seems perfectly natural now . . .*

LAWRENCE'S LIFE

1885	0 years	Birth 9.11. Nottingham, England. Son of Arthur Lawrence, miner and Lydia Beardsall, school-teacher. Dornford Yates, minor novelist, real name Cecil William Mercer, born the same year in Kent, England. Father, solicitor
1901	15	Brother Ernest dies. Lawrence falls sick with near-fatal pneumonia **ARIEL'S ENTRY INTO STORY**
1902	17	Leaves school to work in Haywoods factory
1904	19	Passes King's Exam, First Class, First Division. Dornford Yates admitted to Oxford after studying at Harrow, where he gets a 'Third' three years later in 1907.
1905	20	Begins to write. Produces first poems, influenced by his first girlfriend, Jessie Chambers
1906	21	Gains Nottingham University College Teaching Certificate
1908-1911	23-26	Teaching Assistant in Croydon, London. Hates confronting 'so many pairs of eyes.' Affairs with Louie Burrows, Helen Corke. Engagement to Louie. First novel: *The White Peacock* (1911)
1912	27	Elopes with Frieda von Richthofen, German woman of noble ancestry and wife of Nottingham University Language Professor. She leaves behind **three young children**

1913	28	First book of poems. *Love poems and Others*. The novel *Sons and Lovers* published to great acclaim
1912-1919	27-34	Joins the literary set in London, makes friends with John Middleton Murray, Lady Ottoline Morrell, Katherine Mansfield; meets Aldous Huxley, Betrand Russell, members of the Bloomsbury Group, etc. Also wanders with Frieda all over Europe. Idyllic days in **Taormina**, where they live on and off from 1919 onwards
1914	29	Marries Frieda in London with 'neuralgia in my left eye and my heart in my boots'. **World War I** Dornford Yates joins WW I, embodying the 'barbarism' against which Lawrence protests. His first book, a collection of his short stories, appears in magazine form. He is to write thirty more books which are as 'gentlemanly' and different as anything could be from Lawrence's iconoclastic writings
1915	30	*The Rainbow* is published and banned. One thousand copies confiscated and burned by Magistrate's orders. Dornford Yates posted in Egypt and the Balkans
1917	32	Lawrence accused, with Frieda, of spying and expelled from Cornwall. Dornford Yates sent home from active army service on account of severe rheumatism

1918	33	Publication of Lawrence's *New Poems*. **End** of World War I
1922-26	37-41	Travels to the South Seas, Mexico, **Ceylon, Australia**, etc. Acquires Kiowa Ranch in New Mexico and lives there two years. Calls it 'the greatest experience from the outside world I have ever had.' Dornford Yates moves with American wife Bettina whom he later divorces, to Pau in France where they spend the next several years
1923	38	Lawrence publishes the poetry collection *Birds, Beasts & Flowers* and *Kangaroo*, a novel set in Australia, embodying his theory of the Superman
1928	43	*Lady Chatterley's Lover* printed privately in Florence and the famous obscenity trial begins.
1929	44	Paintings exhibited in London and confiscated. *Collected Poems* in two volumes and *Pansies* published, and the latter banned. Publication of the study *Psychoanalysis and the Unconscious*
1930	45	Dies peacefully in Vence, France from the lung infection that had plagued him since he was fifteen. Frieda is with him. She dedicates a memorial to him in Taos and dies there herself nearly twenty-six years later in 1956, survived by her third husband, Antonio Ravaglia. Dornford Yates lives on thirty years after David Herbert

Lawrence, moving to Umtali, Rhodesia in 1941, then still a colony, and finally breathing his last there in 1960. There is no record of the two writers ever crossing paths, but for the odd coincidence of a single collection of Lawrence's rebellious poetry being found hidden many years later behind a respectable row of twenty Dornford Yates novels in an obscure convent in Tempke, India. **End of dateline**

A truth about David that emerges from my boring fact-sheet: *he began his life as a writer publishing poems and he ended it publishing poems.* The novels came in between, punctuated always by the poetry—but always obscuring it. His poems are David untethered, a mountain goat pursuing his instincts alone and inward and his novels are David unleashed, a savage bull in the toreador's arena in full view of a mocking audience.

David detests that audience, its bourgeoisie consumerism, its stupidity, its capacity to turn him into a 'broken-backed snake'! In this, he is like William, avenging himself on his public through his bitter writing. Hell, for him, I discovered, was an English editor's office.

> *Applicant for post of literary critic: here are my credentials, Sir!*
>
> *Editor: Er—quite. But—er—biologically! Have you been fixed?—arranged—you understand what I mean?*

Applicant: I'm afraid I don't.

Editor (sternly): Have you been made safe for the great British Public? Has everything objectionable been removed from you?

Applicant: In what way, quite?

Editor: By surgical operation. Did your parents have you sterilized?

Applicant: I don't think so, Sir. I'm afraid not.

Editor: Don't trouble to call again. We have the welfare of the British Public at heart.

I realize I have lessons to learn from David even in this mockery, for I know now that I am an illicit child, biologically 'fixed', which gives me a private vendetta to attend to when I return to Tempke. David is not mad in the way Sylvia or William were supposed to be, the whole world agreeing on their asylum-worthiness even when they wrote the most lucid testaments in the world, but read a poem like 'Editorial Office' and it's obvious. David's normality is so high-pitched, his fury at his mental castration so brimming, that you cannot call him less demented. David, like William, wanted to 'change the system'. In the end, he said

In the end, we go insane.

It is the penalty of fear and meanness, being meaner than our natures are . . .

We must change the system, and make living free to all men, or we must see men die, and then die ourselves.

For my Homerton class, I read and reread David and dream of living with him and slowly it dawns on me. The deadly simplicity of David's novels is his peacock's dance. His autobiographical displays, so self-hurtful and proud, are his weapon, his love sword. David cannot be cool and secretive like Sylvia. He is like William! I place my light finger on one of his 'Pansies': *men and women should show tenderness towards one another and leave one another* ***alone!*** He had thundered these words once in a public brawl—and I think meant them.

❁

Today, I borrowed *Lady Chatterley's Lover* from the Homerton Library to try and understand the hate that David harboured against his times—and almost at once I found my answer, as if it was just waiting for me. I discovered that David wanted to call the novel *Tenderness* and I knew immediately that the word was the KEY to understanding David. The most important people in David's life were always women: his mother Lydia, his lover Jessie, his wife Frieda—and all he ever wanted from them was tenderness in love. *Lady Chatterley's Lover* has many passages like the one below copied out by me and *every one of them* is a commentary on love:

> He too had bared the front part of his body and she felt his naked flesh against her as he came into her. For a moment he was still inside her, turgid there and quivering. Then as he began to move, in the sudden helpless orgasm, there awoke in her new strange thrills rippling inside her. Rippling, rippling, rippling, like a flapping overlapping of soft flames,

> soft as feathers, running to points of brilliance, exquisite, exquisite and melting her all molten inside. But he drew away at last, and kissed her and covered her over, and began to cover himself. She lay looking up to the boughs of the tree, unable as yet to move. He stood and fastened up his breeches, looking round. All was dense and silent, save for the awed dog that lay with its paws against its nose. He sat down again on the brushwood and took Connie's hand in silence.

Two humans holding hands in a dense silent wood, an awed dog beside them—that was David's answer to Sylvia's question. *What's love anyway?* Catch him as Paul Morel in *Sons and Lovers* or as Oliver Mellors in *Lady Chatterley's Lover,* he remains constant in his views, Afi.

Afi, listen, I take your cold hand and tell you this, *this* is the main result of my Sylvia scholarship. *Nothing changes.* Nothing changed in David between these books, one written in 1913 nearly at the start of his writing career and the other privately printed in Florence in 1928, only two years before his death. To the last, David is his creation Mellors passionately declaring: *it's astonishing how Lesbian women are, consciously or unconsciously, it seems to me they're nearly all lesbian* and that he *could kill them* for this trait! Murderous, murderous David but this is the way he feels, truly. Afi, listen!

David was a great lover but his greatest horror was always what he called a *cold-hearted fucking.* In his nightmares, he saw himself besieged, *besieged* by ranks of silly hags and button-downed torturers and nurse-Standishes against whom he had to hold his heroines. Like Connie. Connie was his 'talisman', Afi, she was a Pari-angel David created who understood, who *really* understood what David's real life women Lydia and Frieda failed to, however much he loved them. *The core of his life was the right relationship with a woman.* David could, as he put it, *talk himself into Persepolis and Timbuctoo* with Connie, with Ursula and with Miriam, who were both his fictions and his reality. And that is why he had no need, no need at all, of other angels in his novels. But in his poems, especially his late animal poems, David entered a different universe where the human element disappears and chaos reigns.

> *Man cannot live in chaos. The animals can. To the animal, all is chaos, only there are a few recurring motions and aspects within the surge.*

Afi, you will not get this but I guess you could say that I, Pari, was to be that primitive surge in the blood of which David spoke. My mission was to explore with him an animal world beyond human tenderness, into which only *I* could lead him—where Lydia would not go, nor Frieda. William sought the Future but David's poetic enterprise was to celebrate *the immediate present ... where there is no perfection, no consummation, nothing finished!* And who will deny that this is a world animals and angels know best and that only poetry can explore?

Afi, wake up!

Dornford's Madonna

Added to Pari's Notebook

Until it found its way into the rubbish-heap piled under Afi's bed, **The Madonna Triptych** was propped up for ages against the wall of my room in the Convent, opposite the mirror big as Nauru. It *had* to be leaned up against the wall or it would fall flat on its face because the fact is that its hinges were a little loose and one of them broken—but it was still very beautiful. Gowri used to polish it from time to time and then it shone like my mother's jewelry.

After I got out of the hospital in England and went to study English with Miss Marsh in Homerton, I really wanted to tell her about the Madonna Triptych and David and Dornford because she was interested in literature and history and art. I knew she knew a lot about David and she has allowed me to do a term paper on him—but Dornford? Miss Marsh had not even heard about Dornford! I know this because I tried to tell her about him in Tuesday's class.

David and Dornford Yates were born in the same year just a month apart, I told her, and their first names began with 'D' and they were both English authors. These were superficial comparisons, Miss Marsh replied, smiling, even if there really was a writer called Dornford, which she doubted! 'Dornford' was a pseudonym, I said; his real name was Cecil William Mercer. Miss Marsh's smile grew broad like a full moon at this. Well, whoever he was and whatever cover he was hiding under, she said, I should forget this person and concentrate on David for my term paper because he was a great writer and this Dornford Yates certainly was not! I asked Miss Marsh if she had read any books at all by Yates. Of course not, she answered, he didn't sound like a real person. But then, finally, she did look him up and she had to admit I was right. Still, there was 'no comparison' between David and Dornford, she insisted. No one read Dornford Yates anymore and she hadn't even heard of him till I brought him up! Then how did she know that he was not a great writer, I asked her. She said there were things everyone knew and it was 'common knowledge'. But how could one have common knowledge about someone one hadn't even heard of? I didn't have the courage to say this to Miss Marsh of course and in my heart of hearts I also knew that she was right: Dornford was *not* a great writer but I could not 'forget him' as she advised because I remembered how bravely he had defended David and the others in the Convent Library long ago, his books like a great solid wall between them and the prying world. So in my head I tried and tried to find a link between David and Dornford and at last I found one—or even two. True, I did not tell Miss Marsh about my discoveries because she would laugh at me but I wrote them down in my Notebook.

The first link I made was very weak and I knew Miss Marsh would dismiss it right away: David and Dornford both loved America and they didn't think much of brown people. But so *what,* said Sylvia in my head at once, that was like saying that both she and Ginsberg loved Blake and didn't care much for Inuit writers (mostly because they didn't know any) or that the moon was similar to a scimitar, *similar scimitar moon smile scimitar scimitar.* Pari, that's plain silly! Then I told Sylvia that one of Dornford's first stories was called *Busy Bees* (1911) and Sylvia began to listen . . .

❁

My second link was better because it was directly about Dornford. Dornford knew about Sylvia's question. The clue was hidden inside one of his books called *Gale Warning* (1939), written when Sylvia was only seven years old and David had been dead for nine). In this book, a thriller (a genre David would never dream of reading or writing), the heroine is called Audrey (David would not have named any of his heroines 'Audrey' either)—but once, just once in the whole book, the hero slips up and calls her something else. Guess!

He calls her *Madonna,* God promise, and these are the exact words he says to her which I by hearted from page 157: *Madonna, of course you provide the love interest.*

Love interest! It was a Sign. So Dornford *knew* about the Madonna Triptych. He knew about Sylvia and William and David, though he had chosen to keep very silent about their secrets. Dornford was *noble* and now I needed to tell him about the other things hidden in its Design.

❁

The Triptych of Tempke, a description by Pari:

The panel in the middle was the biggest and it had Raphael's most famous painting (by the way, I found all this out later from William, but back in Tempke I had no idea at all who Raphael was. William knew a lot about Art, being an Engraver himself and he worshipped Raphael above all others. So you can entirely trust the information he gave me, beginning with the painting in the centre. Raphael, William told me, had painted this Madonna for the ceiling of the Sistine Chapel in Rome in 1513 or 1514).

The rest I could see for myself, even if the painting in my convent room was only a reproduction, a 'duplicate' like most things in Tempke—*like 'Dornford', a pseudonym*—but full of True Lessons, William said.

Raphael's Sistine Madonna is tall. She is dressed in blue and white with red petticoats and she's standing on a thick cloud carpet. She holds her baby Jesus effortlessly in one arm and seems ready to walk out of the painting any minute. You can guess this because the outline of her strong leg is clearly visible under her skirts, and though the Madonna's head is modestly covered like any housewife wearing a sari in Tempke, you *know* she is no ordinary married woman, no mere Parineeta. She's beautiful like my mother and she looks as if she might walk out of the frame completely or disappear behind the curtains anytime. What is most clear is that *she is her own mistress.*

Then there are the baby angels in the painting, leaning out of their heavenly alcove and totally ignoring all the drama-bazi going on above their heads. William told me that these angels were known as putti in Italian, which almost sounds like a Hindi word, and right away, I knew that the bold putti in Raphael's picture were actually *Mona and Afi* in disguise. The older one on the left was Afi, sporting small turkey wings and a finely disinterested expression. He has one hand propping up his chin, the other resting coolly on the parapet, while Mona beside him has her arms defiantly interlaced and glued to the wall. Didn't I *know* who they were, these tricksters? It's clear to me, Pari, that neither of them want any part in the 'Nativity Play' being staged for the Madonna's benefit on the earth below her cloud canopy. They're bored to distraction and *planning wickedness*. I can detect this because I have seen these exact expressions on Afi's and Mona's faces (like when we discussed guano deposits in Australo-Pacific Nauru, swinging off the roof long ago).

The *second* panel to the right is also by Raphael: *The Crucifixtion*, 1502-3, with Jesus on an ebony cross, his whole body bare and polished like ivory and a single nail neatly piercing his crossed feet and his outstretched hands delicately smudged with blood. But look closely at Jesus' face and you will notice at once that it is quite a bit like *David's*. There are angels in this painting, too, full-grown woman angels fluttering around their Saviour with their turkey-wings arched and their dancers' feet tiptoeing on tiny pieces of cirro-cumulus. And what by the way do you think these angels are holding up for David the Pessimist but the *Heineken beer mugs from Tempke Convent*? DHL, agonized by the sins of the world and feted with pitchers of wine by graceful lady angels inside Raphael's painting, just as he was in real life!

There David hangs, Raphael's sixteenth century valleys

stretching out behind him as they did years later in his own painting of coifed nuns crossing that same Tuscan field, their modest eyes averted from the naked male lying there basking in the sun. There was, William had explained to me, a Pattern in all this: a Heavenly Design, a Lesson. *Art sometimes anticipates our lives, as Chance connects them and the combination of the two we call Destiny.*

What connects the three parts of a Triptych? What joins Sylvia's story to William's and David's? In the case of the Madonna Triptych, as I finally discovered, guided by William's deep knowledge of Raphael, all three paintings were by the same man, Master Raphael, about the same man, Jesus—and Jesus, of course, was *Everyman.* He was Afi and William and David and Doctorji and Dornford and Havelock. He was my father and Sylvia's father and my father's khaini-chewing bodyguards.

In the end, I did come to realize these connections, even though the last panel had been completely pasted over with a glossy blue picture of Krishna. Once William had taught me how to take off the overlay with a wet towel overnight and gently pull off the paper and then finally to stick the Krishna-layer back again after we had investigated the painting below so no one would suspect it had been tampered with, it all became clear to me by stages. (Later, I managed to repay this kindness of William's by revealing to him a new method of Engraving about which I have told you already.) And once I'd laboriously peeled off Krishna and his gopis and put them aside to dry, I had the chance to look more closely at what I had uncovered and the reasons for the cover-up became clear . . .

The last—or rather the first, since it was on the left—of the Triptych paintings showed a 1509 ceiling fresco by Raphael of Adam and Eve in the Garden of Eden with the Serpent coiling around the Tree of Knowledge that rises up between them. In this painting, both Adam, muscular and tousle-haired, and Eve, fair and apple-breasted, are *stark naked.* The fig leaves they wear are not even *apologies* for fig-leaves.

Raphael's Garden of Eden is a tropical garden, its undergrowth lush and the creepers in the background extending menacing fronds just like a murderer's fingers and the whole scene quite a lot like the outer reaches of the Convent garden that it was Afi's job to tend. In this painting, Eve is fair-haired, it's true, but her face bears a distinct resemblance to Sister Lydia's and as for the Serpent, whom Raphael has painted with the green coiling body of a Snake and the face of a Woman, it is *unmistakably* Sylvia, auburn-haired and smiling beguilingly at Adam and Eve. So much delight in wickedness, such bare *seduction,* no wonder the nuns felt they had to paste it up, even if they did so with something as rough as a Calendar Picture of a Heathen God!

The Triptych paintings, clumsily joined together, their centre of gravity uncertain, could anyone believe their presence in my Convent room, opposite the mirror as big as Nauru, was not *Destiny,* I asked Sylvia. And she, for once, looked puzzled. The first panel, once uncovered, was so clearly hers, her serpentine body and Realist smile separating Adam and Eve forever. This was the love-garden Sylvia had sought all her life. *Stasis:* her recurrent dream of Paradise before the Fall, before Christ and before Time. In this Paradise, *God topples from the sky and hell's fires fade* and

Sylvia can at last safely shut her eyes without fear. She is alone at the birth of the world, without parents and without children, naked as an animal. In this first Paradise, there is no memory and no pain. *All the world has dropped dead,* but she—Sylvia—finds herself miraculously rejuvenated, her madness cured by perfect love . . .

Then there's the Madonna in the middle calmly holding her Baby Jesus firm while the putti plan their tricks below—and it's certain this panel belongs to William. This is the birthplace of his *Songs of Innocence and Experience,* his beloved cherubs and chimney-sweeps perfectly anticipated in Spiritualist language by Raphael his Master.

As for David, the last Pessimist panel has to be his, for was he not eternally thrown into agony like Isa Masih on the Cross, his gut pierced by an unhappiness so deep no one could salve it, not Frieda, nor Jessie Chambers, floating about him with soothing words and beer-mugs and wine-pitchers, nor his mother Lydia suffering and pleading below.

David and Dornford, Dornford and David—Madonna men . . .

Piano

Try as he might, Afi, David could never retain his calm when there was a woman in the vicinity, except for Lydia, of course. Sylvia may have insisted that she was the poet with the most massive Electra complex of her age but it was *David* who was Oedipus Rex, stricken with so much love for his mother, Lydia, that it consumed him alive. Lydia, David's high fine Madonna and his lost angel, was far more of a refined and ascetic nun than Sister Liddie of Tempke Convent with whom she shared her name but practically nothing else. His mother was David's first guardian and his first teacher of poetry, his still centre and the source of his perpetual restlessness, the perfect woman he knew he would never find again. From which it follows, Afi, that the times I was closest to David were also when I was closest to Lydia, being *her* . . .

It is on account of Lydia's profound influence on the poet David was to become that I found myself on that enchanted evening in Taormina, unaccountably singing to David as I had once sung to William—an experience he has recorded in a famous poem:

Softly, in the dusk, a woman is singing to me
Taking me down the vista of years, till I see

A child sitting under the piano, in the boom of the tingling strings
And pressing the small, poised feet of a mother who smiles as she sings . . .

The only woman with whom David felt really safe was his mother. He never trusted the 'insidious mastery' that any other woman might exert over him—for it was bound, as he says, to betray him. Even Frieda, who was 'the only woman in the world' for him could hardly be accused of unflinching faithfulness.

David had a distinct image in his mind when he wrote that poem about Lydia. It was of the house to which his parents had moved in 1891—the house in Walker Street, with the most glorious view of the valley from its great bay-window in the sitting room. He was just six at the time but his memory of the freedom and beauty he glimpsed through that window never left him, nor the sense of womb-like security and closeness he felt towards Lydia, nestling under her skirts in a position that his senior contemporary Sigmund Freud would surely have noted. I know about all this because Miss Marsh made us read a lot for our essays, so I knew that David did not only write novels and poems. He had published books with titles like *Psychoanalysis and the Unconscious* and *The Fantasia of the Unconscious* in the successive years 1921 and 1922, so David knew about slips of the tongue, etc. I am not a 'literary critic', but many of them say this. The lasting source for David's poetry could have been 'the inviolate presence of natural beauty and its violent destruction by quarrying', the ever-present threat to nature from man and the parallel threat to Lydia—also from man and from one man in particular, *his father.*

David never forgave Arthur as I will never forgive my father and he could never forget Lydia as I will never forget my mother. Brave, beautiful Lydia, but most of all—unfortunate Lydia. David recalled her distraught on so many occasions that he had to wait nearly another couple of decades before he could capture that pure, liquid picture of her in his poem, although he *never* admitted that it was a poem about Lydia—or, more accurately, *for* her.

'Piano' is one of the few serious poems David wrote which actually rhymes. Usually, he was impatient with rhyme or any hint of deliberate craftsmanship even in his poetry, let alone his prose. He would have nothing to do with covering up his feelings in a decent veil of poesy, not him, not rebellious David, Lucifer incarnate! But this poem is different. It is as if Lydia's piano is playing in his ears again, as if he has regained in it the redeeming, nursery-rhyme innocence of childhood just before the shocks at school and in life took over.

But the truth is that it took the even more shocking news of Ernest's death to wring this poem to his mama out of David. He was almost twenty-two by then—about the same age as Ernest when he died. And the bleeding wound of his brother's death was still fresh upon the family . . .

Robert and Ernest, dead brothers of live poets, what did they contribute to the sadness and self-abomination in William's and David's poetry? That was the sort of question Miss Marsh asked in English class and I remembered Sylvia in my head. *There are two, there are always two.* Except that in the case of David and his brother Ernest, as I slowly found out, one was so much dearer to the mother that the hurt to the one who lived almost killed him.

What follows is the story of Lydia and her sons, Ernest and David.

You *must not* neglect Lydia, please.

Pari's Notebook, London, 1901

My first glimpse of Lydia was of her praying.

She was at chapel after her return from London, having failed to save Ernest. Ernest, her favourite son, her darling, destined to rescue the entire Lawrence family from obscurity and humiliation, was dead—and I could literally *see* Lydia's guilt eating into her with the unforgiving bitterness of biblical wormwood. I was resting high above her on my caryatid perch in the small old church which anticipated *exactly* those remote museum caryatids, *pillars of white bronze, pale-face authority,* whom her other son David was to castigate so roundly in a poem not yet conceived and I saw this sad woman with a huge, gaping smoke-filled hole in her heart. I saw the grief rising unstoppably from within her, choking the breath out of her. She reminded me of Meena Kumari from the Tempke cinema hall, of William when he was down.

Lydia so truly did not want to live that I—an angel—was tempted to do at that moment what all angels are powered to do but which is unthinkable. I almost descended to let my wing brush her soul so that she could die *that instant.* But David, he was incomparably braver than I. I did not have the courage to put Lydia out that day but just a few years later, David was less of a coward. He was willing to risk eternal hellfire to help his mother out of her rigid, whimpering pain as she lay dying of cancer in the year 1910 and he did not give a toss about conventional morality when he acted. Afi was there too at that moment, supervising the 'exit' and he can tell you, breath by breath, of David's terrifying courage when it came to his mother. Or, you can read David's own description of Paul Morel at his mother's bedside in *Sons and Lovers* but what you cannot doubt is David's devotion. And that is why, despite his unreasoning rage and his cruelty and debilitating shyness, I choose to sing to David, taking him, as he puts it, down 'the vista of the years' back to his mother on the black day that Ernest died.

David's passion for his mother and for Frieda, for all his women, is blinding. Like Afi's tears, it is 'a raw phenomenon of nature' which is why, I suppose, Afi was posted there that day. A dead brother, beloved and mourned, can be a tremendous poetic catalyst, the critics have written, as Robert was to William once. This Afi knows as well as I do, and his angel tears stain the cold, damp chapel stone, falling on Lydia, putting out the church candles one by one and gathering in small, miserable puddles around the many tragedies in her life—small ones arising out of her soulless drudgery in a colliery town, and large ones such as—well, her other son, George! But Lydia's mourning Madonna mind is so full of preoccupations that she just fails to notice the dark unseasonal rain, her head hanging low and depressed over her unopened Bible, her eyes blinded.

She is still thinking of George, her eldest, forever getting into scrapes, running away to join the army, knocking up poor Ada Wilson and then having to marry her. Feckless George, so like her husband, Arthur. She, Lydia Beardsall, from a family of superior stock, had married Arthur Lawrence out of her own free will and conscience, setting herself against all her genteel relations—because she loved him. *Loved* him. How could she have known that Arthur would drink her hopes away, that he would prefer the coarse company of his mates to dainty evenings with her and the children? It was in his *blood,* he was bred rough—that was all she could conclude.

Her mind fell back upon a familiar litany of grievances. If we were able to look into Lydia's personal hymnbook, I suppose we could say it contained two sorts of constant entreaty. She deeply, *deeply,* willed the wrath of God down on the manifold ways in which every member of Arthur's family appeared bent on mortifying her—and she called upon Him to save her children. Walter! How could she bear the thought of him? Committed for trial at the Derby assizes and the story all over the papers! That brother of Arthur's had no more sense than to murder his own son by throwing carving steel at him in a brawl. For Lydia, to whom nothing in the world meant more than her children, Walter's behaviour was incomprehensible. *Brute!* She had married into a family of brutes.

Those were days when David would watch her day after day red-eyed at the family table, she able to eat nothing and he unable to do anything and his heart and his mind felt sick to bursting. He did so badly at school then that there seemed no justification for him to remain there. The best he could do was to be like Ernest—Ernest, the only one among them who could still make Lydia's eyes light up . . .

And so David left school at sixteen, abandoning his still half-articulated but devastatingly intense desire for another kind of life, the bookish life that Lydia herself had encouraged him to aspire to as a child—all for the sake of his mother. What did it mean, this soul-killing job that he took at the surgical goods factory in Haywoods? *It meant that at sixteen, David was prepared to die for Lydia*—but she, like David himself, had a knack sometimes of not seeing the obvious even if it loomed large and threatening as a behemoth in her face . . .

Lydia saw only Ernest, who had landed himself a job for 120 pounds a week in a London firm, more than her husband earned in a single month! Ernest had recently come home on holiday and what a difference it made to his mum. She baked him cakes each day and hung upon his every word. He held her mesmerized with his dashing tales of London society and his high-stepping fiancée, Louisa, who called herself 'Gypsy' Dennis. Now there was a spirited gal for you, said Ernest, and all Lydia could do was nod, high spots of colour in her cheeks and her heart aglow. The intensity of her listening at the time blocked the other two children out completely—David slouching in his bitter corner and little Emily who finally wandered out into the garden after an illusory butterfly, bored with so many facts that were totally out of her ken.

Who knew then that within that October, returning from the Nottinghamshire Wakes, brimming with confidence and bonhomie, Ernest would be dead?

I knew but I was bound and trussed by ropes of air, garroted by light. If I had shown Lydia the future that day she might have thrown herself on the tracks at Nottingham station. As it was, bound by no ropes but those of a heart-stilling anxiety, I witnessed her rush like a madwoman to London the moment she got his landlady's telegram, the pins in her hair half-fixed, her flimsy green shirt under her coat quite askew. Indeed all her existence was somewhat misaligned at the time and how little she guessed it. Lydia was not prepared. No, she wasn't at all prepared . . .

In London, she lost her way again. It took her ages to find the poky South London flat that was Ernest's London abode. She had imagined a grander space, more *airy* perhaps, but what of it, it didn't *matter* any more. What mattered was Mrs Parks standing there, waiting at the door and dearie-ing her up to Ernest immediately.

Lydia's memory of those first moments is sharply auditory—Mrs Park's series of clucking 'Dearies' and the quick, heavy thump of their boots in unison, negotiating an endless series of stairs. Then, as the landlady lets her into Ernest's room, her world turns at once visual and silent . . .

There lay Ernest, a stiff slab, like Afi, radiating heat beneath his white sheet, an iron ingot fresh from the blast-furnace—and the doctor beside him, cold as a bar of stainless steel and refusing to hold out hope, any hope at all. Ernest had contracted secondary blood poisoning from his erysipelas infection and there was nothing he could do—*nothing.* At which moment another strange thing happened . . .

Everything in Lydia's world *simply lost colour,* as if someone had poured an acid bleach over it. I, Pari, was there and I saw this. The doctor, still talking to the landlady as he packed his bag suddenly turned into an elongated black silhouette in Lydia's eyes. There he stood, twirling his embarrassed hat in the narrow doorway and politely waiting and waiting to say goodbye to Lydia. He would have to wait forever, though, if that was his intention—because Lydia did not look in his direction again. Never again.

She paid no attention to the landlady either, but that was all right because kind Mrs Parks was no longer herself. She had metamorphosed into a squat shadow barely visible against the dark walls. And Louisa? Louisa 'Gypsy' Dennis hovering like a winged moth over them both—Ernest and Lydia—was redundant as well. What could she do for Lydia, what could she do for Ernest? Nothing, nothing, *nothing*.

Lydia turned her face to the wall and Ernest died without recovering consciousness the next day.

And Lydia returned to Nottingham because she had to. She could not tramp the streets of London all day. She had a home. She had other children. But what did she find? She found she *could not bear* to look at them. They might as well have been grey wool puppets, lying neglected on some half-forgotten shelf. *She* did not care. David, always sensitive to Lydia's moods, began to spend longer and longer hours at the factory. Once again, he was destroying himself for her and once again she *did not see him*. Perversely, he became more and more careless and restless, not protecting himself from the chill at nights when he returned to his gloomy home and finding it impossible to sleep. And all through that time, Lydia never *once* waited up for him, not one single night. He hoped for a single look, a single expression of interest but it never came.

In a way, it was as if Lydia *wanted* him to die.

Watching over them, I felt sorrier for David than for

Lydia. At least she knew why she was grieving but David was shut out like a dog outside a door. *He* could not see the fury of bitterness and rage and sheer anguish flooding her mind like water gushing into a pit-shaft and drowning the life within. All he saw was a mother who did not care whether he lived or not. By Christmas, he had willed himself to die like Ernest and contracted double pneumonia. Still, Lydia paid not the slightest heed, wandering about in her Hades underworld of sorrow, quite oblivious to David's condition.

Until one day, almost by accident, Dr Evans uttered his magic formula. It was the simplest sentence in the world, but it opened the doors of Lydia's prison and enabled her to exit into daylight again. **He may die, Missus**, Dr Evans said to Lydia. He said it in black and white, not mincing words—and, miracle of miracles, Lydia heard him! Well, not him perhaps, but that single tolling word, 'die'. It brought her back to earth—and to David.

Lydia came back to David that terrible Christmas of 1904. She nursed him devotedly all through the unforgiving winter. She gazed into his eyes, exactly as she had into Ernest's. He became her beacon, her torch-bearer, leading her, Demeter, his mother, ever up and up *the darker and darker stairs* and in the process releasing her from the vision of those other ghastly London stairs, until she was redeemed at last from Pluto's dread grip, *the halls of Dis.* It was the best present he could have had, a glowing Bavarian gentian.

Later, decoding David's errant life, the critics I read all agreed:

> *The interval between taking the King's Scholarship Examination and going to college in September 1906*

proved to be perhaps the most significant period of Lawrence's life so far.

In the first place, in the spring of 1905, he started to write. It was, perhaps, the most natural outcome of the years he had spent reading and discussing literature; yet he began writing with a strong sense of the oddity of his ambition. 'What will the others say? That I'm a fool. A collier's son a poet!' he remarked, scathingly, to Jessie Chambers. It was poetry that he began with . . .

Yes, it was poetry that he began with and this was no ordinary collier's son. This was a son over whose brother's death an angel had watched and who had returned to his Madonna mother's arms from the unquiet dead . . .

Batty

Pari's Notebook, Italy, 1915

The first poem I instigated David to write was on a buttercup yellow morning in Florence, though I have to confess it was not a poem I *intended* him to write. All I was doing—quietly, by myself, without fuss—was attempting to observe his habitat before I took the risk of entering his life. One of the things I knew about him was that David's respect for animals, like William's, was total. I also knew he was as fearless in the face of Death and just as able to envision angels as William. In these respects, he could have been the son William never had—but David belonged as firmly to the twentieth century as William did to the eighteenth and that fact alone made him so different from William that I wasn't really sure how to approach him. Therefore, before I used up my once-in-a-lifetime chance to ask Summa's advice, I decided to just wait and *watch* for a bit, not disturbing David, just patiently practicing my bat-impersonation as I had once done in Broad Street with Voltaire, hanging upside-down in the classic Transylvanian style and peeping from behind the ancient, moth-eaten, poison-blue brocade drapes of David's high-ceilinged Florentine room.

What could be more innocent? So there I was, enjoying myself, acting batty without a care in the world when he suddenly strode in, upsetting all my plans. As I mentioned, I'd tried a bat-disguise with William (and I was a bat once with Ted too, you can check his poetry) but those occasions occurred under the conventional cover of darkness. Only with David did I lay my ambush not in menacing darkness but openly in the glowing Italian sunlight. Truth to tell, I half-expected him to fall apart at my ridiculous, anachronistic Vlad-impression when he made his impetuous entry into the room that day but as usual he did not act predictably. One of his bursts of intolerant fury overcame him instead. So aghast was this man who loved animals to find his privacy invaded in broad daylight that it was I who found *him* comical. This misadventure he recorded later in 'Man and Bat':

My room, a crash-box over that great stone rattle
The Via de' Bardi . . .
When I went into my room at mid-morning
Why? . . . a bird!
A bird
Flying round the room in insane circles
In insane circles!
. . . A bat!
A disgusting bat
At mid-morning! . . .
Out! Go out!

This was rich and so *very* David, rounding on me with words like 'insane' and 'disgusting' and summarily ordering me out of his life, without a thought for his own embattled state! There might have been a mite of truth in his accusation of insanity but who exactly did he think he was? Did he think he could be a Poet without Inspiration? I, Pari, was grown up now! I knew my responsibilities. Had I not emerged from the shadows, out of a faraway convent, to shock him out of his debilitating postwar malaise? And if I'd never appeared to him, would he have writtem poems at all? Novels maybe, but poems? But I suppose the truth would look different from David's point of view. If he'd had a taste for the occult which, unlike William or Ted, he emphatically did *not,* I think his phrase for me, for *any* interfering angel who appeared unsolicited in his poetry, would have been **accursed succubus** and he came close enough that morning in Florence.

Round and round and round
With a twitchy, nervous, intolerable flight,
And a neurasthenic lunge,
And an impure frenzy;
A bat, big as a swallow.
Out, out of my room!

Whose neurasthenia was it, I'd like to know! When Frieda and David finally married in that mad April of 1914, it was he who entered the pact, as he put it 'with neuralgia in my left eye and my heart in my boots.' And now I was the twitchy and nervous one, was I? Calling an angel 'impure' was bad enough, but to accuse her of neurosis and even to get her sex wrong, that was typical of the man, of men in general, not barring William. As Havelock scandalously insisted in his time, all humankind is similar in this. *Men and women have a bit of both sexes in them*—and who should know this truth better than an angel, whose *nature* it is to be ambiguously sexed—the exact opposite of David's 'sensual gods.'

Gods, strong male gods were David's obsession. Poseidons rising from the sea and peasants strong-armed in the field. I understood this early on, but—*who else was God?* Was love God, as it said on Jesus' red sparkly heart in Tempke convent? Was this the answer to Sylvia's question, after all and could I go home now because it was answered? No, of course it wasn't that simple. This much was clear from David's paintings—which was another thing he turned out to have in common with William. Like William, David painted so that his soul could speak and like William, his canvases got him into loads of trouble.

Sub-meditation: One of my favourite paintings by David, because it so closely reveals his nature, is of a line of demure Italian nuns, eyes downcast, walking their way home to their convent right past a young man lying quite starkers and oblivious in a sunny Tuscan field with his penis pointing heavenwards like a beacon. What is this image trying to tell us? *I* think it tells us of David's confused sexuality (Miss Marsh would like this answer, she would call it 'insightful'). What I see in the painting: somewhere there, in the infinite, invisible open space between the naked, muscular peasant and the over-clothed nuns, stands a bisexual angel. From David, Afi, I learned about sex, just by *observing* him, nothing else. Angels always came second to gods and animals in his hierarchy because he thought them sexless. I knew this but I also knew that David was stuck with me, Pari. He talked of sensing gods everywhere but it's *me* that he saw.

> *THE GODS! THE GODS!*
>
> *People were bathing and posturing themselves on the beach and all was dreary, great robot limbs, robot breasts robot voices, robot even the gay umbrellas*
>
> *But a woman, shy and alone, was washing herself under a tap and the glimmer of the presence of the gods was like lilies and like water-lilies . . .*

But today, I was no coy water-lily of a woman posing for my beloved's delectation because the Florentine bat-war had become a war that David had to win! The funny thing is, David was a pacifist and the First World War was total anathema to him. *The war is just hell for me. I don't see why I should be so disturbed—but I am*; and another time, he'd called it, Christ-like: *the spear through the side of all sorrows and hopes.* So there was no doubt about David's opposition to war and yet, some battles are so deeply territorial that *all* men must win them and at such times, neither William nor David had much hesitation in turning Raphael's gentle Christ into a sword-wielding fanatic. The war between David and myself (impure symbol, Antichrist!), neither quite male nor female, neither entirely beast nor angel, was such a Holy War. It *had* to be won.

I, bat-winged, turkey-haunted Pari from Tempke in middle of nowhere, had entered David's innermost sanctuary, the room where he wrote, his temple, where even Frieda was a visitor and he was determined to throw me out for the sake of his 'sacred inward peace'. It was as simple as that.

My meditation's done, but David's still choppily at war.

The venetian shutters I push wide
To the free, calm upper air;
Loop back the curtains . . .
Now out, out from my room!
So to drive him out, flicking with my white handkerchief: ***Go!***

Oh, so now we are to have a truce of *his* choosing. A white flag for peace! I choose to ignore it—completely.

But he will not.
Round and round and round
In an impure haste,
Fumbling, a beast in air,
And stumbling, lunging and touching the walls, the bell-wires
About my room!

Naturally, the last thing I'd do now was go. I swooped down at him instead, breaking all our accords. My usual pattern with David, as with my aunt, was based on a series of truces. At dusk, I tempted him and during the day I teased him, sniper warfare. And evenings and nights, I tended to abandon him because this was a man who, for all his electric attraction to women, needed large expanses of isolation. That was the general nature of my pact with him. But sometimes, things did not quite work out as His Holiness desired. On the morning of the bat, for instance, I reflected something of his own stubbornness and insisted on circling endlessly round his room and round and round and *round* in his brain, his neurasthenic, unsettled brain, until his nerves came close to breaking point. This was war after all, for *both* of us.

Always refusing to go out into the air
Above that crash-gulf of the Via de' Bardi,
Yet blind with frenzy, with cluttered fear.

I was enjoying myself for now it was David who was 'blind with frenzy, with cluttered fear'! *He* was the bat. If only he could see himself lumbering around the room while I drove him to the brink of expectation and then withdrew. It was as good as sex and *far* more unusual. I told you, Afi, I learnt about sex from David just by *observing* him.

At last he swerved into the window bay,
But blew back, as if an incoming wind blew him in again.
A strong inrushing wind.
And round and round and round!
Blundering more insane, and leaping, in throbs, to clutch at a corner,
At a wire, at a bell-rope:
On and on, watched relentless by me, round and round in my room,
Round and round and dithering with tiredness and haste and increasing delirium
Flicker-splashing round my room.

This competitive thrashing and whirling went on for a bit. We were caught, as Miss Marsh said in class, in exactly that chaos of the 'urgent, immediate Now' which David had so often celebrated, the unthinking thrill of the chase. To live in an eternal present, David believed, was the unique gift of animals. Humans had no such luck! He says it in this very poem: *the human soul is fated to wide-eyed responsibility in life.* But in his role of poet and lover, David had a contrary ambition. He wanted to get as close as possible to his intuitive, animal self, to shake off the petty confines of human morality, to be *free*!

That was the theory, at any rate. Being locked in battle with a maddened, fearful animal was another matter, though. David's hominid prejudices got in the way. He was bewildered by my antics, not exhilarated.

Something seemed to blow him back from the window
Every time he swerved at it;
Back on a strange parabola, then round, round, dizzy in my room.
He could not go out

No, he was wrong. I *would* not go out. I *could*, but I *would* not. David, of course, had his own explanation:

I also realized . . .
It was the light of day which he could not enter,
Any more than I could enter the white-hot door of a blast-furnace.
He could not plunge into the daylight that streamed at the window.
It was asking too much of his nature.
So I switched on the electric light, thinking: Now
The outside will seem brown . . .

Electricity: banisher of demons to the outer darkness! This one single invention, it is my angelic conjecture, made the principal difference between William and Catherine's meek submission to 'visions' in the eighteenth century gloom of candlelight and David's nineteenth century combatant energy. David was born only sixty years after William's death—a paltry half-century and a decade—but in the interim came electricity, steam engines, aviation and the Birth of Technological Man. For all his William-like hatred of industrial encroachment, it came down to this. David was a true modern in his everyday dependence on electricity—which makes me doubt if he could ever have survived in a place like our Tempke where there were power cuts for *ten hours* at a time. William could have, but not David. And he, only the second collier's son ever to go to university, was smart enough to recognize both this affinity and difference that he had with William in an explicit poem:

The dark, satanic mills of Blake
How much darker and more satanic are they now! . . .
And now the iron has entered the soul
and the machine has entangled the brain, and got it fast,
and steel has entered the loins of man, electricity has exploded the heart

Whether this cry from David's explosive heart had anything to do with me and the fragile continuities I sought between my poets, you will perhaps glean in the end, but of the *facts* there is no doubt. In the last resort, electricity was for David a weapon against nature, a basic tool of modern warfare; but then again, maybe the ancient Chiroptera of Italy were behind the times in this, more denizens of William's time than David's. Also, this particular mimic-bat he was tangling with was *me* and I had no intention of being zapped by a light switch, as David discovered that morning:

But no.
The outside did not seem brown.
And he did not mind the yellow electric light.

In fact, I *liked* snuggling into the soft aureole of the beam, its soothing corona. Reining in my frantic chirping, I began to wilt into sleep:

> *Silent!*
> *He was having a silent rest . . .*
> *Flying slower,*
> *Seeming to stumble, to fall in air.*
> *Blind-weary.*
> *Yet never able to pass the whiteness of light into freedom . . .*

The whiteness of light, of moonlight—well, you could say I was a bit of a connoisseur there. I, Pari, had *already* passed into freedom. I was an angel. If I stumbled and fell in air, it was only because I was exasperated with David, his determination *not* to look me in the eye at any cost.

It was an old failing of his. In his books, David was willing to spit in the eye of reality any time. Those recurrent accusations of obscenity he found a nuisance, never an embarrassment, but give him actual people in an ordinary room and he was stricken. Facing his class of recalcitrant school children in Croydon, Havelock's happenstance birthplace, he could only wail helplessly. *How can I meet the challenge of so many eyes?* Once, he even read at Harold Monro's Poetry Bookshop in London, with his *back turned to the audience.*

For some reason, the human gaze shamed David to the depths of his being. With animals, it was different. David usually had no problems in this area. He positively enjoyed mind-reading a snake or a mosquito, and so this instance with me can be labelled a bit uncommon. Maybe it was because I was not a hundred percent bat and David somehow sensed this. Well, if he would not confront me, I could *compel* him. I could just lie there, Afi-like, till he was *forced* to look.

Till he fell in a corner, palpitating, spent.
And there, a clot, he squatted and looked at me.
With sticking-out, bead-berry eyes, black,
And improper derisive ears,
And shut wings,
And brown, furry body.
Brown, nut-brown, fine fur!
But it might as well have been hair on a spider; thing
With long, black-paper ears.
So, a dilemma!

And so, and so, I stared David down in all my squatting ugliness. I faced him with a dilemma and my bead-black eyes. What would he do with me now—with my nut-brown, palpitating, fallen body, encased in its fine angel fur? He had to do *something* if he was to win, if a poem was finally to result out of this battle of wills . . .

Racism, 1922

I felt the tremulous revulsion running through David as he gazed down at my dark, flaccid form. He was ready to kill me—but something even worse, much, *much* more malicious than a death wish, also fluttered in the air between us.

It was David's incipient racism.

Hidden in this first encounter of ours was all his stark Conradian horror of the dark races, a knee-jerk fear that came to fruition years afterwards on his visit to faraway Ceylon. That disastrous day David's uncontrolled ranting spilled from his heart onto paper: *I don't like the silly dark people, or their swarming billions or their hideous little Buddha temples, like decked up pigsties, nor anything.* I thought I loved him and that an angel could forgive, *must* forgive, anything in her poet, but these sentiments of David's—I have to say that I, Pari, an Indian angel raised in the wilds of Tempke was unprepared for them. They literally sent me up in flames at the edge of the jungle!

I became a combustible angel then, burning and stinging David so bitterly that he turned unsteady on his feet and full of sickness. Some people thought it a tropical stomach bug he'd acquired—and maybe that was a contributing cause—but the roots of David's illness lay deeper. He was totally *disoriented* by Ceylon as he had almost never been in his life before, except during his mother Lydia's illness and death. That is why he wrote of his Ceylon encounter: *I'm not quite sure where I am: sort of look round for myself among all this different world.* David became as faceless as Afi was to me in Gabriel's Gazebo; he could not face our dark race just as he could not face the harsh, stark innocence of the children he taught at Croydon or the eyes of his expectant readers in a London bookshop.

That stir of distant alienation, an otherness so profound that it defeated his poet's soul and turned him into an instant Nazi, David felt it in Ceylon, writing shamelessly to his aristocratic friend Lady Cynthia Asquith that the natives were *in the living sense lower than we are.* Despite his contempt for the prim and proper English middle class, David, I have to report, came out an utter snob in that encounter. He lost the profoundest war of all on his Ceylonese travels. His own strutting primitivism confronted an even deeper racial primitivism within himself and lost—and *was* lost.

So put out was David by that series of events that he *never ever* said much about his trip to that island again—which was unusual for him because writing was his therapy and he put everything down on paper—well, *almost* everything, but some things do not get told.

That is why I, Pari of Tempke, Summa's serving minion, practically a no one, am here. I am an angel charged with revealing the dipping graph of self, that occasional but profound loss of humanity amongst poets. And now, in

Florence, facing my beady gaze, David anticipates something of that uncontrollable disorientation, a visceral disgust that against reason reduces humans to the level of animals and makes of animals 'impure' humans.

He squatted there like something unclean.
No, he must not squat, nor hang, obscene, in my room!
Yet nothing on earth will give him courage to pass the sweet fire of day.
What then?

Yes, what then? Your play, David.

Hit him and kill him and throw him away?
Nay,
I didn't create him.
Let the God that created him be responsible for his death . . .

David is such a mass of contradictions! When Lydia died, he showed how he was capable of an incandescent courage and a capacity for mercy-killing that would do an angel honour—and now he cannot bring himself to destroy a worthless bat!

I admit a God in every crevice,
But not bats in my room . . .

So he's cravenly ready to leave the little business of my death to Allah, to Krishna, to Christ, to Zeus, to Jehovah, to Buddha, to a Mayan Thunderbird, to all the world's zillion, creviced deities, who are all of course more than willing to oblige!

He fell again with a little thud
Near the curtain on the floor.
And there lay.

I could have pleased David by dying then—but I stayed the hand of those waiting gods. Little would be achieved by dying on him so soon . . .

Ah death, death
You are no solution!
Bats must be bats.
Only life has a way out.
And the human soul is fated to wide-eyed responsibility
In life.

Too right, David.

So I picked him up in a flannel jacket,
Well covered, lest he should bite me.
For I would have had to kill him if he'd bitten me, the impure one . . .

Yes, maybe he would have killed me had I bitten him, but then what would have been the point? To kill me *after* I'd bitten him—that would merely be a mean revenge, the kind of pettiness David hated. Then it would have been David who'd have blood on his hands. *He'd* be the impure one. I could not allow that, at least not yet—and so I lay still and limp as a Ceylonese banana skin in his all powerful, god-like hand.

And he hardly stirred in my hand, muffled up.
Hastily, I shook him out of the window.
And away he went!
Fear craven in his tail.
Great haste, and straight, almost bird straight above the Via de' Bardi

But just to set the record straight, I went of my own free will and not because of cowardly fear as David had it, and I went in great haste because I had another engagement—with Summa, as a matter of fact. Further, I flew straight, not because I was 'almost bird' but because I was an angel.

Yet in the dusk I returned one last time, as I always did with David.

And now, at evening, as he flickers over the river
Dipping with petty triumphant flight, and tittering over the sun's departure,
I believe he chirps, pipistrello, seeing me here on this terrace writing:
There he sits, the long loud one!
But I am greater than he . . .
I escaped him . . .

And this time, calmer, David sees himself as *I* see him, from my batty perspective—a demented sap pegged eternally to his table, filling a white void with endless, meaningless squiggles. He is able to put himself in my bewinged, up-side-down place, reversing our roles and giving *me* the last ironic, deluded words in his poem: *I am greater than he, I escaped him.* Despite his foolish arrogance and the racist sickness that sometimes invaded his gut, it is this quality of sudden epiphany, a true apprehension of otherness, that makes David an immortal poet and in the end ensures that, throughout his short life, neither he nor I, chasing each other 'blind-weary', to use David's own language, will ever quite manage to escape each other. Can *this* be love?

Tuesday: the day of my English class at Homerton. I'm walking down the tow-path to college and puzzling over a new poem of David's that I've found. It is his poem to 'clever women'—women like Sylvia or his own Frieda, never satisfied with simple definitions of love or anything else. David holds a low opinion of them. Clever women are fools when it comes to love, he insists, so I'm wondering now whether my sweet, round-faced Homerton teacher classifies as 'clever' or a 'fool', two of David's favourite words and neither complimentary. Miss Marsh is not canny like my Tempke nuns. She's earnest and English and so bent on being kind to all the bewildering hues in her multicultural class that she never bats an eyelid when I turn up dressed for her lessons in the bizarre combo of a sari and a moth-eaten, bat-beaver fur hat! My teacher may be clever but she misses the point completely when she just *assumes* that it is in this incongruous attire that I am, for some peculiar reason, most comfortable. Maybe she thinks in her clear, charitable mind that this is the manner in 'my culture' because I've noticed how regularly she reiterates her wondrous ideal of multicultural Britain to all us wild creatures snarling in the bright, comfortable cage of her bright, comfortable class. In *this* country, she keeps saying, with a slight but unmistakable emphasis on the 'this', anyone can dress as they like, eat as they like, inter-marry and always feel welcome. By law! She concludes triumphantly. So *blissfully* unaware is my dear English teacher of the uncontrollable bouts of racist fever to which her countrymen are periodically subject—and that I, Pari, have witnessed at very close quarters—that it sometimes makes me giggle to myself in a mad, silly fashion *right in front of her*. But my sweet teacher politely pretends to be blind as well as deaf on these occasions. So what would David think of Miss Marsh's capacity for love?

My poor teacher! She is so much nicer than David, who would *die,* I think, rather than agree with the soft-sop she produces in class, that I feel much, much sorrier for her than for him. He will write himself out of cultural disaster because of his capacity for brute epiphany but can *she*? What will she make of David's hatred of 'clever women' and dark Orientals in one and the same breath? She who is in this class to instruct me in the literature of 'her' country, to tell me about William Blake and Sylvia Plath and David Herbert Lawrence, does she have any idea at all how *intimately* I know them? That I am a lately escaped madwoman who has come to her country for therapy and that I commune with these English poets on a daily basis? If I told her I dress like a joker in an ancient fur-hat and sari because this is my idea of expiation for the sins committed against my mother, just as it once was William's crazy route to salvation, how would she react?

Would she even understand a tenth of what I was trying to tell her, would she read David's poetry and gasp in sudden shock how *my English books had managed to* ***blind me into angelhood***? For this is what David wrote in his address to clever women, clear as Raphael's rays of golden Italian sunlight.

Close your eyes, my love, let me make you ***blind!***

Miss Marsh, Miss Marsh, David knew about blindness all right, insisting in poem after poem that the only cure for it was not 'cleverness' but love. Love was the radar that could look beneath surfaces; love was the instrument to dismantle the schoolbooks and unpack the bourgeoisie library of English Literature that David hated with all his furious heart. So *I* was beginning to see why David was important in the larger scheme of things, why his poems might hold some part of the answer to Sylvia's question, but I don't know if my teacher remotely understood what David meant when he declared:

They have taught you to see
Only problems writ on the face of things,
And algebra in the eyes of desirous men,
And God like geometry
Tangling his circles to baffle you and me.

I would kiss you over thy eyes till I kissed you blind;
If I could—if anyone could!
Then perhaps in the dark you'd get what you want to find:
The solution that ever is much too deep for the mind;
Dissolved in blood . . .
That I am the hart, and you are the gentle hind.

Miss Marsh was gentle as a hind, no doubt of that—but I think she'd 'go for a six' as we say in my cricket-smitten country if she had to unpack the secret of David's racism, the complex hatreds that lay beneath the surface of his vigorous and manly defense of free love. Nor would she ever quite comprehend that I, we—*all* of us motley crew of Tanzanians, Nigerians, Sri Lankans, Pakistanis, Swedes, Italians, etc. assembled in her Cambridge class had minds just as complicated as David's. We did not belong neatly to Asia and Africa and Europe, as she imagined in her unsoured ignorance. We belonged as much to her tiny insular country as *she* did and we belonged because we have *read* ourselves into her country. We had witnessed David in the full glory of his Superman racism and we'd forgiven him because we loved him, loved his *writing*. That was why we sat there humbly taking notes in her class on 'multicultural England' a subject about which the lowliest of us could tell her a thing or two, because *we were a populace in love*. We were in love with the forbidden language, the literature of her country, for reasons of history, for reasons of a *violent* history—and although I *sound* demented when I proclaim these things in my perfect Sunday School voice borrowed straight from Father Sinha, impotent orator of Tempke, I'm really at my sanest! I, Pari of Tempke, believe I speak for all the Swedenborgian angels of low pedigree, for all those excluded, invisible legions of love Summa would not sniff at. Does my teacher get this when she prattles on about the universal values of great literature, though? I don't think so. At least Sister Lydia in Tempke Convent long ago, caught in the act of love and wickedly bribing me with the Library keys *knew* she was dissembling when she praised Great Literature, but Miss Marsh, I think, really believes what she says when she so sincerely advises us:

> Write about what you know, class, write about the sights and sounds and smells of your own country and everyone will be interested!

It's at this stage that I want to throw questions like rat-pellets at my so complacent, my so calm English teacher: *How* do you know what 'my' country is? Who is *everyone*? Do you know anything at all about the histories of the people in this room, teacher? Many things have happened in these past years, of which you know maybe about Perestroika and the end of the Cold War, you know about Lech Walesa in Poland and a little bit about the struggle of Sandinistas in Nicaragua, but what do you know of the battles of the Naxalites in Bengal, what do you know of the slaughter of the innocents in Tempke? And what do *I*, sequestered in my English-speaking convent, know of these things either? *Do we care, do we really care? What's love without knowledge, anyway?* What gives you authority over our class, teacher, your knowledge of the rainbow-hued world or just your white firang skin and a birth-certificate? *If generations of your countrymen can write about 'my' country, why can't I write about yours with equal freedom?* Why must I write about what *you* think I know rather than what I *imagine* I know? If David can rant against Sri Lanka with such passion, a place he visited for less than a week, what prevents me from writing about my arguments with *him*? Who is more blind, you or me?

Of course, if I had asked Miss Marsh any of these questions out loud, I really would have been mad, as mad as David and William who conjured up angels in their verse at the drop of a hat! The difference between her and me is becoming plainer each passing minute. When she finishes with us, my clever teacher goes home and feeds her English children honey and crumpets. She bestows on them the same devoted attention that she expends on us. What she does *not* do is mix up her worlds. Poetry does not invade her home, it does not shoot her through her heart when she's not looking. That is why she is normal and I am not. The only honey and crumpets *I've* ever tasted are the crumpets Catherine baked for William or Frieda for David. That's my madness. I hang around my poets' lives and pretend they are mine. I live on soul-food rarified as Biscuit Baba's Parles—poetry prasad, you could say. Would Miss Marsh understand what prasad was, immortality for the asking, a love potion from the gods? David would, *instantly.* Miss Marsh, I suspect, would think I was being even madder than usual . . .

But I am no longer mad, not really. Dr T told me that recognizing my madness was half the battle and the drugs would do the rest—and it's true, my olanzapine doses keep me calm as a hypnotized rabbit. If you want to be sane and untroubled like my English teacher, then keeping calm is half the battle and not saying what you think is the other. I know this now. *So what if I want to stand up on my hind legs and howl like a wolf from time to time?* So what if I am thirsty for my father's blood and dream of faceless Afi's sneakered feet and his lithe body twisting in my arms?

This is not the time for vulgar displays.

Never seek to tell thy love, William had said, and he was right. So I keep my head down as usual and take down my teacher's notes diligently, occasionally pushing the fur hat down over my bat-eyes. Be calm, Pariel, I tell myself, be calm and *learn,* and your time will come . . .

Not I, but the Wind!

The messages I have from Summa and Afi fifteen years after the bat poem was well over and done with are not in the least poetic. Summa's consists of a bald announcement: *Rehearsals over Etna. Come if able,* while Afi's communication is even more cryptic: *Class D Fire at Etna!* That's all, but since Etna's the only word in common, it doesn't take an Einstein to guess that they are going to be across the bay from David and Frieda and me at Taormina . . .

Taormina has been hot and smoking for a whole year.

The central and north-east craters of Etna, active from 15 March 1919, will continue this way until July 1923. From the topmost floor of Fontana Vecchia, the remote Sicilian farmhouse retreat discovered by David just a month before Etna started to show off, the plumes of smoke are visible right across the Bay of Naxos.

Fontana Vecchia nestles by itself among fields and gardens, far away from the town and the madding crowds, its isolation making it a fortress. *Here one feels as if one had lived for a hundred thousand years,* David writes to his friends in damp, doomed old England. Taormina is almost as far south as it is possible go in Europe and he is ecstatic about having found this exact spot, instinctively knowing himself to be at ease here, *in the garden and up the hills among the goats.* Frieda cooks in the kitchen. For a brief while, they are as happy as children. David is six once again and Lydia sings at her piano. Etna's rumblings, the crater-haze darkening the sky, even Frieda's bouts of restlessness which are always a danger signal, can do nothing to quell his happiness. They are living, as he puts it, *in the world's morning . . .*

Frieda, less contented, is usually up long before David. There are moonbathed nights when she cannot sleep and then there are nights when she can, which are worse. Ach, the heat, she mutters, not daring to mention the children even to herself. They are grown now. Charles is twenty, Elsa eighteen and little Barbara Joy sixteen, *sixteen!*—but in her dreams they still wear blue uniforms on their way to class. Each day she stands by the mimosa bushes in a muddy lane and tries to catch them as they leave the house. Look, I am your Mama! she says, pleading, but they seem to think she is a witch, some kind of horrid banshee. *Run, children, run!* she hears the breathy voice of their aunt behind them and soon after, the awful scrunch and slush of their fleeing boots . . .

All this happened once. It really did—or did it? Frieda's mind flows away from her like a gush of water. It was all so long ago, the divorce, the elopement and the years of roving like hunted beasts afterwards—they've erased everything. What's left now? Pincer-talons of panic grip her. The children's faces, what were they like? She's forgotten, she's forgotten what they looked like, how they talked, their English accents. Did Barbara have a lisp, was it Elsa—*neither*? Frieda, half-awake in the whispering Sicilian half-light, is convinced she will never see her children again.

Frieda maddened, Frieda distraught—this is the same unfathomable woman David documented in his first book of poems, dedicated to their tumultuous relationship:

At home, we leaned in the bedroom window
Of the old Bavarian Gasthaus . . .
You looked into my eyes, and said: "But this is joy!" . . .
But the shadow of lying was in your eyes
The mother in you, fierce as a murderess, glaring to England
Yearning towards England, towards your young children,
Insisting upon your motherhood, devastating.

David has never quite been able to combat it. Over the years it has come to live with them, a sort of semi-permanent shadow, that looking-back look in Frieda's eyes, the look of 'Not Lot's Wife, but Mother!'

Yet how I have learned to know that look in your eyes
O horrid sorrow
How I know that glitter of salt—dry, sterile, sharp, corrosive salt!
Not tears, but white sharp brine
Making hideous your eyes . . .
The curse against all mothers . . .

Her heart shrunk to the size of a tiny, dead pebble under the influence of that baleful curse, *Lydia's curse, now hers.* Frieda twists away from David in their Italian four-poster, as large as a football field and about as clean and bare of the rubble and detritus of their lives. The sheer size of the bed makes it seem that they are alien angels floating in space, absolute, utter strangers. Who is he, this thin pale man in his thin pale pyjamas sound asleep beside her? And how could she have given up her whole life for him, no, *more* than her life, her liebe kinder, the darlings of her heart. And now she cannot remember their faces, the faceless ones, the Afis!

❁

The sun is already attacking the eaves fiercely at five in the morning with sharp little knives of light. Frieda floats in and out of sleep like a wounded, exhausted warrior. Once, she reaches out and places her protective hand on David's soft, untroubled penis. She does this for only a few seconds, careful not to arouse him. Somehow, the gesture calms her down, as if she has skilfully managed to rescue a small rodent from a trap without hurting it. And in the half-dream in her head at the very same instant, her son Charles wanders into the dour Nottingham bedroom where she lies stiffly beside her first husband, Ernest Weekly. He cannot find a clean pair of socks, Charles wails, and they're late for school! At once, she swings out of bed and marches him to his room. Then she dives under the bed and finds his missing sock for him before kissing his warm cheek and packing him off. Her body feels young and lithe. *Das ist gut.* Frieda begins to feel warm, happy, restored—but that's before her dream changes again . . .

Elsa and Barbara sit on high stools waiting for Frieda to plait their hair. The preparations are elaborate. First, she brings in the silver-backed comb. Then she fetches their bright ribbons embossed with gold roses and lays them out neatly—purple for Elsa and red for Barbara. Her girls are lovely, obedient. They wait patiently, without protest, for the rituals to be properly completed. At last she is ready. She lifts her comb and parts Elsa's dark mass of hair in a swift, straight line right down the middle and suddenly it turns into a knife plunging into a mass of spiders. Hundreds of them, squirming and wriggling over her hands, her body, climbing up to her face. Her knife, *where is her knife?* It's gone! All she can see and hear are her daughters running screaming from her. And their red and purple ribbons falling like streaks of light to the ground . . .

Frieda wakes from her nightmare with murder in her heart. She dream-walks swiftly down to the kitchen and picks up the long-handled broom lolling in its corner. Then she attacks, she attacks with zest! Her victim is one of the myriad harmless spindly-legged spiders that routinely crawl about the villa floor. In general, she has an amicable relation with these beasts but today she's merciless, a goddess in spate. She fails to note that the spider she has chosen is heavily pregnant, slow to move and no more able to resist death than a drunk in a shoot-out. I am overcome by a senseless desire to repeat David's bat words to Frieda: *Death is no solution!* But then I think, maybe, on rare occasions, it could be—say, when a sucker is prepared to die anyway. As I was . . .

You could speculate, if you wished, that I was the spider Frieda killed without compunction that morning on behalf of her lost children, the animal sacrifice she made to her fate while David slept peacefully upstairs. And that is why, on the same day that David later met his Sicilian snake, but earlier, *hours* earlier, I too wrote Frieda a poem, to commemorate another ritual occasion. I, Pari, felt for Frieda as I had felt for Lydia and as I felt for that maternal spider and this is the poem that came out of that sudden love-letting:

OTHER SPIDERS

Kill her, kill!

Unbearable her long-legged crawl
Spreading inkstain progress on my wall

Something ancient stirs in me
An unwanted jerking in my belly

A red mist gathering

Against that dark striated shape
Drive sharpened stakes

Stone her!

No weapon too cruel for her
Who turns me back a million years

Who is myself

Tangled in a trap
She-creature driven back and back

Though in the last outburst of her dying
I lose again to a simple cunning

From her body's broken splatter
Baby spiders scatter

In wild uncontrollable smoky whorls
Hydra-headed chronicles

Of the revengeful past
These bend back my will

Though I plunging kill, kill again and kill!

There's nothing like a little, harmless violence to soothe the nerves, Sylvia had said. Besides which, whoever said eliminating a mere spider is any sort of crime. Killing me unwound Frieda. It lifted the curse against love, at any rate, temporarily. For the rest of the day, she moved about the house in a strange state of almost bucolic grace, unusual for her but helpful. Meanwhile, I propped up my poem, in a passable imitation of Frieda's own handwriting, by the ormolu jewel-case on her dressing table. It would be interesting to observe what she made of it.

In the event, though, it was not she but David who found my poem first. I should have guessed. David had strong proprietorial instincts where paper was concerned. He thought he owned every bit of paper in the neighbourhood whether he did or not! So waking late that morning, he casually swiped my poem off Frieda's table and read it through without a hint of trespass. Then there he was, craning his head out of the upstairs window and impetuously demanding:

'Who wrote this? Did you, Frieda Lawrence? Did you write this?'

Frieda is at her vegetable patch far, far below, in another world and still lost in her state of grace. She can barely hear him, up at his angel window.

'Write what, Lorenzo?'

'This!' He folds the poem into a paper plane and sends it nose-diving, where it lands gracefully in a bed of tomatoes some yards away from Frieda. She walks across, de-planes the sheet and reads the rhyming English lines with slow, pedantic care, frowning. She's almost done by the time he makes his way to her.

'Your poem?'

'No! Yes . . . I did, I did kill a spider this morning, but . . .'

Frieda's green eyes, with their tawny lioness flecks of gold that have thrown so many men off kilter so many times, supinely ready to be devoured by her and no regrets, turn hazy.

'I cannot remember writing this. It's crazy! I had a bad dream. About the children.'

David is used to the bad dreams about the children, so used that he feels worn out by the mere mention of the topic. Wisely, he chooses another tack. 'It's your hand. Did you copy it from somewhere?'

'I don't know.' She looks unhappy, but then Otto Gross' words come back to her like a curative potion. They are words she has carried like a charm long before she met David, ever since her brief, impassioned fling with Otto in Vienna the year after Barbara was born. *Suppress nothing.*

'I *should* have written it.'

'*Did* you?'

'No. Did *you?*'

'No!' He is vehement. Frieda looks him in the eye and says:

'I'm glad. It's *my* poem. I can't remember copying it or writing it or anything but so what? I forgot Barbara Joy's face last night. Still I love her! I felt those feelings—those feelings in the poem. That's what's important. So it's mine. Give it to me!'

Suppress nothing! David believes in the doctrine of the gut quite as passionately as Frieda and his instincts are fox-fine. He *smells* something odd going on here. Killing and love and death are his themes as much as Frieda's, but his blood tells him this argument is not about ownership. It's about guilt and expiation, it's about the unspoken sorrows that beset them both: *hydra headed chronicles of the revengeful past,* it could be his line—but if it's his, it's Frieda's. Everything he has is hers. He hands her the poem, gravely.

'Here, take it!'

She mock-curtseys in return and sticks the poem in her broad-brimmed gardening hat (Frieda is a great one for hats, by the way. Maybe it's her aristocratic Prussian ancestry showing up. I make a note to myself: someday I must try out my magic jade's fur on Frieda). At the moment, it's my poem she's wearing though! David and I watch spellbound as it flutters bravely there for a few seconds, an exotic ostrich feather, a victory pennant, before another of those boisterous gusts straight from Etna blows it far away and out of sight forever . . .

'Not I, but the wind! The wind wrote the poem and the wind took it away.' Frieda exclaims, inspired. She is quoting, once again, from her favourite poem in that first book David wrote for her, *Look we have come through!*

Not I, not I, but the wind that blows through me!
A fine wind is blowing the new direction of Time
If only I let it bear me, carry me, if only it carry me
If only I am sensitive, subtle, oh, delicate, a winged gift . . .
The rock will split, we shall come at the wonder, we shall
Find the Hesperides!

Many years later, long after David is dead, Frieda will work on a memoir of her life with him and its designated title will be exactly this—*Not I, but the Wind!* But for now, the words have a different function. They are a winged gift from me, David's angel, to split the curse against mothers and reinstate peace in Fontana Vecchia. Also, I'd like to draw your attention to the poem's mysterious last stanzas:

What is that knocking?
What is that knocking at the door at night?
It is somebody who wants to do us harm.

No, no it is the three strange angels.
Admit them, admit them.

Summa, Afi and I, the three strange angels—it's a good job that David opts to admit us. His decision has far-reaching consequences and you can observe them straight off . . .

Here's Frieda now, smiling irresistibly at David in the hot sunshine, handing him a ripe tomato—a golden apple of the Hesperides—and he kissing her smack before going back into the house and his writing. Perfect, luminous happiness! *What's love anyway but such abrupt delight?*

'I'm off to find an animal of my own to slaughter,' David announces cheerfully, waving down the gravel path. And a truer word was never spoken, as it turns out.

In the part of the world I come from, benighted Tempke, it's said that Sarasvati, Goddess of Wisdom, decides to sit on a person's tongue once every twenty-four hours. Anything the poor mutt utters at that moment comes true. My guess is that Sarasvati smartly decided to exercise her option to land on David's tongue on this day in boiling Taormina, at almost noontime . . .

Lunch in an hour! Thirst compels David to pad down the stairs and back to the garden. He's heading for the water trough, still in his pyjamas and jauntily picking up a pitcher on the way. It'll only be a few minutes before he's back, bounding up the stairs, slaked and rejuvenated, his pitcher full, to assault chapter three of the *Fantasia* with renewed vigour—but that's not the way it goes. Chance, seldom on the side of the angels, intervenes . . .

He's almost at the trough when he sees it.

The Snake

A snake! Not just any snake, but the *vipera aspis hugyi,* Sicilian sub-species of the deadly asp viper, reddish, almost golden in the high sun overhead, the distinctive red-orange saddles down its back glowing like Promethean fire, like Sylvia's hair. It's poisonous, this snake. It could wipe out any man it cared to. David knows the local lore:

On the day of Sicilian July, with Etna smoking.
The voice of my education said to me
He must be killed,
For in Sicily the black, black snakes are innocent, the gold are venomous.
And voices in me said . . .

If you were a man
You would take a stick and break him now, and finish him off.

Frieda killed her spider and was released from her agony. She didn't think twice before she acted. David, giant-killer, is less certain. He hesitates, standing Greek statue-still under the great carob, dark green and splashed about with flowers the colour of blood. Here's an animal readymade for slaughter—not a stupidly nictating, harmless old bat this time, but a lethal agent—and yet again, he cannot bring himself to raise his hand against it! What kind of a warrior is he?

Hamlet, says David sardonically to the voices in his head, consider me Prince Hamlet! And he resigns himself to wait for the snake, using the human logic of the queue as his justification—*for he was at the trough before me.* Match, set and point to the snake, of course! Nor is David's wait destined to be short, for the asp is in no hurry at all, trailing his slack body over the edge of the stone, resting his throat lazily before he sips from the clear, dripping pool made by the trough's leaky tap. His movements are slow, silent, ruminant, reminding David for a moment of a most dissimilar beast—of my gau, the Indian cow, subject of my many debates with William in another life:

He lifted his head from his drinking, as cattle do,
And looked at me vaguely, as drinking cattle do . . .

Wonderful accuracy! Those sleepy movements and that quick escape back into its fissure, which so enrage David a little later on, show how exquisitely self-forgetful are his descriptions in this poem—but they do something else as well. They give him plenty of time to argue with me, Pari, angelic producer of all those dissenting voices in his head.

Recall the naturalists' books, David. They tell us that the mountain-dwelling viper asp of Central Europe is active in spring and autumn but hibernates all summer in rocky crevices, which accounts perfectly for those sleepy, bovine movements David noted. And the same books also inform us that this snake never forsakes its ground but cleaves to the same territory for all its life—as I will never forsake Tempke. So whose terrain was this: David's, who was only a bird of passage in Taormina, or the snake's, native of Sicily born and bred? This insistent question, *my* question, now winding its sluggish way through David's head, refuses to go away. Once again, as on the day of the bat, it stays his hand and makes him defy any counter-suggestions:

And yet those voices: If you were not afraid, you would kill him!

David *does not want* to kill the snake. He's immeasurably honoured by the asp's noonday visitation. This snake's a peaceable guest, the king of the underworld seeking his hospitality, why should he be killed? But the voices I've generated are powerful and David *must* 'come through' them if he is to get to salvation. Everybody knows there's no true poetry without conflict. That's why I exist and that's why the voices mock back and forth: David's a coward, a perverse fool to imagine that he can establish any kind of relationship with this alien creature. *Only by killing it* can he prove his mettle!

Boo to you, duckies! David scornfully tells off his voices, his resolve still firm and his heart taken by his visitor. And finally, he's rewarded . . .

The serpent seems to be done. It dreamily lifts its head, seems to lick its lips in pleasure and looks around the garden 'like a god, unseeing, into the air'. David is enchanted. The accursed voice of his education—me, in short—suggested a killing, but it was wrong and his 'blood-consciousness' was right. The affinity, the brotherhood he felt with the snake was real. He has come through, guilty of no fratricidal murder!

Ah, but if only it were that simple, what happened next would not have happened.

Meditation (mainly for David's ears): The sad truth is that instinct blows in an opposite direction from reason. Far from feeling a natural bond with them, humans instinctively fear serpents. *This* is to be your downfall, David, your human inability to accept the unwholesome truth. You feel no fear at the sight of your king, only curiosity. In this, you're *too much* of an educated modern man, not too little. It's the bad, old Oedipal tragic irony recycled once again, the same old story in every culture.

This may not be the moment to bore you with the innumerable Naga legends of the Hindus, the bejewelled serpentine sons of ancestral Kadru who live in the underworld of Patala, supporting the universe, nor with Vishnu's Sesha Naga, immense cobra eternally coiled over the head of a god, sublimely vicious—yet I must mention them. You can only summon up a bilious disgust for the swarming gods of the dark peoples, I remember that from our Ceylonese encounter. But choose Australia instead, David—the far end of the Colonies where you and Frieda are shortly to travel. And you will find the aboriginal elders there equally cautious. *They* class snakes with women, fire and other such 'dangerous things'! So, when you embrace that *soft, blue, humanless sky of Australia, the pale, white unwritten atmosphere of Australia. Tabula rasa. The world a new leaf . . . without a mark, without a record,* remember this: even in that untouched land was the spill of the snake's venom, his cold, fearful rustle . . .

Sure, other Taorminas, other unwritten Edens are to come,

but in a way they are all here already—the smouldering future written into the flux of the present. Here's Frieda, a woman haunted by spidery dreams and the great fire burning across the bay in Etna and the strange appearance of a serpent in David's garden—danger signals all, as the wise aborigines knew in their unwritten kind of way. Prophesying backwards, modern naturalists, the psychologists and the biologists dolefully agree: *Snakes and spiders are always scary. They are the most common objects of phobias and have been so for a long time in our evolutionary history. Even Indiana Jones is scared of snakes. In cultures that revere snakes, people still treat them with great wariness.*

By the time he produces his novel *The Plumed Serpent* about the Aztec snake-god Quetzalcoatl perhaps five years after the Taormina encounter, David comes entirely to agree with that last sentence. *The Lords of Life*, he writes, *are the Masters of Death.* But today it is a slightly different story. Today, David will not acknowledge his basic human weakness and insists on rationalizing his next—and at first glance, distinctly odd—act:

A sort of horror, a sort of protest against his withdrawing into that horrid black hole,
Deliberately going into the blackness, and slowly drawing himself after,
Overcame me now his back was turned.

I looked round, I put down my pitcher,
I picked up a clumsy log
And threw it at the water-trough with a clatter.
I think it did not hit him,

But suddenly that part of him that was left behind convulsed in undignified haste,
Writhed like lightning, and was gone
Into the black hole, the earth-lipped fissure in the wall-front,

At which, in the intense still noon, I stared with fascination.

Why did David end up attacking the very snake for whom he felt such respect? Why was he filled of a sudden with an uncontrollable revulsion that forced him to fling a log at his hapless guest? Was this revulsion not of a piece with the revulsion he felt against harmless bat me that long-ago Florentine morning, the contempt for the dark races that paralyzed him in Ceylon? David claims in his poem that it was his horror at the snake's unexpected withdrawal into the earth's grimy bowels, the craven retreat of a grand monarch, that guided his arm. But mark the deliberate nature of his actions—he puts down his pitcher, looks around, finds a log and *then* proceeds to heave it at the trough! These are the moves of enmity, not of disgust. Okay, he misses, but what's more important, he also misses the point—just like dear Miss Marsh whom he would so despise. His sling-shot was predictable, *totally* so, and this had little to do with his 'accursed human education'. On the contrary, it was his instinct, his breathy, sweaty, sexy, animal instinct that pushed him into the act which so shamed him:

And immediately I regretted it.

How paltry, how vulgar, what a mean act!
I despised myself and the voices of my accursed human education.

That morning of the bat, I would not let David kill me, nor would I bite him so that that he could feel justified in killing me, in taking his petty revenge, but this time he has come to it himself. He has acted murderously out of his instinct (whether he's ready to give it this name or not) and out of his own free will—as I *knew* he would—for that's part of the human package that I will carry back with me to Tempke, a lesson in raw revenge . . .

All poets need their albatrosses. To write, they must become killers and David, in his heart of hearts, is getting ready to confront this unpalatable fact. *That's* what's eating into him.

And I thought of the albatross,

And I have something to expiate
A pettiness.

So, for all the following week, David goes about his expiation with the ascetic enthusiasm of a Trappist, hair-shirted and cranky. Sex, which is Frieda's panacea for most kinds of bruise, he irritably refuses, as he does her penetrating observation that he is punishing his penis just because the snake withdrew. It's as well Frieda's tough, because the malevolence with which her Lorenzo attacks her now would destroy most women. He cannot, he tells her, *abide* clever, greedy women—and he doesn't forget to be cruelly caustic about her early worship of his body either.

'Remember how you praised me, Frieda? *Why are you ashamed,* you said. *That little bit of your chest that shows up between the gap of your shirt, why cover it up?*

> *Why shouldn't your legs and your good, strong thighs be rough and hairy?* Mein Gott, Freida, your greed!'

Frieda says, 'Enough!' and leaves the bedroom, but David is relentless. He trails after her into the long, dark corridor.

> 'And then you said, Otto Gross's brilliant disciple Frieda said to her young husband: *Oh, men are the shyest of creatures, they will never come out of their covers. Like any snake slipping into its bed of dead leaves, you hurry into your clothes.* How did you learn about my snake, Frieda? And is that all he means to you, witch woman—sex? Sex, sex! Woman, you are insatiable!'

Under her breath, Frieda mutters *schweinehund!* and sweeps downstairs, David in hot pursuit:

> *'And I love you so!* You have not changed, Frieda. All you know is this body—this, this *machine* . . . You drooled over it, Frieda. Drooled!'

David's imitation of Frieda's German accent is growing thicker by the second.

> 'What an instrument, your body! What a tool in the hands of the *Lord!* And do you remember my answer, Frieda, my darling?'

Frieda is now at the kitchen sink, furiously scrubbing potatoes, her back to David, but David has no intention of letting up. He bounds up the stairs and is back in a few minutes with a copy of *Look we have come through!* Planting himself square beside Frieda and her bowl of half-clean, half muddy-brown, half pallid-white, potatoes, he keeps at it:

'It's there—my answer. Shall I read it to you?

Frieda picks up a knife, sticks it into the heart of a particularly offensive mixed-race potato and moves from the sink to the far trestle table, leaving David stranded by the sink, from where he begins to declaim loudly:

Now I say to her: "No tool, no instrument, no God!
Don't touch me and appreciate me.
It is an infamy.
You would think twice before you touched a weasel on a fence
as it lifts its straight white throat
Your hand would not be so flig and easy
Nor the adder we saw asleep with her head on her shoulder
curled up in the sunshine like a princess
when she lifted her head in delicate, startled wonder
you did not stretch forward to caress her
though she looked rarely beautiful
and a miracle as she glides away, delicately away, with such dignity
And the young bull in the field, with his wrinkled, sad face,
You are afraid if he rises to his feet,
though he is all wistful and pathetic, like a monolith, arrested, static.

'Is there nothing in me that makes you hesitate?
I tell you there is all these.
And why should you overlook them in me?'

David the white-throated weasel, the lovely adder, the bull, splendid in his isolation—should Frieda not be impressed? But she's staring at a small harmless hopping flea observing her from the very edge of the table, thinking: I've overlooked so many things in David. Was it worth it? Was it *worth* losing the children? He needs to sleep, he looks so wild . . . and I, I need to get away, to go into town, to perhaps have a coffee . . . That handsome fellow in the municipal office—what is he, I wonder, an officer, a clerk? Not a businessman, certainly not a businessman! He looks too splendid for a clerk. Those moustaches! I need a new hat. When Lorenzo falls asleep, I'll maybe . . .

❁

The flea is still there—*arrested, static,* a bull in miniature. Frieda says:

> 'Lorenzo, there's shopping to be done. When I have finished here, I'm going into town. Will you come with me?' She knows what his reply will be.
>
> 'No!'

'I'll be back by evening, then.' If David was bent on insulting her to assuage his own wounds, Frieda knows how to thwart him too. She's asserted her independence by the simple expedient of ignoring his barbs and going shopping on her own. Over her movements in town, he has no control.

He may not admit it, but David is becoming tired out by his own exertions by now. His perennial cough's a little more insistent and the episode of the snake is already turning blurry in his mind. In a war of attrition, one needs to recoup. David abruptly turns on his heel and trudges upstairs, leaving the kitchen to Frieda . . .

Now in temporary possession of the field, Frieda efficiently chops up her potatoes, cleaning each like a child being readied for school. She dresses them tenderly with basil and mint and olive oil and covers the flecked blue dish with a wet cheesecloth, all the while imagining her own children chattering happily around this healthy salad the prosciuto slices and fresh-baked bread. By these means, she succeeds brilliantly, at least for the time being, in forcing thoughts of David to the far margins of her consciousness. *Suppress nothing but that which you suppress deliberately,* Otto should have said. On this day, in smoking Taormina, Frieda deliberately erases her Lorenzo from her mind. Then she casts off her hausfrau apron, wipes the table memory-clean, sighs luxuriantly and exits, leaving the kitchen in sole charge of a small, keen, brown, winged flea . . .

❁

Upstairs, David has fallen into a narrow trough of sleep, coffin-dark. Good—that gives me time to rush into town ahead of Frieda and to make sure my fur hat is prominently displayed in the window of *La Chapeau de ma Tante,* the unlikely French milliner whom Frieda favours in downtown Taormina. A fur hat in a Sicilian summer? Only if it's an excellent bargain, which I ensure that it is . . .

David is still asleep when I get back. I crawl idly all over the bedpost, my brown insect body merging with the brown of the ornate brown wood carvings of the four-poster. If David were to wake now, he would kill me in horror. A hopping flea in their bed, how careless Frieda has grown of late! But I know David is unlikely to wake, he is sleeping the dreamless, draining sleep of emotional exhaustion and I can watch the shallow, consumptive rise and fall of his chest in quiet peace for a long time yet and dream of the pleasure in Frieda's eyes when she finally spots my hat.

It's getting, I find, to be a habit, the way I naturally identify with her. Sylvia, Catherine, Frieda, where would their husbands be without them? I may be these poets' Inspiration but these women are their life-blood. As I watch over David now, my antennae sensing the warmth of his body and inviting me to move closer to him minute by minute, I also realize something else: Frieda, despite her multiple affairs, her attraction to other men, will always be there for David when he needs her most desperately, and she will be there with him at the moment of his death, as Catherine was with William . . .

David will die in Frieda's arms as once he woke to life and to poetry in Lydia's. From him I have learnt about **a whole hidden history of love**, how men depend on women not so much to love them as to *conceptualize love.* Nurturing mothers and wives, selfless nuns, clever antagonistic wasp-women whose fierce embrace can crush any man to death, Miss Marsh my innocent English teacher, there's no imagining love without them. *What's love anyway* but the *idea* of love?

I see now why I was sent to David's poems. David is like Afi, surrounded by women, drawn to animals, searching for love among violent uncertainties and getting beaten up for it. *Pessimist* David, Raphael's ivory Christ speared in the side but never short of Mary Magdalens to comfort him back to life, is immortal as an angel himself. Ergo, he has no need of me. It was *I* who needed him to help me answer Sylvia and that task is partly accomplished, so now all I have to do is check with Summa but I'm almost sure I'm right. My mission with David is over. I just have to wait for David to display the first stirrings of wakefulness or for Frieda to return and then I can be off—but the minutes pass into hours this night and there are *still no signs of Frieda.*

The clocks chime all through the night in various crannies of the calm old Italian house but Frieda is not back, *not all through the night.* Then, at about five in the morning, finally, I hear the click of the garden gate and the tiptoe of Frieda's feet up the trellised stairs. I spot her in the hallway mirror the minute she comes in. She's wearing my fur hat and looking happy—at least, I think so, although the gloom makes it hard to be certain . . .

Despite the near opaqueness of the pre-dawn mirror, I note that Frieda pauses to admire herself in it for a second before pulling off her hat. David, by the way, has written a cruel poem about this weakness of Frieda's, which is not hers alone according to David in his kingly wisdom but the weakness of all women:

Don't you care for my love? she said bitterly.

I handed her the mirror, and said:
Please address these questions to the proper person!
Please make all requests to head-quarters!
In all matters of emotional importance
please approach the supreme authority direct!—
So I handed her the mirror.

And she would have broken it over my head,
but she caught sight of her own reflection
and that held her spellbound for two seconds
while I fled.

No woman can love a man more than her own image in a mirror. David has asserted this most triumphantly, as if it is a self-evident truth. So it is left to me, Pari, his angel, to ask the obvious question: what are David's own poems but *one vast cracked mirror big as Nauru in which he endlessly observes himself?* Is this not an act of blind self-love far greater than a woman's fleeting glance into a mirror?

But I cannot wait for David's convoluted response. The time is fast approaching when I must flee too, before Frieda turns her rapt attention from the mirror and spots me—a *flea,* alarmingly close to her unrumpled pillow and her sleeping husband. Also, it now appears she's decided not to slip stealthily into the sheets beside her Lorenzo, but take a long soak in the bath instead.

Then, in fresh petticoats, I observe her trip down to her dear kitchen and put on the kettle, humming an aria from *Madame Butterfly.* A modern marriage and a woman restored, this could be love, too—but what of David?

I make a decision. I will not wait for David's uncertain awakening. Frieda is back and I am certain she will treat him to fresh salad and herbs when he finally rises from his extended slumber in the molten, Sicilian dawn. She will mother him. She will bind his wounds with her special dressing. Whatever she has done during the night to recover her own peace of mind and protect herself against David's barbs, she has come back to him in the morning. That is sufficient.

All I have to do now is to cross the bay to Etna and discover what a Class D Fire is . . .

Appointment in Etna

The magnificent, swinging tent hangs suspended a mile or two over Etna's fuming crater. Ah ha, Gabriel's Gazebo has relocated! So that's what Summa and Afi's messages were about. Until May, the gazebo was as far away from Sicily as it could possibly be. I had seen it dangle like a jewel against the icy background of the Northern Lights, caressed by solar winds and swaying gently over Iceland's fir-tops. According to Finnish legend, it had taken just a single arctic fox to start the whole show off. All he did was spray a jet of snow into the air with his frantic feet, till the whole sky glowed and sparked with myriad colours—red, blue, green and royal purple! Or you could go with the physicists' accounts, which attribute the northern Borealis to charged particles from the sun hitting the earth's atmosphere in sudden bursts of speed and skewing her magnetic field to produce an opalescent dance of ions—red, blue, green and royal purple! Whichever way, the Arctic Aurora was a hard act to follow, but Etna in season, afire for the festival of Vulcanalis, celebrated in all Sicily, offered it a run for its money.

Etna's big. It is, in fact, the largest mountain in Europe and has, as the Library encyclopaedias confirm, periodically destroyed villages and people—in 1669, 1689, 1843, and it will do so again in 1928, 1979 and 1987. Etna is a god, a towering master of Life and Death. So Taormina 1919 is not unusual, but if Afi and Summa are there this year, directing operations, it's a safe bet that something is afoot. I don't think I'll be sorry about the snap decision I've taken to leave David in Frieda's care and fly to Etna this morning . . .

My target glows hotter and brighter by the minute as I glide hesitantly towards it, but I need not have worried. Afi's visible, long-distance. I would have recognized him anywhere—face or no face. Today, he's wearing firefighter's garb. The sneakers have been replaced by shiny black fire-retardant boots, and his non-face is considerately zipped up in a snazzy black visor. Then, there's the rest of him, magnificent in a crimson tunic, complete with a red instruction booklet tucked into a top-pocket, his wings the sensational hue of Bollywood blood. Stupefied, I blink and stumble in my flight-path, bat-like, doing a David in spite of myself. I don't think I've *seen* so much concentrated redness ever before. Unfazed, Afi looks up and greets me cheerily:

'Hi there, Angelica. Ready for the guided tour?'

I ignore the slight emphasis on the 'red' of 'ready', which I gather is Afi's idea of a pun and politely enquire after his health. In reply, he waves the fire-fighter's hose on his shoulder (yes, it's the Ginsberg dream-hose all right) and uncoils what looks like a thick black he-man bracelet of tubing around his arm but which turns out to be a *snake* (yikes!). Then he puts words to his joie de vivre:

> 'We're fine, doing great! Meet Coluber. He's harmless, see. *Coluber viridiflavus viridiflavus,* also known as the western whip snake, a genuine Sicilian. Trust me, he won't bite. Coluber's no asp viper. He's a peaceable soul. Here, hold him! By the way, how's your Poet?'

'He's well. Asleep, actually—or was, when I left Fontana Vecchia.' I don't know how much Afi knows about David's current state of mind, but that reference to the asp is suspicious. Is he pulling my leg by any chance?

I resolve to stall until we meet Summa, sum of all mothers, Most Superior Angel. Then I can consult them both. Besides, the present situation's tense and demands all my attention.

Afi is holding Coluber out to me in the friendliest possible way. I have to remind myself that I'm an angel and snakes are about as dangerous as cotton-wool to me. Then I gulp and take the little whip snake into my hand. He feels dry, like grass, against my skin, and suddenly I'm not afraid, not afraid at all. This is a cousin of the emerald grass snake Afi and Mona and I spotted as children from the convent parapet as we flew over Nauru, guano paradise of the world. He is a good omen.

'Come, I've a little present for you.' Afi is off. 'No, I don't mean Coluber,' he says, reading my thoughts again.

We are moving into an area curiously lit by tiny cold fires under our feet. 'Revonlulet', Afi announces casually.

'What?'

'*Revonlulet*—luminescent fungi that feed of rotten wood, aka foxfires.' So that's where the damp, slightly sweet, sickly smell is emanating from! Given my previous experience with him, I'd taken it for granted that odd smells in the vicinity came from Afi, but then, I should have known. Afi might have an obliging nature but nothing about him was to be taken for granted. Last time he was a specialist in ice-sculptures, this time it's fire he's playing with! And what a mine of information he is, as knowledgeable about flora and fauna as he was in the days when he tended the nuns' garden and put splints on wounded dogs—which reminded me that I had a question for him.

> '**A Class D Fire**—you mentioned it in your message. I'm afraid I don't know what that is either.'

Pleased, Afi flourishes his lurid red fireman's booklet. 'Thought you'd never ask!'

He opens the booklet at a page that lists *Types of Fire from A to D.*

> 'Class A', I read. 'Ordinary combustibles: wood, cloth, paper, rubber, plastics.'
>
> 'Go on.'
>
> I go down the list till I get to D.
>
> 'Metals: magnesium, aluminium, lithium, metal dust. Highly dangerous. Use Halon 1211, bromochlorodiluoromethane, etc. Can cause dizziness and loss of coordination, obscures vision, can cause choking. Caution advised.'
>
> 'The malady and the cure—both equally parlous,' Afi chuckles. 'That's what we've got up here at Etna. A

> flaming Class D with elements of B thrown in: liquids, fulminating gases, the works! Which is why we need art, Angelica—to distract us while we prepare to die.' Cheerful is Duplicate Afi.

We're moving out of the cool revonlulet forests and onto a sort of marshland where occasional lights shine in the distance for seconds and then disappear. I know what these are—*ignis fatuus*, the will o' the wisp, friar's lanterns, misleading illusions that lead you to your doom.

'Nature's poetry.' Afi remarks, no hint of sarcasm in his tone. 'A form of art, in a way. Aren't they lovely?' Afi conjures up a small, squat boulder and leans comfortably against it. 'Sit, Pari.'

But I notice uncomfortably that it is getting dark. Occasional claps of thunder rent the air. Shouldn't we be moving on?

'It's an illusion—this darkness. Just as much as the *ignis*.' Afi is emphatic. 'We've only been going about twenty minutes, Ariel, don't you know that?'

I do, but wherefore the illusions? 'I made them up. Special effects for Vulcanalis. Fire's our theme, I need hardly tell you.'

What am I afraid of? Afi's a fellow angel, a bonafide member of the angel fraternity. No reason for fear—and yet my wings feel suddenly fragile and *David*, of all people, materializes as a voice in my head. He's talking out of his angel poem, *Lucifer*:

Angels are bright still, though the brightest fell.
But tell me, tell me, how do you know
That he lost any of his brightness in falling?

I don't know, of course. I know nix about Lucifer except that he's *persona non grata* and ancient history, but David's as unrelenting with me as he was with Frieda:

He only fell out of your ken, you orthodox angels,
you dull angels, tarnished with centuries of conventionality.

Right, I accept. I'm dull and raw, a mere apprentice angel, but whatever Afi's failings, *he* cannot be accused of orthodoxy. So David's telling me something—but before I've time to ask, he's dashed frenetically onto another of his verses, *Old Archangels*:

And so, the official archangels
Orthodox Michael, and that whispering Gabriel
Have had their term of office, they must go.

Here we are in Gabriel's own gazebo and here's David bad-mouthing him on his own turf, a trait I've learnt to live with—even respect—by now. Then David says, very distinctly in my head:

Look about you, look him in the face!
It is Lucifer's turn, the turn of the Son of Morning
to sway the earth of men
the Morning Star.

Looking Afi in the face is not something I have the stomach for just yet. The last time I did so, I was perversely reminded of William's desolation each time I left him. This time he has a visor on, but the effect's the same. I'm beginning to understand in my bones the panic David felt when exposed to the challenge of a roomful of eyes. It's the same with Afi, in a way. To confront his facelessness is to look into the mouth of a flaming crater or at the sun without protection.

The glare of truth, like the light of naked love, is unbearable, there's no help for it, you just *have* to turn away. I know that today. But that day, alone with Afi in the woods, coward that I was, I chose to look up instead—where the illusory noonday darkness showed me exactly the sign I'd expected, the Evening Star, which is also the Morning Star, beaming serenely over Etna. ***Lucifer's star*** . . .

'Hey, relax.' Afi sounds royally amused. 'I won't eat you, even if I am Lucifer, and neither will Coluber.' Coluber! I'd forgotten him. He's found himself a cozy corner of my wing and fallen asleep. Somehow, his insouciance reassures me.

'Put him down.' Afi points to a dark hideout underneath his boulder. 'And let me give you your present.' He digs into one of his innumerable fireman's pockets and pulls out an ornate, you could even say, lurid, plaque. It says, in large Gothic lettering: **Champion of the Bhutan Vanguards: Cosmic Batter.** This legend is followed by a terribly intimidating table that looks something like this:

D.H. Lawrence	**Official Record**	**Cosmic Batter**						
	YEAR	TEAM	POS	BA	AB	H	HR	RBI
	1987	Vanguards	OF	.251	287	72	6	31

KEY

POS-Position; BA-Batting Average; AB-At Bats

H-Hits; HR-Homeruns; RBI= Runs Batted In

Champion of the Bhutan Vanguards: Cosmic Batter

What I know about baseball would fit comfortably on the back of a postage stamp, but this I do know. If a poet has been elevated to a ranking American player, if he features in the computer games of the twentieth century, then he has arrived at the pinnacle of success. At the very mention of America, though, David invades my headspace again, 'batting on and batting on' as Afi whispers to me coolly. But David's off the mark now, agitatedly reciting his 'Evening Land' piece without pause, a hero of the homerun:

Oh America,
The sun sets in you
Are you the grave of our day? . . .

I confess I am afraid of you . . .
The catastrophe of your exaggerate love,
You who never find yourself in love
But only lose yourself further, decomposing,
You who never recover from out of the orgasm of loving . . .

Even the winged skeleton of your bleached ideal
Is not so frightening as that clean smooth
Automaton of your uprisen self,
Machine American . . .

Dark, elvish
Modern, unissued, uncanny America
You nascent demon people
Lurking among the depths of your industrial thicket
Allure me till I am beside myself,
A nympholepht.

Two lines of the poem still to go and David falls abruptly into silence. He's gone! As if he wants to leave me with a puzzle, with that strange last word: nympholepht. Now it buzzes like a mad bee in my head, singing, stinging: *nympholepht, nymphy, nympholepht,* ***bite****, nympholepht*! But what David doesn't reckon with is Afi by my side.

'Confused, Parineeta?' enquires my erudite fireman, off the mark at once, his voice balsam-soothing. '*Nympholepsy*, Greek, denoting *a frenzy of emotion for the unattainable.*'

Whoa, not only can this enigmatic fellow, this faceless funnyman, match David's erudition, he can actually *pronounce* the word silken-tongued, which is more than David managed. I'm impressed. The bee in my head settles into a corner and a new thought starts to hum. I begin to realize that there's more to this solitary tête-a-téte with Afi than meets the eye. *Questions:* why has Gabriel's Gazebo been so uncharacteristically deserted all the time we've been here? Why are the two of us romantically alone in this wilderness, with my gallant companion going to such lengths to present me a plaque of David as an American baseball player, of all the weirdest things? Romance! David's views on this 'bourgeois' variant of love are sharp. *This* is what he set down in black and white on the subject of romance:

> *What's romance? Usually a nice little tale where you have everything as you like it, where rain never wets your jacket and gnats never bite your nose and it's always daisy time.*

Romance may be Bollywood cinema (about which Multicultural Miss Marsh knows less than nothing), where the rain never wets Amitabh Bachchanji's jacket, but *it is not love*. David, prophet of the future, has made that clear to me. So what am I doing in this enchanted forest glade allowing Lucifer Afi to shamelessly serenade me? And why has he, Summa's most aristocratic nephew, so politely tolerated that long-winding Coluber of a Ginsberg-echoing American poem from David, when he could, by Summa's orders, have whisked me away to Etna's exciting fireworks any time he wanted? So there *had* to be a plan. There had to be a *reason* why Afi was so patiently supplying me with the meaning of odd words like 'nympholepht'. And *then* I see it!

David said it himself

> *. . . to be limited by a mere word is to be less that a hopping flea, which hops over such an obstruction at first jump . . .*

I'd been a flea in David's own territory, hopping out of his poetry into his life and then back again. No one knew better than Summa's darling nephew that this was my appointed role, which, I suppose, was why he'd blown David's American poem into my head so deliberately. *That* was the lesson: *one should never get stuck on a word.*

America was not a word, it was a Class D Fire, a catalyst. If my ridiculous role was to hop in and out of my poets' lives, then America's role was to turn all men into frenzied lovers of the unattainable. *What's love, anyway?* Love was America holding out her seductive *steel-straight arms* to the whole wide world. I saw it now. In all my long conversations with William, I never quite managed to convince him, despite Ginsberg's terrible wailing, despite all my wiles, that America was the greatest love-hate puzzle of the future. Yet now in a single poem, David had changed all that. He had painted in the early twentieth century an exact picture of America in the future. *Winged Angelfire America:* that was Afi's real present to me—not that absurd baseball plaque, but a nice big chunk of the answer to Sylvia's question. He had answered her in the most general, the most *social* terms possible. *What's love, anyway?* It is America exuding her *love, like a poison gas* . . .

Poison gas! Afi, monitoring my thoughts as usual, rises to the occasion, producing a not unpleasant but extremely pungent sulphurous odour—and the smell achieves its intended double goals at once, as I'm sure Afi knew it would. It sends me reeling and staggering to him and it magically clears my head . . .

'Happy, Angel?' he asks, this jaunty fireman who can read my thoughts at will. Then, light as a zephyr, he lets me move away from him. The sulphur reek's gone and in its place, here is Afi bowing with a flourish to the drumroll of thunder that he has managed to summon out of the inky air apparently for this exact triumphant minute.

'Y-yes.' I answer him a little doubtfully. 'I suppose I ought to be getting home.'

'Which home is that, Pari?' Afi asks and the gentleness in his voice troubles me so much I can hardly speak for a moment. I gulp again.

'Tempke,' I reply, 'No, I mean Cambridge. To my aunt.'

'It can be arranged. Leave it to Lucifer!' I can hear him smiling. 'Here, don't forget Coluber.'

Coluber, slippery green garden snake and the decorative balance-sheet of David, Cosmic Poet and Baseball Hero, I find both equally hard to hold on to in this smoky wilderness. I find myself trembling without cause. *Where am I?* Who is this creature beside me? How will I ever get out of here? Summa, Durga Mata, I need you, *Summaji*!

'And here I am!' says Summa, descending majestically out of nowhere and touching my shoulder. She is in a forest-green dress enmeshed with little fires, blue wood fires, white sulphur flames, tiny red-tipped fusillades. She looks like a Christmas tree—but I've already got my present. David's future is assured. Now all I want to do is to get home safely.

'Afi will take you home,' Summa announces calmly. 'I have another engagement.' *Afi?* Is Summa leaving me in his charge? 'Don't panic, child.' Summa advises and then she's gone!

I'm alone again with Afi.

'Come.' Afi relieves me in a single efficient stroke of both Coluber and of David's batting averages and puts his arm once again around my shaking shoulders. His arm, that's all, his *arm*, okay, but I cannot describe what I felt at that moment, the all-encompassing *warmth* of that embrace. I did not care where Afi took me or whether he was the devil himself. All I knew was that I wanted to be with him forever just like in a Mills and Boon novel . . .

Epilogue

Last Gathering of Angels

The Return of Ariel

Sylvia did not drown the world in moonlight. How could she?

I did not kill Sylvia. How could I?

There are no answers, only doubts.

The doubts are written down below.

Scepticism is a great gift, Voltaire had declared and William agreed with him. So did Sylvia. We were born to ask why we were born but no one had answers. The truth was a fiction, a stupid cocoon, and that is why no one, *no one,* could face Pontius Pilate's terrible question, not William, not David, nor Ted, nor the nuns. Ask them, Pari, Sylvia said, holding me up by my hair, ask them!

And so I must ask you:

Whose voices have I ranted in all this while, in which forked tongues? I have spun you this crazy tale of English poets who live permanently suspended between fervent belief and ludicrous disbelief. I have drawn on convent clichés of a secluded childhood lived among nuns and painted you a portrait of an evil father out of a fairytale and a victim mother who ended her life dangling in mid-air. I have spoken in stolen voices, childish to worldly flippant. I have inflicted upon you a patchy jeremiad of illicit angelic fancies and you have wondered, where's my *plot*, what exactly is the *point* of my tale? Drugs, depression, mad hatter meanderings, you've thought, so what's so new, Pariel? In return, I have confessed to you a bookish madness, which appears so wildly implausible coming from a young chick raised in the Indian wilderness of Tempke that you don't even bother to *respond.* And to top it all, shudder shudder, I have insisted that my shoulders sprouted gold-tipped wings when I was thirteen and that I am a Recording Angel turned to an Avenging Angel during the course of these flexi-time chronicles! I have asserted that I flit in the upper reaches of the uncontrolled imagination where deception and insanity merge like the illusory colours of an artist's palette. So now at the end of my story, here's a question as simple as Sylvia's: *why on earth should you believe me?*

You do not, in the common course of things, have much time for winged monsters or little green homunculi manning metal and plastic starships. I am cured now and back in the Convent and I can appreciate this but I have many questions still. How about the run-of-the-mill do-gooders canoodling in your local haunts or Rotarians in their comfy clubs determined to save the world or the woman who feeds snarling bands of neighborhood mongrels on weekends? There they exist in all their ordinariness and you accept them *unquestioningly* at the peripheries of your life as you do the amazing African American Ripley woman who can pop out her eyeballs eleven millimeters at will and back again, or Mr Paterini the journalist. *None* amongst my poets would have found the wacky Mr Paterini, driving coast-to-coast from Maine to Texas in the company of an eighty-four-year-old Dr Harvey, who'd once stolen the great Mr Einstein's brain and secretly maintained it in a Tupperware container for the next half-century, in the least bit odd. On the contrary, they would have gassed down the wild American freeways with them happily, finding in them exact kindred spirits. David wrote:

> *You must fuse mind and wit with all the senses*
> *before you can feel the truth.*
> *And if you can feel truth you can't have any other*
> *satisfactory sensual experience.*

The feel of truth: is that what love is at bottom, the imagined sensuality of angels and animals, fused together? Is that why we need Sylvia's 'incantations' to raise the angels of love from their darkened graves? I, Pari of Tempke, am dying for love of Afi. I confess this with all my heart at the end of my story—but who am I? And who is Afi?

Where is he? If I do not answer Sylvia's question down to the edge of the future, I will lose him. Afi will be blown into a wilderness so hellish that I shall never find him. This chills me. I go cold when I think of Afi doomed in that new world none of my poets could ever comprehend—William, David, even Sis Liddie. So now I think: *what would Sylvia's question look like to the angels of the future?*

All through the twentieth century, Walter Benjamin's learned Angel of History, facing the past wide-eyed but blown towards the Future by a wind of irresistible violence, has been forced to find new hiding places. He has been a victim of countless attempts at **murder**. Miss Marsh made us read this Benjamin essay and then showed us pictures of his 'Paul Klee modernist Angel'. She also made us read 'Virginia Woolf's stake-sharp appeal to suffragette women'.

> *And while I was writing, I discovered that . . . I should need to do battle with a certain phantom. And the phantom was a woman, and when I came to know her better I called her after the heroine of a famous poem,* ***The Angel in the House****. It was she who used to come between me and my paper. It was she who so tormented me that at last I killed her . . . She died hard. Her fictitious nature was of great assistance to her. It is far harder to kill a phantom than a reality. She was always creeping back when I thought I had despatched her. But to continue my story. The Angel was dead; what then remained?*

Virginia's question was just as hard as Sylvia's: *what remains when an Angel dies?* Is she replaced by other phantom angels? Feminist angels, Pessimist angels, Realist angels, Spiritual angels, Chance and Destiny angels, can any of them define love? *Can any of them really command the future?*

Ever since they were invented, the alpha-wave medium of television and the nutrient agar of cinema have drawn unto themselves all manners of angel variants. Fusion angels bent on sensual assault, offering you truth on a golden Tai-chi platter. Vampire slayers who punch Evil so hard it miraculously dissolves into instant harmless dust and bureaucrat angels operating out of sedate offices tastefully done up in cottonwool clouds and cerulean monotones, swooping down on unsuspecting moony-eyed fools with the zeal of insurance agents and aiming to settle the balance sheets of their mundane lives once and for all. Leather-jacketed and jack-booted angels, judo busting and Luger-toting angels who think nothing of gunning down a whole K-Mart in pursuit of their vengeful quests—have we not witnessed these legions step out of the back alleys of Hong Kong and Los Angeles into our living rooms? And have we not politely welcomed them all, out of their Disney studios and Hollywood homes, these rampaging gangsters of the future, into the rabbit warrens of our lives as if our nun-less souls were being saved? Have we not allowed them to colonize our headspace—giving them time, energy, space?

Come to think of it, these are measures common to *all* angels, past and future.

Time and energy and space are the dimensions in which I, Pari, move, as they are *yours*—though you may be constructed of flesh and bone and I out of the four eternal elements. No difference at all! Or same difference, as Sylvia's Americans say—and at this point, the grounds for doubting me grow ever more shifting. Newtonian gravity ceases to hold you so firmly down to earth. Your head begins to buzz like a summer bee imprisoned under glass and the moment I lift the confining cover you can do nothing but spiral dizzily upwards into the angel air as if your life depended on it—which makes *you* as much a soaring angel as me or as any of Virginia's or Sylvia's phantoms.

What is an angel after all? She is a line, an image, a thought that flies at a tangent to the rounded earth and will not be beaten down into ordinariness. An angel is a whiff of hope, a fragment of immortality, a half-imagined Apsara out of Kalidasa's book, the scent of fresh blood, not true exactly but real. That's why we believe in angels, we even believe we *are* angels when there is something to be done that's out of the ordinary. Like a poem to be written, Sylvia said, a revenge to be planned or a slaughter. Do not doubt me anymore. Please do not. I am sane now.

I am Pari of Tempke. Come with me!

In November 1989, the Berlin wall fell and I returned to Tempke. The same year, about thirty million turkeys were slaughtered in England, about thirteen million of them for Christmas. Of course I was back home by then and planning my revenge—which, as it happens, did not turn out at all as I expected because Chance, long silent, spoke again. And Chance, as I told you right at the beginning, is hardly ever angel-friendly!

I discovered the cruelty done to turkeys all over the world by chance. My Homerton teacher, proud of her multicultural class, declared one day that we should write essays for a National Competition on our 'own' literature. Miss Marsh said she would pick the three best and it would 'help our class integrate better'. We didn't, of course, understand what she meant and there was pandemonium at once—thirty turkeys all gabbling and pecking together. In the end, to shut us up, my teacher gave us instructions on *exactly* what we had to do. Me, I was the quietest one, eyes fixed on the floor, easiest to handle, so I got my reading early. I had to study these books about by some writer whom some mullah had ordered to be killed. I didn't see why he was 'mine' but she said he was a great writer from India and I should appreciate him. He was very original. But I have to tell you, if Sister *Maria* had read him, she would have written **'Very Poor'** in red ink on the margins. The writer mixed up Hindi and English, although the nuns said we should *never* do this. Maybe that's why they wanted to kill him, I don't know. I desperately needed Sylvia's help to understand this person's books but she had vanished, gone up in fumes of olanzapine for the time being and I had to struggle through them alone. It was hard. In the end, I got a B+ which was not a good grade and my essay was not among the three best, but I *had* found out something. In a book called *Shame* by this writer there is this mad girl, like me, whose mother hates her neighbour's turkeys because they make too much noise. So one night the mad girl goes and tears the heads off *two hundred and eighteen turkeys* and pulls the guts out through their necks. The girl is only ten, so her father in the story asks, how is this *possible*, what gave the child such strength?

I had the same question. I had seen Jahangir, how big he was, how strong, how difficult to hold. No one, not even an akhara wrestler from Benares or my father's khaini-spitting bodyguards, could manage to kill two hundred turkeys in a day. The writer was exaggerating; he was like William and Sylvia and David, he was deliberately twisting the neck of truth and drawing its guts out, but it made me curious. I decided to go to the library and find out exactly how turkeys were killed. It would help when I went back to Tempke and tried to find out what happened to Jahangir.

This is what I discovered about the life and death of turkeys . . .

Wild turkeys fly like angels and roost high up in trees but there are very few wild turkeys left in the world today. Today turkeys are reared mostly so that human beings can eat them. Americans eat turkeys for Thanksgiving and the English eat them for Christmas. Indians do not consider turkeys edible, by and large, but there are exceptions. In India, there are always exceptions. In America, the President releases a 'freedom' turkey before Thanksgiving (which is giving thanks to God for bringing English people to America) but this turkey is lucky. Chance saves him. Other turkeys are not so fortunate. 'They are usually kept either in large, windowless broiler sheds or in pole barns.' (In many parts of the world, it is the same with humans. They are kept in large windowless sheds called prisons or hospitals. Sometimes they are killed.)

Broiler sheds contain flocks of around 10,000 birds and as the birds grow and approach slaughter age they become tightly packed. The litter is not often changed in the sheds and so they become covered in bird faeces. Turkeys do not scratch around like chickens and this means the litter gets spoiled very quickly. The light in broiler sheds is low intensity so as to minimize aggression. (What about aggressive humans, should they be kept in low intensity lighting too?)

'Turkeys reared in pole barns are less densely stocked but the natural light in pole barns combined with a large flock size encourages aggression and cannibalism among them. Because of this, debeaking is regarded as essential and almost all the turkeys reared in pole barns are debeaked'.

Debeaking involves slicing off about one-third of the beak with a red hot blade when a turkey is around five days old, which can be extremely painful. Studies on debeaked chickens have shown their pain to be prolonged and indefinite. Male turkeys may also be desnooded soon after hatching. The snood is the part of the turkey's wattle arising from the forehead and lying over the upper beak. Desnooding is done to reduce the risk of cannibalism in intensively stocked turkeys.

The natural lifespan of a turkey is around ten years but turkeys are slaughtered at between twelve and twenty-six weeks, depending on the size of bird being produced (that means that Jahangir was not more than six months old when he was brought to the schoolyard and would be five and a half years old if he was alive and well today).

Pole-barn and broiler-shed turkeys are seldom well. Diseases affecting them include colisepticaemia, rhinotracheitis and pasteurella, which can be fatal. Because of their large size, lameness is a big problem in male breeding turkeys. Studies have shown over ninety per cent of these male turkeys suffer degenerative hip disease. Young birds unable to find feed and water points and die as a result are called starve-outs. (Starve-outs, by the way, are common among humans too. If you came to mushahar Tempke, you could see this for yourself. *Write about what you know*, my teacher said.)

Turkeys are much larger and stronger than chickens and can be nervous and easily frightened, so catching and transporting them before slaughter causes them considerable distress. On reaching the slaughterhouse, turkeys are removed from their crates and hung upside down in shackles on a moving line. Turkeys may legally hang shackled for up to six minutes before being stunned. Since they weigh anything from 5 to 28 kg (12 to 60 lbs) at slaughter, the pain caused to heavy birds whilst they hang in shackles is awful. This pain is worsened by the fact that many of the birds and especially the larger ones suffer from diseased hip joints.

Stunning involves the birds having their head and neck dragged through an electrically charged water bath. Some birds may be stunned using hand-held stunners instead. Following stunning, the birds have their throats slit before entering a scalding tank which loosens the feathers for plucking. A study found that some birds were still alive on entering the scalding tank. This means around 35,000 turkeys enter the scalding tank alive each year.

Turkeys reared for meat are hatched from eggs laid by special breeding stock. Male turkeys, called 'stags', that have been selectively bred for size are too broad-breasted and heavy to mate naturally. Because of this, turkey breeding is dependent on artificial insemination (AI). Breeding stock are kept in single sex pens. AI completely frustrates natural mating instincts and is distressing for both males and hens. Male turkeys are milked of semen at least once a week and the hens inseminated using a length of tubing inserted into the birds' vagina. Once the birds are past their peak of semen or egg production they are slaughtered and made into pies, pâtés and other processed foods.

After I did my research on turkeys and found out what could have happened to Jahangir if he had been born in England or America, I lost my taste for murder. I decided once and for all to abandon my plan of killing Dr M and my father by stabbing them. I had practical reasons for this choice as well as moral ones. If it is so hard to kill a turkey that no one (except in novels) can manage it alone but need so much equipment and so much help, it would be difficult for me to eliminate men as powerful and cunning as my father and Dr M and *I did not want to fail in my attempt.* I did not want to fail because then *I* would be the one who was dead—and I did not want to die. I did not want to die like my mother.

Besides, I had learnt that there were other ways of being cruel—creative ways. I was sane now and I was beginning to believe what David had whispered to me for long. Creativity and cruelty were related activities amongst the human species—but I remembered David's discomfiture at the prospect of killing a mere bat and I was confused. Was that not a contradiction? When I was with him, this Christian anguish that was his Durga mother's too, was always apparent to me—and puzzling. *Hit him and kill him and throw him away? Nay, I didn't create him. Let the God that created him be responsible for his death!*

I think Sylvia felt the same too, her words coming back to me very clearly after my turkey learning. The encyclopaedia that I had by-hearted said *categorically* that turkeys are not so much related to chickens as to wild pea-fowls and pheasants and this is what I remember: Sylvia writing her poem 'The Pheasant' in an eerie Devon pre-dawn spring the year before she moved to London to die.

You said you would kill it this morning
Do not kill it. It startles me still
The jut of the odd, dark head, pacing

Through the uncut grass on the elm's hill.

O Jahangir, Jahangir, Emperor of the World, *who* tore your wings from your body?

I had five questions before returning to Tempke. Four of them had been answered, three while I was with William, almost without my knowing it—and one while I was with David.

Why was my mother wearing her fur hat when she hanged herself?

Answer: To revenge herself on my father.

Why did my father hate me?

Answer: Because I was not his child, not really.

Why did Dr M's leather-lidded eyes flicker when my mother was mentioned?

Answer: He felt guilty about my mother because they loved each other and she killed herself because she was going to have Dr M's baby and also because my father would destroy her anyway when he learnt of it. So my mother was not insane. She was rational but Dr M was evil and so was my father. And they were going to be punished by me, Pari, angel daughter of Sonali, who had carved SONALI and IRAP inside her arm with the 'I's joined forever. My arm had healed now, and the pattern had become a bit indistinct but this much was certain. I was returning to Tempke to finish the job. Dr M and my father ***would not get away****.*

What's love, anyway?

Answer: Okay, I lied a little when I said this question had been answered. What I've learnt is more complicated. There are some questions that are hydra questions, thousand-snake questions or something of the sort. All my poets knew about them, that they raised doubts like dust-storms, that they never really went away. The more you asked them, the more clichés and confusions sprang, e.g. Love is Poetry; Love is Jesus God, Love is Biscuit Baba in a Holy Trance; Love is the Star to Every Wandering Bark (by the way, 'bark' means a boat here and it's **not** *about a dog and it's Shakespeare); Love is Never having to say You're Sorry; Love is the World's most Elaborate Ruse and it is Mona and Afi and Badshah the Turkey; Love is the nuns selflessly rearing perfidious Afi and it is Lakshmi and Gowri oiling my hair; Love is the Doctorji's snow-flake Taj Mahal; Love is my mother hanging bird-broken from her Tempke ceiling; Love is Durga Mata with all her Children at Puja-time and Love is Raphael's Madonna weeping at her dead Son's feet and it is Lydia disconsolate; Love is all the synonyms in Ms Gupta's Hindi Amarkosh: prem, pyar, sneh, vatsalya, etc; Love is Tenderness and Love is the Cremaster Muscle; Love is Romeo and Juliet, Sunil Duttji and Nargis, Sylvia and Ted, Willam and Catherine, David and Frieda; Love is Cupid-Madana with his Nickelodeon Arrow on St. Valentine's Day and it is circulating packs of Mills&Boon; Love is reading English Books in a Convent Library and imagining you are English, Love is Blind, Love is the Greatest Empty Signifier in the Universe, Love is Attitude and Attitude is Everything in Life according to the*

Heineken poster, so Love is Everything in Life—which means I have to get back to Afi soon, as soon as I can get back to Tempke and find the answer to my last question:

Why was Badshah the turkey murdered?

When Afi deposited me in freezing Cambridge after my interlude in his arms amongst Etna's fires, I became convinced of one thing. *I had to return to Tempke.* I told my aunt I had never been more certain of anything in my life. I did not want to complete my degree at Homerton. I wanted to go home. At once! If my aunt refused to listen, I would *stop taking my olanzapine cocktail*! Write to my father, phone him *now*, I tormented her. Book my ticket! I have to go home.

I planted myself all day long at my poor aunt's kitchen table with my mother's hat jammed on my head and I refused to budge.

I would not eat.

I would not sleep.

I would not move, even to go to the bathroom.

Hour by hour, I ground down my aunt's resistance with my bad behaviour. Not mad—*bad*. She was becoming exhausted. She had phoned the hospital twice already but it was not a crisis and the hospital was unresponsive. I had already had one outpatient appointment and got my supply of olanzapine and the next one was still months away and all my aunt could truthfully assert to date—and she was a very truthful person—was that I had *threatened* to stop taking my medication, not that I had *actually* stopped taking it. That was not good enough for overworked Addenbrooke's. Was I violent? No. Was I showing manic symptoms? Well, I was sitting there wearing a hat and arguing with her. Wearing a hat, was I? That's common enough in this country, Miss, *I* wouldn't worry.

Finally, my aunt whose shoulders had practically folded into her chest by then, asked for Dr T, as a last resort. Was he on call? Would he speak to me on the phone? No, Dr T was not available. Any other doctor? No. If there was an emergency, please call this number for an ambulance, but my aunt who had seen me dashing around her house cackling like a turkey in the early uncontrolled phases of my madness, knew well enough that my behaviour had been *exemplary* ever since I returned from the hospital and that nothing I had done qualified as a crisis, not by any means.

Of course, I had absolutely no intention of dropping the olanzapine—it was my ticket to freedom!—but my aunt did not know that. To her my threat was horribly real. Without the drugs, she did not know what I would do, whether I would jump out of the window or throw her out instead. I was bigger and stronger than her. There was *no way* she could bundle me into the car and take me to the hospital without my cooperation and the Emergency Services would not like being called in on false pretexts.

The truth is that my aunt was timid. I had observed this from the way she took orders from my father. There was something else I had observed. My aunt was an 'immigrant' and she just wasn't sure of her rights. I had attended enough classes in Homerton to know that Britain might be 'multicultural' but the multicoloured ones, like my aunt, were not so sure that they were British, although they *were*. By law! as my Homerton teacher proudly proclaimed, but by law alone—*and not in their heads.*

Because I had spent most of my life living inside other people's heads, places I had no business to be in, I had learnt something basic. Doctors, nurses, teachers, *everybody* exploited a person's weaknesses when they wanted to control them, just as my father had exploited my mother's guilt until she was broken. So now *I* played upon my aunt's weaknesses which were her timidity and her honesty—yes, her honesty!—and I *won.*

My aunt caved in. She wrote to my father, she called her circle of phone-friends and got me a first class Air India ticket through her 'contacts' on a flight that would leave in two weeks.

Two weeks! In two weeks, I would see Afi and Mona again, in two weeks I would be revenged . . .

❁

Before I left, I bought presents—a hair-dryer for Mona, necklaces and matching earrings from Marks and Spencers for Lakshmi and Gowri, a mirror for Sister Liddie though I knew nuns were not allowed vanity, hand-cream for Sister Maria's gnarled hands, a yellow-striped tiger-tie for Afi, chocolates for everyone. I even bought a dining set for my aunt and a remaindered *India Discovered* by John Keay from Heffer's for my Homerton teacher, placing the free book mark on the Havell page with the painting of the turkey.

I did not buy anything for my father or Dr M but I did

invest in a couple of sharp kitchen knives—the sort Frieda used in her kitchen—just to be on the safe side. Then I packed my suitcases, got my final supply of prescription olanzapine and valium from the doctor's clinic and waited.

There were still six idle days to pass. I spent my time going for long solitary walks, hoping to catch a glimpse of Sylvia. I tried walking past the willow tree in the Granchester meadows about which both Sylvia and Ted had written. I gazed upwards at the boarded-up windows of the house on Eltisley Avenue where Sylvia and Ted had lived for a while and tried to imagine their ferocious arguments and passionate making-up afterwards. I sat on the college backs, watching the girls and their boyfriends kissing without shame and the American tourists pointing loudly at the colleges and laughing and I thought sadly of Sylvia in the first delirious phase of her romance with Ted.

Was Sylvia really like these people by the river, carelessly happy, living for the moment, their books unread and lying face-down beside them, sun-bathing *hedonists*? Once a man came up to me when I was thinking these thoughts and offered to buy me a drink at the *Granta* but I ran from him like a wild ghost. A ghost, by the way, is someone who does not know how to live for the moment. She is always out of time, always straining to reach the past or the future or some other place. Sipping wine with a stranger from the towpath, a romantic interlude, that was a Mills and Boon thing but I knew that I, Pari, could never, *never* do a thing like that. For me, *only Tempke and my poets were real.* AFI WAS REAL. The rest, the young man from the towpath, the doctors and nurses, they had to be endured.

I was excited, really excited about going home to Tempke, but my wings were hurting again and Sylvia had gone, which were both bad signs. I was also on the verge of stopping my olanzapine so that I could see her again, just once, but I knew I *mustn't* . . .

❁

Then, on the last night before I am to leave, when I'm tossing in my bed like Frieda in agony, all sorts of animal thoughts pouring into my head and unable to sleep even after a double dose of valium and thinking anything, *anything*, was better than this Sylvia-less existence, the mercury drops without warning and ***Sylvia* enters** . . .

She is not alone. She is with her friends Loubelle and Deedee and Betsy and Doreen, all released straight out of the *Bell Jar*, out of Belsize and all chattering away in their American accents. They also have this photographer man with them. I don't know, I can't recognize him, his face is indistinct in the dull moonlight but Sylvia and the other girls are in the light. They're whispering and giggling in high-pitched voices about posing for some fashion magazine. Then Sylvia announces, not looking at me, offhand but gaily:

> This is the *last* round of photographs before we go back to Tulsa or Biloxi or Teaneck or Coos Bay or wherever we've come from!

I say, *I'm* going back too!

Sylvia replies, still not looking at me, because she never does when she is saying something important. She explains about the girls.

We're supposed to be photographed with props to show what we want to be.

At this point, everyone gets very busy posing. They pay no attention to me at all. Sylvia's friend, Betsy, holds up an ear of corn. It's supposed to show that she wants to be a farmer's wife and then the girl called Hilda holds up a bald, faceless head! Sylvia explains to me that it's a 'hat-maker's dummy.' It shows that Hilda wants to design *hats.* I can't believe it! I want to quickly fetch my mother's hat from my suitcase, where it is tightly packed in already for Tempke with her saris, just to show them—but by the time I get to the suitcase, the flock of girls is there already. So I help them open the lock and then the girl called Doreen begins to rummage and rummage inside the suitcase like a rat. I can't stop her. Finally, she gets what she wanted.

She is holding up one of my mother's golden embroidered saris. She says:

> It's to show that I want to be a social worker in India!

Then she turns to Sylvia and confesses, I don't really, I only want to get my hands on a sari!

But Sylvia's not listening because it's finally her turn. What does *she* want to be? The girls turn and stare at her. I stare at her too. We all wait for her to answer. The air in the room turns very still and even the photographer man stops fiddling with his equipment. Sylvia says slowly:

> I don't know. I don't know what I want to be.

Oh, sure you know, the photographer man says. His voice sounds sweaty and encouraging. You can hear he wants to get the shoot over and done and go home. Then the girl called Jay Cee pipes up:

> She wants to be everything.

She's being witty, Sylvia explains to me. Then she turns boldly to the girls and the photographer and says unblinkingly:

> I want to be a poet.

The girls seem happy about this. They pay me no attention. I don't even think they can see me or I would have warned them, *don't* let Sylvia choose to be a poet. *Don't!* But they're busy again, scouting about my room looking for something for Sylvia to hold. Jay Cee says:

> What about a book of poems?

Surprisingly, the photographer man objects. No, that's too obvious. It should be something that shows what *inspired* the poems. Finally, Jay Cee unclips the single, long-stemmed paper rose from her hat. Sylvia can hold that.

The photographer fiddles with his hot, white lights.

> Show us how happy it makes you to write a poem.

Sylvia's not paying attention. She has spotted the sudden bee nuzzling into the paper center of her rose. She *makes* herself look away from it, look away at all costs. She lifts her head like a startled animal and stares blindly outwards. She stares and stares through the frieze of rubber-plant leaves in my window to the blue sky beyond . . .

Hey, I hear the photographer protesting. There is the same awful foreboding in his Afi-voice that I'm beginning to feel in the pit of my stomach.

Hey, you look like you're going to cry!

Then Sylvia's tears come cascading down like William's spears of heaven, like Afi's unrelenting hail. It seems as if she won't ever stop. She buries her face in the lumpy pink velvet of my aunt's curvy antique love-seat, arrived from God knows what garden sale here in my bedroom, and she weeps. She weeps and she weeps, until my eyes are streaming too. An immense relief from the salt-tears and miserable noises that had been prowling around in me all day destroying my Frieda-sleep floods the room . . .

When I lift my head, the photographer has vanished. Jay Cee and all the girls and Sylvia have vanished as well. I feel as limp and betrayed as Sylvia. The olanzapine has worked at last and I have somehow become the skin shed by the same terrible animal that once attacked her—not the animal, just the *skin*. It is a relief to be free of the animal, but it seems to have taken my spirit with it, and everything else . . .

Sylvia's gone and, with her, many of my reasons for being alive. To find other reasons I had to return. *I had to return to Tempke.*

❁

Next morning, my aunt comes into my room at six-thirty. She announces briskly:

Pari, come on, we've got to go! I've phoned for a taxi.

I can tell she is so happy to be rid of me that she is determined not to say anything about the Sylvia-mess in the room with **my mother's saris** strewn helter-skelter all over the place.

She just gathers each one up in silence and proceeds efficiently to fold it, holding up the shimmering six-yard pieces with both arms wide and the middle tucked under her chin, as generations of her ancestors have done down the centuries. After all that stern hanging and shaking, each sari turns into a docile twelve-inch by twelve-inch neat flat square package in less than twelve seconds with no resistance to offer at all! That is the fate of saris and it could be *the fate of the women who wear them.* But my aunt, quite unaware of these ironies, ruthlessly stacks up my mother's saris which are now mine, one on top of the other, glistening strips of chutney-green and magenta and turquoise and gold and rose, and stuffs them into the open, hungry mouth of the suitcase without pause. Then she squashes my mother's hat underneath the large folded pile as if it is a dangerous animal that might escape otherwise. Her lips are folded too as she says:

This is my present for Dada. Don't forget to give it to him, Pari, and I see her bending and shoving a dark-red shirt and a bottle of Suave men's cologne into the bag's open flap. Zipping the suitcase smartly shut, she hands me the key to put in my handbag.

The Cam-Cab Panther Taxi man rings the bell half an hour later. We're off!

❁

My father did not come to the airport. He sent Ramprasad the driver, not even Lakshmi. But I did not cry. I thought about how I had flown through the clouds at 169 miles per hour so that I could return to Tempke and I swallowed my tears. Then Ramprasad tried to touch my feet and even then

I did not cry. I did not let him see that I wanted him just to hug me after such a long time, not touch my feet as if I was a stupid **stranger**. I wanted him to tell me about everything that had happened while I had been away—but of course I knew that would not happen. So I sat alone in the backseat of my father's Ambassador, my English suitcases wobbling behind me and I stared and stared sightlessly at rice-fields and the dhabas and the OKAY TATA trucks by the roadside until Tempke came into focus and I meditated—or at least I tried. I borrowed a superior voice from the ratpat library of voices in my head and I meditated on Tempke.

Tempke, Tempke the changeless. Not a hair on its head has whitened in the five years that I've been away, which is logical because time and history always left our town out of their calculations. This is the truth. Tempke, like Nauru island in the far-off South Pacific, is one of Great America's many invisible others, a place at the world's faceless margins . . .

It is hard enough to imagine Homerton and the man from the Cambridge towpath in Tempke but it's doubly hard to imagine America—Sylvia's Statue of Liberty America. Here, on the outskirts of Tempke, I feel myself dizzily alone and my wings ache from the strain of trying to reach out to Sylvia in these final dangerous hours. As soon as I land in my town, I sense in my fragile bird-bones that the great arc of history whose pattern I have traced in my notebooks, beginning in 1757, the year that William was born and the Battle of Plassey fought, is about to come to as certain an end as the twentieth century. And in the next millennium—*which is not Sylvia's*—we are to witness the rise of an America very different from the one that my Poets knew, an America with which even Tempke will have to contend, an aching, bee-enraged, newly colonizing America.

For William, America was the epitome of freedom and even David, when he was not seething against her 'western, brutal, faery, quality' saw America as *that far-off retreat which is the Future to me.* And Ted, of course, held America embodied in his arms, his fatal love, Sylvia—the original American Beauty, all guns and roses and a peculiarly modern ideal of freedom symbolized by a free-floating plastic bag. And now, I spot a change! I see that plastic bags have invaded the paper economy of Tempke, jamming up the necks of its narrow riverine outlets and twisting up the insides of its Brahmini cows whose fatal characteristic it is that they will ingest *anything,* including the strange idea that Jesus speaks directly to a great American leader in his up-curling Danbury Stetson and causes him to speculate thus:

> Which country would Jesus bomb next, I wonder?

Jesus: whom the nuns of Tempke worship without a single doubt, Jesus in his Triptych Madonna's arms, Jesus whom William passionately called upon to save his beloved England from a heartless industrial future, Jesus, stand-in for so many powerful gods across the world with whom David had bitterly argued in his stark couplet entitled 'Retort to Jesus':

> *And whosoever forces himself to love anybody*
> *Begets a murderer in his own body*

How would this Jesus, still centre of so many pleas, a host of divine plastic bags netting his thorned head for eternity, deal with the Judas kisses of history? How would he prevent the begetting of a murderer in my own troubled body, a body that has known so many forbidden loves? How would *he* manage to resolve Sylvia's million dollar question? Did Jesus really *get* it?

I, Ariel, was back in Tempke seeking answers—minus my poets, but with revenge in my heart.

Tempke, immortal city. The changeable elements here are just two—the weather and the people. And, as my father's steely grey Ambassador ploughed through the pavement-less Main Road, the weather was certainly doing its bit to keep up Tempke's reputation as a mover and shaker. The unpredictable November rain was getting heavier by the second and dissolving great embankments of brown slush and foul multicoloured rot and plastic debris with a will. Children with matted-straw hair and holes for eyes were still scrabbling for scraps in the slimy, open drains which make you want to retch and the cool off-white cows still ridding themselves unhurriedly of *gobar* at the traffic intersection where the railway-line sliced right through our town's underbelly and sternly held up higgledy-piggledy lines of cyclists and hand-carts and rickshaws at the Level Crossing so that the slow Goods Trains and fast Passenger Trains of the Northern Railways could trundle through to their unknown destinations. These patterns of life in Tempke are Eternal.

Write about what you know, my English teacher had taught us, but what's the point of such descriptions? I could shut my eyes and imagine Tempke any time, anywhere. Its scenes are pasted forever inside the walls of my head, like the film-stars lining the walls of Ratan Talkies. But (Sylvia knew this) it's what you *cannot* so easily summon up in your head that's troubling. The soul of a town like Tempke lies in the barely visible things that go on behind the scenes, what its people are secretly up to . . .

Now that I'm back, it seems that I have never been away but, once I've had my bath and had my hair oiled and plaited and been cuddled endlessly by Lakshmi, I realize this is an illusion, because she is not Ramprasad and she has news for me. The things that have happened in Tempke in my absence, the events that have passed me by so lightly, are about to twist my life out of shape for a second time . . .

Lakshmi sits herself comfortably on the floor of my old room with the single bar old electric heater radiating warmth and informs me that I am grown up now and cured—and marriageable. She can tell me everything! Then she hands me a rich bowl of jhal-muri and begins to gossip non-stop. Her friend in the purple sari has married a rich man and moved to Allahabad where her husband has a sweetshop business. The young boy with the amputated arms—the shameless one after all the Baba had done for him!—ran away to Madhepura and set up his own rival establishment where she has heard he calls himself Sahasra Hath Bal Bhagwan and gives people aashirwaad with his feet. They don't touch his feet, he touches them with his! Also, Mrs Palit's brother has become the Burra Police Inspector and my father has bought two more properties in Chotanagpur and already been twice to see, no, not Jagganath Mishraji, but the new leader from Chapra Zilla everyone is talking about, Lalloo, aiasa kuch. This fellow is very low-caste, an Ahir, but they say he is going to win power in the 1990 elections with his new slogan: raghuvanshi-yaduvanshi bhai bahi, anya jati kahan se aayee. Even Father Sinhaji likes him. He says he will finally do something for Tempke's poor people! As if, I think to myself distractedly, *not if he has comings and goings with my father.* But, to tell the truth, I'm hardly listening. I find myself sifting restlessly through Lakshmi's downpour of words for certain items—which, when they come at last, are so stunning that all I can do is push them away to the slushy embankments at the edges of my mind to deal with later in the last of the four hours allotted to me. *Time is running out for me as it did for Sylvia* and I must be brief.

There is so much left to tell and so little time in which to do it.

From Lakshmi I learn three items that put all my plans in a spin. One, Mona Bebi has decided to become a nun, two, Afi is now working for my father and three, Dr M has got a disease that makes him shake so much he has had to stop working!

Chance, I notice, is speaking again, voluble and unstoppable, through its new messenger, Lakshmi. Consequently, my wings have begun to bristle so much it's becoming uncomfortable for me to turn around in my bed. Still, I resolve upon one single thing before I plummet into jet-lag's flightless abyss . . .

I have to meet Mona as soon as possible.

Finally, it's recess! Mona's free of her duties from four to six-thirty and I am meeting her for the third time this Thursday. We pace briskly up and down just as we did last week, arms interlinked, down the path that leads to Mother Mary in her Grotto down at the end of the garden. The awkwardness of our first meeting is past and the terrible shock of seeing Mona in a lay sister's white dress with her short, prickly widow's hair, the clipped thorn-bush springing from her head! Of course, if Sylvia were around, she would not have failed to remark on the extreme inappropriateness of the gift I had selected for Mona in my ignorance: *a hair dryer, you bought her a hair dryer!* But Sylvia is *not* around and I am still not sure how I am to plan my revenge. When we were young Mona was the leader, *she* decided. Now I have to manage on my own, learn to listen and act, but the more I learn, the more confused I get. It's like getting twenty phone calls at once!

Some of the things Mona tells me I am prepared for, in a way—how she found her Vocation under Mother Superior's constant guidance and, anyway, being a nun is a really good deal if you're not interested in boys and how Sister Liddie the Beauteous startled everyone by running off with the music teacher—no, not the Accountant—three years ago. Well, the news about Liddie doesn't surprise *me* too much, but then, by chance, casually, Mona gives me another piece of information that's dynamite—good dynamite. *Jahangir is alive!*

We're discussing our favourite subject—Afi.

He has disappointed the nuns, Mona declares roundly. They sent him to Ireland to study to be a doctor but he came back last year with a diploma in *veterinary science* instead!

What's *that*? As if you need *firang* qualifications just to attend to animals! Had he lost his head? On top of that, everyone expected him to become a priest but he said he couldn't because he wasn't sure of his faith anymore and he went off to work for my father—yes, Mr Honorable Dey himself—where he's in charge of managing the new poultry and farming wing of my father's always diversifying business. What an insult!

Faithless Afi, Mona cannot get over his perfidy and so this is not the moment to confess to her that I think I *love* him. She wouldn't believe me anyway because I haven't set eyes on him for five years (or so she thinks!) and, even more importantly, because it may be all right to play as children, but no one in my position would ever be allowed to consort with someone so low caste as Afi, *never ever*. Mona cannot hear these secret thoughts, of course. She's telling me now that Afi still comes and helps the nuns out with the garden when he can and sells them produce from my father's farm at cut rates. He's got them this year's turkey at a very cheap price, but it just isn't the same! Mona seethes. Afi has lost his shine for the nuns! He has *lost* his standing in their eyes and in hers. But not in mine, I think, *but not in mine* and into my ears seep David's glowing lines about Lucifer's fall:

In the dark blue depths, under layers and layers of darkness
I see him move like the ruby, a gleam from within
of his own magnificence,
coming like the ruby in the invisible dark, glowing
with his own annunciation towards us.

A poem's a kind of kiss, a gleam from within the heart of a ruby: it is Afi's resolute heart. I feel I'm being told something here, that, under the layers of darkness, an angel is announcing to me: you're getting closer, Pari, *much* closer, although Mona's chattering away and I can't really concentrate. She's saying, very, very animatedly:

> He was so *different*! Afi was so *good* when we were children, Pari! He listened to everything I said. Do you remember how he helped me save the turkey for you? What did you call him—Badshah or something? Afi sold all the bird shit in the convent for twenty rupees in the market. You gave him the idea, right? He was the one who stole your Badshah from the garden in the night and left him with his uncle in the Adivasi village. Then he gave his uncle ten whole rupees to look after Badshah, imagine! Of course his uncle was very happy! Afi was so clever and he knew everyone. He went and got throwaway feathers and goo from the bird wholesellers in the market and arranged them here early in the morning before Sister Maria got up to feed the turkey and it had gone! No one came to know, not even the police, Pari! They all thought it was *our* turkey's feathers—but they weren't. Afi even saved five rupees for ice-cream for us. He was so good then and we saved your turkey for you, Pari! I don't think you remember, you were too sick! But you can go and see him now if you want. Afi has him still. He keeps him in the farm and feeds him grasshoppers and seeds. You should go and see him, Pari. He will be so happy to see you!

I don't know whether Mona is saying Jahangir or Afi will be happy to see me. It doesn't matter anyhow, it's all a happy, miraculous jumble in my head and the cleansing words are still tumbling out of Mona's mouth.

> When you got sick and went away to England, we were so sad, Pari! Then Afi went away. I was so lonely and then Mother Superior said God is the Best Friend of All, but now you're back, I'm so happy! You look so well, so pretty!

I love Mona. She may have decided to become a nun—a *nun*, of all things! But good humans, like good poems, are unpredictable. Yes, I, Pari, made this up too, not Sylvia. I'm not a child anymore and I see the truth. And the truth is that Mona's my true friend under that concealing, maddening habit, maybe my *only* friend. These days, she's stopped snapping 'Forget it!' and 'Shut Up!' and replaced them with 'It's God's will', but what she means is the same. Arguing is a waste of time. Let's be practical. So, in the last resort, I feel I can rely on Mona if I'm really in trouble. But there is a problem.

The problem is, Mona is going to be a *nun*, not a doctor, not a deep sea diver, not a lion trainer, but a *nun*. If I tell her what I have discovered about my father she may have to confess it to Father Sinha or someone. Or she may think I am unwell again and tell my father because it is her Duty. With a nun, you have to pretend extra-strength, because nuns are always reporting things to Higher-ups who then report it to God. That's the problem with nuns. Also, the one thing my stay in Addenbrooke's hospital has taught me is to *pretend*, always pretend to be normal, to be just like other people, even to your best friend. That's the safest, so now I say in a happy, made-up voice that sounds fake in my head but true to Mona:

> I remember, I remember. Mona, I'll go and see Badshah. I'm dying to!

❁

But before I can allow myself to see Jahangir and Afi, I have one more visit to make. I choose my sari for it with special care, a red Chanderi with a narrow green border and golden stars all over. Last, I pull out my mother's hat and tuck it under my arm. People in Tempke are not like people in England who know all about multiculturalism and try very hard not to stare. Tempke people would *definitely* point and stare and think I was mad if I wore anything as absurd as a hat and walked around the streets. So I have to *carry* the big, fat hat until the last minute.

When I'm done, I shout out to Lakshmi downstairs that I want to visit the poor, sick Doctor Sahib and she should ask Ramprasad to fetch a rickshaw. Lakshmi is cooperative and excited. She loves going to town. She quickly wraps herself in a shiny orange nylon sari with a rainbow pallu and puts on her new earrings and chain and her huge stick-on maroon bindi and is ready at the door.

At Dr M's, I tell Lakshmi to wait outside, I won't be long. Then I fix my mother's hat firmly on my head and walk into his study . . .

I am not sure exactly what will happen next. The corridor,

which used to be bustling with patients, is eerily silent but he's there all right, my *father*. I notice one change immediately. The goofy Glaxo boy has been replaced by a sad family—two neat, meek children sandwiched between their neat, meek parents against a depressing background of brownish yellow. The slogan says 'do ya teen bas' and has a big red triangle beside it. It's the official Family Planning poster, which seems to me pretty ironic—but I'm not in a laughing mood.

Doctorji, my father, is sitting quietly at his desk with the slightly chipped Taj Mahal paperweight intact, thinner and smaller than I remember him, a flaxen-headed ghost. When I last saw him, he was *the only white man* I had seen in my life. Now I have seen the ghost-people in their hundreds, David's 'Great British Public' crowding England's sleety streets, the poor and the old struggling with their baskets of washing in the Laundromat, their mottled blue hands fumbling with their passes at the Coach Station. I have seen young ghost-mothers feeding their babies with messy cereal in strollers parked precariously on kerb-sides, I have felt ghost-nurses jabbing needles up my defenseless arm and I have heard the voices of ghost-teachers instructing me solemnly in the intricacies of their native English. Today, Dr M is not alone, he is part of his pack of people—from England. When I challenge him, I will be challenging them.

I swallow hard and say in an unnaturally loud and jolly way

I'm back. Doctorji, I'm back!

He looks up and peers at me though the uneven shadows of his dim room. It is bright noon outside but Dr M's room is cool and shady. I can see him bend forward now, staring and shaking. Ignoring me, he walks painfully over to the drink-cabinet and pulls it open. At once, the bottles and glasses in there begin to tinkle and shake as if they all want to speak to him in chorus, as if they want to warn him to stay his unsteady hand so that they will not meet a shattering, violent end any minute.

Dr M is trembling so much by now, his outlines have turned blurry as if he really is a ghost, but he manages somehow to pour himself his chota-peg of whisky and gulp it down, faint lines of wetness dribbling down his chin. He wipes them off sloppily with his mottled hands and lurches back to his desk.

I am still parked there in my red sari and hat, waiting for him. Startlingly, he looks straight at me and echoes William's faraway belligerent English words with unexpected force.

Go away!

Then he repeats himself with terrible despair all over again, but this time he's added some words and there is an irritable, whining note in his voice.

Go away, O go away, Sonali, for Christ's sake!

Sonali! That is my *mother's* name, Sonali, the golden one. Retribution! I get it, I get it right away. My broken mother is not, it seems, quite dead. She is alive and kicking in at least one of Tempke's withered hearts. Satisfaction, warm and flush-making as my mother's hat upon my head, envelops me. Chance may have got to Dr M first and robbed me of my angelic revenge but I cannot complain. Dr M has been punished exactly, *exactly* right.

I sense the fear rising in him as I approach him now, my dark hair a streaming waterfall under William's English hat and my bangles of engraved gold and red glass tinkling as energetically as Dr M's terrified whisky glasses were a moment ago, my anklets sounding in his ear like distant, reminding cowbells . . .

Dr M is *finished*! He's leaning backwards now, his Parkinson's wraith hands held out in front of him to ward off my mother's phantom presence, his jaw in rictus as he strains to make out my form against the dappled sunlight of the room, his breath raspy and uneven. Then, without warning, my mother says sharply in my ear in Bangla, *bas, that's quite enough, Pari!*

Yes. Yes, it is, Ma.

I turn obediently on my heel and walk back to the door, shutting it softly once and for all on my father, who is my father but not my father. The rest can be safely left to Chance.

Now I have a plan at last! I know how I can bring my other father, the powerful one, to his knees. We barely talk, so I can't be sure what he's thinking. The rule is, if I leave him alone, he leaves me alone—that's the way it is, that's the way it's always been.

It was only when I went in for 'inappropriate attention-seeking behaviour' that he mercilessly packed me off to England. Dr M used the phrase and it's been stuck in my head ever since. Dr M always talked about my 'condition' as if I didn't exist, even when he knew I was in the room—although I've finally fixed that failing! My father was the same. He never asked my opinion, not a word said, not even when he deposited me in the convent at age seven, not even then, but maybe he thought I was too young. Well, I'm going to *prove* to him that I'm not so young anymore.

These days, I'm sure he's planning to get me married off but he won't ask my opinion about this either. He'll just *act* when he's ready. He'll act on *my* behalf as if I have no mind of my own, no will, as if I am one of his endless properties. This is what I hate most about my father. Dr M stole my mother's heart but my father stole her *mind.* Between them, my mother was sucked dry. I *hate* them. Now my father is getting ready to steal *my* mind. I know this, that's why I have to act fast. My teacher at Homerton gave us notes once: *postcolonial peoples are rendered pathologically powerless by the patriarchal processes of colonization.* I memorized that sentence because it had so many p's in it. Now I like it because it sounds true, in a way. *I'm* a 'postcolonial person' because I'm pathologically powerless. It's true! I'm a fluff-head and my mind is like cotton-wool! I'm out of control, okay (well, not totally at the moment because of the olanzapine) but I *was* out of control because everyone was always trying to control me, especially my father. *He* always decided. He's Isa Masih, he's Jesus God, Brahma Vishnu Maheshwara, but *I'm going to stop him now*! I heard him the other day speaking to someone in Calcutta, discussing my marriage prospects. O yes, he wants to get rid of me all right, but with his reputation intact and my grandfather's land all to himself and he wants to act soon, since I show no outward signs of madness these days. That's why *I* must act soon.

Besides, I'm *not* mad anymore.

I see things more clearly than an angel. I see them as clearly as God my father.

A good plan must be as simple and perfect as a circle: SONAL-I-RAP.

My plan is this. *I will seduce Afi.* Then I will announce to my father without flinching that I am going to have Afi's baby. I am going to *marry* him and I am going to tell Mona, Mrs Palit, Lakshmi, everyone. My father will *melt* from sheer mortification and then I will run away with Afi! This is such a fine plan that, after my success with Dr M, I am walking on air. My wings feel glossy. I don't need Sylvia so much anymore. I almost don't need my olanzapine . . .

What I have not anticipated in my plan is Afi's sheer *stubbornness.* He loves me. I know he does. *What's love, anyway?* It isn't something you talk about, always. If Afi doesn't love me, why does he request me so respectfully to come to the farm *at the drop of a hat,* as Sylvia used to say? Any excuse will do: checking the pink-slip accounts, showing me his new layout for the farm. Why are his dark hands moist when he hands me papers to check? Tell me. They're dry for other people! And why does he take me for rides when he is sure my father is out of town? Why does he ask me to *hold on tight* when I get behind him on his new motorbike? Tell me why! This elongated vehicle of his, paid for by my father's munificence to loyal employees of whom Afi is now one, this powerful beast with its black puma body and red handles and 'THUNDERBIRD' edged with zig-zag fire-flames tipped with yellow-blue embossed on its sleek side, what do we feel when we ride it?

That feeling between us is *love,* haunting us like the trail of fumes left behind by the bike as we fly away from ramshackle Tempke. Trust me, it's love. *Love* follows us all the way to the horizon, the blue rim of small Adivasi villages where Afi does business with the men while I sit with my hands cupped round a warm cup of chai at a rough wooden table. Sometimes the women take me into their houses and give me bead-malas, tiny red and black and white beads like seeds strung together. I wrap the fertility-malas round my wrist and hold it up for Afi to admire and I know he wants to grab my wrist and kiss it. There are other parts of me that he wants to kiss.

Afi does not have to *tell* me he loves me. *I know it.* Love's there, waiting on us. We both feel it. It may be Mills and Boon but it's also Havelock, the grip of sex invincible as eagles' talons. I have not lain with Ted and Sylvia and discovered in painful stages the truth about my mother's fatal love for nothing. Nor have I been an apprentice for so many years to William and David, love's greatest experts, without learning to diagnose the signs of love as accurately as any doctor—and Afi is stricken, even though he flatly refuses to admit his symptoms.

Not only does Afi not kiss me, he does not even *touch* me unless he has pretexts like asking me to hold on to him when we're on the motorbike. This is frustrating because, from the first day that I stepped out of my father's grey Ambassador into Afi's small, whitewashed office, clutching the yellow tiger tie I have carried for him all the way from bleak England like a ray of sunlight, I knew there was going to be something between us. The good thing, the *best* thing, about my father is that he's out of town on business for at least half the week, sometimes longer if he's off to foreign countries, so I can do what I want with the car, with Mona, with Lakshmi, with my plans—and at the moment my plans are totally focused on Afi.

Afi's 'office' is not really an office. It has little hammocks with sick birds and a basket with a ginger cat in the corner and a cupboard full of seeds and medicines and syringes and five or six medical books on his desk along with my father's accounts. I can see at once that Afi is a messy person but the animals trust him. A faint odour of manure, like musk, pervades the room and a familiar hint of tears. It's November cold but Afi's office is warm. It's waiting for me . . .

He is not there.

I have not seen him for five years. I'm nineteen now and he is twenty-three. What will he look like? Mona said he hasn't changed *outwardly*, referring to his disloyalty to the nuns, but I am only concerned with Afi's looks, his face, his body, and I can forgive the rest. Easily. After a time, though, I get bored in the office and walk towards the vegetable plots. They are as neat as his office is messy, and I'm staring admiringly at the sheen on Afi's brinjals when he creeps up on me, feet sneakered.

Hullo, Didi, he says, I heard you had come back.

My first thought is, Didi, why is he calling me Didi? He's *older* than me. He used to call me Pari. I force myself to look at him, which is always hard for me. He's taller, that's the other thing I notice, not that much taller, maybe four or five inches more than me, which would make him five ten at most. His nose is flatter and more flaring than I remember, but his cheekbones still slant and his eyes are still irresistibly long-lashed, a wild fawn's guileless eyes. Afi never had any trouble looking people straight in the eye even when he was not telling them the exact truth. I see a vein throbbing in his neck where his white shirt is open, a button missing.

Have you come to inspect the farm, Didi?

That's Afi again. *No, I've come to inspect you.* Aloud, I ask, deliberately,

Why are you calling me Didi? My name is Pari.

It's one of those rare occasions when I've seen Afi uncomfortable. He loses his poise.

I, I . . . You . . .

Afi stops. There's an expression in his eyes that I recognize from my mother. It's *humiliation,* something like that, maybe shame, but he recovers in a trice. He's quick, he always has been. His eyes are inscrutable as he says:

You are the Malik's daughter . . .

Not to you! Call me Pari.

At that moment, I fully realize my power. I *am* the Malik's daughter. No one knows about Dr M and my mother or the Glaxo baby in her stomach—or if they do, they don't dare talk about it. I am the only daughter of the richest man in Tempke and, mad or not, that gives me power over Afi, Afi his *em-ploy-ee.* The prophetic voice of Sylvia's chatterbox

Belsize nurse comes back to me. Gently, my voice caressing, honey sweet, I say to my love:

> We're *friends*, Afi. Don't you remember? Call me Pari.

Again that expression like a flash. To smooth the awkwardness over, I joke.

> I haven't come to see the farm—or you! I've come to see *Badshah.* Mona says you have him.

Afi relaxes at once. Come, he smiles. No 'Pari', yet, but at least he's dropped the 'Didi'!

❋

The next thing I know, I'm with Jahangir in a hedged enclosure and the years fall away. Afi watches us, leaning against a young silk-cotton and humming softly in his white shirt. Badshah Jahangir, tame as a dog, his wattle a little weathered but still a proud flag of independence, cocks his head and comes high-stepping to me as he always did and I repeat my old charm over and over in his ears *badshahrukjahbadshahrukjahjamumkhashatutkhabadshahturukjah!* It still works, that old spell, and we are in Paradise, Afi, the Badshah and I. It's as simple as that—but not that simple, as I discover . . .

❋

In the high childishness of my angel encounters, I was able to make Afi my hero. I could summon him up out of my dreams and make him rescue me from the mouth of Hell. Sylvia knew how it worked: *I dreamed that you bewitched me into bed, sung me moon-struck, kissed me quite insane, I think I made you up inside my head!* So when I was in England, I had watched the white boys and girls kiss together and do all sorts of things, any boy with any girl. Because I could not do that, because I looked away every time, I had no boyfriend in England. Afi was the only boy I really knew and he meant love to me. I *wanted* him, but he was a servant and it would make such a scandal that even my mother's death would fade into insignificance before it. This was why my plan to seduce him was so *perfect.* It would make my father heart-attack furious, he would be so mad he would not know *what* to do.

The trouble was that Afi was as aware of this fact as I was and so he was equally determined *not* to touch me in that way. However hard I tried to tempt him, Afi resisted. He would not bite the hand that fed him, he was not a namak-haram. Nor was he a poet, ready to give up everything for Inspiration, nor a rescuing angel who would bail me out of desperate situations.

The rules of dreamland are kinder than the rules of a small town. In Tempke, Afi was just a young man wanting to make a living on his own, wanting to be free of the nuns, wanting to be free of being a charity boy all his life. That's why he'd sold himself to my father, no question, whatever Mona might say, and now his fear and respect for his new master easily won over his desire for me. Yes, this was the same high-spirited Afi who had taken such a major risk when he rescued the Badshah just for fun—*and for me*—but now he was grown up. To live in Tempke, he had to live by the codes of Tempke town. This was the wall between us that Afi, for all the longing in his soul, knew he could never scale. It accounted for that expression in his animal eyes—humiliation, maybe anger, maybe shame, the sure knowledge of defeat should he reach out for a forbidden thing. To break such a barrier down required superhuman skills. It needed my own angel gifts, not Afi's human wistfulness—but time was running out for me and I had no idea at all how the wall separating us was to be dynamited . . .

Then Afi himself shows me the way.

One morning, he takes me down to an unused patch in one corner of the farm, beyond the vegetable rows and the poultry sheds and even beyond Jahangir's enclosure, to show me a new experiment. He is trying out something which, if it succeeds, will make some money and then maybe he can start a small business of his own.

My heart goes out to Afi, my love. I want to put my arms round him and tell him that he *will* have that chance to be free, I'm going to arrange it somehow, I'm his *angel*, but he has forged ahead towards a plot of man-high bushes with large, pink flowers.

They're hybrid rhododendrons, Afi informs me, spelling out the name carefully for me—RHO-DO-DEN-DRON. He's heard that bees bred on these specially grafted hybrid bushes produce honey with special properties, intoxicant honey, medicinal honey. He's almost ready to harvest the first lot and he already has interested customers. He hasn't told my father yet because my father might think he's misspending the farm funds but he's sure the profits will please my father in the end. Afi's exaggerating a bit, I can tell (he always did) but his enthusiasm is real—and infectious.

Excitedly, he points from a safe distance to the bulging,

crawling drop-down nests hanging from their bright canopy of pink and green. The bees are temperamental, he tells me. When the weather turns bad or when an unpleasant wind blows, they sting more frequently. Bees hate strong-smelling things, they dislike bright colours. They're sensitive! Once he brought his salesman friend, Rajan, to see the bees, and Rajan had been drinking, not much, just one or two country beers but the bees attacked him. They had to run really fast!

Bee stories pour out of Afi. He has high hopes for his rhododendron bees, I can see that, and in any case, I am in love with the way he is holding out his taut hand before me like a signal, warning me.

No closer, Pari, no closer!

I register with a thrill Afi's unselfconscious return to the past. He's calling me Pari. The sky is angel blue above us and I turn towards Afi instinctively, thinking his guard is down, *this* is the right moment to kiss him, when I hear a distinct humming in my ear. At first it's distant, then it's much, much closer and it's a human voice I recognize well—*Sylvia's.*

I should have known.

Bees attract Sylvia, they bring out what she calls her Electra-self, her Daddy complex, and now she has followed them unerringly halfway across the world, Sylvia who wanted to call her last book, the book *I* helped her to write—'Daddy', not 'Ariel'. In her draft manuscript, she'd printed **D-A-D-D-Y** in bold capitals across the title-page and written 'A Birthday Present' right under. *That* was how she was going to punish her father, her bee-keeping, traitorous father, with stinging poetry, but in the end I think she got more savage, animal satisfaction from just *scratching* his name out as if she was rubbing *him* out in the process.

That's also how the book became mine in the end—by default. As for my Ariel wings, I know now that they were borrowed from a nameless, dead turkey and my voices were borrowed too. Borrowed from my poets, from my English books, from Havelock and John Keay and Dornford and all sorts of other unlikely messengers. I, Pari, was all *made up* of borrowings. *Nothing, nothing,* about me was real. *What to do, whattodoo?* I don't want to but I feel myself falling headlong into self-pitying meditation mode. I can't help it. Sylvia turning up unexpectedly does this to me. And then, as I gulp and swallow air, Afi's voice receding further and further into the distance, *David,* of all people, comes to my rescue. Four lines, he says cryptically, just four lines, elocuting them at a brisk clip and vanishing before I have time to recover!

I never saw a wild thing
sorry for itself.
A small bird will drop frozen dead from a bough
without ever having felt sorry for itself.

I have no intention of dropping frozen dead from a bough but I can see David's point. This is a crisis and I should hardly be wasting time whining. I *must* shake off Sylvia and attend to Afi.

I try to do this and when I come through my meditation, Afi's still talking about his beloved rhododendron bees. He hasn't noticed a thing. He's saying:

> You have to move *slowly,* they find it harder to see you then! *I've* been stung when I've moved too quickly, so you have to be careful, Pari. *No closer!*

Sylvia's very close, though. *She* hasn't given up. I feel her breath and I hear her high, clear, nasal American tones ringing in my ears. She's reciting her poem 'Stings':

It is almost over
I am in control
Here is my honey-machine

A third person is watching
He has nothing to do with the bee-seller or me
Now he is gone . . .
And here is the square of white linen
He wore instead of a hat
He was sweet . . .

The bees found him out
Moulding on to his lips like lies
Complicating his features.

Yes, it is almost over and I am in control. Sylvia has spoken. She has instructed me with her always uncanny precision in the use of the honey-machine that will destroy my father.

This, after all, is what David also wrote: *life is for those who put honey on our lips and those who put salt.* Sylvia has just put honey on my lips, I know it. Afi is to be mine. We will ride into the M & B sunset on Thunderbird, we *will.* And so, I turn to him and order him as my father's daughter one last time.

Afi, I'm tired. Take me to the car. I want to go home.

The next week, I meet no one, not Afi, not Mona. I just wait for my father to return from his business trip—which he does on Friday.

I take a special interest in my father's dinner that evening. I ask the cook to make ilish maachh, and my father's favourite, home-made pantuas. I make it a point to sit with him at the dining table, something I usually avoid. Finally, I broach the topic. I tell my father that Afi has started a bee-farm and he thinks it will bring in a lot of money but he's been hesitant to tell my father. My father should know what's happening, though. He owns the property after all, but I think Afi's idea is a good one because when I was staying with Pisi in England, I learnt that English people love trying new types of honey, faraway honey. If Afi's hybrid rhododendron honey can be exported from our farm to foreign countries, it would be good business. I keep my voice neutral through all this, as if the only interest I have in the world is to turn my father's business ever more profitable. Why don't we go together to the farm on Sunday, I suggest with my heart in my mouth. My father can wear the new red shirt and cologne that Pisi sent him. That would make her very happy!

It is almost the first time in my life that I have spoken at such length to my father. I'm so nervous, the *soles* of my feet are perspiring though it's almost December, but I can see he is intrigued by my sudden normality and that his brain is ticking. He's thinking, I sound coherent, not mad at all, maybe he doesn't have to offer such a big dowry. He's wondering, perhaps she's right and there's money to be made in this honey business. He's weighing in his mind whether to punish or reward Afi for his initiative. Anyway, he's listening intently, neatly separating out the fine ilish maachh bones with his teeth and piling them up on the side of his plate, then cutting the two pantuas in his silver bowl into exact halves before placing them carefully into his mouth, never saying anything the whole while. My father is a deliberate man, but in the end, luck and my father's curiosity are on my side. He says:

> Tell Ramprasad. We leave at nine-thirty on Sunday.
> Be ready, Pari.

❁

On Saturday morning, I wear a plain cotton sari for the outing. I don't want my father to suspect anything and I don't want the bees to get *me* by mistake. The drive is almost twenty minutes long. As usual, we speak very little. Afi is not in his office when we arrive, but the Thunderbird's parked out front which means he's somewhere on the premises but probably away working in one of the plots at the back. This is just as well.

I lead the way to the bees, emboldened by Afi's lucky absence. There they are! I urge my father:

> Closer, closer! You can see them better from closer!

Fearlessly, my father marches up to his destiny. When he's as close as he's willing to get, I do it. I throw the stone I have hidden in the palm of my hand as hard as I can at a bulging bee nest. My childhood was spent hiding bits of glass and crockery in my kerchiefs, my uniform, even my underpants, so I could cut myself. I'm an *expert* at this.

What I'm not so good at is aiming.

My stone hits the nest all right, but not dead centre. A few confused bees emerge from the hive. They don't seem inclined to sting my father. O God, I think, what will happen now, but then my father moves in a rush and the bees don't like that. They swarm at him in sudden terrible rage, the cologne and the red shirt tipping them over the edge.

My father's enveloped in a big, black hum. I can hardly see him. Success! I feel its scent intoxicating me. Flinging caution to the winds, I shout at him:

> Afi and I are going to get married! I will be Parineeta, just like Ma! You can't stop us! I love him!

Where did those lying words come from? Except for the last three maybe, they are pure fantasy, but they have an instantaneous effect. I hear a sound like a distant roar coming from within the hum. My father stumbles towards me, shouting and cursing in his bee blanket. It's awful.

I'm transfixed.

I can't move. I'm like my father's Ambassador stuck grrh-grrh! in thick Tempke mud.

Then I see Afi come running up to us because of the commotion. I see him sprint back to the shed and fetch a real blanket from God knows where and wrap it around my father. He flaps the bees off smartly, getting stung a little himself in the process, but invincible, and bundles us both into the car in seconds. Hospital jaldi chalo! he orders Ramprasad.

This quick action of Afi's saves my father.

In return, my father, powerful even from his hospital bed,

has Afi beaten up so badly that the doctors fear he may never walk again. **All it took was a couple of phone calls . . .**

If Afi survives his terrible thrashing, it will be no thanks to me. It will be because the nuns who, without a thought for his disloyalty to them, moved him to the nunnery, bandaged from head to toe, gently, very gently removed the bloodied sneakers from his broken feet and nursed him devotedly once the doctors had given up, saying, take him home, there is nothing more we can do. If Afi survives, it will be because he has a young, strong body and the will to fight for his life. *Ordinary people make poetry, ordinary people resist.* That's what William thought, that's what David said. And if Afi survives, it will be because he had friends in every gully of Tempke, all petty goondas, all nobodies in my father's book, just hangers-around, but they have hearts, these loafer friends of Afi's who picked him up and rushed him to the same hospital where Afi had taken my father the day before. They threatened the doctors with dire consequences unless they attended to Afi *then and there*! If Afi survives, it will be because there are angels in Tempke but *not one of them is me.*

As for me, spoilt and olanzapine-soaked, all I could do on that dreadful day I was to run to Mona, sobbing, *I will never go back there again. Never!* Mona doesn't ask any questions. She just holds me in her arms and rocks me back and forth; she smoothes my tangled hair and murmurs, it's all right, Pari, it's all right, it's not your fault.

But it *is.*

It is my fault, although Mona doesn't guess it—and when we hear about Afi, it becomes my fault a thousand times over. Nobody knows why Afi has been pulped and left in a bleeding heap in the wet marketplace. Even Afi doesn't know.

Mona is totally unaware of my perfidy. She has done everything for me. She has arranged for Jahangir to be looked after by one of the odd-job boys who works for the convent, she has got Lakshmi to bring me my English suitcases packed with my things from the house and she has persuaded Mother Superior to give me back my old room, where *everything* is exactly the same except that the half-hinged Madonna Triptych is gone.

In its place is a full set of **Bapuji's Three Monkeys**, perfectly new, perfectly whole: *hear no evil, see no evil, do no evil.* Mona may be a junior nun, but she has willpower. Some day she will be MS herself, it's just the aura around her. I don't know how she managed to convince Mother Superior without money or anything else on her side or how she worked on Lakshmi but she has efficiently achieved it all on my behalf and asked for nothing in return, like Bapuji. So I do not dare to tell her the cowardly, lying thing I have done, because then she will despise me and I will lose my only friend. So I keep quiet, but every day my insides hurt. I swell and bleed and I rot from the guilt inside me, as my father does on the outside.

What have I done?

I have destroyed a man. Because of me, because of my stupid, half-witted declaration of a Mills and Boon love, Afi may never walk again. Love has begotten a murderer in my body, just as David predicted.

Not just any man, I have mowed down Afi, Afi who trusted me.

❁

The pointless days pass slowly into weeks. Christmas is almost on us. The nuns practice *Noel* and *Hark the Herald Angels Sing!* with the schoolgirls, a young turkey fattens once again in the schoolyard, and we all take turns at nursing Afi round the clock, changing his bandages, turning him over in his heavy plaster, feeding him Horlicks and soup and dalia mash, one teaspoon at a time through the bluish pink O that must be the mouth in his faceless face.

Afi drifts in and out of consciousness, recognizing no one, a living dead man. Each time I bring myself to look at him, the bees within me grow outraged. They spring into my hair and up my nose and within my gullet, and they bite and *bite.* It hurts so much, this shame, it is so strong that it drives out even my madness. That pure, shining triumph I felt at my victories over Dr M and my father has disappeared into a black snake tunnel and all I feel is pure misery, my mother's misery pouring into me and William's dying song sounds in my ears like a dirge. *All through this morn and through this night, some are born to dear delight and some are born to endless night.* Endless night and living death, they equal Afi's corpse-like form in the nunnery, alive only in name and brought to this state by *my* insanity.

Two, there are always two, it's perfectly natural. For the first time in my life, I think seriously of the route that Sylvia took. What's love, anyway, if it all came to this in the end—these dreaded, trampling *hooves* of hers?

I have to think clearly.

When everything hurts, when everything is a blind blur of pain, how does one think of the best way out? I know of no other way but reading, I have never known any other way. I can tell no one my shameful secret. Who to tell? All I can do is to beg my English books for help. Havelock, not much older than me when he had his epiphany in unknown Australia, has the coolest, the wisest advice: *thinking in its lower grades is comparable to paper money and in its higher forms, it is a kind of poetry.*

Paper money, my father's estate, I am done with that now. He has shown no signs of fetching me back from the convent because of what we both know and the others do not. My father had Afi beaten up on account of what I told him and he knows I know this. I hold his reputation in my hands. That's why he will keep me at a distance. We're done with each other forever and he has reclaimed the Thunderbird from Afi. Our debts are settled. But not even my father suspects that what I told him was a lie, an unspeakable lie. No one knows this but me.

Should I kill myself then? *Should I?* Is that the only way?

Thinking in its higher forms is a kind of poetry, Havelock repeats patiently and little by little, it becomes clear to me that he's advising me to return to my poets, to William and to David. He's telling me that poetry is a form of prayer and that I should go down on my knees and pray to the gods I have created.

So I pray. I pray to Bapuji's three silent monkeys. *Do no evil.* And David, closer at hand these pessimist, aching days than he has ever been, responds at once, speaking as he always does, only in intensities, but confidently, *very* confidently.

Thought, I love thought
Thought is the testing of statements and the touchstone of the conscience
Thought is gazing onto the face of life, and reading what can be read . . .
Thought is pondering over experience and coming to a conclusion.

❁

In the purgatory days by Afi's bedside, in his tincture-iodine smelling room, not knowing if he will live or die, I try to make what sense I can of David's words, I examine my conscience, I gaze on the faceless face of life that is Afi's, and I come to a conclusion.

I, Ariel, have no right to my wings.

Harder, *much* harder than killing myself is to chop off my angel feathers with my own hands. It is the worst punishment I can imagine. Never to be intimate with William and David again, to live a life without Sylvia, the mere thought is unendurable. *Will slicing off my wings save Afi?* Is there any chance that he will forgive me when I tell him what I did? How *can* he forgive such betrayal? Afi is human. Yet I know that the sacrifice of my wings is the only way I can atone, the only penance that matches the awful senselessness of my crime . . .

❁

Knives: That night, I lie low till the last nun in the convent has retired and the swish of every habit is still. Then I collect Sylvia and William and David and Havelock in the midnight darkness and take them back to their original resting place, the secluded cemetery in the Library behind the stalwart, undisturbed rows of Dornford Yates. This space, once exclusively occupied by my books has, I notice, been encroached upon by a few tattered Mills and Boons while I've been away—and I evict them as summarily as my property-conscious father would have done, replacing them reverently with my beloved haul. *In Gratitude For Services Rendered.*

Some other schoolgirl will find the magical hoard some day, but my time is over.

My best companions are no longer mine.

Behind the bare crisscrossed branches of the babul tree outside the library window, I see the moon. It is smiling a crooked, curving smile. *Fear no evil.*

A Sign! I have to go.

As I leave the Library forever, I cannot help glancing at silken John Keay still majestic on his glass-topped table and the Old Brown Mahatma, bare-bodied and bespectacled in his wobbly wooden frame above, presiding over the serried shelves. Silently, I put them in charge of the key to Sister Liddie's life-changing English gifts. For I am done with them now and though my wings droop to the ground with the sadness of the thought, sweeping up the dust as I slip-slop listlessly back to my room, I do not look back.

Back in my room, I waste no time mourning. I know I have to tackle the suitcases in the corner. First, I look for my mother's hat and it is right there, in the lighter one on top. Next, I begin the search for the knives, the just-in-case knives that I brought to use against Dr M. and my father. They aren't hard to find either, nestling in the fishnet flap of the heavier suitcase below, yielding themselves up to me in their outer sheaths of Best British Cardboard. I grasp them in my hands and their firmness comforts me. They have a role to play now.

I extricate my English knives from their plastic scabbards—a lustrous pair, the one smaller, serrated and the other large and plain-edged, and lay them on the bed.

I am nearly ready.

In my room with the mottled mirror as big as Nauru, I turn on the dim electric light with its conical hat of white enamel edged with navy blue, suspended by a long swinging wire from the ceiling. Reflected winkingly in the mirror I see the Mahatma's Monkeys waiting for me to act: *hear no evil, see no evil, do no evil!* They watch, cheering me on in expectant silence as I place my mother's fur hat firmly on my head, tear off my blouse and stand bare-breasted and silken-winged and stare at myself.

I will look different soon—*human.*

It is shivering cold and I can spot the goosebumps on the parts of my skin on which the yellow overhead light falls. Other parts of me are shadowy and dark. In the mirror, I have become a tawny creature of contrasts, half yellow, half dark-brown, rearing naked in the night like some exotic animal.

Two, there are always two, it seems perfectly natural now. Somewhere in the old convent building, I hear the water pipes echo faintly to a racketeering tune I've heard before.

Clickety clack! *Somebody's done for,* clickety clack!

Sylvia's here.

I can sense her right behind me, ready to assist with the ritual.

There is no time left.

I pick up a knife.

It's the big, clean one. I lift it high and hack and slash at my left wing.

Hack! There is an immediate crunchy, crackly noise. Pain, like *lightning,* courses through every part of my body, even my eyeballs, my toes. Bits and starry pieces of gold and blue and plumy white float about in front of my eyes. The pain is so searing that after a while all I can concentrate on is the slashing and the cutting.

Hack, hack, *hack*!

My left wing is nearly off, but I'm finding it impossible to get at the root. I twist and writhe and contort but I just cannot reach that part of my shoulder—until Sylvia the Realist steps in to help me with the serrated knife. She's very cool and clinical as if she is still in Fitzroy Street, with the blue seersucker covered kitchen table between us, slicing bread for breakfast. Her knifed hand expertly finds the exact jointed place where the wing is attached to the bone and then she holds my shoulder firm and moves the serrated edge back-and-forth until my wing finally falls to the floor.

I see it. I actually *see* it tumble to the floor, a great mutilated mass of cartilage and feather and gristle and I want to scream. It would be mad to try and describe the pain of this operation. Pain is a strange thing. When it's there, it blots out everything else but there are no words to describe the sensation of it later. Pain escapes the nets of memory, of history. You are most likely to catch its ascetic, torturer's face in a poem but, mostly, pain is an expert in the art of torment without leaving a visible mark. Pain is just pain, animal, unspeakable. This I have learnt from all my poets.

My pain when my left wing fell was beyond screaming or shrieking, it was the soundless blood-letting of a rabbit slaughter. And then my other wing, my lovely right wing, had to be torn from me. I required Sylvia's help even more desperately for this because my hand wouldn't reach the bony knot at the wing's node—but finally it's *done* . . .

My wings are severed.

I will never see Sylvia again. I will never cut myself again. I will never fly again.

History's in the can, the poetry lesson's over and my time is up. Only the debris remain, like the items in the raddi-dump under Afi's bed. I *must* go to him soon . . .

But before I lose my manic angel will, I, Pariel, know what I need to do. *I have to destroy the evidence of my fallen wings forever.* Learn to forget them! In a frenzy of panic, I grab the terrible objects and stumble with them all the way up my grandfather's wrought-iron staircase to the roof, but it's locked—how could I have forgotten?—and I'm forced to stagger down to the ground again. *Forgetfulness is human.*

Once I reach level ground, I toss the wings as quick as I can into the waiting anonymousness of the Convent backyard. The pain from this is so blinding, I find myself running blouse-less up and down the gravel outside my room, panting, a wild animal on the loose . . .

Tempke winters are wet and it's begun to drizzle quite heavily. The moon has vanished completely. One of my mother's half-English, half-Bengali nonsense rhymes suddenly pops into my head. *Rain-come, jhama-jham, path-e hoilo kada, I have not fallen down fallen down my dada!* I sing the meaningless lines endlessly, the chill winter wind blowing against my burning face.

With only a condemned young turkey once again scratching somewhere in the outer darkness for company, I run and run bare-breasted and barefoot till I'm ready to die . . .

If anyone had seen me at that moment they would surely have confined me to the lunatic asylum in Ranchi and had me chained to the floor, but no one did and in the end I managed to drag myself by some primitive effort of will up the five long stone steps back to my room and there I collapsed like a broken egg, a splatter of elementary albumen and yolk across my white linen bed . . .

It seemed like Eternity but it did not take long, the slashing of my wings.

When I woke, it was at the usual time, a quarter to five. My shoulders ached like mad and I felt exhausted, but I also felt relief somehow and a curious weightlessness. I had come out of my ordeal and I was still alive! It was a Madonna miracle. Last night's events seemed to have occurred in some dark, distant universe—but I had no time to ruminate. I had to relieve Sister Maria on Afi's watch at *five-thirty*. I quickly bathed, plaited my hair and started down the wet gravel path, its tiny grass feathers sprouting on either side with brilliant raindrops, the night's dreadful downpour converted into jewels . . .

The ancient Tamil poet's monsoon voice spoke to me gently: *all is well.*

Pari! Pari! they cry
these poets . . .
Yet it's not only Pari
the rains too
keep the world going
in these parts

Yes, the ancient poet was right. The rain, the angel-fine Tempke rain had saved me. It had washed away my guilt. Everything was going to be fine!

Then, without warning, I saw it.

I spotted the small dead animal, lying dead centre ahead.

Awful, malicious **omen**! I could almost smell its foulness and my stomach began to turn. Vomit, vomit, vomit! *Ulti ulta, ulti ulta, hahaha!* In my head, my voices took up the chant too: idiot Pari, trust you to believe a Tamil poet from God knows where! Oye, you've been fooled! *Again!* The whole thing made me want to *die,* but I knew I had to go forward.

I had to get to Afi. There was no way out. I *had* to go on.

If I hadn't been so afraid of stepping on the creature, I suppose I would have screwed my eyes tight shut as I came closer to it, just like Sylvia: *I shut my eyes and the world drops dead, I lift my lids and all is born again.*

But then I did come closer and I nearly laughed out loud from relief.

It was not an animal at all! It was my mother's fur hat, which must have fallen off when I was running crazily up and down in the pitchy night. How stupid I felt and how impossibly happy! You will not believe this but that heavy wet hat, dripping water from its cold insides like an endless bucket of tears, like P.C. Sorcar's magical *Water of India*, actually felt light as air in my hands. It took on its own flighted life, a perilous but still attached wing hanging from my shivery fingertips carrying me effortlessly all the way to Afi's sickbed . . .

❁

Morning had not yet entered Afi's room when I got there.

Everything was bathed in smoky semi-darkness and Sister Maria was snoring her usual bearish snore in the big armchair by Afi's bed. It was hard to see things clearly but I knew every inch of the room anyway. There, safely stowed away in their usual box under the bed were my beloved pair of diaries, *AN INVESTIGATION INTO LOVE* and *AN INVESTIGATION INTO DEATH* and the remaining stub of my pencil. And, although I could not see them, I suppose the Madonna Triptych and the Heineken poster were there too, watching out for me from down under, encouraging me: *ATTITUDE IS EVERYTHING IN LIFE. Be brave, Pari!* But I refused to look in their direction.

I just went straight to the little dead fire in the corner, now full of small grey lumps of used-up coal, each a baby pigeon huddled soft and warm in its cold nest, and here I put my mother's hat tenderly down to dry. And only then did I turn to him, my charge—Christ in bandages, betrayed by love . . .

Afi's face was the usual ghastly death-mask.

The second I laid my eyes on him, only the slight bird-movements of his chest confirming that he lived, my heart stopped. All my old misery came flooding back. I could not bear that heavy, stone-slab look of him, so grounded, so *wingless,* he seemed dead already. *I should have loved a Thunderbird instead.* What was the point of it all? I had shorn myself of my wings. I was no longer Ariel, I was not Pariel, I was just stupid Pari, who could even cast away my olanzapine, maybe, and drag on, but *what if Afi died?* How would love survive? If I lived and Afi died, would anything make sense anymore?

The confusion in my head began to turn the uncertain morning in Afi's room into twilight. It sent a fearsome odour crawling up my nose. This was the same suffocating incense smell that suffused Biscuit Baba's tent at kirtan time or the acrid smoke scent of a poor man's funeral pyre lit with dank wood at dusk and refusing, just *refusing,* to come alight. It was the same black back-and-forth dread that used to grip me in Addenbrooke's hospital, sulphurous and hell-hot one moment, icy rigid the next, sending me reeling into William's arms, to David, to heartless Summa in her high heartless altitude. *Where was I? Had I made one more numskull mistake? Why* was Sister Maria still snoring? Was it really morning?

One thousand phones began suddenly to jangle in my mind all at once and I felt my breath come to a jerky stop, the panic very sharp and stale within me, strangulating me. I could not breathe . . .

Helpless, I was totally *helpless* in that instant. If it had not been for my beautiful turkey neck, I think I would have died, but then my neck suddenly acted all on its own as if it had a wound-up spring inside and it saved me! It took over, just as my hand had once done with the Taj Mahal paperweight in Dr M's clinic—and this is what it did.

My turkey neck craned crookedly up at the small, grilled window which was the only oasis of light in Afi's room—and it spotted my saviour . . .

There he was, no mistaking him. General Wallace! The identical wise old poulter whose precipitate action had once helped deliver William from death's door, now doing his best, apparently, to make a sterling contribution to the guano deposits of Tempke Convent, Chotanagpur. And he was not alone. He had an acolyte with him, a small bedraggled tuntuni bird, an enthusiastic local recruit singing its eternal migrants' song: *mae ka khaun ka piyun, ka leke pardesh jaun.* Chance to the rescue or was it Destiny—it didn't seem to matter that much. What mattered was that I had been given a *Sign.*

Again that soaking wind-chill of relief, mindless, angelic . . .

So it was morning! It *had* to be morning. Pigeons only spatter in daylight, at night they fall spellbound into one-legged, wing-tucked sleep. Afi could tell you, the pattern's been unchanging from the dawn of time whether the sun breaks in Australia or Bihar. The General and his little witness confirm it and that coal-soaked scent of death, he sputters patronizingly, it's just from some ordinary kitchen chulha, you witless child!

Breathe, breathe, *breathe* . . .

Now I breathe in morning freshness and I breathe out night terror, again and again and again. I keep time to the soundless rise and fall of Afi's heart until my hysteria starts to fade. In Bangla, my mother's hanging-from-the-ceiling, broken-hearted language, members of the General's

Columbiform species are called *paera. Paera*—it sounds so close to that other outcaste word *pariah* that in my mind the two senses have long since merged. General Wallace the Pariah, what's he doing up here on Afi's windowsill?

There is only one question on my mind and I put it to him, mutely.

Will Afi live?

Whatever the General's faults, he cannot be accused of indecisiveness or dawdling.

> Of course! Of course! What a silly question to worry about!

And gurgling cheerily, he flutters into the sunrise without a backward glance, leaving me with no option but to turn back to Afi in a single marvelous moment of forgetting.

By Afi's bedside that morning, I somehow manage to forget my gutless past and even the loss of my angel wings. I just forget *everything.* All I can think of is that Afi will live because General Wallace has declared it. His prophecy rises like the wispy tendrils of water vapour from my mother's English hat, now smoking contentedly in its forgotten corner, and hope spirals in my heart as in the finest of fine Mills and Boon.

Yippee and thank you, General, thank you! I declaim, so moronically overcome with joy that the most simple inference of all eludes me until later, much later, when Sister Maria has risen heavily and lurched out of the room like a red lumbering sun and I am alone with Afi. It's then that a sudden, curious thought, Sylvia's deadly afterthought, flaps into my mind from out of that blue void into which the General has vanished.

Whose question was the wily old bird answering, mine—or Sylvia's?

Afi's room spills slowly over with soft, feathered, December light.

Bending over his motionless body, I speak at last to his waking soul: Tell me, Afi, sweetheart, *what's love, anyway?*

Acknowledgements

This book has spent a long time in denial. For years, it made its home a dark bottom drawer, refusing to face the cold light of the world or the luminous puzzlement in an unknown reader's eyes. Now that it is being published, I must begin by thanking my first readers for their faith in the novel: V.K. Karthika, Anna Webber and Usha Mudiganti Rao. It seems no accident to me that these are all wonderfully well-read and self-confident women.

To J.M. Coetzee, I owe perhaps the most enormous debt of all, not only for reading the novel with penetrating thoroughness and austere precision but for not mincing his words. He was the one who asked the unflinching question: why should anyone bother to read an exhausting rant from a madwoman? Even if one granted that it was 'a stroke of genius' to invent a character like Pari, who intimately engaged with major figures like Plath, Blake and Lawrence 'in a space simply not available to discursive criticism', did the novel do anything to explain the 'life crises' that beset these writers? Pari might be 'a possessed possessor' and her prose 'clever and verbally creative' but was that enough to make her a convincing character? As he put it: 'I won't pretend that I haven't struggled with it, which is odd, because it is a very lively and intelligent book, with lots going on all the time.' I replied, rather defensively, that it was this very oddness, this sense of struggle, which reflected our postcolonial condition, our collective schizophrenia. Being raised in India on a diet of English literature, even in this day and age, was a quite maddening fate. We had after all imbibed our marvellous command over English from 'non-native speakers' and learnt to write in it largely on the basis of reading about countries and climes that we'd never experienced first-hand. John said he could not comment on the postcolonial aspect of the novel but the main task of a writer anywhere was to make what might be inaccessible, such as the fantasies of a mad person, reachable and readable. This was a technical problem and could only be solved through craft. He was entirely correct of course and I have thought hard about these matters in the months since John Coetzee made his insightful comments.

I have cut and pruned and sheared the text of the novel. I have tinkered with the chapters and made the technical feature of the psychiatric notes on Pari's condition more prominent even if real doctors may think them amateur. Most of all, I have taken the risk of letting Pari speak for herself in the first person, demented though she is. I have tried, too, to make this a book where you can leave out a whole section, the one on William Blake for example, without losing the plot. Yet, the textual problem remains uneasily resolved because, for one thing, the main character is one who has lost the plot from the very beginning. For another, anachronisms kept popping up in the book however sternly I dealt with them. The most egregious of these historical swaps is a direct allusion to Marsha Keith Schuchard's work on the erotic art of Blake which Pari could not possibly have read since it was published in 2006, eighteen years after the episode described in the book. I have kept this reference in for two main reasons: first, because I thought it uniquely illuminated the relationship between William Blake, his wife Catherine and Pari's peculiar obsessions; second, because it is one of the great, out-of-control luxuries of fiction not to be trammelled by a necessary allegiance to temporal fact. Finally, as John Coetzee pointed out, this book needs readers who are as crazily familiar with Plath and Blake and Lawrence to really get a sense of it. My great hope is that there are enough such ensnared readers of English literature and especially poetry, educated in convents and the like or sequestered in English departments across the world or maybe just people who are English-lovers through odd historical happenstance. This novel is dedicated to them.

Three authors whom I must thank for the serendipitous contributions they have made to the book are: John Keay, whose *India Discovered* has augmented the turkey imagery in the text and so much else, especially in the early chapter 'Wings of Glass'; Marsha Keith Schuchard, whose explanation of 'why Mrs Blake cried' I have already mentioned and who will, I hope, find it in her heart to forgive me for my unusual appropriation of her intrepid scholarship; and Allen

Ginsberg, whose *Indian Journals* and irresistible torrents of poetry reveal how powerfully imagination can sometimes sweep away our sane attention to the Aristotelian unities of time, place and manner. I am very grateful to this wise triad: an ironically inclined colonial historian, an academic whose field is English literary studies and a politically awakened poet of the American sixties.

I thank Souvik Mukherjee for a last minute posting and David Godwin for his early support.

Steven Pinker is to be thanked for the the passage on the evolutionary fear of snakes quoted on page 327.

A special salute is due to Nick Ceramella for inviting me straightaway to give a plenary at a centenary conference he organized in Lake Garda last year after he'd read my chapters on Lawrence. Nick wrote: "'When I read the first sentence 'No one calls him by his name. He is Lorenzo to Frieda and Bert to his mother but I think David suits him best' that was enough for me to say to myself 'I want Rukmini to come on board. She shows she knows where she stands.'" Such kind words from a devoted 'Lawrencian' are to be treasured.

Pradipta Sarkar and Achala Upendran, the two young copy editors assigned to work on *Mad Girl's Love Song* deserve every credit for being quite unfazed by its rampant literariness. Pradipta assured me that her college education in Kolkata naturally led her to empathise with the characters in the novel while Achala informed me that she had a friend just like Pari, which was certainly comforting. Pradipta also found the remarkable paintings by the Australian artist Garry Shead that matched the theme of the book so eerily. These paintings have added immensely to the texture of novel and

I am grateful to Mr Shead for the generous access he has allowed to his original work.

Speaking of art, the artists whose woven tapestry figures on the front cover of this novel coincidentally held a show called 'My Image, My Memories' at Gallery 302 in Delhi at a time when the book was still firmly stuck in the bottom drawer. That exhibition was an eye-opener. I wish to thank Rahul Jain and Gunjan Arora for the invaluable gift they gave me. From the minute I walked into their exhibition, it appeared to me that it was Pari whose story they had recounted in their long, winding tapestry, so many yards and yards of it snaking its way all round the gallery. Later, Rahul was kind enough to give me another present, a neat folder of slides from their bildungsroman. The one at the top of these Acknowledgements happened to be the first of these and the caption said: 'CHILDHOOD DREAMS: Aadya dreams of a *pari* (is it a guardian angel or is it herself?) playing out her dreams for the future, seemingly unaware of the manipulative strings attached [italics theirs].' Another section showed Aadya-Pari emerging from what seemed like the pages of a book. I was mesmerised. I was also impressed. These were two men who had chosen a young girl with angel wings for their hero. A nonchalant declaration Rahul made then has stayed with me. They would, he said, cut their tapestry up into bits and sell it piecemeal if Gunjan and he could not find a buyer for the whole. The dire symbolism of this statement only dawned on me later; at the time, I just wished I was the sort of person rich enough to buy artwork on a whim.

Two websites that I relied on implicitly and have quoted from so extensively that I should by rights be hauled up for shameless plagiarism are <http://seagrant.uconn.edu/ publications/ magazines/ wracklines/ fallwinter02/ hatters.php> for the section on hats (pages 189-192); and the 'Vegetarian Society Fact Sheet—Turkeys—Production & Welfare' <www.vegsoc.org/ page.aspx?pid=537—United Kingdom> for the section on turkeys (pages 364-366). Without the help of these websites, the book would have lacked stuffing, so to speak. The baseball reference in the Lawrence section owes its existence to the Cosmic Baseball Association <http://www.cosmicbaseball.com/00bvr.html>. I am grateful to this imaginative site.

My family, friends and students have contributed to this book as they have to the others that I've ventured to write in the past simply by being there. Their scepticism and irreverence kept me anchored even as I ventured into *Mad Girl's Love Song* territory. As for this unbeatable title, I owe it one of the main protagonists of the novel, Sylvia Plath.

This year, 2013, is in fact the 60th anniversary of Plath's only novel, *The Bell Jar*. It is also the 80th anniversary of Havelock Ellis' *The Psychology of Sex* and the 90th anniversary of D.H. Lawrence's *Kangaroo* and the 100th anniversary of his *Sons and Lovers* as well as of his book of poems *Birds, Beasts and Flowers*. Finally, 2013 is the 220th anniversary of *America: A Prophesy* by William Blake. Such a conjunction is unusual. I hope it augurs well.